Praise for the novels of Rachel Reid

"The book that got me into hockey romance.
It's what I would call my sacred text."
—*NPR's Weekend Edition* on *Heated Rivalry*

"Reading this was like rolling around on an autumn lawn
with a pack of rambunctious puppies."
—*New York Times* on *Time to Shine*

"Rachel Reid's hockey heroes are sexy, hot, and passionate!
I've devoured this entire series and I love the flirting,
the exploration and the delicious discovery!"
—#1 *New York Times* bestselling author Lauren Blakely

"It was sweet and hot, and the humor and banter gave it balance.
I'm really looking forward to more from Rachel Reid."
—*USA TODAY* on *Game Changer*

"Reid's hockey-themed Game Changers series continues on its
red-hot winning streak.... With this irresistible mix of sports, sex,
and romance, Reid has scored another hat trick."
—*Publishers Weekly*, starred review, on *Common Goal*

"The Game Changers series is a game changer in sports romance
(wink!), and firmly ensconced in my top five sports series of all time."
—*All About Romance*

"*Role Model* proves that you can take on sensitive topics
and still deliver a heartfelt and sexy sports romance.
Grumpy/sunshine at its best."
—*USA TODAY* bestselling author Adriana Herrera

"It's enemies-to-lovers with loads (and loads, literally)
of sizzling hot hate sex and hot hockey action and
it's all tied up in a helluva sweet slow-burn love story."
—*Gay Book Reviews* on *Heated Rivalry*

**Also available from Rachel Reid
and Carina Press**

Time to Shine
The Shots You Take

The Game Changers Series

Game Changer
Heated Rivalry
Tough Guy
Common Goal
Role Model
The Long Game

THE SHOTS YOU TAKE

RACHEL REID

carina press®

Recycling programs
for this product may
not exist in your area.

ISBN-13: 978-1-335-01532-7

The Shots You Take

Carina Press
22 Adelaide St. West, 41st Floor
Toronto, Ontario M5H 4E3, Canada
www.Harlequin.com

Printed in U.S.A.

This book is for Mom and Dad.
Sorry about the sex scenes.

The Shots You Take deals with the shock and grief of the sudden death of a beloved parent.

Chapter One

April 2024

There was only one person who could make the most painful day of Riley Tuck's life even worse, and he'd just walked into Avery River United Church.

Riley was with his family behind the last row of pews, too close to the entrance to ignore the arrival of Adam Sheppard. And if he hadn't been standing as close, he still would have heard the ripple of Adam's name being excitedly whispered throughout the crowded church.

Adam's piercing blue eyes met Riley's miserable ones, and Riley's useless heart gave a hopeful bounce. Because Riley's heart had always been his worst enemy.

The same could be said for Dad, he thought darkly.

Riley managed a curt nod in acknowledgment of Adam's baffling presence, then turned to his mother. Susan Tuck raised her eyebrows at him, but Riley shook his head. He didn't know why Adam was here, and he didn't care. It wasn't important right now. Not when they were about to say goodbye to their beloved father and husband. He just needed to get through this. He needed to sit through whatever Reverend Walter had to say, then try not to lose it completely while he shared his own memories of Dad. Then he would endure the crush of sympathies from their friends and neighbors in the church basement while everyone ate tiny triangular sandwiches.

And then they would bury Dad's ashes, and that would be it. Dad would be gone, and Riley would have to find a way to cope with that. He didn't have a good track record for coping with misery.

Adam had sat himself in one of the pews at the back of the room. Riley wondered if he'd expected the funeral to be so crowded. When had he decided to come? Had he booked a flight yesterday? Did he rent a car? Why was he here, sitting with obvious discomfort in a pew that didn't offer enough space for his long legs? He was smushed up against Dr. Tanner, and that probably wasn't good for his shoulder, especially after a flight and what was probably a two-hour drive in the rain.

Fuck. Why was he here?

"It's time to go," Lindsay, Riley's younger sister, whispered to him. She nodded toward the altar. Riley forced himself to start walking. He felt the weight of hundreds of gazes as he made his way to the pew at the front and tried not to feel the particular weight of one of those gazes. He sat and stared at the tiny black box that contained all that was left of his father—a man who had always been the loudest and most cheerful in any room. A man who'd coached kids' hockey, played guitar, and helped everyone he could, however he could. A man who'd started selling Pride flags in his sporting goods shop after Riley had come out to his family. A man who had gone to countless funerals and weddings in this same church, who had offered comforting words in the basement, and who had loved those little sandwiches, especially the pickle ones.

A man who had loved people, and who had died alone of a heart attack in his backyard. Even Mom hadn't been home. He'd been found by one of their neighbors.

Riley couldn't see anymore. Lindsay's hand was on his back as he shook with grief.

"If you don't want to speak up there," Lindsay said, "you don't have to. People will understand."

Riley wiped his eyes, blinked at the dark wooden rafters for a moment, then said, "No. I'll do it." He could at least do this, for Dad. And for himself. He couldn't always hide.

Lindsay squeezed his hand. "No one will judge you, either way."

"I know."

Reverend Walter began speaking then, and Riley did his best to listen.

Riley desperately needed some air. The church basement was hot, overstuffed with people. More people than Riley wanted to see, and more laughter than he wanted to hear right now.

He stepped out of the church into the endless cold drizzle of April in Nova Scotia. He realized then that he'd left his suit jacket on a chair inside. He'd be all right for a few minutes, and his warm, sticky skin welcomed the chilly rain.

He rounded the corner of the church, hoping to find more privacy away from the entrance, and spotted Adam. He was alone, leaning against the side of the building, staring at his phone. The roof stuck out just enough there to keep him dry. It was where Riley had planned to stand, but like so much of his life, it was occupied by Adam Sheppard.

"No signal in the church?" Riley asked as he approached him. It sounded angry. He *was* angry. About so many things. But only one of those things was standing in front of him.

Adam glanced up, clearly surprised and possibly even embarrassed as he fumbled his phone into his coat pocket. He was elegantly dressed: expensive wool coat, crisp dark suit pants, shiny black shoes. His short dark hair was flecked with gray now. It hadn't been, the last time Riley had stood this close to him.

"Just wanted some air," Adam said.

Riley's heart clenched, and he wondered if Adam even realized the memories those words dug up. If Adam even remembered; he'd usually been drunk whenever he'd used that code. And it had been so long ago.

I'm bored. Wanna get some air?

The words and Adam's hot breath would caress Riley's ear, making his heart race and his dick hard because he'd known what Adam had really wanted.

Riley blinked away the memory and stepped closer to Adam, getting in his space. "Why are you here?"

Adam looked like he'd slapped him, his eyes huge and sad. "Did you really think I wouldn't come?"

Riley didn't answer. He just stared and waited.

"I'm sorry," Adam said.

Riley scoffed. He wanted to ask "for what" because there was a list, as far as he was concerned.

"I loved your dad," Adam said. "I couldn't believe it when I heard."

"How did you hear?"

"Maggie follows your mom on Facebook. She saw the obituary."

Riley was pleased to notice that the name Maggie didn't feel like a knife piercing him anymore. He liked Adam's wife, truly. And he couldn't blame her for loving Adam any more than he could blame Adam for not loving him.

"Riles," Adam said softly. He put a hand on Riley's forearm, where the damp cotton of his white dress shirt stuck to his skin. "I'm so sorry. I know how much your dad meant to you."

And the thing was, Adam did know. He knew almost everything about Riley.

"Your speech was…" Adam blew out a breath. "Man. It was awesome. Awesome."

"Thanks," Riley said quietly. Adam's hand was still on his arm, warm through the cold cotton. He heard himself say, "I almost didn't do it. I didn't think I could."

"You always sell yourself short."

That's when Riley remembered that he was mad at Adam. "How the fuck would you know?"

Adam removed his hand. "I know it's been a while…"

"A *while*," Riley said, too loudly. "It's been twelve fucking years."

A hint of anger flashed in Adam's eyes. "Is that my fault?"

Riley glared at him, furious at himself for not having an answer to spit back at him. Because yes, it was Adam's fault, but also, no, it wasn't. It was just a fucking mess of a thing that neither of them had wanted to clean up. And now it was too late.

"I tried to reach out. At first," Adam said.

Riley gazed up at the gray sky. He couldn't look at Adam. "Okay."

"You told me not to contact you. You fucking said those words, Riles."

You were supposed to ignore them, Riley thought. *You were supposed to know I needed you.*

"I can't do this right now," Riley said, meeting his eyes. "It's been a fucking week, and I have to go across the street and put Dad in the ground." He gestured to the cemetery behind them. "So, thank you for coming or whatever, but please fuck off."

Adam sighed and looked away. "This was a mistake," he muttered.

"Wouldn't be your first. Goodbye, *Shep*." Riley turned and walked away before Adam could reply, and before Adam could see the tears in his eyes.

Chapter Two

January 2007

"I'm bored. Wanna get some air?"

Riley felt the words against his ear, a soft puff of breath from Adam's lips, and his heart began racing. Now? Tonight? When the team was out celebrating at a club, and Riley had spent the past hour trying to ignore the way women had been pressing themselves against Adam on the dance floor and the way Adam had pressed right back against them, eyes hooded and cheeks flushed. Riley had written the night off as a lost cause ages ago, like so many others.

But now the tip of Adam's nose was dangerously close to Riley's temple, and Riley wanted to tilt his head right here in this bar, to expose his neck to Adam's lips. To expose himself to everyone.

"Yeah," Riley said. "I do."

He met Adam's gaze and saw the thrilling combination of alcohol and lust there. Riley didn't need alcohol to want Adam, but they both needed it for courage. They never did this sober.

"Let's go," Adam said.

Several blocks of walking, five subway stops, and an eleva-

, they were in their apartment, locking the door

before Adam had him against a wall, kissing him hungrily.
Riley's whole body celebrated.

"Riles," Adam whispered against Riley's jawline, and god,
Riley loved it when Adam said his name when they did this.
He loved that Adam knew exactly who he was kissing, and
who he was hard for.

"Want you to fuck me," Riley said in a rush.

Adam hummed his approval, and for the millionth time
Riley couldn't believe this was really happening.

It had taken Riley nearly three years to get Adam to kiss
him for the first time. Not that Riley had been actively trying
to get his best friend to kiss him, or that he'd been expecting
it at all. More accurately, Riley had spent nearly three years
hoping his best friend would kiss him. They'd been rookies together, both making the abysmal Northmen roster in their first
eligible seasons; Adam because of his skill, and Riley because
of his size. They'd hit it off immediately and had been practically inseparable ever since. All that time, Riley had dreamed
of kissing Adam, longed for it, knew it would never happen.

When it finally did happen, they'd both been twenty-one,
drunk, and, at least on Riley's part, so horny he'd been ready to
die. They'd been squished together in a booth at a bar for hours,
out with teammates, like tonight. Adam had been unknowingly
torturing Riley the entire time with the solid press of his thigh,
the warm tickle of his breath against Riley's ear, the little touches
to Riley's forearm. All of it was familiar, but had also felt electric with the promise of more. Riley had no idea, then or now,
how he'd known that night would be different, but when they'd
stumbled into their apartment and collapsed on the couch, it had
made sense when Adam had placed a hand on Riley's cheek, held
his gaze for a breathless moment, then kissed him.

He remembered Adam pausing after the first tentative brush of lips, then letting out a nervous puff of a laugh that danced across Riley's skin. "Is this okay?" Adam had whispered, his voice softer than Riley had ever heard it.

Riley, thunderstruck, had only been able to rasp out, "Yes," and then Adam had been kissing him again. Riley had tipped over, pulling Adam with him, and they'd made out frantically like that, Adam grinding down on him while they'd panted into each other's mouths.

That night, they'd stayed fully clothed. Adam had his forehead pressed against Riley's shoulder when he came, a surprised gasp escaping him. Riley had gripped his fingers into Adam's lower back—not brave enough to grope his ass yet—and came right after. The whole thing had probably taken about six minutes.

Riley wanted tonight to last a whole hell of a lot longer than six minutes. He wanted sex, but more than that he wanted to hold Adam after and kiss him until they were both hard again. He wanted Adam to not run away as soon as the orgasms were over. They'd been doing this for three years and not once had Adam ever stayed.

This—the sex—was the one thing they never talked about. The closest they'd gotten to having a conversation about any of it was Adam breathlessly asking Riley if he "liked doing that" after he blew him for probably the seventh time. Riley had shrugged, not wanting to give too much away, and had said, "Don't mind it," when the truth was that he fucking loved it.

"Will you..." Adam said, now. His voice was rough already, low and raspy and ridiculously hot. "Would you—"

Riley didn't need him to clarify. He kissed him, then sank to his knees. As always, Adam watched him with unguarded amazement. If Riley had a photo of Adam's face in that moment, he'd never need porn again.

"You're so fucking good," Adam said. "Fuck, Riles."

Adam was still wearing his boots, and snow was melting from them into a tiny puddle around Riley's knees. Riley didn't care. There was nowhere else he'd rather be, with Adam looking at no one else but him. With Adam being amazed by him.

He took Adam as deep as he could, held him there, and closed his eyes, letting himself be overwhelmed by the man he was completely, painfully in love with.

"So fucking good," Adam repeated. Then, to Riley's astonishment, he trailed a gentle fingertip down Riley's cheek.

Riley opened his eyes, and met Adam's hooded gaze.

I love you, Riley thought. *I love you so much I might die from it. I might have to tell you. I'm sorry.*

Adam kept staring at him, lips parted. For a moment, Riley thought Adam had somehow heard him. That he was about to say it back.

Instead, Adam said, "I wanna suck you too."

It wasn't a confession of love, but it was still exciting. Riley had been shocked the first time Adam had gone down on him. It had happened only a few months ago, during the summer when Adam had visited him in Avery River. Riley knew it didn't mean anything, really, that Adam was suddenly interested in giving head, but it had felt significant. It had been one of the many reasons those few weeks in Avery River had been magical, and Riley had felt, for the first time in his life, like he'd had a boyfriend.

Now they were back to fucking, whenever they were drunk enough, and not talking about it. But there was something *there* between them. Something new that had followed them from Avery River to their shared Toronto apartment. Riley couldn't ignore it, and he suspected Adam didn't really want to either.

Riley released Adam slowly, and Adam reached out a hand to pull Riley up. Then they were kissing again, and Adam pressed his hand against the bulge in Riley's jeans.

"Bedroom," Riley said.

"Yeah."

After, Adam didn't leave the bed right away. Usually, within two minutes of coming, he would be laughing nervously and saying stuff like, "Wow, shit. That was crazy," and "See you tomorrow, Riles." But that night he lingered, still lying beside Riley after their breathing had returned to normal. Riley took a chance and rolled onto his side so he could stroke Adam's hair a bit and enjoy the view. Adam smiled sleepily at him, captured his wrist, and kissed Riley's palm. He was so beautiful and so sweet like this, and Riley had reached his limit. He had to tell him.

"I love you, you know."

Adam's eyes went wide and alert, and his mouth fell open. Riley's heart possibly stopped beating as he waited.

Then Adam laughed. "Come on," he said. "We're not like that."

Riley was frozen as dread and humiliation washed over him. Adam must have noticed because he stopped laughing. "Riles," he said gently, "this isn't—"

"I know," Riley said. Then he forced a smile that probably looked deranged. "Yeah. I know. Sorry. I was just..." He left the bed in a hurry before the tears came. Before the situation could get any more embarrassing.

Alone in the bathroom, Riley pressed a hand hard against his mouth and blinked at the ceiling. He'd miscalculated. He'd ruined everything. Would Adam even want to be friends with him anymore?

Later, when he returned to his bedroom, Adam was gone. Riley wasn't surprised.

The next morning, Adam was whistling as he entered the kitchen. Riley was sitting at the table, forcing himself to eat cereal despite having a stomach full of anxiety.

"Mornin'," Adam said. "Is there coffee?"

"Not yet. Sorry."

"It's cool. I'll make it."

The sounds of Adam opening cupboards and containers filled the kitchen, while Riley's heart threatened to beat out of his chest. When the coffee started brewing, Adam said, "You think Coach is finally going to switch up the penalty kill today?"

Okay. So they weren't going to talk about it. Riley was relieved that Adam was willing to overlook Riley's confession, but he also wanted to scream. What the fuck did Riley have to do to make Adam interested in talking about all the sex they'd had? Was it really possible that Adam didn't have a single feeling about it?

"Maybe," Riley said, answering Adam's question in what he hoped was a steady and casual tone. "We've gotta do *something* about it."

"Yeah, it's been a mess lately."

Adam stretched his arms over his head, and Riley fixed his gaze on his cereal so he wouldn't have to see the sexy sliver of stomach that always revealed itself whenever Adam did that. He considered, for the zillionth time, moving out. Finding his own place. Giving himself space from a man who couldn't love him back.

He wished he was strong enough to do that. He wished Adam could be terrible, because besides his aversion to talking about the sex stuff, he was a perfect friend. Honestly, his only crime was not being in love with Riley, and Riley could hardly blame him for that.

He wondered, now that Adam *knew*, would the sex end? And if it did, would that be Adam punishing him, or doing him a favor? Either way, it would be agony.

Chapter Three

"I shouldn't have come," Adam said as soon as Maggie answered her phone.

"Didn't go well, huh?"

"I think he wanted to punch me."

"I did suggest you call him first," Maggie reminded him. "He'd be emotional right now. He doesn't need surprises."

"He's always emotional," Adam said automatically. As if he had the right. As if he had any idea what Riley Tuck was like these days. "But yeah. I should have called. Or just, y'know. Stayed home. Left him alone."

"How is he?" Maggie asked in a softer voice. The question made Adam's lingering anger—at Riley, at himself—disappear.

The shitty bed in his shitty motel room creaked as he sat on it, the mattress dipping nearly to the worn carpet. "He looks miserable," Adam said. "It hurt to see him, honestly. I wanted to…" Even though Maggie knew as close to everything as anyone who wasn't Adam or Riley was going to get, he still struggled to get the words out. "Hold him," he finished.

"Oh, Adam."

"You should have heard the speech he gave at the funeral. I don't know how he was even able to do it, but everything he said was so *beautiful*, y'know? He loved his dad so much." Adam had experienced a million emotions at once, as he'd watched Riley read his eulogy. He'd been heartbroken for Riley, but also proud of him, and also surprised, because Riley had never been much of a talker. Adam had shared the anxiety that he'd felt in the room as everyone wondered together if Riley would make it through his speech without crumbling. No one would have blamed him if he hadn't, but he'd gotten to the end, his voice rough and on the knife's edge of bursting into tears. He'd nodded at the full church when he'd finished, looking bewildered like he had no idea when all those people had gotten there. Adam had wanted to take him by the hand and tell him he'd done great. That it was over. He'd wanted to sit beside him with a comforting hand on his back. He'd wanted so many things that he couldn't have, and shouldn't even let himself want.

"I'm glad you went," Maggie said.

"Me too. But now it's over, and I'm not sure I'm much use to him. I should leave. Tomorrow. Tonight, maybe." The bed creaked in agreement.

"I think you should stay," Maggie said. "Give it a few days, at least. Give him time to get used to you."

Adam's wife—his *ex*-wife—was, and always had been, too good for him. She was loving, supportive, funny, beautiful, and a wonderful mother. He'd truly hit the jackpot with her, and he'd tried so hard to make it work, even after he'd finally figured out the truth about himself. For years after realizing he was gay, Adam had kept it to himself. By that point they'd been married for over a decade, and the thought of ending things—of hurting Maggie—made him sick.

But not telling her made him feel worse, and finally, nearly fifteen years into their marriage, he'd broken down and told her. She'd been upset, obviously, and surprised, but later she would admit to him that she'd also been relieved; their marriage had grown stiff and quiet over the years, and now she knew why. She'd admitted that she'd suspected he'd been having an affair. He'd assured her that hadn't been the case, but he'd also told her about Riley. By that point, Riley had been out of his life for years, but Adam still had a long-overdue confession to make to Maggie. He'd told her, through tears of shame, about the one night he hadn't been faithful. Maybe because it had been a few days after her husband came out to her and she'd had time for the shock to fade, but Maggie hadn't been angry. She'd been *sympathetic*, and thanked him for telling her, even as she'd still been reeling from the heartbreak of their marriage ending.

Too good for him, truly, and he was beyond grateful they were still friends.

During the two years that followed that conversation, Maggie had gently suggested several times that Adam get in touch with Riley. Adam had dismissed her suggestions. It had been over a decade since Riley had cut Adam out of his life, and for all Adam knew he could be married now. He was almost certainly doing just fine without the skittish, closeted teammate who'd jerked him around for most of their twenties. Adam would have to navigate his new life—retired, divorced, gay, and in his forties—without the man he was still in love with.

But then, two days ago, Maggie had given him the news about Harvey Tuck. "Riley needs you," she'd said, and she hadn't needed to say anything else. Because if there was even a chance it was true, Adam would be there.

"I'll stay at least another day," Adam decided, out loud. "I don't even know if I'll be able to see him again, though."

"It's not a big place, is it?" Maggie said. "I'm sure you can track him down."

"Maybe. How are the kids?"

Maggie laughed. "How should I know? They're barely ever home."

Adam smiled. Lucy was sixteen now and had a very active social life that left little time for family. Cole was fifteen and kept busy with basketball and video games. They weren't particularly interested in Adam, but Maggie assured him that they weren't interested in her either. They were teenagers, and, because neither of them played hockey, they were mysteries to Adam. When he'd been a teenager, he'd been nothing *but* hockey.

Adam still lived close to Maggie, in a smaller house that was larger than he needed, and the kids split their time between them based mostly on whatever was convenient for everyone each week. Maggie had been dating an engineer named Ethan for a few months now, and the kids seemed to like him. Things were decent between all of them, and Adam considered that a personal success.

He chatted with Maggie for a bit longer, about the kids, Maggie's day, the weather, and then Adam said, "When I saw him today, I couldn't believe how much I missed him. He looked so different, but also the same, y'know?" He blinked away the burning in his eyes. "Sorry. It's selfish of me to be talking about him with you."

"It's fine. You know it's fine."

"You're too good for me, Mags."

"Well, yeah. That's why we're divorced."

That made him laugh, a little. "Still. I promise I won't call you every day about this. I'm just feeling a little alone right now."

"I know." Her voice brightened. "Hey, how about you find

some fried scallops? I remember Riley boasting about a place there with the best fried scallops."

"I've been there before, yeah." God, how many years ago? Seventeen, at least. "They're good."

"Do that," she said. "And don't get a case of beer or a bottle of whiskey, okay?"

"I won't."

"Get some sleep tonight, and try to see him tomorrow."

"Okay. Yeah. I'll try. Thanks."

They ended the call, and Adam gently maneuvered himself until he was lying on the terrible mattress. Adam was used to luxury, and the River Bend Motel had none. It wasn't sketchy, exactly, just old and inexpensive and probably barely making a profit. It was the only hotel of any kind in town, but he doubted the No Vacancy sign got much of a workout.

His shoulder wouldn't thank him for this bed, he could already tell.

It was only three in the afternoon, which seemed impossible. He'd left Toronto on a 6:00 a.m. flight, picked up a rental car at the Halifax airport, then driven nearly two hours to Avery River on the north shore. The funeral had started two hours ago.

Now he was alone with his thoughts, which was a situation he'd been finding himself in far more often since retirement and divorce. Besides spending time with his kids, which was getting to feel less and less required, at least from Lucy's and Cole's standpoints, Adam didn't have much going on in his life. He was still in demand as a hockey celebrity in Toronto, was still friendly with his former teammates, and he still went to most of the Northmen home games, but he was finding some of that depressing. It was hard to be in the building but not be on the ice. Maybe it would start to feel easier soon.

None of his hockey friends knew he was gay, and he didn't

feel ready to tell them yet. He loved the guys like brothers, but he wouldn't exactly describe any of them as progressive thinkers. He worried that coming out would create a wall between him and his friends. He also wondered if the burden of hiding such a huge part of himself wasn't creating its own wall. Maybe it would be easier to come out so he could find out who his real friends were.

As far as his sex life went, he'd been...trying things out. The apps were an exciting and efficient tool, especially now that he wasn't terrified he'd be recognized. He wasn't *hoping* to be, but he'd made peace with the inevitability of it if he chose to hook up with men in the Toronto area. So far there hadn't been any gossip, but he expected that wouldn't last forever. Adam didn't particularly want to issue a public statement announcing his sexuality, but he didn't hate the idea of people just...finding out. There had to be an easy, organic way of being openly gay, right?

He really didn't know, and he had no one to ask. Though he'd been hooking up with men for the past couple of years, he didn't have any gay friends. The closest he'd come to making one was a guy he'd fucked three times, but then that guy had moved to Vancouver.

In summary, Adam was lonely. He was used to being constantly scheduled and busy and focused on winning and self-improvement. He'd been the captain of a top-ranked NHL team, a husband, and a father, all since his midtwenties. Now he was a largely unnecessary father with a busted shoulder, fumbling his way through hookups.

And he was in a motel in Nova Scotia, trying to, what? Win the heart of a man who hated him now? Of course not. He wasn't that delusional. He only wanted to try to repair some of the damage between Riley and himself. He wanted to apologize, and maybe he wanted Riley to apologize too, because it hadn't all been Adam's fault. Most of it, probably, but not all. Adam had made some bad decisions, but he hadn't been the one to throw their friendship away. He never would have chosen to do that.

The truth was, before it all went to hell, Riley had kind of been Adam's whole world. Obviously there'd been hockey, but Riley had been such a big part of that too. Even after Adam was married with kids, Riley had been a part of the family. Lucy and Cole had no memory of "Uncle" Riley now, but he'd adored those kids. If Maggie had found it weird, having Riley around so much, she'd never said anything. Maybe she'd thought it was part of the hockey wife package.

Adam probably should have realized then that he was gay and in love with his best friend. Or maybe he should have realized far sooner, during the many times he'd had sex with Riley before Adam was married. Or the one time he'd had sex with him after he was married.

Adam had been horrified with himself after that one time, but in the moment, when he'd been deep inside him and he'd had Riley's huge hands on his hips, all Adam had felt was relief and joy. Like he'd been exactly where he should be.

It had been the end of everything. The end of Adam trying to have it all. He'd panicked afterward, and no doubt hurt Riley badly. And then Riley had gone to Dallas, stopped talking to him, and left Adam reeling while also trying to make the most of the situation he'd put himself in. It hadn't been awful: marriage to a woman he truly liked a lot, two wonderful kids, an impressive hockey career, and a whole lot of money. But through it all, there was a giant Riley-shaped hole in Adam's life.

"And that," Adam said to the empty hotel room, "is exactly why you're staying for at least another day or two." He had no plan, and no expectations, but he was here. And it was a start.

Chapter Four

There was a gathering at Riley's parents' house the night of the funeral, because that's what people did here. Especially when someone like Harvey Tuck died.

"Here," Lindsay said, handing Riley a paper plate full of food. "Eat."

"Not hungry," he said, but he took the plate. Lindsay sat beside him on the love seat in the sunroom at the front of the house. They were mercifully alone in there. Riley had needed an escape from people.

"There's ham," Lindsay said. "You like ham."

"Thanks." Riley did like ham. "How are Katie and Allison holding up?"

"They're going to miss their grampy," Lindsay said, "but they seem okay. Josh has been a rock for all of us, God love him."

"That's good. I'm glad you have them."

Lindsay sighed and leaned her head against his bicep. "I want you to have someone."

"I've got Lucky." He nodded at the large, golden-brown lump snoring away on top of the heat vent in the corner.

"I saw Adam Sheppard was at the funeral."

"Yep," Riley said stiffly, recognizing the obvious segue. "I think everyone did."

"Did you talk to him?"

Riley's hand started shaking. He set the plate on the floor. "Not much."

"Nice of him to come."

"Is it?"

"Is he staying in town for a bit, or—"

"I don't *know*, Lindsay. Jesus." A horrible silence filled the room, then Riley said, "Sorry."

"It's okay. It's been a hell of a day."

Riley exhaled. "Yeah. Fuck."

"I keep expecting to see Dad in there, with everyone," Lindsay said, nodding behind them at the crowded house.

"Me too."

They were silent a while, then Lindsay said, "You should stay here tonight. Sleep on the couch or something. You shouldn't be alone."

"I won't drink. I promise."

"That's not what I meant. But that's good. It's probably tempting."

Riley ran his hand through his hair. "Yeah." He waited a beat, then said, "I think I'll go to the store tomorrow. Not to open it, but just to, I don't know. See what needs doing."

"It might help," she agreed. "Good to stay busy, they say."

"They do say that."

"Well..." Lindsay stood and brushed down her skirt. "I left poor Josh talking to Sherry Greenlaw, so I'd better rescue him."

Riley managed to smile.

"He's going to hear about her plans to keep the deer away from her tulips this year."

"So that battle continues, does it? I miss so much in Halifax."

She pointed at the abandoned plate of food. "Eat. Before Lucky wakes up and notices a plate full of ham."

"Yes, ma'am." Riley picked up the plate but didn't eat. Instead, he stared out the window at the rain that was still spitting against the glass and thought about the last time he'd seen Dad. Had it really only been five days ago? They'd closed the shop together, then, as usual, had lingered outside the entrance, chatting in the cold even though they'd been working together for hours and would again tomorrow. Riley had planned to drive to Truro later that week to pick up some gardening supplies ahead of the planting season and had asked if Dad needed anything from town. Dad had said no and then had proceeded to list several things from four different stores that Riley could pick up if it wasn't too much trouble. Riley had assured him that of course it wouldn't be too much trouble, and he should let him know if he needed anything else. It had been a dull conversation, really. Completely unremarkable, but Riley would replay it forever, probably. He didn't know how long they'd stayed outside talking, but he did know that he'd thought Dad had looked tired. He'd figured it was only because Dad had been busy lately, with the minor hockey season wrapping up and the upcoming awards banquet (now postponed).

Alone in the sunroom, Riley said, "Of course you waited for the hockey season to be over before you died."

An unhinged-sounding laugh escaped from him, which woke up Lucky. The dog stood and stretched, then noticed the plate of ham.

"Yep," Riley said, then held out a piece of ham for him. He watched Lucky happily devour it and wished, for the millionth time, that he could trade lives with his dog. "You don't have a single regret in the world, do you?"

Lucky licked his own nose, his tail thudding against the floor in the laid-back manner of someone whose concerns were mostly ham related. He didn't have to deal with the grief of burying his father, plus the heartache of coming face-to-face with the love of his fucking life, all on the same day. Riley was sure Lucky missed Dad in his own way. Of course it was impossible to know, really, but Riley was pretty sure Lucky had noticed Dad wasn't around.

"He's not coming back," Riley said, more to himself than to Lucky.

Lucky sat with a sigh and stared at the ham.

"Dad's gone, and Adam Sheppard is here." Riley massaged his own forehead. Lucky rested his head on Riley's knee and gazed up at him with sad eyes. "Yeah," Riley agreed. "It's fucked."

Adam probably wasn't still in town, though. Why would he be? Riley hoped he was already back in Toronto.

It *was* nice, though, that he'd bothered to come. That he still thought about Riley at all. Riley had assumed Adam had long forgotten about him. It would have been easy for him to move on from…whatever they'd had. It had never meant much to Adam.

It had meant everything to Riley.

Anyway. Adam was gone, and Riley could go right back to not thinking about him. Or trying not to think about him.

Lucky shifted so his head was leaning toward the ham. Riley scoffed, then gave him another piece. "I guess we should mingle." It was the last thing Riley felt like doing, but the house was full of people who'd loved his dad, and he could keep it together for a little while longer.

As soon as they were back among people, Lucky took off, weaving through the crowd in search of whoever seemed most likely to give him attention. Riley drifted like a ghost toward the kitchen, hoping no one noticed him at all. He gave quick nods of acknowledgment to a few people—Jessica and Addie, who were the high school kids who worked part-time at the shop; his cousin Cory; Robert from the hockey board—but didn't linger. Holding a paper plate that needed to be disposed of gave Riley a mission.

There was a small cluster of people in the kitchen, but they'd formed a tight conversation circle that Riley could easily bypass. He disposed of his plate, then busied himself for a while rinsing out the empty bottles and cans that had collected around the sink.

"There he is," said a voice Riley knew well. He turned to see his oldest friend, Darren, crossing the kitchen with his husband, Tom. "God, come here." Darren wrapped Riley in a hug and kissed his cheek. "I'm so sorry, love."

"Thanks." Riley glanced over Darren's shoulder. "Hey, Tom."

"How are you holding up?" Tom asked as he took his turn hugging Riley. Darren wasn't a small man, but Tom was *huge*. Taller even than Riley, and built like an offensive lineman. He had a thick beard and a kind face, and he absolutely adored Darren. Riley liked him a lot.

"I'm doing all right," Riley said as Tom released him from his bear grip.

Darren held his hand and squeezed it gently. "It's us. You can be honest."

Riley exhaled. "I'm barely holding it together."

"Of course you aren't. What can we do to help?"

A shaky, humorless laugh escaped Riley. "Nothing. I mean...right?"

Tom nodded, his warm brown eyes full of sympathy. "Do you need any errands done, or maybe some help around your house? It's planting season..."

"No, it's fine. I'm okay," Riley said. He really was. He'd already put a lot of work into starting his seeds for spring, and everything was going smoothly in the greenhouse. "It's just a hobby anyway."

Darren looked horrified. "Don't pretend that garden isn't your life."

Riley smiled a bit. "I've got a handle on it. Besides, it's still sugar season. You guys are busy enough."

"Never too busy for you," Darren said. "Especially now."

"Why don't you come to dinner this week sometime," Tom suggested. "Just us."

Riley appreciated the clarification. Darren and Tom often hosted dinner parties for what they liked to call the "who's who of queer Maritimers." They were popular hosts, with their beautiful cabin-style house on their scenic and secluded maple farm. "Yeah," he said. "Okay, maybe."

"You can come every night if you want," Darren said earnestly.

Riley glanced around the kitchen, which was heaving with food containers that hadn't even been opened yet. "I think I'll be good for dinner for a while." If he ever felt like eating again.

"The invitation is there. Anytime." Darren hugged him again. "We love you."

"Love you too." Riley had grown up with Darren, though they'd traveled in different circles. Riley had been a local star hockey player with hockey player friends, and Darren had been...well. Probably pretty lonely. He'd been singled out as "different" from an early age. Riley hadn't paid much attention to him until they were teenagers. By then Riley had figured out he himself was attracted to men, and he'd also noticed that Darren—tall and slim and blond—was sort of beautiful. They'd fooled around in high school, before Riley had gone to play junior hockey in Moncton, and then again during his summers home. It was an easy arrangement that was certainly convenient in a small town. When Riley went to Toronto, he'd stayed in touch with Darren, and they'd hooked up during that first summer too, but it had never been romantic. Eventually, Darren met Tom and fell hard in love. Riley had been deep in love with Adam by then, and jealous that the man Darren loved actually loved him back.

"You guys should head home," Riley said. "It's getting late." It was already dark, and the farm was a twenty-minute drive away.

"Can *you* head home?" Tom asked. "This is probably torture for you."

"Kind of. But it's okay. I'll stay a bit."

"I'm texting you tomorrow morning," Darren warned. "And if you don't reply I'll *call*. I swear to god."

"Okay, sweetheart," Tom said affectionately, "don't threaten your friend." He clapped Riley on the shoulder. "Get some sleep tonight, okay?"

"People keep suggesting that," Riley said. "I'm starting to think I don't look amazing."

His friends laughed politely at his sad joke. "You're stunning as always," Darren insisted.

They left, and Riley stayed for another hour or so. By that point he was barely registering what was going on around him. Mom found him leaning against a doorframe with his eyes closed.

"Riley," she said gently, "go home, sweetie. People are leaving now anyway."

"I'll help clean up."

"We have plenty of people who have offered to help with that, but I'll be shooing them out soon too. I need to go to bed."

Riley nodded. "Yeah. Okay. Is Lindsay...?"

"She put the girls to bed and conked out with them. Josh is still mingling, God love him."

"She married a good one," Riley said.

"She did. She learned that from me, you know."

They both smiled sadly. She deserved so many more years with her husband. They'd been an amazing couple. Absolute relationship goals, in Riley's opinion.

"Did you talk to Adam Sheppard at all?"

Riley rubbed his forehead. His family was not subtle. "A bit."

"I was talking to Deb, and she said Adam is staying for a few days."

Riley blinked. Deb co-owned the River Bend Motel with her husband. "Why?"

"Maybe he wants to reconnect with you."

Riley barely managed to stop himself from rolling his eyes. Adam could reconnect with the bottom of the fucking sea for all he cared. "He'll leave soon."

"Well, Deb is certainly excited about her celebrity guest. And it might be nice for you to catch up with him. I know you drifted apart, but you were such good friends once."

"Maybe," Riley said, just to end the conversation. If they kept talking about Adam Sheppard, he was going to punch a wall.

Instead, he wrapped his mom in a hug and said, "I love you."

"I love you too. Now please get some rest."

"Okay."

He left a few minutes later. He may have taken an unusual route home that happened to take him past the motel, but no one needed to know about that except God and Lucky.

Chapter Five

The following morning, Adam knocked on the front door of the Tuck family home. He shoved his hands in his coat pockets while he waited, then took them out, thinking it might appear disrespectful somehow. His stomach swam with nerves.

Voices sounded inside the house—muffled at first, and then someone he was pretty sure was Riley's sister, Lindsay, calling out, "It's Adam Sheppard."

The knob turned, the door opened. Adam took a small step backward. The woman who opened the door stared up at him, and yes. He was sure this was Lindsay. He'd caught glimpses of her yesterday, but the last time he'd spoken to her she'd been an undergrad. She'd be in her late thirties now, but didn't look too different than she had back then: about half a foot shorter than Adam, with a slim, toned body, and long, wavy hair the same reddish-blond color as Riley's.

"Hi, Lindsay," Adam said. "It's been a while."

She smiled. "Surprised you remember me."

"Of course I do. I'm sorry about your dad," Adam said. "Harvey was a great man."

"He was. Thank you."

"If there's anything I can do…"

Lindsay's eyebrows raised. "I don't think there's much that can be done about the situation."

Adam's gaze dropped to the black rubber mat under his feet. "No. I know."

"Are you looking for my brother?"

Adam's glanced back up. "Is he here?"

"No."

"Oh." Adam put his hands in his pockets again. "Sorry to bother you. And sorry for...sorry."

He turned to leave, but stopped when Lindsay said, "You any good at drying dishes?"

Adam eagerly whipped back around at the invitation. "Sure. Yeah. I can do that."

Lindsay stepped back from the door, and Adam followed her into the house.

"We had a gathering here last night, so now we've got containers we need to wash and return to people," Lindsay said as she took Adam's coat and found a place for it in the closet. "I know people aren't in a hurry to get them back, but I need something to do. Seems like you might too."

"Yeah," Adam said gratefully. "I do." His chest felt tight as he gazed around the front hallway of the house he'd enjoyed spending summers in nearly two decades ago. It looked the same: soft yellow walls decorated with framed family photos and watercolor paintings of boats, worn wooden floors, and an old barrel serving as a table for keys and sunglasses just inside the door.

Lindsay led him to the kitchen. "My husband, Josh, took our girls to the park, since it finally stopped raining."

"How old?" Adam asked.

"Josh? He's thirty-eight."

Adam snorted.

"Sorry," Lindsay said. "That was a tribute to Dad. The kids are eight and six. Katie is the oldest, and then Allison."

"Fun ages."

"Sometimes." She opened a drawer and pulled a dish towel from it. She handed it to him and asked, "How old are yours now?"

"Lucy is sixteen, and Cole is fifteen."

"Holy. I forgot how young you were when they were born."

"Yeah, well. Maggie and I kind of put the cart before the horse there."

Lindsay smiled, but it looked sad. Adam wondered what she was thinking. How much did she know?

"How is Maggie?" she asked.

"Good. Great." He folded the towel in half, and then again. "We're, um. We're divorced now."

Lindsay's brow furrowed. "Oh. I'm sorry. I didn't know."

"We're still good friends," he said quickly, "but we're not together anymore. She's with someone else now." He realized how that sounded and added, "Not that she left me for him or anything like that. There were…other reasons. But nothing she did. She's wonderful."

"That's good," Lindsay said, though she sounded like she wanted to ask a million questions. Instead, she went to the sink and began to fill it with hot water. The sink was full, and she'd started scrubbing the first plastic container before she asked, "So you're single now?"

"I am."

She didn't say anything as she finished washing the container, then handed it to Adam. Finally, she said, "It's been a while since Riley's seen you, hasn't it?"

Twelve fucking years.

"We sort of drifted apart, I guess." It was both accurate and the total opposite of what had happened between them. Drifting apart sounded gentle. Adam had felt more like he'd been ripped in half. Or that he'd ripped himself in half.

"But you came anyway."

"I did." Why were these containers so impossible to dry? Water seemed to gather and stick to every part of them.

"When are you leaving?"

"Not sure yet."

Lindsay handed him the lid to the container. "Riley's going to take this the hardest. Losing Dad, I mean. We're all devastated and shocked, but Riley... I'm going to worry about him the most."

Adam swallowed, then nodded. Of course Riley would take it the hardest.

"He's worked hard," she continued, "since he retired from hockey. He was in rough shape when he first moved back here. I know you weren't really in his life anymore by then."

"I wanted to be," Adam blurted. "I tried to be."

She turned to face him. "He's not the easiest person to help. Sometimes you need to stay on him, y'know?"

Adam held her gaze, but barely. He was so ashamed. "I wish I had."

She nodded. "Is that why you're here now?"

"Something like that."

"Because I don't really know what the deal is with you and him, but I do know that he doesn't need anyone adding extra pain to his life right now."

Adam wanted to argue that he'd never do that, except obviously he couldn't promise that. Pain seemed to be all Riley and Adam had been able to give each other in the end. "I'm not here to hurt him," he said, because that, at least, was true.

"Good." She turned back to the sink and began washing another container.

After a moment, Adam gathered some courage and asked,

"So he's doing better, you said? Since…" Since he'd completely fallen apart, at least according to hockey gossip.

"He's a lot better. I won't get into it with you, because it's not my place but, yeah. He's better."

Adam took the container from her and began drying it. "Glad to hear it." Then the question that he'd been determined to hold back burst out of him. "Does he…have anyone? Living with anyone, like? Um…"

"He's single, if that's what you're asking." She ducked her head so Adam couldn't see her face. "He doesn't share everything with me, but no real boyfriends that I know of."

Boyfriends. It was ridiculous that after everything, the easy acknowledgment that Riley was gay was so shocking. "That's too bad," Adam managed.

"Is it?" Lindsay's tone was light, almost teasing.

Adam's cheeks heated, and at that moment Susan Tuck entered the kitchen.

"Adam Sheppard," she said brightly. "My god, look at you. Come here." She embraced him in a hug, her head level with Adam's chest.

"It's good to see you again, Mrs. Tuck," he said. "I'm sorry for your loss."

"Thank you. And it's Susan, of course. How are you these days?"

Adam was surprised by how cheerful and steady she sounded, given the circumstances. "I'm good. Retired now, so that's different."

"I heard. I also heard the Hall of Fame rumors already. It's a legacy to be proud of, that's for sure."

"Thanks," he said, because he *was* proud of his career. He may have fucked up the rest of his life, but his hockey career had been close to perfect.

"We missed seeing you here in the summers," she said.

"I got busy with the kids and all that," he said apologetically. Adam had loved those summers, spending days at the beach or puttering around the bay in Riley's family's boat. The first few years Adam had simply enjoyed being away from his own stern parents, who would have focused solely on his conditioning and on marketing opportunities. He'd been enchanted by Riley's family, by this small town, and by Riley himself. And that fifth summer...god, if Adam could choose one part of his life to stay in forever, it would be that fifth summer in Avery River.

"You could have brought the kids," Susan said, "but I suppose there were other reasons."

"There were," he agreed, and hoped she didn't expect him to explain those reasons, because that would be impossible. What could he say? That he'd maybe accidentally broken Riley's heart? That he was here now to try to fix it?

He knew it was unlikely that anything he could say or do would repair the damage he'd caused, and maybe Riley was years past caring about him at this point. That would make sense. Why would Riley still be carrying a torch for a man he hadn't spoken to for twelve years? It was ridiculous.

Except Adam knew it wasn't impossible. Adam was *proof* that it wasn't impossible.

He blinked when he realized Lindsay had asked him a question. "Hm? Sorry."

"How's your shoulder?"

"Oh. You know. Better some days than others."

"You had tendon repair surgery last year?"

"Yeah," he said, surprised she knew about that. "Last summer. Third time, though."

"And you're doing your physio?" She smiled. "Sorry, professional curiosity."

"Are you a physiotherapist? I didn't know."

"She sure is," Susan said proudly. "The best in Nova Scotia."

Lindsay shook her head, still smiling. "Hardly. But I do specialize in joint pain, especially shoulder, elbow, and knee injuries."

"Oh," he said. Then, "I'm getting joint replacement surgery soon. I guess it's a real mess in there at this point."

Lindsay huffed and turned back to the sink. "I'm going to shut my mouth now because you don't want to hear what I think about the way you hockey idiots never let anything heal properly."

Adam smiled. "Sounds like I just heard it."

"And you really don't want to get me started on hockey players and their mental health. When Riley—" She stopped abruptly. "Anyway. Ignore me. I'm exhausted."

"Riley?" he asked, because he couldn't help it.

"Nothing," Lindsay said, at the same time Susan said, "Where is Riley today, anyway?"

"The shop, I think," Lindsay said.

Susan scoffed. "He doesn't need to do that. We're closed for the week. People here understand that."

"I know. But he needed something to do."

Susan sighed. "I should bring him some of this food. He's barely been eating."

"I could do that," Adam said quickly, before he could talk himself out of it. "I could bring him his lunch."

Both women stared at him. He scratched his wrist. "I'd like to talk to him. Y'know, see him. Before I go."

"Well," Susan said, as she shared a glance with Lindsay, "that would be nice of you. Do you eat ham?"

Chapter Six

Riley had made a mess of Tuck's Sporting Goods. What had started as a minor decision to swap the placement of the hockey tape shelf unit and the batting glove rack had turned into a full teardown of nearly every display in the shop. Riley was now standing in the middle, bewildered by how things had gotten to this point.

"Should've left those gloves where they were," he muttered.

Lucky was staring at him with an expression that seemed exasperated.

"Yeah, I know," Riley sighed. "We're gonna be here awhile."

He wanted to crumple to the floor and cry, but he resisted. He needed to put the store back together, one piece at a time. He was halfway through restocking the hockey stick rack when the door chime, and Lucky, announced a visitor.

He had his apologetic but firm explanation that the shop was closed today ready to go, but then he saw Adam coming through the door. Just like yesterday, Riley's stupid heart bounced.

"We're closed," he said, just to be a dick.

"I can see why."

And, yes. God. Now that another person was here, Riley

could see exactly how chaotic the store looked. How chaotic *he* looked. Why did it have to be Adam? "Just rearranging some things."

"I can help."

"No thanks." Riley turned his back to him and began fussing with the hockey sticks that he'd already placed in the rack. Just hearing Adam's voice again—deep and slightly soft, but always steady—was making Riley's stomach ache. There was a reason Adam had been named captain of the Toronto Northmen at only twenty-four; he had that *thing*, that easy competence that made people respect and admire him. He seemed like someone who always knew what to do, what to say. Like someone who never made mistakes or bad decisions.

Riley knew better.

"Who's this?" Adam asked.

Riley glanced over his shoulder and saw Lucky enthusiastically sniffing the full-looking shopping bag Adam was holding. "Lucky."

"Sounds like there's a story there."

"No story," Riley said. "Named him that because he's lucky to be a dog."

Adam laughed, quick and nervous. "It does seem relaxing, I guess." When Riley didn't reply, Adam said, "I brought lunch. Your mom gave it to me."

"When did you see Mom?" Riley didn't like the idea of Adam bothering his family.

"I was just there."

"Why?"

"I was looking for you."

Riley snorted. "Why?"

"I thought we could talk, maybe."

He shook his head, then continued to place hockey sticks in the rack.

"Or not," Adam said. "If you don't want to."

"I'm busy."

"And I offered to help."

Riley threw the stick he was holding against the rack. It clattered to the floor with a satisfying amount of noise. A heavy silence followed, then Lucky began whimpering. Riley scrubbed a hand over his own face, feeling like an asshole. He turned and crouched, holding a hand out to Lucky. "I'm sorry," he said gently. "It's okay."

Lucky went to him, pressing against Riley's bent legs. Riley glanced up at Adam. "I'm not at my best right now."

"Be weird if you were."

Riley scratched Lucky's ears, then stood so he was eye level with Adam. "What is this? What are you doing?"

"Bringing you lunch?"

Riley took a step toward him, then another. He must have looked as angry as he felt, because Adam took a step back. Good. "Leave me alone. Leave my mom alone. Fuck *off*."

Adam nodded, infuriatingly calm. "Okay." He placed the bag on the counter next to a pile of mouth guards. "You should eat, though."

Riley glared at him.

Adam held up his hands, palms out. "I just want to help. However I can."

"You can help by leaving."

The pain in Adam's eyes was obvious, but Riley refused to feel bad about it. Adam was a man who wasn't used to not being adored, and Riley couldn't do that. Not again.

"Yeah," Adam said, "okay. I'm sorry." He took a step toward the door, stopped, and said, "I'm staying at the River Bend, Room Four, and my phone number is the same as it's always been."

Then he left. The door chime tinkled behind him. Riley

stared at the door for several seconds after it closed, and that's when the guilt began to settle in. He glanced down at Lucky, who was gazing up at him with questioning eyes.

"It's complicated," Riley said. "We've got a lot of history. You don't need to worry about it."

Later, when he was dusting shelves, he told Lucky, "I know he seems nice. He's perfect, right? Adam *fucking* Sheppard."

Later still, when he was picking at a ham and cheese sandwich, he said, "You don't know what it feels like, to have your heart stomped on *repeatedly*. It took me years to get over him, okay? So it doesn't matter how helpful he wants to be or how good he fucking looks." He sighed and tossed Lucky a piece of ham. Adam really looked good. His gray-flecked hair and stubble, his fancy millionaire coat, and those fucking eyes. "He's bad for me. I needed to be an asshole to him. It's for the best."

Much later, when the sun had set and Riley had gotten most of the mess off the middle of the floor at least, he said to a sleeping Lucky, "Why is he staying? It doesn't make sense."

Riley was behind the counter, his ass resting against the top of it, staring at the framed photos on the wall. There were a few of Riley from his years with the Northmen, and one from his brief stint with Dallas. There was one of Riley and Adam hugging after a goal Adam had scored, Adam smiling and Riley yelling in his ear, arms wrapped around him tight. They'd been playing together for five seasons when that photo was taken, and they'd been fucking for two of them.

There was a photo of Dad wearing an Avery River minor hockey jacket and smiling. Riley stared at it until his eyes burned. "I don't know if I can do this," he confessed to the photo. "I can't be you. I wish I could be."

He knew what Dad would say: "You just need to be Riley Tuck." Riley wasn't sure that was true, though. This town needed Harvey, and Riley was a poor substitute.

His gaze traveled back to the photo of the goal celebration. God, they'd been so young. Like different people. Riley had been so hopelessly in love with Adam, he'd have done anything for him. And he'd been stupid enough to think Adam had felt the same way.

He sighed, then pushed off the counter. He wasn't going to be calling or texting Adam, that was for damn sure. Adam could stay at the River Bend Motel for as long as he fucking wanted, sleeping on a lumpy mattress and thin, scratchy sheets. Riley had heard from plenty of people how uncomfortable those beds were.

It was probably hell on Adam's shoulder.

Whatever. Fuck him. Riley had things to do, unlike *some* recently retired superstars. Like right now he was going to go check on his mom, then hopefully get a halfway decent night's sleep, then get back to cleaning up his mess at the shop tomorrow.

"Come on," he said, gently nudging Lucky awake. Lucky grumbled as he lifted his head, probably irritated by having to do something that wasn't sleeping or eating—the two things Riley himself had been unable to do for days.

"Sorry your life is so hard," he said.

Lucky woofed quietly in agreement, then followed him out of the shop.

After leaving the shop, Riley went to his parents' house and found a living room full of people staring expectantly at him.

"What?" he asked.

Mom, her sister Ruth, Lindsay, Josh, and even the two kids all had more or less the same expression on their faces. That expression said, *So how did it go?*

"What?" Riley said again.

"So," Mom said, "how did it go?"

He shrugged.

"Oh, Riley," Lindsay sighed. "Were you rude to him?"

Riley curled his fingers until his nails bit into his palms. "I wasn't rude to him," he lied. If Adam was going to show up in Riley's town twelve years too late, at a time when Riley was already an emotional wreck, he could fucking expect some rudeness. "He didn't stay long. Whatever. Thanks for the lunch, though."

Lindsay gave him a questioning look, then changed the subject. "Josh is going to take the kids back home tomorrow. I'm going to stay a bit longer."

"How will you get back to Halifax?"

"I'm, uh." Lindsay glanced at Mom, who nodded, then said, "I'm going to take Dad's truck. We were talking about maybe selling it, and I know someone in Halifax who's interested."

"Oh," Riley said. He felt like he was falling backward into a pit.

"I've never liked driving that big old thing," Mom said. "May as well let someone else make use of it."

"Right. Yeah. Makes sense," Riley said tightly, then he turned and escaped to the kitchen. When he got there, he placed his hands on either side of the sink and stared out the dark window, hoping he wasn't about to throw up. He watched a raindrop trail its way down the glass, joining a blob of water that had pooled in one corner. He watched more drops do the same, and he breathed. Even though he'd seen the tiny box that held Dad's ashes go into the ground, the idea that the man would never drive his beloved truck again seemed impossible. That Dad would never pull into Riley's driveway, ready to help with whatever home improvement project Riley was working on. That he'd never show up at the rink again with a tray of coffees and a big smile. That he'd never pull a silly little float in Avery River's Canada Day parade again.

"Hits you like a ton of bricks, doesn't it," Mom said from behind him.

Riley turned and saw his mom standing in the middle of the kitchen with open arms. He went to her and hugged her tight. "He loved that truck," he said.

Mom sniffed, and said, "Did he? He barely ever talked about it."

Riley managed to laugh.

"We probably should have buried him in it," Mom continued.

Riley laughed harder, even as tears streamed down his face. "Jesus, Mom."

They broke apart, and he saw the tears in Mom's eyes too. "You have to laugh when you can," she said, "otherwise you get swallowed up."

Riley nodded and wiped a hand over his face. Swallowed up was exactly how he felt, by grief, by anger, and now, with Adam here, with the old feelings of longing and misery that had plagued him for years.

"You look tired," Mom said.

"I'm exhausted," Riley admitted.

"Go home. Get some sleep. Come by in the morning to say goodbye to Josh and the girls, okay?"

"I will."

"And take some eggs. Jerry dropped off two dozen this afternoon, and Sandy gave me two dozen yesterday. They think I'm drowning my sorrows in soufflés or something."

"I'll take some. I'm glad Lindsay is staying."

"Me too, of course, but I told her it isn't necessary. Still, it'll be nice to have her around a bit." She paused a moment, then added, "Adam seems like he'd like to help."

Riley took a step back. "Yeah. Well."

Mom patted his arm. "You boys were such good friends."

She headed for the fridge, and Riley's heart twisted in his chest. They'd been fucking *great* friends, and maybe if they'd been able to leave it at that, they'd still be great friends.

He left a few minutes later, Lucky in the passenger seat of his truck, panting happily. He drove to the end of town, then turned left toward the ocean. His house was about fifteen minutes away from his parents' place, down a dark stretch of road lined by thick forest. Eventually it met up with the road along the ocean, where there was a mix of small summer cottages, large vacation homes that had been recently built, and some of the original houses in the area. Riley owned one of those houses. He'd bought it as a fixer-upper a few months after he'd quit hockey, thinking it would be good for him to have a project to work on. He hadn't been the handiest guy in the world at the time, but he'd since learned a lot of skills over the past decade of renovating it. He was proud of his home.

Lucky ran ahead of him, as always, as if the dog could unlock the door. He paced impatiently on the front stoop as Riley gathered the food Mom had unloaded on him from the back seat.

"Give me a second," Riley grumbled. When he finally got to the house, balancing the food while fumbling the key from his pocket, Lucky stood with his front paws on the door. "It would be easier if you moved," Riley said.

He got the door open, despite Lucky's refusal to move, then carried the food to the kitchen while Lucky tore around the house, inspecting every room as if there'd be a surprise there. Riley put the food in the fridge, which had been mostly empty, then made his way to the living room, where he promptly collapsed on the sofa in an exhausted heap.

"Fuck," he said to no one. What a day.

What was Adam expecting? A chat? There was no way they

could talk about anything without talking about *everything*. And Riley really didn't want to talk about *everything*.

Things like, "Do you remember when I told you that I was in love with you and you laughed in my face?"

Or, "Did you ever tell your wife about the night we won the Cup?"

Or, "Do you even care what happened to me after that, or were you just relieved that I was gone?"

Adam had hurt him deeply and repeatedly. Riley had barely survived the pain, and that wasn't an exaggeration. After Riley went to Dallas, Adam had broken more records, raised his kids, and loved his beautiful wife. During that same time, Riley's life had been mostly undiagnosed depression, alcohol, sleeping pills, and weighing the pros and cons of ending it all.

It was Lindsay who'd told him to come home, during a tear-filled phone call when Riley had, for the first time, admitted out loud how bad he was doing. How he didn't think he could play hockey anymore, and that it might actually kill him if he stayed in Dallas. Nothing personal against the city of Dallas—Riley hadn't given it a fair chance—but it was over two thousand miles from home, and at that time he'd felt every single one of them.

Quitting the NHL at the age of twenty-nine was the hardest decision he'd ever had to make. He'd worked his whole life to get there, and he'd still been in decent physical health. If his brain had cooperated, he probably could have had at least five more good seasons in the league. Maybe even ten, like Adam had managed. Instead, he more or less fell apart over one and a half seasons in Dallas: he'd missed practices, he'd been scratched from the lineup and benched a few times, and he'd even gotten into a fight with a teammate during a practice. Some days he'd been so depressed he couldn't force himself to get out of bed. Other days he'd been too hungover to function. At the time it was basically unheard of for an NHL player to quit for mental health reasons. Honestly, it had been unheard of for an NHL player to *have* mental health issues. So Riley had been vague, claiming that he simply felt it was the right decision for him. The hockey world mostly translated that as Riley being a lazy drunk who had gone nuts. A wasted talent. A joke.

Dallas hadn't been sorry to lose him.

Things got better after he'd come home. He quit drinking, found a good therapist in Halifax he sometimes saw in person but usually talked to on the phone, and, through his family doctor, had been able to figure out the most effective antidepressants. Riley liked living in Avery River, and with time, he made a nice life for himself. A full life, even without a partner or reliable regular sex. Being a single gay man in a small Nova Scotia town wasn't ideal, but he wasn't celibate. The apps worked here, even if the pickings were slim.

Lucky, either satisfied or disappointed that everything in the house was as they'd left it, returned to the living room and jumped up on the sofa. He slumped over Riley's thighs and rested his head on Riley's chest. Riley idly scratched Lucky's ears and continued to stare at the ceiling. He'd hung a vintage chandelier made from iron and stained glass in the center, a piece that he'd fallen in love with in an antiques store four years ago. He'd decorated the whole living room to complement the rich jewel tones of the geometric glass pattern. His sofa and matching armchair were from the forties, both reupholstered in dark teal velvet and accented with embroidered gold and blue pillows. A large Persian-style rug spread over the refinished wood floor, ending just in front of the brick hearth that supported his cast-iron wood stove. It was a cozy, beautiful room, and Riley felt comfortable here. Even now, when that comfort was spiked with loneliness.

He closed his eyes and listened to Lucky breathe and to the

rain outside. He thought of Adam, then cursed himself for thinking of Adam. Fuck Adam.

Adam, who had seen the mess Riley had made of the shop. Who had offered to help fix it. Who had traveled to Nova Scotia to attend Dad's funeral. Who wanted, for whatever reason, to be there for Riley. As if they could simply be friends again.

Riley was spiraling, and when he spiraled he made bad decisions. He wouldn't make a bad decision. Not tonight. He would drag himself upstairs, go to bed, try to sleep, and forget about Adam Sheppard.

Chapter Seven

Adam had to admit to himself that he'd run out of logical reasons to stay in Avery River. Riley didn't want him here, and Adam had probably done all he could to help. That had amounted to drying some dishes, delivering lunch, and fucking off when asked.

Still, he couldn't make himself check out of the River Bend Motel.

Riley wasn't going to text him. Of course he wasn't. It was ridiculous for Adam to even think he still had his number saved, but he hadn't been able to resist trying to find out. As if the fact that Riley still had Adam's number in his contacts would mean something.

Adam had spotted the framed photo behind the counter at the shop, the one of Riley and him celebrating that huge goal. Adam had the same photo on display in his own house, back in Toronto, even though it hurt to look at. They'd been fucking magic together back then, on the ice. And off the ice...well.

Early in their second NHL season, they'd been praised by a hard-ass Northmen beat reporter for having "something special." Adam had read the article aloud to Riley across their round IKEA kitchen table in the apartment they'd shared, and still remembered the way Riley had tried to hide his pleased smile by stuffing a spoonful of Raisin Bran in his mouth. It had been thrilling, having someone else notice and announce that Adam Sheppard and Riley Tuck had a rare, magical connection. Adam had felt it every single day.

Kissing Riley for the first time had simultaneously been the most terrifying and easiest thing Adam had ever done. He'd been just drunk enough to not overthink kissing his male best friend, but not drunk enough to forget how fast his heart had raced, or how sweet Riley's surprised gasp had been before he'd kissed Adam back. It had been about halfway through their third season in Toronto, and they'd both been twenty-one. Kids, really.

Later, when the orgasms were over and the alcohol had worn off, the overthinking had started. Adam had been so desperate to convince himself that it hadn't meant anything— that it had just been sex, a spontaneous experiment—that he'd immediately begun to spout cliches. "We'll pretend that never happened," and "Man, how drunk were we, ha ha?"

Of course he hadn't been able to pretend it hadn't happened, and of course it had happened again. And again. Eventually he'd stopped pretending he didn't want it, but he'd never admitted what Riley had really meant to him. He'd never allowed himself to acknowledge it, because there was no way he was *gay*. NHL players weren't gay.

Adam could blame the concussions he'd suffered during his hockey career for how slow he'd been to figure himself out, but the truth was he'd never been very smart about things that really mattered. And the other truth was that Adam the NHL player *was* gay and had always been gay. The truth was that he'd been in love with Riley, and probably still was.

The harshest truth was that he didn't deserve to be.

Adam went to the bathroom to brush his teeth and ended

up frowning at himself in the mirror for a full minute. "Don't you dare tell him," he instructed himself. "He needs a friend, not this mess."

Adam could do that, he decided as he spit toothpaste into the chipped sink. He couldn't undo the past, but he could be here now for Riley.

He got into bed and grabbed the book from his nightstand that he'd almost finished because he'd had plenty of time to read. He was two pages into the last chapter when a knock on his hotel room door startled him. It was late, almost eleven. "Who the hell?" Adam muttered as he left the bed.

When he opened the door, he was surprised to find Riley. It was raining again, and his hair was clinging to his temples and forehead. His eyes looked wild, and for a moment Adam worried he was about to get punched.

"Hi," Adam said cautiously.

"Hey."

"You, uh, want to come in?"

Riley stepped past Adam, his arm brushing Adam's chest. He stopped in the middle of the room, then glanced around like he wasn't sure how he'd gotten there.

"You can sit," Adam offered, gesturing to the metal desk chair with the cracked vinyl seat.

Riley didn't sit. "Why are you here?"

"Well," Adam said slowly, "this is my motel room."

Riley's jaw clenched, and he snorted, almost like a bull. "Fucking answer the question."

"Okay. I'm here for you."

His answer only seemed to infuriate Riley further. "I don't want you here. I don't need you."

The words seemed to bounce off the thin walls for a moment, hopefully drowning out the shattering of Adam's heart. He swallowed hard and waited. Riley's head dropped, and his hands curled into fists at his side, then released, then curled again. Adam recognized this from years of living together: Riley was trying to calm himself.

"I get it," Adam offered. "I shouldn't have come."

Riley paced the room for a moment, then said, "Did you think I'd actually *want* to see you?"

"No. I didn't think that."

"Then why. The fuck. Are you here?"

Adam scrambled for the right words, and ended up blurting out honest ones, "Because I wanted to see you. I wanted to make sure you—" He stopped himself when he realized how stupid the end of that sentence was going to be.

"You wanted to make sure I'm okay? Well, I'm fucking not."

"Of course not. I know. And I'm making it worse. I'm sorry."

Riley huffed and looked away. He had a well-groomed beard now, which really suited him. Adam had only ever let his own facial hair grow beyond stubble during the playoffs, and had always been keen to shave the beard off as soon as he could. Riley looked good, though. Rugged and handsome. His reddish hair was lighter than it used to be, closer to strawberry blond, which hid any gray hairs he might have.

"I don't know what I'm supposed to say to you," Riley said.

Adam took a careful step toward him. "You can say anything to me."

Riley met his gaze and held it, anger flashing in his eyes. "Can I?"

Adam's cheeks heated with shame. The words "I'm in love with you, you know" echoed across seventeen years, followed by the sound of Adam's dismissive laughter.

"What would you like to talk about, *Shep*?" Riley crossed the room in long strides until he was inches away from Adam.

"You gave me your hotel room number. What were you hoping for?"

Riley's eyes were like storm clouds, and his voice sounded like distant thunder. Adam's lips parted involuntarily, and he may have gasped.

Riley's gaze dropped to Adam's mouth. He placed a hand on Adam's chin, holding him there, tilting his head back slightly. Adam's heart raced and his cock stirred.

"Maybe," Riley said, "you thought I'd want to escape my problems by sucking your dick for a bit, hm?"

"N-no."

Riley studied his face for a moment, so close Adam could feel his breath on his lips. He shouldn't want Riley to kiss him. Not like this.

"Nah," Riley said. "Of course you don't want that. You're too sober, right?"

Adam closed his eyes. "That's not—"

Then Riley let him go and retreated to the other side of the room. He raised a fist at the wall, but stopped himself before punching.

Adam sat on the bed, breathing hard. Riley wouldn't hurt him. He wouldn't kiss him, but he wouldn't hurt him either.

Riley paced a bit, then sat in the chair Adam had offered earlier, knees spread with his elbows resting on the metal arms. For a long moment, there was silence, then Riley said, quietly, "This week has been a nightmare."

"I understand."

"It's too much," Riley said. He flapped a hand next to his temple. "Too much, y'know?"

"I know." Riley had never been good at managing his emotions, and there'd been many times in the past where Adam had helped him through that. It had scared Adam, sometimes, when Riley would sink so low he couldn't function, or get so worked up that he couldn't breathe. But what had scared him the most had been Riley leaving Toronto without a word to Adam, after secretly asking for a trade. Adam had felt sad for himself, but he'd been worried sick about Riley. Who would take care of him in Dallas?

"I'm sorry," Riley said.

Adam hadn't been expecting an apology of any kind from Riley. "It's okay."

"No. That was fucked up, just then, when I—I'm sorry."

Adam swallowed. "It's okay," he said again. If either of them was fucked up, it was him for getting aroused by a furious Riley.

A long, heavy silence filled the room, then Riley said, "Dad would have liked you being here. At the funeral."

Adam knew how much it cost Riley to say that. "Thank you."

"I made a mess of the shop."

"It can be fixed."

"I don't want anyone to see it. I don't want—" Riley's voice was breaking. "I wrecked Dad's shop."

Adam took a chance and placed a hand on Riley's knee. "Let me help. I've got two hands and one functional shoulder."

Riley's gaze dropped to Adam's hand on his knee, then back up to Adam's face. "Still bothering you? The shoulder?"

"It's better than it was before my last surgery, but it's still a bastard most days."

Riley looked like he wanted to say something about Adam being a bastard himself, but he managed to hold his tongue.

"Honestly, I forget what it's like to live without pain," Adam said, probably too cheerfully. It really wasn't a joke.

"Sorry." Riley's gray-blue eyes were so sad, and Adam was overcome with the desire to take his hand, pull him onto the bed, and wrap himself around him. Adam suddenly became very aware of how little he was wearing compared to Riley: a snug white T-shirt, loose-fitting black sleep pants, and bare feet. That he was sitting on a bed, and that Riley was alone with him in a hotel room, like so many times before.

Adam pulled his hand away. "Did you eat your lunch?"

"Some of it." Riley exhaled hard. "Thanks for bringing that."

"I went to Paula's for some scallops."

Riley's lips curved up slightly. "Must have caused a commotion."

Adam smiled. "I signed some things. Was in a few selfies."

"Normal day in the life of Adam Sheppard."

Adam couldn't deny it. He got recognized a lot pretty much everywhere in Canada. "I don't mind. I like meeting people."

Riley grunted, folded his hands between his legs, and stared at the floor. "I can't deal with this right now."

"With what?"

Riley moved a hand in the space between them, back and forth. "This. Us."

"I'm not asking you to. I just want to help."

Riley shook his head. "No thanks. I'll be fine."

"Riles—"

"I'll be *fine.*" Riley stood up. "And don't call me that."

"All right, I won't. But I don't want you to be alone."

Riley stared at him. "I have friends, you know."

Adam's stomach dropped. He was such an idiot. "Right. Of course."

"Anyway," Riley said. He sounded so tired. "Like I said, Dad would've liked you being here. So thanks, I guess. But I think we're done here."

Adam nodded miserably. "Got it."

Riley stared down at him, and for a moment, his eyebrows pinched together and Adam thought he saw regret in his eyes.

Or maybe he was only shocked by how pathetic Adam looked, sitting on a shitty motel bed, trying not to cry.

"Goodbye, Adam."

"Bye," Adam said, but Riley had already left.

Chapter Eight

The next morning, Adam decided he couldn't leave things as they were with Riley. He stopped by Paula's to arm himself with coffee and two of the delicious-looking cinnamon buns (still warm!) that were piled on a platter next to the cash.

"You won't regret those," Paula herself said as she rang him in. "We're famous for them."

"I'm sure I won't."

"Is the second one for poor Riley?"

Adam paused in the middle of entering his PIN. "It's—yeah."

"Such a sin," Paula clucked. "Harv was one of a kind. Well, I suppose Riley didn't fall far from the tree. Looks like him too, only..."

"Taller," they both said at the same time.

Paula smiled. She was probably in her sixties—about Riley's mom's age—a white woman with short gray hair and kind eyes. She was dressed very casually and wore no makeup, like someone who had been doing this job a long time and wasn't trying to impress anyone. "You tell Riley to come by anytime for a hot meal. No charge. And give him this." She grabbed a loaf of homemade brown bread off a shelf behind her. "His favorite."

Adam stashed this piece of info away like a treasure. He'd take anything he could get. "Thanks. I will. And I'll tell him."

She glanced at a table where two men who were probably in their fifties were sitting, both staring at them. "Oh, for pity's sake, fellas. Just ask him." She turned back to Adam. "Arnold and Jeff over there are die-hard Toronto fans."

Ah. Adam put on a smile. "Do you have a pen I could borrow?"

Fifteen minutes later he parked in one of the three spaces in front of Tuck's Sporting Goods. A truck that likely belonged to Riley was already there.

Before exiting the car, Adam took a steadying breath and said, "Don't fuck this up, Sheppard." He carried the tray with the coffees and cinnamon buns in one hand, and the bread in the other.

There was a Pride flag sticker on the shop's glass door, just above the handle. That definitely hadn't been there when Adam had last been in Avery River. The bell chimed as he walked into the store, and Riley glanced up from where he'd been breaking down a cardboard box.

"Fucking hell," Riley muttered.

"Hi."

"What now?"

Adam lifted the tray in his hands. "I brought coffee. And cinnamon buns. Oh, and this bread is for you, compliments of Paula."

Riley glared at him, then said, "Nice of her."

"She's great," Adam agreed, ignoring how annoyed Riley clearly was. "She said you could come by for a free meal anytime." He set everything on the counter, then glanced around. There was a lot of work to be done. It was absolutely ridiculous that Riley thought he could put the store back together on his own. "Cream and sugar," Adam announced as he pointed to one of the coffee cups. "Just how you like it." He was proud of himself for remembering that.

Riley slowly approached the counter, as if worried Adam might attack him. He looked every bit as exhausted as he had the night before, and the day before that. "I take it with milk now. No sugar."

"Oh." There was no reason for Adam's heart to deflate as much as it did at such a tiny thing.

He brightened a bit when Riley wiggled the coffee cup that was marked with CS for cream and sugar out of the tray, then peeked into the paper bag that sat between the cups.

"Couldn't resist the cinnamon buns. You know my sweet tooth." Adam laughed nervously. "I mean, I still have it. Still love dessert."

Riley took a sip of his coffee.

Adam tried for a subject change. "Where's Lucky?"

"Asleep in the back. We went for a long walk on the beach this morning."

"Sounds romantic."

Riley held his gaze for a long moment, eyes narrowed, while Adam squirmed. "Sorry," Adam finally said. "I'm nervous."

"Is that what you think?" Riley said. "That I'm all alone here, no one to love me but my dog?"

"No," Adam said quickly. Leave it to Riley to jump to the most extreme conclusions. "I'm sure you...date...people. Have relationships, um." He swallowed, but it didn't stop the next question from escaping. "Are you? Dating a...person?"

Another endless, agonizing moment, and then Riley said, "A man. I would be dating a man, because I'm gay." He let that hang there a moment, then added, "I'm a gay man. You know, that thing you said we definitely weren't? I am."

Adam's heart pounded in his ears. He was mortified by the reminder that he had, indeed, said that. Most horribly he'd said it just minutes after being inside Riley, still tingling from how good it had felt. After Riley had looked at him seriously and said, "I love you, you know," and Adam's whole world had stopped. His heart had been pounding just like it was now. Riley had been breathtaking in that moment, flushed and messy and vulnerable, holding his heart in both hands for Adam to take. Adam knew now, like he'd known then, how hard it must have been for Riley to say those words. To offer himself to Adam.

And Adam had laughed at him. Laughed at him and had said something like, "Dude, we're not like that. Come on." Because Adam was a fucking coward.

He could be brave now. This was where he could tell him. *I'm gay too.* The opportunity was gift wrapped, but instead he said, "So you're not dating anyone now?"

"Jesus Christ," Riley grumbled. He set his coffee on the counter, then walked to a stack of boxes against the far wall.

"I just mean," Adam said, the words tumbling out of him now like the world's most useless fountain, "it must be challenging, in a small town like this?"

"Finding men to fuck, you mean?" Riley asked flatly as he extracted a box cutter from his back pocket. "Or do you mean hiding? Because I don't do that anymore." He sliced open the top box, his back still to Adam.

"That's good," Adam said. "Not hiding. That's good. That's great. And it's been okay? Everyone's been...okay?"

Riley huffed, and Adam was sure he was rolling his eyes. "Everyone? No. But the people I care about are cool with it."

Adam nodded enthusiastically, even though Riley wasn't looking at him. "Glad to hear it. It's nice to be supported."

Riley did turn then. He looked Adam directly in the eyes

and said, cold as ice, "Yeah. It is." Then he thrust the open box at him. "If you want to help, you can hang these practice jerseys up. Smallest to largest, left to right. That rack over there. I'll get you some hangers."

"Right. Okay. No problem." Adam walked to the mostly empty rack, then set the box on the floor. His shoulder complained from carrying the box, and his back complained from putting it down. He ignored both, removed his coat, and draped it over the hockey stick display next to him. He would do an amazing job of hanging up these jerseys, and he would keep his mouth shut.

"Here," Riley said from behind him. He was holding a large plastic bin full of hangers. "If you see any holes or stains on any of the jerseys, let me know."

"Got it."

Riley headed to the back room with two unopened boxes, leaving Adam alone with a box of jerseys and his thoughts. The mindless task of inserting hangers into shirts did nothing to distract his brain from everything Riley had just said and all the memories his words had kicked up. All the regrets.

What if Adam hadn't laughed at Riley's declaration of love all those years ago? What if Adam had let himself feel all the things his heart had been screaming for, instead of immediately throwing up a wall? What if he'd fucking appreciated how lucky he could have been—how lucky he *had* been—to have someone as wonderful as Riley Tuck be in love with him?

It would have been impossible, he told himself now, the same way he'd told himself for years. *We never could have been together.*

Riley emerged from the back wearing *glasses* and frowning at a piece of paper. Adam shouldn't have been surprised by the reading glasses—they were both over forty now, and Adam had started using them himself a few years ago—but he was. The glasses, the beard, the faded red hair, the dog, the exhaus-

tion in Riley's eyes—they all reminded Adam of the time he'd
lost. He'd known Riley when they'd both been young, at their
physical peaks. Now Adam's body felt like it was falling apart,
and Riley looked...

Adam forced his lungs to take a breath. Riley looked perfect.
Sad and tired, but so handsome and strong. So comfortable in
who he was. Adam had never known *that* Riley.

Riley muttered something at the paper, which made Adam
blink and turn his attention back to the jerseys. He wrestled a
small jersey onto a hanger, his fingers feeling thick and clumsy.
It wouldn't have been impossible, being with Riley; it would
have been *difficult*, and that wasn't the same thing. They would
have had to hide, but hadn't they done that anyway? If Adam had
been braver, they could have hidden together. They could have
teased each other when they'd worn their reading glasses for the
first time, when they'd both started to get gray hairs. They could
have picked out a dog together, and a house. Adam could have
caressed Riley's face one morning, observed that his beard was
filling in, and Riley could have shyly admitted he was growing
it out. Trying something new.

Adam swallowed hard, then took the next jersey out of the
box.

He worked in silence for about half an hour, wishing Riley
would talk to him. When he'd hung the last jersey, Adam
said, "Done."

"Okay," Riley said, without any interest in his tone. He was
on the other side of the shop, seemingly making some repairs
to a clothing rack.

Adam sighed and walked over to a pile of baseball socks near
some empty wall hooks. "Want these hung up?"

"If you want."

Adam hung baseball socks neatly by size and color. Then
he did the same for jockstraps, batting gloves, and belts. He

shelved tennis balls, batting helmets, mouth guards, and water bottles. Other than giving quick confirmations that Adam was putting things in the right places, Riley ignored him. Lucky came to check on him a few times, so Adam chatted the poor dog's ear off out of boredom.

"I heard you went on a beach walk this morning. That sounds nice. I should check that beach out myself. Haven't been near the ocean for a while."

"I'll probably go to Paula's again tonight for dinner, unless you have a better recommendation. I should try something else, but those scallops are next level."

"You know what I like about baseball uniforms? The belts. They look so classy, right?"

Lucky listened to him with a definite air of anxiety. He kept glancing toward Riley, as if silently asking him, *"Who the hell is this guy?"*

No one important, I guess, Adam thought.

He'd just finished shelving the water bottles when Riley said, from behind the counter, "You haven't eaten your cinnamon bun yet."

It was an invitation, and Adam took it. "Forgot about it. Not sure how," he said cheerfully as he approached the counter.

Riley didn't say anything.

"What kind of dog is Lucky?"

"No idea."

Lucky was medium sized with short, golden-brown hair, a white belly, a black nose and muzzle, and short, floppy ears. He was, Adam thought, a good-looking dog. A friendly looking dog. "So he's a mix? You don't know which breeds?"

"Nope. Probably not the smartest ones, though." Even as he said it, the fondness was clear in Riley's expression.

"Must be why I was getting along so well with him."

Adam swore he saw Riley's lips curve up, but then Riley turned away.

Adam took a bite of his cinnamon bun. "Holy shit," he said, his mouth still full, "these are amazing."

Riley was busy with something on the computer that sat on the counter. He was wearing his glasses again, which hid most of the bags under his eyes. Despite the obvious lack of sleep and the emotional upheaval, Riley was nicely dressed. Adam wouldn't have thought less of him if he'd been wearing sweats, but his dark green plaid shirt was crisp and clean, and even looked like it had been ironed. He wore it untucked with black jeans and black boots. His beard was neatly trimmed, and his thick hair, which had been shaggy and permanently messy in his twenties, was now stylishly cut short on the sides, but fell in red-gold waves on top. He looked like an L.L.Bean model.

"You've got glasses now too, eh?" Adam said.

"Just for reading."

"Same." When Riley didn't react to that, Adam attempted to casually lean on the counter. "Yours look good on you."

Riley pinned him with a flat stare, then removed his glasses.

Adam sighed. "Seriously? You'd rather not be able to see than take a compliment from me?"

Riley squinted at the computer but didn't reply. The phone rang then, and Riley answered it. "Tuck's...no, um, sorry... he's not. This is his son."

Adam froze.

"Right," Riley said. "No. He isn't. He's no longer with us... no. I mean he died." He winced as he said the words, but his voice remained steady. "Thank you. So, yes, I'd be in charge of accounts payable now."

Adam wanted to grab the phone from his hand and tell this person to please fuck off, but he knew that wasn't reasonable.

Finally, the call ended, and Riley went back to staring at the computer screen like nothing had happened.

"Riley," Adam said gently.

"I'm fine." His hand was trembling above the keyboard.

"Maybe I could answer the phone for you."

Riley slammed a fist down on the counter, causing the mouse to fall to the floor with a clatter. "I can answer the fucking phone."

Adam took a step back, giving him space. Riley hung his head, the way he'd often done before, when his emotions had exploded out of him.

"It's okay," Adam said.

Riley shook his head. After another moment, he said, "It's getting worse. Like the shock is wearing off, and now it just... it hurts so fucking much."

"I'm sorry," Adam said, because he didn't know what else to say. He wanted Riley to keep talking.

Riley stood straighter, as if shaking off the weight of his sadness. "Lindsay is going to stay a bit longer. Her husband and kids drove back to Halifax today, but Linds is gonna stay with Mom."

"That's good."

Riley nodded, then stared into the middle distance. "She's going to sell Dad's truck."

Adam's chest tightened because he *got it*. How real that decision made everything. How final. "Shit," he said. "That's a lot."

For a moment, Riley's gaze met his, and Adam saw gratitude in his eyes. Then Riley blinked and looked away. "It's just a truck. I don't know why it bothers me."

"I do," Adam said gently.

Riley blinked again, and then again. His eyes were wet. "Yeah," he said. "Shit."

He covered his mouth with his hand, then turned his back

to Adam. Without hesitating, Adam walked behind the counter and put a hand on Riley's shoulder. "It's okay."

Riley's large body shook under Adam's palm, his face turned away. Adam wanted so badly to pull him into his arms and hold him. To kiss his temple and whisper comforting words. But that wasn't what this was. This was a man who probably wished anyone but Adam was here with him now.

Finally, Riley blew out a breath, and said, "Sorry."

"Don't apologize," Adam said quickly.

"I shouldn't—" Riley didn't finish his sentence, but Adam jumped on the opportunity.

"You can, though. You need someone right now, and it can be me."

Riley braced his hands on the countertop. "It really can't."

Adam's heart sank. "I know I haven't been a good friend," he tried.

Riley snorted.

"But," Adam continued, "I miss you."

"You *miss me*?" Riley turned his head to face him, eyes burning with anger rather than tears now. "Are you fucking serious?"

"Yes?"

In two long strides, Riley had Adam pinned against the wall. "You don't get to *miss me*."

Adam had reached his limit. He bumped his chest against Riley's, refusing to cower. "Why not? You fucking ghosted me, Riley. You went to Dallas without a word to me about it, and then fucking quit hockey? I tried to call you! For weeks I tried to call you and text you. Then when you finally talked to me, it was to tell me to stop contacting you."

"Because I had to fucking spell it out for you."

"Then how am I the asshole here?"

Riley's jaw was so tight Adam worried his teeth would shatter.

"I could have helped you," Adam said desperately. "Whatever you were going through, I could have helped."

"*You* were what I was going through!"

Time seemed to freeze as both men breathed loudly and angrily against each other. Then Lucky wandered out from the back room, looking concerned.

Riley walked away, and Adam closed his eyes, heart racing. Of course he knew he'd hurt Riley badly, back then, but that couldn't have been the entire reason he'd left Toronto. It couldn't have been what had made Riley quit hockey. One drunken mistake couldn't have been responsible for all of that.

He knew Riley was about to tell him to leave—not just the shop, but Nova Scotia—and Adam needed to think of something he could say that would change Riley's mind. But there was nothing. Of course there wasn't. Adam would have no choice but to leave, and that would be it. He'd never see Riley again.

And that was when Susan Tuck entered the shop.

"Thought I'd drop in because I have to go to the credit union to deal with about a hundred things and—God Almighty, Riley. You've been busy in here."

"Just moving some things around," Riley said.

"I'll say." She turned to Adam, and her face lit up. "Adam! Keeping him company, are you?"

Adam hoped his smile looked easy and not full of anxiety. "Just brought him a cinnamon bun."

"Did you now?" She crouched to give Lucky a scratch. "I'll bet Riley appreciated that."

"Yep," Riley said tightly.

"And how are you today, Adam?"

"Fine. Good." He wondered how long he would be trapped in this awkward standoff.

And then Susan found a way to make it more awkward. "Lindsay told me about your divorce. I'm sorry to hear it."

There was a clatter from across the shop, where Riley had apparently backed into a display of sunglasses.

"Uh, yeah," Adam said. "We're divorced. But we're still good friends. It's very, um, amicable." This wasn't how he'd wanted to tell Riley. "We've been pretty private about it. No social media posts or anything."

"That's good," she said. "Especially for the kids."

"It is." He glanced quickly at Riley, whose brow was furrowed as he gazed at the floor. He could only guess what he was thinking. *You threw me away to be with her, and now you're not even with her.*

"Well," Susan said. "I should—"

"Do you want me to go to the credit union with you?" Riley blurted out.

Susan waved a hand. "No, no. I'll get through it. But maybe you could come by the house later?"

"Of course. I was going to anyway."

"Adam, you can come too if you like. It would be nice to catch up more, but I understand if you've got better things to do."

"I, um…" There was no way Riley wanted Adam to accept the invitation, right? "I'd be happy to. If Riley doesn't mind." He caught Riley's gaze, but couldn't get a read on what he was thinking.

Susan glanced between them, perhaps realizing the tension that was filling the store. "I'll let you boys get back to work then."

She gave Riley a quick hug and kiss before leaving. Lucky

tried to follow her out, then sat and stared through the glass door. After a long silence Riley said, "You're divorced."

Adam took a deep breath. "Yeah. For over a year now, officially."

"You didn't tell me."

"When should I have told you?"

Riley shook his head. "Never mind."

Carefully, slowly, Adam walked toward him. "I was going to tell you. I just didn't want to unload my shit on you right away, y'know?"

"It's fine. It's—I guess it's none of my business, really." He began straightening up the sunglasses display, as if the conversation was over.

Adam *wanted* it to be Riley's business. He wanted it to matter to him.

"You staying in town another night?" Riley asked.

"Yeah." *Ask me why I'm divorced.*

"Why?"

"You know why." The words were out before Adam could stop them, and they hung in the air for what felt like forever.

"I don't mean—" Adam stammered. "I just want to help. To be a friend. Whatever you need."

"A friend," Riley repeated.

Adam sighed. "I know we've got a lot to talk about, and that now isn't the time. Like I said, I'm not here to unload more shit on you. Not when you're in so much pain. If me being here is going to hurt more than help, then fine. I'll go. But I wasn't kidding when I said I've missed you. We were best friends, and I still care about you, okay?"

Riley's jaw clenched, and for a moment Adam thought he was about to be angrily backed against the wall again. But then Riley exhaled and said, "How'd the kids take it?"

It took Adam a second to realize he was asking about the

divorce. "Not too hard, honestly. I think the fact that I wasn't around a whole lot for most of their lives probably helped. But also, Maggie and I are still friends, and I live about five minutes away. We've got a pretty good arrangement."

"That's good," Riley said, though he looked confused.

"We're better as friends," Adam offered, as a watered-down version of the truth.

"A lot of people are." Riley caught his eye, just for a moment, then looked away.

Adam exhaled. "Look, um. I know you don't want me to go with you to your mom's house, and I totally understand that. But maybe we could get a beer or something later?"

Riley folded his arms across his chest. "I don't drink anymore."

Jesus, Adam sucked. "Oh. Okay. Maybe we could—when did you stop drinking?" He winced internally at his own bluntness.

"Been about ten years, I guess," Riley said, as if it was no big deal.

As far as Adam could remember, Riley hadn't been a particularly heavy drinker, at least not compared to really any of their teammates. Going out and getting drunk had been part of the lifestyle. But maybe Adam had missed something. "Ten years? Wow. And it's been good? You feel better?"

Riley's eyes told him that he knew Adam had no idea he'd had a problem. "Sure. Yeah. I feel better."

"It must have been difficult, though."

"Easier once I got home. If you remember, the local tavern is lacking a bit anyway."

Adam smiled, delighted that Riley was referencing anything to do with the summers they'd spent here together. "They haven't renovated?"

"I don't even think they've *cleaned* it since you were last there."

Adam got a brief and wonderful glimpse of Riley's smile, and felt the lightest he'd been since arriving in town. "Is your jersey still on the wall?"

"Yup. And yours. Right next to it."

Adam froze. "Really?"

"Really."

It seemed impossible that all this time their friendship had been immortalized on the wall of Riley's local bar. Had Riley stopped drinking just so he wouldn't have to look at it?

"I want to see it."

"Why? Your jersey is probably hanging in every bar in Toronto."

"Not next to yours," Adam said before he could stop himself. "I mean, I remember when I signed it for them. Do you?"

Riley smiled slightly. "Yeah. I remember. We'd been out on the boat all day, totally sunburned. Got a couple of pints of the worst beer on the North Shore."

"Then you suggested the bonfire on the beach," Adam added. He managed to avoid blurting out that it had been the best day of his life, possibly. Riley had taken him to a small beach that wasn't as popular as the others nearby. They'd been alone, stretched out on the sand with the fire burning in front of them. Adam had been amazed by the stars above, more than he'd ever seen before, and he'd been enchanted by the man next to him. They'd slowly inched closer until their shoulders were pressed together, then their legs tangled, and then they'd been kissing. Then Riley had been pressing Adam into the sand as his hand slid inside Adam's shorts.

Adam had been sure they'd both known the day would end that way, though they'd never kissed in Avery River before. After that night, they kissed a *lot* in Avery River, stealing privacy whenever and wherever they could get it. It had been like an intense summer fling inside of their weird few years of sporadic "just friends" sex. Adam had gone back to Ontario more confused than ever. A few months later, Riley had told Adam he was in love with him. And then Adam had fucked it all up.

"Did we have a bonfire that night?" Riley asked lightly. "Hard to remember. It was a long time ago."

That was a spear to the fucking stomach. "Maybe I'm wrong."

For a long moment, Riley held his gaze. He was as sure of that bonfire as Adam was.

"Anyway," Riley said. "The jerseys are still there, because nothing ever changes at the Dropped Anchor."

It seemed the conversation had ended, so Adam pointed to a box and said, "Want me to put away whatever's in there?"

"You've done enough." Riley sighed. "And, um, thank you. For your help."

Adam eyed the general upheaval of the shop skeptically. "I can do more."

"I've got it. Don't worry about it."

Adam tried to give him a hard stare so he'd know he was being stupid, but he was distracted by how lost Riley looked.

"Riles," he said, then corrected himself, "Riley, I mean. You don't have to do this alone."

"Yeah, well. You don't have to do it at all, so..." He walked past Adam, toward the counter.

Adam grabbed his wrist. "You're being stubborn."

Riley spun back around. "I'm stubborn? You're the one who showed up in my shop after *I told you not to.*"

"Fine, we're both stubborn." Adam was still holding his wrist. "I'm not letting you do this alone."

Riley stared at him, then shook his head. "I don't get you."

Adam shrugged instead of saying, *"You get me more than any-one ever has."*

Riley's gaze kept dropping to Adam's lips, then away, then back again. He jerked the arm Adam was holding, yanking Adam closer.

"Why?" Riley asked.

Adam gave the same answer as before, but this time it was barely a whisper, "You know why."

Lucky began whimpering by the door.

Riley took a giant step back, his eyes wide with what looked like horror. "I know," he said to Lucky. Then, to Adam, he said, "I need to take Lucky out for a bit. You should go."

"Are you sure?"

Riley was already at the door. "I'm sure. Come on. I need to lock up."

"I could come tomorrow," Adam said as he grabbed his coat.

"Don't."

Riley exited the shop with Lucky, and Adam had no choice but to follow. Outside, Riley walked away without a word. As Adam watched him leave, he said to himself, "Milk. No sugar," and began making plans for tomorrow.

Chapter Nine

July 2006

"We'll probably be here for a while," Riley said.

Adam glanced over his sunglasses at the front of the boat, where Harvey Tuck, behind the wheel, was chatting with the man who'd pulled his own boat up next to theirs. "That's cool. I've got nowhere to be."

To demonstrate, Adam folded his arms behind his head and slid lower on the bench seat, bare legs outstretched in front of him. He tilted his face up to the sun and smiled.

Beside him, Riley stood. "I might swim."

"Yeah?" Adam watched him pull his shirt off. His broad shoulders were tanned and dotted with freckles, and his golden chest hair glistened in the sun.

"You comin'?"

Adam glanced uneasily at the dark water surrounding the boat. He didn't trust the ocean, even the calm waters in the harbor they were puttering around.

"You're not going to get eaten," Riley teased.

"You can't promise that."

"I'll fight any sharks off." Riley flexed his biceps.

Adam believed him. Riley was always quick to fight any-one who touched Adam during games. "All right," Adam said, removing his sunglasses. He didn't trust the ocean, but he did trust Riley. "Fuck it. I'd love to watch you punch a shark."

Riley executed a perfect dive off the small swim platform at the back of the boat. Adam, not interested in venturing too deep below the gentle waves, eased himself in via the ladder.

"It's fucking cold," he complained when he was only shin deep.

Riley laughed. "Come on, Ontario. Let go of the ladder."

Adam descended another step, his breath catching in his chest. "No. What the hell. No, Riles."

"You get used to it. Just jump."

This was Adam's fifth summer visiting Avery River, and he knew from experience that, yes, eventually his body would adjust to the frigid water, but he suspected it was only because his body simply stopped functioning.

"Ah, Jesus," he yelped as he went as deep as his waist. "I'm never going to be able to have kids. My balls just fell off."

"That'd be a shame," Riley said, and Adam was pretty sure he didn't mean about the kids.

They hadn't touched each other since he'd arrived three days ago. Not like that. They hadn't last summer either, not the entire three weeks that Adam had visited. Or any of the summers before that. He knew he shouldn't be touching Riley like that anywhere, but for some reason it made sense during the hockey season. Not all the time, but sometimes.

They weren't gay. Adam just liked having sex with his friend sometimes. He liked doing everything with Riley, so why not a bit of sex? It didn't mean anything, and no one had to know. It was just for them. A way of burning off adrenaline after a game, or nerves before one. A way to kill time when they were stuck in a hotel for a few hours. A way to feel good when there was no reason not to.

But one day Adam would meet the woman he would want to marry. And he'd have to explain to her why his fucking balls had fallen off.

"I seriously can't even fucking breathe," Adam complained, slightly panicked. He glanced over his shoulder at Riley, who was treading water happily. "Are you a merman or some shit? How are you so comfortable?"

"You're basically all the way in now anyway. Just swim, Shep."

Adam squeezed his eyes shut, muttered, "Fuck," and let go of the ladder. He screeched a bit as the water numbed everything below his chin, and Riley laughed.

"I h-hate you," Adam panted as he swam toward Riley. "Fu-fuck you."

Riley disappeared beneath the water.

"No," Adam said. "Don't. Where are you?"

Beneath the water, a hand clasped his ankle. Adam yelped and yanked his leg away. Riley popped up beside him, splashing water everywhere. Adam shoved him as best he could, but he was treading water and Riley was basically a cement wall.

He was also breathtakingly beautiful in that moment, all smiles with the sun glinting on his wet hair. Was that a normal thought to have about your best friend? Even one you've been recreationally fucking for a couple of years?

"See? It's nice."

"Yeah," Adam said distantly. "Nice."

Hours later, sunburned and thirsty, they entered the Dropped Anchor together. Harv had told them the owner had some jerseys for them to sign.

The kindest way to describe the Dropped Anchor was to call it a dive bar. A more honest description was a total dump. Just a sad, dark rectangular room full of white men of various ages. An older model television in one corner showed sports—baseball at the moment—and was the only source of entertainment.

"Benny," Riley said as he approached the bar. "What's happening, man?"

"Not a damn thing," the man, Benny, said. "The Jays are losing."

"Fine with me. I'm a Red Sox fan."

Adam gasped. "I didn't know that. Why are we friends?"

Riley looped an arm around his neck. "Because you need someone to fight sharks."

By then, Adam had started to hear his own name being murmured throughout the tavern. It was something he'd gotten used to, as much as anyone could get used to it. Over the past season he'd evolved from an exciting young prospect to a full-blown hockey star, complete with an invitation to the All-Star game, and being named Toronto's new captain only a couple of weeks ago. He was getting recognized a lot these days.

And, of course, everyone in town knew he was here, visiting Riley.

"Dad said you have some jerseys you want us to sign?" Riley said.

"Is that why those are here? No one tells me anything," Benny grumbled as he ducked down behind the bar. He resurfaced with an overstuffed plastic bag. He thrust it at Riley. "Here you go."

"You got a Sharpie or something?" Riley asked.

Benny patted his chest. "No."

Riley shot Adam an exhausted glance, and Adam had to press his lips together to keep from laughing.

"I got one," someone called from the end of the bar, a white man wearing worn and stained work clothes. He nearly fell off his barstool as he held the pen out. "I always have one on me for work. You can borrow it. You can keep it, um, Mr. Sheppard."

Adam smiled and took the pen. "I don't need to keep it. And you can call me Adam. Or Shep."

"Yes sir, Shep," said the man, who was at least ten years older than Adam. "And if it's not too much trouble, would you sign something for me?"

"Of course. My pleasure."

They laid the jerseys out on the bar and took turns signing. Riley was wearing a tank top that had really huge arm holes, exposing skin from his armpits to nearly his waist. When he leaned over the bar, Adam could see his nipple. He forced himself to look away.

By the time Riley and Adam were finally alone at a table with pints of beer, they'd signed the jerseys, a couple of ball caps, several five-dollar bills, and a bunch of scraps of paper torn from a notebook someone had.

"It's fucking wild, right?" Adam said as he leaned back in his chair, sun drunk and happy. He tapped the toe of his sneaker against Riley's ankle. "We can make someone's whole fucking day just by writing our names on a piece of paper for them."

Riley tapped Adam back, the side of his ankle brushing against Adam's calf. "You can, maybe, *Captain*."

"Oh fuck off. Like you're not a star."

Riley grinned and wrapped his right arm over his head, grabbing the elbow with his left hand to get a good stretch. It made his biceps look huge, and also exposed his hairy armpits, which Adam found fascinating for some reason. Most dudes had hairy armpits. *Adam* had hairy armpits. And huge biceps. And eyes and lips and strong hands. Riley wasn't special.

They finished their pints, and then another round, talking and laughing as if they were old friends catching up, instead of two guys who should, by all rights, have nothing left to say to each other.

Adam was just tipsy enough from the weak beer to be wondering if there was somewhere private he could go with Riley. It would go against their unspoken rule of never fooling around in the summer, but he'd been pretty hot for Riley all day. The tank top wasn't helping.

Something must have shown on his face because Riley tapped his foot against Adam's ankle again and said, "I was thinking we could go to this beach I know. Maybe have a bonfire."

Adam smiled. "Sounds cool."

He learned, when he was back in Riley's brand-new truck, that Riley had planned ahead. When Adam asked about firewood, Riley said he had everything he needed in the back of the truck. Adam felt a familiar twist of pleasure and panic, his usual reaction to anything Riley said or did that seemed romantic.

"Is beer one of the things?" he asked as a way of avoiding feelings.

"Yep. Got it on ice in a cooler."

Adam wondered what else Riley had deemed necessary for this beach date. Blankets? Champagne? *Condoms?*

It's not a date, dickhead, Adam scolded himself. *You might fool around a little. Whatever.*

But the romance factor got cranked way the fuck up when they reached their destination. The beach was a small, lonely crescent of sand, dramatically lit by the vanishing sun. Gentle waves lazily lapped at the sand, and other than a couple of gulls, he and Riley were alone.

"Not many people come to this one," Riley said. "There are so many around, and this one's small and doesn't have parking or bathrooms or anything."

"It's awesome," Adam said.

Riley looked pleased.

They made their careful way over some rocks to the sand below. Adam wasn't looking forward to navigating those rocks in total darkness later, but that was a future problem.

"We should make the fire before the light is gone," Riley said.

Adam had no idea how to make a bonfire, so he sprawled on the blanket Riley had indeed packed and watched him work. Secretly, Adam was pretty turned on generally by Riley being good at stuff. Especially macho caveman shit. By the time the fire was blazing, Adam was half-hard.

Riley flopped on the blanket beside him. "Beer?"

"Yeah. Cool."

Riley handed him a can. It was icy cold and dripping wet. Heaven.

For a long time, they just lay next to each other, drinking beer and talking and watching the fire. The waves kept a steady rhythm on the shore, and a crescent moon hung high above them. It felt really fucking magical.

"Have you ever seen the northern lights?" Adam asked. He was flat on his back, and Riley was sitting beside him.

"Nope."

"Me neither. I really want to. Where do you have to go to see them?"

Riley nudged him. "North."

"Yeah, but *where*? Like is there a cool place to travel to see them?"

"I dunno. Iceland?"

"Sounds right. I heard they have hot springs there. Didn't Cheesy go there with his girl last summer? I should ask him."

"I think you have to go in the winter, to see the northern lights."

Adam scrunched his nose. "Well, that fucking blows. I don't have time to see anything in the winter."

"Someday, maybe."

Adam reached his arms over his head and gave his whole body a stretch. "Someday, Riles. You and me, sitting in a hot spring, watching the northern lights."

"You and me," Riley agreed quietly.

In the firelight, Adam could see the way his gaze was fixed on where Adam's T-shirt had risen. Adam rested a hand there, letting his fingers idly tease at the exposed skin. Riley kept watching.

Adam *liked* the way Riley always looked at him. There was no question about it. He liked that he could spark heat in those wintry gray eyes just by exposing a bit of skin, or by smiling at him a certain way. Adam smiled at him that way now.

He liked that Riley was hot for him. It made Adam feel less weird about being hot for Riley.

Riley bent the knee that was closest to Adam, which meant he was probably getting hard. Adam sat up so he could get closer.

Riley turned his gaze to the sky, so Adam did too.

"Jesus. I've never seen so many stars," Adam said, legitimately awed.

Riley inched closer. "You can see a bit of the Milky Way there."

"Oh wow," Adam whispered. He brushed Riley's leg with his bare foot, then draped it over Riley's shin.

"And I think that's Jupiter."

"Where?"

"The really bright one. Look." Riley took Adam's wrist in his hand and guided it up. "Stick your finger out."

Adam did, and Riley rested their heads together so he could almost see what Adam was seeing. Adam's heart started racing.

"There," Riley said, very quietly. "See it?"

Adam looked at the end of his own finger and saw a star that was brighter than most of the others. "That's Jupiter?"

"Yeah."

"That's crazy that we can see it, y'know?"

"I know."

Adam turned his face, just slightly, toward Riley's. For a moment, he felt Riley's breath against his lips, and he wondered if they were really going to do this. Then his question was answered when Riley's lips brushed his own.

It got really heated, really fast. One minute they were gazing at the stars, the next they had their hands down each other's shorts. The combination of the darkness and being outdoors and it being Riley had Adam so keyed up that he couldn't even be embarrassed about how quickly he came. Whatever. He was young. He could do another round.

He and Riley had never gone more than one round in one night. They weren't like that.

Maybe tonight could be like that. Maybe tonight could be…different. It was a scary thing to want, but Adam fucking wanted it. It felt safe here, so far from their teammates, and hockey journalists, and Adam's parents.

Riley came less than a minute after him. They lay next to each other when it was over, both breathing hard.

"I gotta clean off," Riley said when he'd caught his breath.

"You mean…" Adam glanced warily at the pitch-black ocean.

"Yeah. Come on." Riley kicked off his shorts, which were barely still on his body anyway. Naked, glowing in the firelight like a god, he reached for Adam.

And how could Adam refuse?

Chapter Ten

April 2024

Fuck Adam Sheppard. Fuck his helpfulness, fuck his beautiful eyes, and fuck how cute he'd been while talking to Lucky. Fuck the way he'd licked cinnamon off his lips, and especially fuck how achingly familiar it was to hear his voice again. To have him in Riley's space.

Why did Adam have to mention the bonfire?

Riley was at his mom's house now—without Adam because there was no way Riley was going to let him invade more areas of his life. Not even after Adam had worked his ass off at the shop without complaint, because he'd known, no matter what Riley had said, that he needed help.

What a fucking dick.

"I hope you're in the mood for lasagna," Mom said when Riley entered the kitchen. "We've got three of them."

"One for each of us," Lindsay said cheerfully. For the first time in a week or so, there were no additional people in the house. Riley was grateful.

"Paula gave me some brown bread."

"Keep that for yourself," Mom said as she gestured toward

a corner of the countertop, where a stack of loaves of various breads sat. "I'm going to need to buy another freezer as it is. Here, sit. I made tea."

They all sat at the round kitchen table, and Riley tried to ignore the empty chair. Lindsay poured tea into mismatched mugs from a teapot covered in a handmade cozy that looked like a hen. Riley's mug had the Toronto Northmen logo on it.

"How'd it go at the credit union?" Riley asked.

Mom sighed heavily. "Oh, you know. Nothing too complicated, but it was still...hard. At least I didn't have to explain much about the situation. Not in this town."

"You should have let me come with you," Lindsay said, at the same time Riley said something similar.

Mom waved her hand. "It's done. But—" she looked at Riley "—what do you think about taking over the shop officially? Owning it yourself, I mean."

"Me? But shouldn't we share it?" He glanced uncertainly at Lindsay.

"It's yours," Lindsay said firmly. "I haven't even worked a shift there in over a decade. And you love it."

He did love it. But would he still love it, now that Dad wouldn't be working alongside him? "It seems unfair, though."

Lindsay laughed. "Unless you're secretly earning millions under the table at that shop, I don't think we're being all that generous here."

Riley huffed. The shop was definitely not earning millions. It did all right, as the only sporting goods shop in the area. They certainly lost business to the larger chain stores in New Glasgow, Amherst, and Truro, and these days they lost even more to online stores, but Tuck's had been a fixture here since the fifties, and people were loyal. As long as Tuck's stayed on top of the trends, stocked what people were looking for, and provided friendly and knowledgeable service, they'd survive. It didn't hurt that Riley was something of a local celebrity.

"But what about you, Mom?"

"I'm almost seventy. I'm happy to help out if you need me at all, but I'm not interested in being in charge." Mom had been the secretary at the school for nearly thirty years before retiring, but had worked at the shop during the summers. It had never been her passion, but he knew she cared a lot about the family business she'd married into.

"I'll do my best with it," Riley promised. "I'm not Dad, though."

Mom reached across the table, and Riley gave her his hand to squeeze. "He was so proud of you, and the work you put into that store. I know he was never worried about the shop's future."

It was nice to hear, even though Riley's eyes went misty. "Thanks."

"So I heard Adam helped out today?" Lindsay asked.

Riley took a long sip of his tea, swallowed, then said, "He did."

"You must have had lots to talk about," Mom said.

"I guess." Riley was stuck on the things they *hadn't* talked about, and the things that had only been hinted at. Like the *fucking bonfire*.

Since Adam had mentioned it, Riley's brain had been running a clip show on a constant loop: Adam, nearly twenty-four years old, glowing in the firelight and smiling up at the stars; Adam on his back, sand clinging to his neck and arms as he pulled Riley closer; Adam arching and gasping Riley's name as he came into Riley's fist; both of them cleaning themselves in the ocean after, laughing and stealing kisses in the moonlight. Riley had been absolutely euphoric, dizzy with how much he'd loved Adam, and wishing this could all be real. That this could be their lives every day, instead of being reduced to sporadic moments when all of the conditions were perfect. When Adam was just tipsy enough, just horny enough, just weak enough to want Riley.

The summer after that one, Adam had married Maggie. There hadn't been a wedding to speak of—they'd eloped to Niagara Falls when they'd learned Maggie was pregnant—which had been the only small mercy. At least Riley hadn't had to endure the agony of watching Adam get married. He'd only needed to endure the agony of watching Adam *be* married.

"It's weird seeing him again," Riley said. "I don't know."

Lucky wandered in after wrapping up his inspection of the entire house. He squeezed between their legs under the table and lay down, tail thumping against Riley's ankle.

"I've been getting messages from all sorts of people who I haven't talked to in years," Lindsay said. "I get it."

Riley was sure it wasn't the same situation, but he nodded.

"You should invite him to stay with you," Mom said. "You've got that lovely guest room, and lord knows he can't be sleeping well on those lumpy old things at the River Bend."

Absolutely fucking not. "No one is forcing him to stay in town."

Mom and Lindsay exchanged a look that Riley didn't like. He knew they didn't understand why he was so angry with Adam. They didn't know, because Riley had never talked to them about it. Even if he'd wanted to, he'd never known *how* to talk to them about it. Adam had always insisted he was straight, and though Riley had his doubts about that, especially when Adam was fucking him, it certainly wasn't his place to share those doubts with anyone. Riley had long suspected that his family might think he'd had unrequited romantic feelings about Adam, and that that had caused the rift between them, at least in part. It would have been an easy assumption to make, given the way Riley was sure he'd always looked at Adam. The way he'd talked about him.

And, anyway, it was true. The feelings had been unrequited.

"It would be nice for you to have some company," Mom said. "I know I'd feel better if you weren't alone out there at that house."

Riley could hear what she wasn't saying: we expect your father's death to break you, and someone should be there to help.

Well, it wasn't going to be Adam Sheppard, that was for fucking sure. Adam Sheppard, who was *divorced* now. Who Riley had already nearly kissed *twice* in less than twenty-four hours, despite hating him. Distance was crucial.

"I'm fine. And I have friends." Then he blurted out, "I'm actually heading to see Darren and Tom after this."

Mom brightened. "Oh, that's good. Would they like some bread?"

Riley stayed with his mom and sister for a while, eventually eating lasagna and then helping with the dishes. The whole time, his head was swimming with Adam Sheppard. He could still feel Adam's fingers around his wrist, and Adam's breath against his lips when he'd said, "You know why."

Riley hated how weak he'd felt in that moment. He hated the sharp flash of excitement that had rocked him when he'd learned Adam was divorced. He hated that twelve fucking years hadn't been enough time to get the man out of his system.

Now he sat in his truck in Mom's driveway and texted Darren: Can I come over?

Darren replied quickly, telling him of course he could. About twenty minutes later, Riley was driving up the long unpaved road that wound its way through maple trees to Darren and Tom's house. He was glad he'd come, already feeling lighter with how normal this felt. Darren and Tom were his friends now, not Adam. His social life was easy and comfortable and openly queer, with no misplaced feelings. His sex life was equally uncomplicated. He would feel better after spending time with his friends.

Darren greeted him with a kiss, while Lucky was greeted by Darren and Tom's two Great Pyrenees, Josephine and Claudette.

"Did you get some sleep?" Darren asked as they watched the dogs happily dance around each other.

"Some."

"Good. Have you eaten?"

"Yeah. Sorry if I'm interrupting your dinner."

"Absolutely not. Tom is reheating some cassoulet. Come sit. We'll let the dogs play out back for a bit."

They went to the living room, with its high ceiling and giant stone fireplace. Riley sat on what he'd come to think of as his usual end of the sectional sofa. Darren took the dogs to the large fenced-in area behind the house, then joined Riley on the sofa, one cushion away. "So how are you?"

"I don't know," Riley said. "Not great."

"Have you talked to your therapist?"

"Not yet."

Darren made a disappointed noise.

"I *will*," Riley said. "Jesus Christ, I've been kind of busy. It takes a while to get an appointment anyway."

Darren stared at him, eyebrows raised, until Riley said, "Which is why I should make the appointment now."

"Right now," Darren said. "Get out your phone."

He watched as Riley dutifully booked an appointment online for two weeks from today, and insisted Riley put himself on the waiting list for last-minute cancellations.

"There. Done," Riley said. "Happy?"

"It's about *you* being happy, love."

Tom emerged from the kitchen carrying a tray with a water pitcher, glasses, and a bowl of something. "Hi, Riley. I can make coffee if you like."

"No, water is great, thanks."

Tom placed the tray on the coffee table, then poured water into a glass. "Rough day?"

"Weird day." Riley decided to start with the easiest thing to explain. "The shop is mine now. Or it will be once I sign some paperwork. Feels strange."

"Oh," Darren said sympathetically, "that's huge. Are you okay with it?"

Riley shrugged. "Guess I knew it was coming, or at least that I'd be in charge of it. Still. Dad kind of *was* the shop, y'know?"

"He was a big part of it," Tom agreed, "and I know I'm from away, but to me you're just as big a part of it."

"He's right," Darren agreed quickly. "Avery River loves you."

"Not like him, though. Dad always had time for everyone, and he was friends with everyone. I've never been great at talking to people. Hard work I can do, but the rest of it…"

"Like what? The hockey stuff?" Darren asked. "I'm pretty sure you know hockey stuff."

Riley smiled a little. He was, in his opinion, a pretty uninspiring hockey coach, and he never had anything to say at any meetings for the local hockey association. He hated organizing fundraisers or participating in them. Dad would throw himself into local events and festivals year-round. He'd been the kind of guy who made a great Santa at the annual Avery River Christmas skate, or who was never uncomfortable visiting people in the hospital or a nursing home. He'd loved people, and he'd loved his town.

"All of it, really," Riley said. "I just want to be good enough to be his son."

Darren and Tom made identical noises of protest, then Darren said, "You're more than good enough. Everyone knew how proud he was of you. You know how we knew? Because he never fucking shut up about it."

Riley laughed, but his eyes were wet. "Yeah. I know."

"He was proud of your hockey career, he was proud of you for being strong enough to quit, he was proud of the work you did at the store. Fuck, Riley, he was proud of you when you came out. Do you know how awesome that is? Your dad is the reason they fly a Pride flag outside the rink now. That was not a man who wished his son could be *more*, you know what I'm saying?"

Riley nodded, then a sob escaped him. "I miss him."

Darren wrapped his arms around him, then Tom was somehow behind him with a hand on his shoulder. They let him cry, and when he was done, Tom handed him his water.

"Thanks," Riley said. He took a sip. "I'm so tired of crying."

"Do you want to hear some gossip from Halifax?" Darren asked.

"God, please. Yes."

They talked for over an hour, the air soon filling with laughter instead of sobbing. Riley listened to outrageous stories about people he barely knew, or didn't know at all, and munched on spiced almonds. The dogs had tired themselves out, and Tom had let them in so they could rest in front of the fire. Tom and Darren ate bowls of cassoulet from their laps and drank wine because they knew it wouldn't bother Riley if they did. Riley loved that about them, how they didn't treat him like he was broken. Everything was just matter-of-fact: Riley didn't drink because he chose not to, he took antidepressants because he needed them, and he didn't talk much because that was just who he was. He didn't need to be fixed, and no one needed to be careful with him.

Maybe it was the coziness of a moment, and the safety Riley felt, that made him say, "There's something else going on. Maybe I should talk about it."

Darren leaned in, all ears. "Of course. Anything."

God, Darren was going to love this. But how could Riley talk about Adam without outing him?

Carefully, he supposed.

"There's this...guy."

Darren pressed his fingertips to his lips in excitement.

"Calm down," Riley said. "This isn't that kind of story. It's just...someone I haven't seen in a long time has been in town this week, for the funeral, and I don't know how to feel about it."

Tom nodded, but his brow was pinched. Darren said, "We may need a tiny bit more information, love."

Riley exhaled. He could do this. "He's someone I...let's say had a crush on. But a long time ago."

"How long ago?" Darren asked.

"It's been twelve years since I'd last spoken to him."

He could see Darren doing the math in his head. "Is this a hockey player?" Darren finally asked. "Oh! That superstar guy. Everyone was talking about him at your mom's house after the funeral. What's his name again?"

"It doesn't matter," Riley said, at the same moment Tom said, "Adam Sheppard." When both Riley and Darren stared at him, Tom said, "I used to live in Toronto, remember?"

"All right," Riley said. "Fine. Yes, it's him."

"Okay, so you had a crush on this guy when you were teammates?"

Calling it a crush was such a massive understatement, but

Riley nodded anyway. "You can't tell anyone. I'm not here to out anyone, I just—" Shit. *Shit.* Riley hadn't meant to say that.

Darren's eyes widened. "So not just a one-sided thing then?"

"Fuck. Never mind."

Tom put a hand on Riley's arm. "You know we won't tell anyone."

Riley held his gaze for a moment, then nodded. "It was more than a crush," he admitted. "But that's all I'm going to say about it. Anyway, he showed up at the shop today to help me out. He brought coffee and cinnamon buns and did a bunch of work."

"Oh," Darren said. "That sounds…terrible?"

"It *is* terrible," Riley insisted. "He's making me remember things I've worked hard to forget."

"Bad things?" Darren looked fierce, like he'd murder Adam without question if Riley asked.

"Bad things, yeah. But the good things are maybe the worst of it."

"You still feel something for him," Tom guessed.

"No," Riley said quickly. "I don't. I *can't*, I—fuck. I'm so messed up right now, but he's suddenly here and, I don't know. It's been a long time, but it almost feels like it hasn't been."

"He's still hot, huh?" Darren said.

"God," Riley sighed. "He's even hotter."

"I mean," Darren said slowly, "this doesn't sound like the *worst* situation."

Riley was going to have to dig a little deeper to make his friends understand. "He broke my heart," he blurted out. "Like, fucking crushed it. And then he did it again."

"When? Today?"

"No, back then." Even though Riley had just said he wouldn't go into detail, he heard himself saying, "We used to fool around sometimes, nothing serious. At least not for him.

But I was in love with him. I told him, he laughed at me, and I had to keep going somehow. We stayed friends, and I watched him get married and have kids and be heterosexual, while I fucking fell apart inside. Then, years later, he kind of threw himself at me, and I was so fucking happy. I thought maybe he was going to choose me after all, but instead he freaked out after and said it was a mistake and it could never happen again. That he loved his wife, that he wasn't gay. All that."

"That," Darren said, "is fucked up."

"And I know I'm an asshole for sleeping with a married man, no matter our history. I fucking *know*, but I wasn't strong enough to say no. Not if there'd been a chance he might choose me."

"Jesus, Riley," Tom said. "How come you never told us before?"

"Mostly because I just want to forget about him."

"But now he's here," Darren said. "He's still here?"

"Yeah. He doesn't seem to be in a hurry to leave."

Darren and Tom exchanged a look.

"So, he knows you're gay, obviously," Darren said, "and he decided to come for the funeral, despite not talking to you for over a decade, and now he's hanging around just so he can spend time with you?"

"Does his wife know he's here?" Tom asked.

"Oh. That's the other thing. He's divorced now."

Darren and Tom shared another look.

"So," Tom said, "if he's hot and divorced and only in town for a few days, maybe it wouldn't be so bad if you..."

"Tom!" Darren scolded. "That is terrible advice. This isn't some old fling—this is the monster who broke Riley's heart."

"*Monster* might be a bit much," Riley said, though it felt good to hear someone say it. "But still. I'm way too fucked-up right now to deal with Adam."

"I know the timing is awful," Tom said gently, "but maybe he has regrets about how he treated you. If you still have feelings for him, maybe—"

"Too fucking late," Darren interrupted. "Right, Riley?"

"Yeah," Riley sighed. "Way too late."

Chapter Eleven

June 2010

"We're going to win the Cup! We're going to win the fucking Cup!"

Riley was screaming the words in Adam's face. They were on the bench, and Adam's expression was stoic, as if it was too early to start celebrating. As if having a 5–1 lead with just over a minute left to play wasn't enough of a guarantee.

Riley put a hand on Adam's shoulder and shook him, "We fucking did it, Shep!"

Adam watched the clock, and Riley watched him. A smile broke through, lighting up Adam's face. "We're going to win the Cup," he said.

They were going to win it at home, in Toronto, where the fans had waited decades for this moment. They'd won the series in five games and had dominated Chicago for this entire final game.

The whole bench was standing; the whole arena was standing. The noise was deafening but Riley kept adding to it, screaming until his voice was hoarse. His heart was racing, his dick was half-hard. Every part of him felt like it could burst, but in the best way possible. Finally, the last seconds ticked away, and the Toronto Northmen spilled out of the bench, throwing their gloves and helmets and sticks aside. They crashed into each other, forming a chaotic pile of bodies on the ice. Riley ended up flat on his back, Adam on top of him.

"We fucking did it, baby," Adam yelled. His nose bumped against Riley's. All around them, their teammates were holding each other, straddling each other. Adam and Riley didn't look any different, but they *would* look different if Riley gave in to the urge to roll Adam to his back and kiss him into the ice.

Instead, Riley kissed his cheek. "We did it."

Adam raised his head and held Riley's gaze, and for a moment everything felt still and silent. Riley recognized the flare of heat in Adam's eyes, even though he hadn't seen it in years. Not since Adam had gotten married.

Then Adam blinked and rolled off of him. He stood, and immediately hugged one of their teammates.

"We won the fucking Cup!" Adam yelled in Riley's face. He was grinning from ear to ear, his eyes wild with adrenaline and alcohol.

"Yeah we fucking did," Riley yelled back. He was pretty drunk himself. They were at a club where the team had been steadily drinking after steadily drinking in the locker room. Riley couldn't even remember how they'd gotten here. Was it next to the arena?

He remembered Maggie being in the locker room for a bit, and he remembered Adam kissing her, holding her in his strong arms while she wrapped her legs around his waist. He remembered them smiling at each other, foreheads pressed together.

But Maggie wasn't here now. The families had gone home to let the Northmen celebrate as a team. Adam would go home to Maggie at the end of the night and then spend the summer with her and their kids, but for now, he was with Riley.

He'd been touching Riley all night. An arm around his shoulders; a hand on Riley's knee; a hug from behind, draping himself over Riley's back. Or, like now, when he was holding Riley's face with both hands.

"I love you," Adam declared loudly. "I fucking love you, Riles."

Riley kept smiling, though his chest suddenly hurt. The thing was, Adam told Riley he loved him all the time, but he said it the *right* way. The way that was acceptable. Riley had said it only once, and it had been the wrong way.

So he didn't say it back now either.

Adam's expression turned serious, and for a moment, he looked confused. His gaze fell to Riley's lips, and his brow furrowed.

Then he laughed and let go of Riley's face. "Fuck. I'm hammered."

Riley managed to smile back. "I know."

"I'm gonna stop drinking now."

"Good idea."

"Yeah." Adam looked around, then nodded. "Fuck. I live really fucking far away."

Riley laughed. "Yeah."

"You live near here."

"Dude, I have no idea where we even fucking are."

Adam waved a hand. "We're at that club that's fucking… near you. It's called…fuck, I don't know. It's near you."

Even drunk, Riley could see where this was going.

"Can I crash at your place? I don't—I don't want to go home like this, y'know?"

It would hardly be the first time. Riley lived close to the arena, and sometimes Adam would stay in his guest room when it was convenient. Absolutely nothing sexual had happened between them for years, and Riley had no reason to think tonight would be different.

"Yeah," he said, "all right."

"We won the fucking Cup," Adam panted against Riley's lips. He had Riley pinned against the wall, just inside the door of his apartment.

"I know," Riley said, then kissed him hungrily. He hadn't dared to hope for this, not after so many years. Not after Adam making it clear he'd never feel the same way as Riley did.

"Oh fuck," Adam gasped. He was already rock-hard and grinding into Riley. "I fucking want you so bad, Riles. Missed you."

Those words made Riley's blood sing. "I missed you too. God, Shep. I fucking missed you."

Riley wasn't drunk enough to not know how wrong this was. But he'd wanted it for so long, and he'd been turned on for hours, and he had no defenses left. This felt *right*.

They stumbled their way to Riley's bed, grabbing each other and kissing along the way. When Adam was spread out naked on the bed, he grinned up at Riley and said, "We won the Cup." That sent Riley into a giggle fit, but he did his best to kiss Adam everywhere while they both shook with laughter.

Later, when Adam was fucking him, Riley could only think about how perfect it was. The man he loved was in his bed, inside *him*, and the dagger hanging over them faded away. There would be a mess to clean up later, but Riley was sure they would clean it up together. Adam couldn't deny them this anymore. It would be impossible now.

"Riles," Adam panted as he thrust into him. "So good."

"I know," Riley agreed. "I know."

A few minutes later, it was over. Adam was on his back beside Riley, his eyes closed and his breathing heavy. Riley was on his side, brushing Adam's damp hair away from his face. The words were on the tip of Riley's tongue, and Riley almost had the courage to say them. To try them again.

But then, Adam's eyes opened, and Riley knew immediately that the switch inside him had flipped.

Adam sat up with a jolt. "Fuck," he said, his voice shaking with fear. "No. *Fuck.*" He scrambled out of bed and swore to himself as he searched for his underwear.

Riley's stomach sank like a stone. Adam wasn't going to choose him. Not ever. And he'd been a fucking idiot to think he ever would.

"Don't" was all Riley could say. "Please don't."

"I can't," Adam said, his voice still shaking. "I fucking *can't.* Why did you—fuck. We shouldn't have—"

"You wanted to," Riley said desperately. "You want *this.*"

Adam shook his head. "No. I want—I need to go home."

Riley crawled to the end of the bed and began to beg. "Adam, please don't do this."

Adam's eyes changed then. There was something more than fear there, more than sympathy. It was like Adam was looking at everything he'd ever wanted, but also knew he was about to walk away from it.

"I'm sorry," Adam said, barely more than a whisper. "I'm so fucking sorry, Riles."

Riley reached a hand out, absolutely pathetic. "Don't go."

Adam squeezed his eyes shut. "I have to." He exhaled hard, his breath shuddering, then began to get dressed.

Riley left the bed and stood, naked and furious, in front of Adam. "You do want this, Shep. Stop fucking lying to yourself."

Despite his damp eyes, Adam's voice was steady when he said, "This was a mistake. And it never happened, okay?"

It was a killing blow. Riley deflated instantly, then watched silently as Adam finished getting dressed. He didn't bother following him out of the bedroom, but he flinched when he heard the apartment door close.

And he knew, in that moment, that he needed to get away from Adam for good.

Chapter Twelve

April 2024

It took twenty-seven years for Riley to achieve his dream of winning the Stanley Cup, and he'd spent the fourteen years since trying to forget that night.

Sometimes the memories hit Riley hard, and last night had been one of those times. He'd left Darren and Tom's house feeling lighter, but then everything had crashed down on him when he'd been tossing and turning alone in bed. Once the sun had risen, Riley gave up on sleep and took Lucky for a walk.

He watched Lucky run ahead of him on the foggy beach, wishing he had the energy to run alongside him. Jogging was Riley's main source of exercise these days, and he especially loved beach runs, but it wasn't happening today.

The sky matched his mood: dark and foggy. The fog blocked the view of any houses lining the two arms of land that curled around the bay, making Riley feel alone. He liked that. Here there was nothing but the rhythmic crashing of the small waves, the sand under his sneakers, and maybe the occasional seabird. There were no papers to sign, no expectations to meet, and no Adam Sheppard.

Except there *was* Adam Sheppard because Riley couldn't get the man out of his head. As he watched Lucky dance around a wave, Riley tried to fight the memories that wanted to drag him under.

This was a mistake. And it never happened, okay?

Riley's chest ached now like it had then.

"Lucky!" Riley called out. "We gotta go."

Lucky glanced at him over his shoulder with an expression that Riley interpreted as, *"But I found something really cool."* It was probably a crab shell.

"Five minutes," Riley said, as if Lucky wore a watch.

Adam being divorced didn't mean anything. It didn't *change* anything. It didn't mean Adam regretted his choices; it didn't mean he'd left his wife for Riley. It definitely didn't mean that Riley should get his hopes up, even a little. He shouldn't *want* to.

Why was it so impossible for Riley to be normal about Adam Sheppard?

"Come on," Riley called out again. This time, Lucky obeyed, bounding over to him with something in his mouth.

"What did you find?" Riley asked when Lucky reached him. Lucky dropped a small chunk of soggy wood at his feet, then sat, excitedly awaiting Riley's review.

"Yep, that's neat," Riley said, and scratched Lucky's ears. "Good job."

They walked back to the house on the narrow grassy strip that ran alongside the road. Riley's house was four away from the start of the beach, up a short hill that gave him a spectacular view of the bay from his bedroom. Riley went to his greenhouse first, to check on his seedlings. This year he'd added some exciting new vegetables to his garden plan, including eggplant and asparagus. Everything was looking good, despite the lack of sunshine lately. He planned to transplant the asparagus

to the garden next week. They wouldn't yield any actual asparagus until next year, but Riley liked that about gardening:
the caretaking, the patience, and the eventual reward.

He liked everything about gardening, which was something he hadn't expected when he'd first started clearing the
weeds that had taken over the yard of the old house before he'd
bought it. He liked being outside, and he liked using his hands.
He liked quiet and solitude and having a task to do that didn't
require a lot of thinking. But later he discovered that he also
liked the mental challenge of planning his garden each year.
Of figuring out the best times to start things from seed, and
when and where to transplant them. He liked trying different
fertilizers and seeds, and he liked learning from his mistakes.
He tracked everything in a hardbound journal, noting what
worked and what didn't. Jotting down ideas for next year. He'd
built the greenhouse five years ago and expanded his single
small vegetable patch into four large ones. By June the cheerful flower garden that wrapped around his house would be in
bloom, and hummingbirds would start visiting his feeders. It
was something to look forward to, and his therapist would tell
him that was important.

His therapist would also tell him that sleep was important.

Riley lingered in the greenhouse, enjoying its warmth and
the smell of soil. His young tomato plants were already adding
their scent to the air, bright and summery. His asshole brain reminded him that, when he'd planted those seeds, he'd thought
his dad would be around to eat the tomatoes they'd produce.
Dad had loved tomatoes.

Riley refused to cry in his greenhouse; it was his happy
place. He went inside the house and cried there instead, leaning against his fridge as he hugged himself and assured Lucky
he was all right. It would pass, and he might get several good
hours before he needed to cry again.

Eventually he went to his bedroom to get a nicer shirt, because he felt better when he was somewhat put together. His phone was still on his nightstand, connected to a charger. When he picked it up, he saw that he had a text from the number he'd never been able to make himself block. Riley squinted at it.

Adam: Are you at the shop now?

Riley huffed out a surprised laugh. Was Adam really this determined?

Riley considered not writing back, but then wrote: Not yet. Soon. Why?

Adam: I was thinking I could bring you breakfast.

"God dammit, Adam," Riley said to his empty bedroom. Couldn't he take a hint? This offer was absolutely ridiculous.

It was also, Riley hated to admit, kind of sweet.

Riley wrote: You don't have to do that.

Adam: I want to.

Riley sighed. He was about to reject the offer, but then his stomach growled, and he decided he could maybe manage a bit of breakfast.

Riley: Fine. Nothing too big.

Less than an hour later, Adam walked into the shop precariously balancing two large paper bags and a tray with two coffees.

"I wasn't sure," Adam explained, "so I got a few things you can choose from."

"You can pick the one you want first," Riley said as Adam began unpacking and opening various Styrofoam containers.

"I already ate," Adam said, and patted his stomach. "Paula's omelets are huge!"

"So you ordered me five breakfasts?"

Adam shrugged, and his cheeks pinked slightly. "You didn't give me much to go on."

Riley had thought "nothing too big" would at the very least translate to "no more than one full breakfast, please," but Adam had never been a great problem solver. At least Paula had enjoyed a lucrative morning. "Thanks," he said, and grabbed the container with bacon and scrambled eggs.

"Sleep okay?" Adam asked.

Riley shrugged and picked up a piece of slightly warm bacon with his fingers.

"It's so quiet here at night," Adam continued. "I forgot about that. It's nice."

"One of the perks," Riley agreed.

"Well, except the heater in my room. That thing rattles like a freight train. I tried to turn it off last night but couldn't figure it out."

It was then that Riley noticed the bags under Adam's eyes, and the way his stubble wasn't quite as tidy as it had been yesterday.

Well, whatever. Adam was free to return to his fancy house in Toronto anytime.

"Can Lucky eat bacon?" Adam asked.

"He can, but he shouldn't. Here." Riley tossed a chunk of scrambled eggs on the floor, and Lucky swooped in to gobble it up.

"How old is he?"

"Eight, but he's still full of energy."

"He seems like a good friend."

"The best," Riley agreed.

When it became clear that Riley wasn't going to share more food with him, Lucky retreated to the back room for a nap. Adam explored the shop while Riley picked at his breakfast.

"Sign any more autographs at Paula's this morning?" Riley asked.

"A couple. I had a bit of a wait."

"People are going to start showing up there with your jersey."

Adam smiled. "I'll enjoy it while it lasts. People will forget about me soon enough."

Riley suspected Adam would be signing autographs for many years to come. He'd broken every record for Toronto defensemen, and a couple of records for NHL defensemen. He'd be in the Hall of Fame soon, and he'd always be a hero to Toronto fans. He was, without exaggeration, a living legend.

And he'd brought Riley breakfast.

"How are the eggs?" Adam asked.

"Fine."

"They're probably cold, aren't they? Sorry about that."

"It's okay."

"There's coffee there too. With milk."

Adam seemed nervous, which was annoying. "I saw the coffee. Thanks."

"Hey, um," Adam said, "there's something I want to tell you."

Riley swallowed a bit of cold toast. "Okay."

For a long moment, Adam didn't say anything, and Riley suspected the noisy heater hadn't been the only thing keeping him awake last night.

"You don't have to tell me anything," Riley offered.

"I'm gay."

Maybe it was the lack of sleep, or the way grief had fucked up Riley's brain, or maybe it was the surrealness of hearing Adam say those words after so many years, but Riley started laughing.

"I'm serious," Adam said.

Riley covered his mouth with his hand, knowing his reaction was horrible. "I know. I'm sorry." He snorted around his hand, then laughed harder.

Adam looked devastated, and that seemed funny too. Suddenly every horrible moment of Riley's life seemed fucking hilarious. Riley waved a hand in an attempt to explain he had no control here. He was rattling apart, and Adam was just going to have to witness it.

"Riley," Adam said, in his captain voice. So serious. So ridiculous. Riley walked away, trying desperately to stop laughing.

Of course Adam was gay. Of course he was *here* and finally confessing this *now* when Riley was teetering on the edge of a cliff. Words Riley had only ever dreamed of hearing him say. Actually, he'd never needed to hear them. He'd just needed Adam to admit that he felt the way Riley did.

He braced himself with a hand on a wall on the other side of the store from where Adam was still standing and closed his eyes. The giddy mirth that had overtaken him began to gain weight, and he stopped laughing. "Jesus," he said. "Fuck."

"Are you done?" Adam asked, clearly and rightfully irritated.

"Yeah," Riley sighed. "I'm done. I'm fucking completely done. Finished." He sounded insane, and he knew it. "Done, done, done."

"I'm just telling you because I thought you should know. Not because...y'know. Whatever."

Riley looked at him from across the shop. "You thought I should know?"

Adam spread his arms wide. "You were right. Totally gay."

If Adam expected Riley to celebrate that win, he was very wrong. The words felt like a punch to the gut. "And when did you figure this out?"

"A couple of years ago," Adam said. "Well, before then. But I told Maggie a couple of years ago."

Maggie. Right. God. "You loved Maggie, though."

"In a way, yeah. I still do. She's great. But it never felt the same as—" Adam's gaze dropped to the floor. "Some parts of it were...forced. It always was, with women."

"There were a lot of women. Before Maggie, I mean."

"Yeah, well. I guess I was trying to prove something to myself. And maybe it wasn't as many as I made it seem like."

Riley slumped against the wall. Every time he and Adam had drunkenly hooked up, like clockwork, Adam would want to go out to pick up women the following night. He'd always invite Riley to come too, as if Riley would share his need to cleanse himself. Riley never joined him. "You know bisexuality exists, right?"

"Of course I do. But that's not me. Believe me, I tried to make that happen."

"I don't think that's how it works."

Adam huffed. "Nope."

There was a long silence, and then Adam said, "So..."

Riley closed his eyes, waiting. But Adam didn't finish his sentence. He just let that "so" linger in the air between them.

"So what?" Riley finally said.

Adam didn't say anything.

Riley groaned. "Are you here because I'm the only man you've fucked? You want to practice being gay on a sure thing?

Because I'm not a sure thing, Adam. Not with you." He felt good about making that clear.

But Adam annihilated him with his next words: "You're not the only man I've fucked."

The wall was the only thing keeping Riley on his feet. Had he been wrong about everything?

"I mean," Adam continued, "you *were*. For a very long time you were. But since Maggie and I separated… I've been seeing what's out there. The apps are helpful."

Adam was gay and hooking up with men all over Toronto. Neat.

Then Adam chuckled. "Gay porn is way easier to access now too."

Riley wanted to scream. How wonderful it was that Adam had waited until conditions had improved before embracing his gay self, while Riley had struggled alone in the shadows during his own NHL career.

"I have to be careful, in Toronto," Adam explained, as if Riley wanted to hear any of this. As if Riley didn't *know*. "I'm not out, really. I haven't told many people." He exhaled. "I was so nervous to tell you, but you were also the first person I *wanted* to tell. Sorry if that's weird."

It was weird, but it also made sense. Adam had been the first person Riley had wanted to call when Dad had died, even though they hadn't spoken in so long. Old habits.

"I'm glad you told me," Riley said, because that, at least, was true. He just wished he'd told him over a decade ago. "I'm sorry I laughed."

Adam began walking toward him. "I know it's not an excuse for everything shitty I said to you back then, but I wanted you to know. I owed you that."

Riley was about to argue that Adam didn't owe him anything, but that would have been a lie. So he nodded and said, "Thanks."

"Are you okay?"

Riley let out a shaky laugh. "Obviously I'm great."

Adam raised a hand, as if he wanted to touch Riley in some way, but then lowered it. "I didn't want to leave town without saying that."

"You're leaving, then?"

"I mean… I'd rather stay. At least to help you get the store back together."

He looked so hopeful, like tidying up Riley's shop would be the best way he could possibly spend his day that Riley surrendered. "All right. Let's get to work, then."

Adam had thought things would feel easier, after saying it. Like his big revelation would clear the air between them, that maybe Riley would be sated, learning that he'd been right all along.

It wasn't easier. They worked in near silence for the first two hours, and things felt more tense between them, not less.

At least the shop was looking good.

"When are you reopening?" Adam asked, needing desperately to talk about something.

"Tomorrow." Riley stood from where he'd been sitting on the floor, rearranging a low shelf. He glanced around the store, then said, "I checked with the staff and they're ready. Not that we need everyone tomorrow."

"You've got staff?"

Riley stared at him like he was a moron. "I don't work here alone."

"Oh."

"It's not a big staff. It was me and Dad and Steve—he's worked here for almost thirty years. You probably met him during the summers you were here. I've got a cousin, Cory, who's been working here awhile. And we usually have a couple of part-time teenagers helping out. We've got Jess and Addie right now. I gave them all the week off with pay."

"And you didn't give yourself the week off?"

"I did, technically. I just thought I'd..." He trailed off.

Adam smiled. "You just thought you'd turn the store upside down instead?"

To Adam's delight, Riley laughed. A single amused puff of breath. "Yeah. Not my best plan."

"It's looking good in here now, though. Better than before, would you say?"

Riley glanced around again, then nodded. "I think so." For a moment, he looked pleased, then his shoulders sagged. "It's going to be weird, without Dad."

Adam could picture it, Riley here alone or maybe with Steve while a slow trickle of locals took turns offering condolences while buying hockey tape. It didn't sound like what Riley needed at all.

"Can I help?" Adam asked.

Riley's eyebrows shot up. "You're not leaving tomorrow?"

"Not that I know of."

Riley huffed an exasperated breath and shook his head. "How long are you planning on staying, exactly?"

Adam squared his shoulders. "My flight home is on Tuesday."

Riley stared at him. "It's only *Thursday*."

"I'm aware."

"You—" Riley let out an exasperated whoosh of air, then walked to the counter.

"I don't know why this is such a big deal," Adam called after him.

"You're right. Everything about it is super normal."

Adam walked over to him, leaving a few feet of space between them. "Listen, I'm retired, and I'm divorced, and I thought maybe I could be useful here. So if you think me sticking around might make things less shitty for you, I'm happy to stay." He smiled. "Feel free to tell me I'm an egomaniac, though."

"You're an egomaniac," Riley said quickly. Then he sighed and added, "But stay if you want, I guess. God knows everyone in town would fucking celebrate it."

"I'm not staying for them." It was probably too much. His earnest words seemed to land on the counter between them with a thud.

But he didn't miss the way Riley's cheeks went pink. Riley ducked his head, probably to hide it, and said, "Come on. We're almost done."

By four o'clock the shop looked perfect. At least Adam thought so; Riley kept finding little things to improve.

"You going to your mom's?" Adam asked, hoping to remind Riley that there were other things he could be doing other than checking the level of a shelf of energy bars.

"Not today. She and Lindsay are at my uncle's house in Pictou. There were some things Mom wanted him to have. That's Uncle Dennis. You may have met him, I can't remember." Riley narrowed his eyes at him. "Is your shoulder bothering you?"

"Oh." Adam's shoulder was throbbing, but he hadn't meant for Riley to notice him rubbing it. "A little bit."

Riley was a hockey player, so he knew that "a little bit" meant "a lot." His expression darkened. "Why didn't you tell me? I never would have let you help if I'd known."

"That's why I didn't tell you."

Riley raked a hand through his hair, clearly distraught.

"It's okay," Adam said softly. "It's not that bad. Really."

"No," Riley said. "No, it's not okay." He walked to the

counter, then to the door, and then back again. "You shouldn't be staying at the River Bend."

"Well," Adam said, "the Ritz was all booked up."

"I have a guest room."

Adam stared at him. "Are you inviting me to stay with you?"

"You fucked your shoulder up helping me, so yeah. I'm offering." Then he rolled his eyes and added, "Since you insist on sticking around."

Adam smiled and said, "Thank you. I'd appreciate that."

To his surprise, the barest hint of a smile curved Riley's lips. "Yeah?"

"I'd really like to see your home, Riley."

"I'll be busy," Riley warned him. "I've got work and other stuff. This isn't—it's just to get you out of that motel, okay?"

"Okay."

"Doesn't make sense for you to be uncomfortable when I've got an empty room for you." Riley seemed to be trying to convince himself of this.

"Right. I get it. Thank you."

Riley took one more look around the store, then exhaled. "Let's go get you checked out of there."

Chapter Thirteen

Riley's house looked like a painting. Old, but beautifully restored with cranberry-red shingles and a cheerful golden-yellow door. There was a weather vane with a whale in the center on the peak of the roof. And beyond the house there was an enormous yard that sloped toward a breathtaking view of the sea.

Adam parked his rental car behind Riley's truck. He was immediately greeted by an excited Lucky, who danced around his legs as Adam exited the car.

"You gonna show me your house?" Adam asked him. "I'll tell you, I'm impressed so far."

"The view is nicer when the sun is out," Riley said, frowning at the cloudy sky.

"I look forward to it."

Riley turned his frown to him, which reminded Adam that he was, understandably, on probation here.

"It's a nice spot, though," Adam tried. "Ocean." He gestured to the water, as if Riley didn't know where it was. "And I saw the beach there. Pretty sweet."

Riley frowned at him for another few seconds, then said, "We can go inside."

Lucky was already at the door, tail wagging frantically. Adam followed Riley up the short wooden staircase to the front porch. While he waited for Riley to unlock the door, Adam touched his finger to a shingle. "These look new. Did you replace them yourself?"

"With help, yeah. Took forever."

"Worth it."

"Thanks." The door opened and Lucky thundered inside. He barked once, over his shoulder, as if inviting Adam in.

Adam removed his boots in the tidy mudroom, then followed Riley deeper into the house.

"So this is the living room," Riley said.

The word that popped into Adam's head as he gazed around the room was *exquisite*. Everything was beautiful and ornate and had clearly been thoughtfully chosen. Rich colors paired with dark wood and pops of gold. All of the furniture looked vintage, and the walls were decorated in dark blue wallpaper with a shiny copper floral print. The woodstove and the large area rug made the room look cozy and inviting. But the showstopper was the giant window that faced the sea.

"Wow," Adam said. "This is beautiful. Did you hire a designer?"

"No. I just put together some things I like."

Adam gazed up at the stunning chandelier above his head and thought about the apartment he used to share with Riley. Drab, white, and undecorated, with cheap furniture and Adam's clutter everywhere. Was this what Riley had dreamed of for himself, back then?

"Pretty different from our apartment," Adam said.

Riley huffed. "A bit."

"Where do you even get a chandelier like that?"

"Antiques stores. I've got some local favorites, and I look online too."

"You've got a great eye for it."

Riley's lips curved up on one side. "It's my gay superpower."

Adam laughed. "I haven't figured mine out yet. Or do you have to be granted your power? Is there a council?"

"Yeah. There's a lot of paperwork, though."

"Pass."

Riley's smile grew. "You're still shit at that stuff?"

The only reason Adam had ever had any important documents, like his driver's license, up-to-date was because Riley—and later, Maggie—had always reminded him. "I'm slightly better," Adam said. "Divorce is a lot of paperwork."

Riley's smile disappeared. "Right." He sat on one end of the couch, so Adam sat on the other. Lucky had disappeared, but Adam could hear him clacking around upstairs.

"Sorry," Adam said. "I don't have to mention the divorce if you'd rather I didn't."

"No," Riley said quickly. "I don't mind. I just still can't believe it."

"Yeah. Well. Add it to my list of fuck-ups."

After a pause that was long enough that Adam thought Riley might actually be mentally adding it to a list, Riley said, "Was Maggie surprised, when you told her you're gay?"

Adam's gaze traced a section of the intricate pattern on the rug under his feet. "When I first told her, she definitely was. But not long after, she told me it made a lot of things make sense."

He heard Riley shift on the sofa. Adam kept his gaze on the floor as he continued, "I wasn't a great husband. I tried, but I know I wasn't. Maggie never made me feel like I wasn't enough, but our relationship was…" He sighed. "I was on the road a lot, obviously, but when I was home, I still wasn't really present. I focused all my attention on hockey, because it was the only thing I was sure of. It made sense. What didn't make sense was having a wonderful wife and amazing kids in a beautiful house and still feeling empty every day."

Adam turned his head and met Riley's eyes. "I made a mess of things. It was selfish of me to marry her. I just thought I could make it work. And I sort of did, for a while. We were mostly happy. I can't regret it completely, because we have the kids and I love them, obviously, but I regret wasting Maggie's time."

Riley didn't say anything.

"So to answer your original question, Maggie has been great about the whole thing, but I still feel like the world's biggest asshole."

Riley didn't try to convince him otherwise. "Do Lucy and Cole know you're gay?"

Adam nodded. "We told them together and kind of rolled it into one big conversation about our decision to split up. Wasn't the easiest day of my life. Cole took it really hard, Lucy was more sympathetic. But it's been a couple of years now, and Cole is older and more understanding."

"That's good." Riley huffed. "I can't believe they're teenagers. I saw them on the ice for your thousandth game ceremony, but that must have been eight years ago now."

Adam smiled. "You watched that?"

Riley's cheeks turned pink. "For a minute or two." He shifted again. "You got photos of them?"

"Yeah! Of course." Adam pulled out his phone and quickly pulled up a recent photo of Lucy and Cole together. Riley moved closer to see it.

"Lucy really looks like you," Riley said.

"People say that. Not sure she likes hearing it."

"Cole is tall. He's fifteen, right?"

"Yep. He's on the high school basketball team. He's good too."

"That's cool," Riley leaned back. "Did either of them play hockey?"

"A bit when they were really young. It didn't take. I'm not sure I was the best advertisement for the sport, given how often I was out of commission at home. Always nursing some fresh injury. It was probably scary for them."

"Probably."

"Lucy was at the game when I fucked up my shoulder the first time. I was down on the ice for a while. She was nine and, yeah. Not a great memory for her."

"Or for you, I'll bet."

Adam didn't like to think about it. "No. Not for me either."

They were quiet a moment, Adam staring at his smiling kids, and Riley breathing beside him.

"Are you hungry?" Riley asked. "I have a whole lasagna in the fridge."

"Starving," Adam said, wondering how long this fragile peace between them would last. "Lasagna sounds amazing."

The kitchen was also beautiful, with weathered wood cupboards, a pale blue tiled backsplash, and butcher-block countertops. The window faced the trees that lined one side of the property.

"I can't believe you did all this," Adam said. "Like, you made a house."

"I *fixed up* a house," Riley said as he turned on the oven. "But yeah. I'm happy with it."

"You should be." Adam studied the ornate light fixture above his head. "That another antique?"

"Yes."

Adam tapped his foot on the gleaming wood floor. "Did you install the floors too?"

Riley opened the fridge door. "I restored the original flooring throughout the house."

Adam whistled. "You must impress the pants off dates you bring here."

Riley snorted. "Dates."

"What? You never tell a guy, 'Hey, wanna see the amazing house I basically built?'"

Riley set the lasagna on the counter. "Nope."

Adam tried not to think about how *he* was here to see the amazing house Riley basically built. "Never?"

"Are you asking if I ever invite men here to have sex?"

"No?" Adam tried.

Riley's eyes narrowed. "I do, yeah. A bunch of times. I don't, like, give them a tour."

"Oh," Adam said. "Cool."

"Anyway." Riley put the lasagna in the oven, then leaned against the counter with his arms folded, facing Adam. "I'd offer you a beer, but I don't have any."

"Right. Of course. That's okay." Truthfully, Adam really could use a drink. "So…"

Riley rolled his eyes. "You can't drop it can you?"

"I can."

"Okay then."

Adam ran his hand over the countertop next to him, then said, "So there are men here? Like, men to hook up with?"

"Why? Are you looking for one?"

"*No.* I just thought it would be harder for you. Here."

"I'm not the only queer in town," Riley said bluntly. "But okay. I'm not really hooking up with locals. Like you said, the apps are helpful."

Adam nodded eagerly. "Yeah. They're great, right?" When Riley looked away, Adam said, "Sorry. I just haven't had anyone to really talk about this sort of stuff with."

That made Riley unfold his arms, and his expression soften. "No one?"

"Not really. Not, like, a friend."

Riley held his gaze, and Adam wondered what he was think-ing. Maybe that Adam didn't deserve gay friends. Adam had often thought the same thing.

"That sucks," Riley finally said.

"Basically, yeah."

There was another long silence and then Riley said, "Is *that* why you're here then?"

Adam threw his hands up. "Jesus, Riles. No. Would you stop?"

"Stop what?"

"Stop trying to make it seem like I'm here for selfish rea-sons." Even as Adam was saying it, a voice inside his head asked, *"Aren't you?"*

"I'm not," Adam said firmly, both to Riley and to the voice.

Riley looked away.

Lucky entered the kitchen, tail wagging, and Adam wel-comed the distraction. He crouched and reached out a hand. Lucky immediately pressed his head against it, so Adam scratched his ears.

"You have a lovely home, Lucky. Did you choose the wall-paper in the living room?"

Riley huffed.

"It's very fancy," Adam continued, ignoring him. "When I lived with your dad he had a *Gladiator* poster in his room."

"You can't prove that," Riley said.

Adam smiled. "If only we had smartphones back then. I'd have so much evidence." To Lucky he said, "It was *framed*."

"We had *cameras*, and it was just one of those cheap poster frames."

"As if I knew how to use a camera. Anyway, Lucky, your dad used to be pretty tacky."

"No, he used to be horny for Russell Crowe. But who wasn't

back then? Also, that poster was only up for a few months. I can't believe you even remember that."

Adam stood. "Was it? Why'd you get rid of it?"

Riley glared at him. "I guess it didn't work out between us."

Adam laughed. He'd missed Riley's sense of humor: dry, a little mean, and lightning quick. Adam had always been the chatterbox, and Riley had always been able to slice through Adam's noise with a cutting remark that would make Adam howl with laughter.

Riley was smiling too, that same bemused little tilt of his lips that he used to always get whenever he made Adam laugh. It was like he didn't understand what Adam was laughing at, and that would only make Adam laugh more.

"Anyway, you were the one who always wanted to watch that movie," Riley said. "Although that makes a lot more sense now."

"I watched it for purely heterosexual reasons!"

"There *are* no heterosexual reasons to watch *Gladiator*, Shep."

Something bounced inside Adam's chest at the nickname. It was the first time all week that Riley had used it without it sounding like a weapon. It was friendly and comfortable.

"There totally are," Adam argued. "It's a classy movie about history."

"Uh-huh."

"I'm serious!"

Truthfully, Adam hadn't thought much about the movies he'd liked when he was younger, and whether or not he'd been attracted to the actors in them. He could say with certainty that he'd liked sharing a couch with Riley for two and a half hours while they watched *Gladiator* together. He'd liked how Riley usually fell asleep against him in the middle of it. The DVD they'd owned reliably froze about two hours into the movie, and what Riley didn't know was how long Adam would stare at the image of a blurry horse, being careful not to wake his friend. He'd loved having the weight of Riley's head against his shoulder, or sometimes even on his thigh, and the soft sounds Riley would make while sleeping peacefully.

God, Adam had been stupid. How could he not have realized how in love he'd been?

Riley's smile faded, as if he was realizing how relaxed he was being with Adam and he didn't like it. He folded his arms again. Adam tried to think of a way to make him smile again, but at that moment the phone rang.

Like, an actual phone that was attached to the wall. It had a *cord*. It was *pink*.

Riley glanced at it, still frowning. "Not sure who that would be."

"You have a landline," Adam said.

"Mostly for emergencies. Cell service isn't always reliable out here and storms take the Wi-Fi out all the time. Not many people have the number." The phone rang again. "Shit, I'll bet it's Darren."

"Darren?"

Riley answered the phone. Adam deciphered that it was in fact someone named Darren calling, and that Riley had been ignoring his texts and calls. That was all he got before Riley made a "do you mind?" face at him and Adam left the kitchen.

It was pretty adorable that Riley still had a landline and that he'd filled his house with antiques. Back in the living room, Adam noticed a record player sitting on a small, sturdy cabinet. The shelf underneath held a small collection of vinyl records. Adam crouched and flipped through them, curious. Riley had always been a country fan mostly, and Adam could see that hadn't changed. Dolly Parton, Patsy Cline, Linda Ronstadt, Waylon Jennings, Johnny Cash, Emmylou Harris. All of the sleeves were well-worn, probably all purchased in secondhand shops. Adam wondered if Riley listened to them very often, and what he did while the music played. His house was so tidy, maybe he cleaned while listening to old crackly records. Adam found himself charmed by the image.

Lucky sneaked up behind him and nosed his thigh, as if letting Adam know he'd been caught snooping.

"Sorry," Adam said. "I was just curious." He slid the Roger Miller LP he'd been inspecting back into the cabinet. "I don't even know how to use a record player. My parents would never let me touch theirs when I was a kid."

"It's pretty easy," Riley said from behind him.

Adam jumped to his feet, startled and embarrassed. "Is it? I wasn't—"

Riley's lips tilted up again. "You've discovered my dark secret: I own a few records."

Adam laughed nervously. "Yeah. Shocking." He wouldn't tell him how thrilling each tiny piece of information about Riley's current life was to learn. He was so different now, so impressive and attractive for completely new reasons, but at the same time Adam could see how this man had always been there, waiting inside the young, emotional, and somewhat chaotic hockey player Adam had known so well.

"Takes a while to heat up a lasagna," Riley said, almost apologetically.

"It's okay." Adam gazed around the room, trying to find a new conversation topic. He landed on the television. "You gonna watch any of the games tonight?"

"What?" Riley said.

"The playoffs start tonight."

Riley's eyes went wide. "Shit. Right. I forgot."

"Toronto doesn't play until tomorrow night," Adam said quickly.

"Yeah," Riley said quietly. Adam watched the color drain

from his face, hating that he'd even mentioned hockey. Of course Riley had probably planned to watch the playoffs with his dad.

He took a step toward Riley. "We could watch together, if you want."

Riley let out a slow, uneven breath. "I'm not really in the mood for hockey. Or anything, really. I should try to go to bed early."

Adam tried not to feel disappointed. "Right. Yeah. Good plan."

"Um," Riley said, "I'm going to go check on the, uh—" He turned and left abruptly, but not before Adam could hear the strain in his voice.

Adam looked at Lucky, who was staring at him with a vaguely accusatory expression.

"I don't think I'm helping much, Lucky."

Chapter Fourteen

Riley wasn't surprised to hear Adam enter the kitchen, and he was too exhausted to attempt to pretend he wasn't crying.

"Hey," Adam said softly.

Riley sniffed and said nothing. He was sitting at the kitchen table, his head in his hands, and probably looked like a perfect reference image for misery. Dimly he registered Lucky resting his chin on his knee.

He heard a cupboard door open, then another, then two more. Then the tap running. A moment later Adam placed a glass of water next to his elbow.

"You want to talk about it?"

"No," Riley said honestly. He didn't want to talk about anything at all. He just wanted to go to sleep, and maybe wake up months later, when the grief wouldn't be as sharp.

A chair scraped against the floor, then Adam was sitting kitty-corner to him. It should have felt more surreal, and alarming, to have Adam here in his home, and maybe it was a testament to how tired Riley was, but it felt...comfortable.

"I don't think I've ever told you this," Adam said, "but do you remember that game about halfway through our first season that both our families were at?"

"I remember." Riley remembered Adam's dad being a total dick after the game. Both Adam and Riley had gotten a decent amount of ice time for two rookies, and Adam had even gotten an assist. Toronto ended up losing, but losing was what the Northmen did back then. None of that had stopped Colin Sheppard from giving a detailed account of every mistake Adam had made during the game. He'd done it in front of the entire Tuck family, minutes after meeting them, all of them standing in an awkward group in the hall outside the locker room.

Riley was pretty sure that Adam's parents had hated him, or at least their son's friendship with him. He'd suspected they knew what Riley was, and how he felt about Adam, and it had disgusted them. Maybe they'd noticed the way Adam looked at Riley, sometimes. Whatever it was, Riley had no doubt they'd celebrated when the friendship had ended.

He was also pretty sure they used to hit Adam, when he'd been a kid, but Adam had never outright said so.

"Dad was...being Dad that night," Adam said. "You know, picking apart my game and—"

"Yeah," Riley interrupted, and lifted his head. "He was being a fucking prick."

Adam huffed. "Exactly. Anyway, I know you were there for that part, but after, your dad caught me alone somehow—he must have created an opportunity, I don't know."

"Probably," Riley said. He leaned back in his chair. "He was good at that."

"He told me I was one of the prettiest skaters he'd ever seen."

Riley smiled. "He wouldn't be the last person to say that about you."

"He wasn't the first either, but man, I needed that compliment in that moment. But he also told me how happy he was that his son—" Adam paused to give Riley a pointed look "—had made such a good friend."

Riley's cheeks heated. "He said that?"

"And he told me if I wanted to spend some of the summer in Avery River, I was more than welcome."

Riley wiped away a fresh tear. That was Dad: knowing exactly what someone needed and giving it to them.

Adam held his gaze, his expression serious, and said, "I *was* lucky to have you as a friend."

This irritated Riley. What was he supposed to say to that? It was absolute bullshit. Did Adam expect him to say it back?

Still annoyed, Riley pushed his chair back, and stood. "Lasagna's probably ready."

As he walked to the oven, he heard Adam sigh heavily.

They ate while Lucky loudly crunched through his own dinner in the corner, and Adam carried on a mostly one-sided conversation about several things: the town, Toronto's playoff chances, the possibility of sunshine tomorrow, food. Riley only half listened, but managed to finish his serving of lasagna.

"I'll take care of this," Adam said as he took both of their plates to the sink.

"The hell you will. Go rest your shoulder."

Eventually, Adam did leave the kitchen, which gave Riley a moment to breathe. He reminded himself that he'd only invited Adam to stay because it was the right thing to do. Adam had hurt himself while helping Riley in the shop, so the least Riley could do was offer him a bed that wasn't being used. It really wasn't a big deal, and surely Adam would get bored soon and leave.

When Riley entered the living room, he found Adam lying on the sofa, his eyes closed. Lucky was resting on his dog bed in the corner.

"You awake?" Riley asked.

Adam opened his eyes and smiled. "Hey."

Riley's heart wobbled. *Oh no.* "I'm going to do some laundry in a minute, if there's anything you want me to throw in."

"God, that would be great. I'm wearing my last clean pair of pants."

The pants in question were dark brown and, Riley couldn't help but notice, exquisitely tailored. He could tell Adam's legs were still thick and strong.

"You sure your clothes don't need to be dry-cleaned?"

"Does this town have a dry-cleaner?"

"No."

"I'll risk it then."

Which meant Adam was serious about staying, at least for a few more days.

For the next several hours, they both just existed in the same space. Adam had his phone out a lot, probably texting his kids. Or old teammates. Or the fucking Prime Minister. Who knew what Adam's life was like these days?

Riley busied himself by watering plants, doing laundry, ironing, deep cleaning his kitchen sink, and, most absurdly, rearranging two shelves of his pantry.

"Need help?" Adam had called out from the living room when Riley had dropped an open bag of split peas on the floor, scattering them everywhere.

"No," Riley had quickly called back. "I'm good." Because everything he was doing was related to a single goal: avoid Adam.

Except now, in the golden lamplight of the living room, with Adam still lying on the couch and quietly reading a book, Riley found himself fascinated. Adam was wearing his glasses, which wasn't a big deal, except they were really nice glasses and Riley hadn't seen them before. The frames were heavy and dark and rectangular, like display boxes that showcased the perfect sapphire of his eyes. Adam's lips were tight, as if the scene he was reading was tense or sad. Riley tried not to notice any of it, just like he didn't care about the way Adam idly curled and uncurled his toes inside his socks as he read.

Riley didn't care. He was only sitting for a moment, exhausted after all of his mostly unnecessary chores.

After a few minutes, Adam rested the book on his chest and said, "Shit, I didn't even see you there."

"Good book?"

"Aw, you know. It's just a spy novel."

Riley had never known Adam to read anything, before. Not that Riley was a great reader either. "What's it about?"

"Spies." Adam smiled lazily at him, then yawned.

"I can show you where you're going to be sleeping," Riley said. "If you want."

Adam nodded. "I'm pretty tired."

"How's your shoulder?"

"It's been worse."

Adam swung his legs over the sofa and sat up. His hair was a mess, and it was annoyingly cute. Riley watched as he stuck a bookmark in his paperback, then removed his glasses.

"What?" Adam asked when he noticed the way Riley had probably been staring at him. "Oh, is it the glasses?"

Riley grabbed that excuse with both hands. "Yeah. Hadn't seen them before." He stood. "Come on upstairs."

The guest room, Adam soon discovered, was every bit as charming and beautifully decorated as the rest of Riley's house. The walls and ceiling were covered in wide, white wooden boards, and the wood floor was stained the same rich brown as the rest of the house. A large rug covered most of the floor, and the bed was piled high with pillows and a blue-and-white-striped duvet. The window faced the ocean, though it was too dark outside to see now, and had a built-in blue velvet bench seat. Lucky had his front paws on the bench, as if trying to make sure Adam saw it.

"Are you kidding me?" Adam said. "Riles, this is beautiful."

"Thanks. I wanted it to be nautical without being too nautical, y'know?"

"Nautical but nice," Adam agreed.

Riley rolled his eyes, but he smiled slightly. "Anyway. The bed should be better than what you were sleeping in."

"Definitely."

Riley was taking up most of the doorframe, leaning against one side with his arms crossed. He would have looked menacing, except Adam couldn't possibly be intimidated by a man who'd made a room as adorable as this one.

"There are some books there." Riley pointed to a small shelf in one corner of the room. "Since you're such a bookworm now."

"I only started reading a few years ago, when I broke my foot," Adam said as he bent to scratch Lucky's ears.

"Dad liked spy novels too. He'd give them to me after he finished them, but I don't read much." He stared at the shelf for a moment, not moving, then cleared his throat and said, "Anyway. Help yourself."

Adam stood and took a step toward him. "Riley…"

Riley raised a hand. "I'm fine. I need to go to bed. Come on, Lucky."

"Okay, but…thank you. Seriously."

"No problem," Riley muttered, though Adam felt like he was causing all sorts of problems for him.

Later, alone in possibly the best bed he'd ever been in, Adam wondered if he was imagining that Riley's hatred of him was thawing a bit. Obviously if Riley hated him, Adam wouldn't be in this bed, in this beautiful house. He wouldn't have fed him and done his laundry. He wouldn't have offered him his dad's spy novels.

Riley had to still care about Adam, at least a little bit. And that was something Adam could work with.

Chapter Fifteen

Adam had gone to Paula's with the responsible intentions of ordering a light breakfast—maybe a coffee and some toast—but then he'd realized he hadn't tried the pancakes yet. So now he was reclining with one arm stretched across the back of his booth seat, full of delicious buttery goodness.

"How'd the pancakes treat you?" Paula asked as she refilled his coffee.

"My god," Adam said, patting his belly, "I might die, but it would be worth it."

Paula laughed. "I've seen hockey boys put away twice as many pancakes without blinking."

"Well, I'm not a boy anymore. Or a hockey player."

"Go on with you. Are you an old man now?"

"Feels like it."

Paula shook her head. "Barely out of your thirties, handsome as sin, complaining about being old."

Adam smiled. He liked the way people talked here. "Handsome, eh?"

"Like you need to take my word for it. Now what've you got planned for today, Mr. Adam Sheppard?"

"I was going to pop into the shop—Tuck's, I mean—to say hi."

"Heard they were opening up today. That's good. I hope it's not too hard for poor Riley."

The customers at the tables around them, who weren't even pretending not to be eavesdropping, all made sounds of agreement.

"I'm sure he'd appreciate it if any of you want to stop in and show your support," Adam said to the whole restaurant. "He did some reorganizing, and the place looks great." To Paula he said, "That reminds me: can I get some coffees to go? Maybe some cinnamon buns?"

"Of course."

"Hey, Shep," said the young man in the booth across from his. "You should come by the Anchor tonight. We're watching the game. Be cool to have you there."

"Yeah?" Adam immediately began to wonder if he could convince Riley to join him. "Maybe I will. Thanks, um..."

The man beamed at him. He was young, probably in his twenties, and spoke with a French accent. "Seb," he said.

"I'll try to be there, Seb."

People were still talking excitedly throughout the restaurant as Adam left with a tray of coffee and a paper bag of cinnamon buns. He supposed he'd have to go to the bar tonight now, though he'd been looking forward to another night in with Riley.

Yesterday had gone well, Adam thought. There'd been a rocky start at the shop, and things certainly hadn't been smooth sailing at Riley's house later, but it had felt like progress. This morning, in the empty house, Adam had watched videos on YouTube of Riley and him playing together. It had hurt, like he'd expected it to, but it had also been a rush to let himself remember how life had felt back then. Back when they'd both been young and beautiful and rich and famous. When the city of Toronto had loved them. When they'd loved each other with a fierceness that Adam could see in those videos. Clips where he would get tripped, and then Riley would flatten the poor guy who did it. Where Riley would score a goal and Adam would hold him against the boards, smiling while yelling in his face, their noses touching. So many videos, spanning nine seasons, and ending with the Stanley Cup win. Adam hugging him, and probably telling him he loved him. Riley would have silently acknowledged it, because he hadn't said any version of those words to Adam since the time he'd tried to say them for real. And Adam, selfishly, had said them all the time to Riley, disguising them as casual, as if showing Riley how to do it properly.

God, Adam had been such an idiot. All the coffee and cinnamon buns in the world couldn't make up for how badly he'd treated Riley.

When he entered Tuck's Sporting Goods, there were a few customers and Riley already looked frazzled. He nodded at Adam, then went back to talking to the woman who seemed to have him pinned in one corner of the shop.

Adam placed the coffee and cinnamon buns on the counter, then casually made his way to the hockey stick rack, which was closer to where Riley was trapped. He heard the woman, who looked about his own age, say the word "Harvey" and then "won't be the same without him," and he saw the way Riley was nodding, his jaw tight and his eyes unfocused. Adam made a beeline for them.

"Hi, Riley," he said cheerfully, then to the woman he said, "Oh, sorry to interrupt. I'm Adam." He held out his hand. As expected, the woman's face lit up.

"Oh my goodness, hi. Of course I know who you are."

"Well, that puts me at a disadvantage." Adam winked and hoped it was charming and not creepy.

She laughed and blushed a little. "I'm Cathy. I went to school with Riley and—" she tilted her head from side to side while rolling her eyes "—I'm a proud hockey mom. Two sons and a daughter."

"That's great," Adam said enthusiastically. "I owe a lot to my own hockey mom."

She seemed very pleased with that. "I was just telling Riley that I've taken on the organization of the end-of-year minor hockey banquet. Obviously we postponed it, and it feels awful to go ahead with it at all without Harv, but it means so much to the kids."

Adam glanced at Riley, but he was staring at the floor. "Of course," Adam said. "Do you need help?"

"Well, actually, Riley, I was wondering about the hosting of it. Harv always did it," she explained, with a glance at Adam, "so I don't know if you, or maybe Susan…"

"No," Riley said. "Sorry. I'm not… I can't."

She nodded sympathetically. "I completely understand. I only wanted to offer. We can find someone."

"When is it?" Adam asked.

She glanced at Riley, as if worried she might offend him. "This Monday night. Is that too soon, Riley? It's just we had things rented and they've been good about postponing a week, but I think if we push it…"

"It's fine," Riley said. "No, it's good. It should happen. Dad would want that."

She smiled at him, her eyes misty. "He worked so hard on it. He always worked so hard on everything."

Riley nodded. Adam could see his jaw tighten.

"There's a lot to do," Cathy said. "But I've got it covered, don't worry."

"Thank you," Riley said quietly. "But if you need help at all—"

"Then ask me," Adam interrupted. "I'm in town until Tues-

day and I'd be happy to help. I could even host it if you want."
He grimaced. "Sorry. That's probably overstepping."

Cathy gaped at him. Then she grabbed his arm with both
hands. "Would you? Oh, that would be so special for the kids."

Adam glanced at Riley, who was also gaping at him. "I
mean, yeah. If you want. It could be fun. Hey, why don't we
let Riley get back to work and we'll discuss the details?"

After giving Cathy a quick goodbye, Riley retreated to the
back room. Adam gave Cathy his cell number, which she was
clearly very excited about, and suggested they meet tomorrow.
As soon as she left, Adam was approached by a man he vaguely
recognized from the last time he'd been in Avery River.

"Hey, Shep. Good to see you again," said the man. He was
stocky, bald, white, and probably in his sixties.

"Steve," Adam guessed, and held out his hand. Steve shook
it happily. "I brought coffee. And cinnamon buns." He gestured to the counter. "Help yourself."

"That's nice of you. Thank you." Rather than grab a coffee, however, Steve stayed put, grinning at Adam. The man
behind Steve—a customer, Adam assumed—stared at Adam
with wide eyes.

"Hi, I'm Adam. Shep, if you like."

The man vigorously shook his hand and said, "Yes, sir, Shep.
I'm Lawrence."

"Nice to meet you." Adam counted backward in his head:
3…2…

"Can I get a photo with you?" Lawrence asked as he fumbled his phone out of his coat pocket. "Would you mind?"

"Of course."

Adam took photos with Lawrence, then Steve, then a woman
who'd just entered the store. He'd just finished with that photo
when he heard, "Egomaniac."

He turned and found Riley standing right behind him, his lips curved up slightly.

"Hi," Adam said, a little breathlessly.

"You brought coffee."

"I did."

"Thanks."

"Everything okay?"

"Yeah," Riley said on an exhale. "Fine. And, uh, thanks. Cathy's great, but she can be a lot."

"No problem."

"You don't have to host the minor hockey banquet, obviously."

"Are you kidding? She said there's going to be pizza. I'm totally there."

For a moment, Riley's eyes almost looked...affectionate. "Did you sleep okay?"

"I slept great. That bed is amazing. Plus I got to listen to the ocean all night. Incredible."

"How's your shoulder?"

"Much better." It was sort of true.

The door chimed, and a group of four people entered the store. They spotted Adam immediately and smiled excitedly.

"Do you want me to hang out for a bit?" Adam asked. "Maybe sign some stuff? Hey, it could be a reopening special—I'll sign anything people buy today."

Riley's brow furrowed. "You'd do that?"

"Sure. I like it here. And I don't have plans today." He snapped his fingers. "Except—would you come to the Dropped Anchor with me tonight?"

Riley recoiled slightly. "Why?"

"They're watching the Northmen game there. I was invited by a young man named Seb."

"Seb Gallant, probably." Riley rubbed his beard thoughtfully. "I guess he's not unattractive."

"Shut it, I didn't mean like that. Jesus, Riles. No."

Riley's slight smile returned. "I know."

"So will you come? I get it if that's too much people in one day for you." Something else occurred to Adam. "Or, oh, right. I get it if you don't want to go to a bar."

"It's not that. Being around people drinking doesn't bother me. I just don't—" He sighed. "I'll think about it, okay?"

Adam clapped his hands together. "All right. You got any Sharpies?"

"I guess he works here now?" Steve said jokingly.

Riley blinked, realizing that he'd been staring at Adam from behind the counter. Adam was near the door, chatting animatedly with three teenagers who Riley was pretty sure were supposed to be in school right now. "He seems to think so."

"He's good for business."

Steve wasn't wrong. The shop had been busy all day, especially as word that Adam Sheppard was hanging out had spread around town. Adam had been there for nearly three hours so far.

"How long is he in town?" Steve asked.

"Apparently forever," Riley grumbled as he checked some inventory levels in the computer.

"Harv would have loved this," Steve said. "Adam Sheppard's here, everyone's laughing, and lots of sales."

Riley realized he was right, and that Adam had kept the energy positive in the shop all day. "He would have," Riley agreed. He glanced at Adam again and saw that he was showing the kids different hockey sticks from the rack.

Steve laughed. "He's making sales now."

At that moment, Mom and Lindsay entered the shop. Lindsay looked at Riley while pointing at Adam. Riley shrugged.

"Well," Mom said when she got to the counter. "It hasn't been a slow day, then."

"Nope," Riley said.

"Did you see our new staff member?" Steve joked.

"I thought he'd be gone," Mom said. "I ran into Deb today and she told me he'd checked out."

"That's strange," Steve said. "Not sure where he'd be staying if not there."

Riley sighed. "He's staying with me." He made the mistake of glancing at Lindsay after he said it. Her eyebrows were sky-high.

"Good on you, Riley," Mom said. Then, to Steve, she said, "I told him to offer up his guest room to poor Adam."

Poor Adam. Jesus.

"I need to get more pucks from the back room," Riley said. "People keep buying them for Shep to sign."

"I'll help," Lindsay said immediately. In the back room, she closed the door behind them and said, "He's staying with you, is he?"

"It's nothing."

"Listen, I have been listening to boring gossip from Aunt Ruth about people I don't know for *days*, Riley. What I actually want to hear about is why my brother is tied up in knots about Adam Sheppard."

"I'm—*what?*"

"Give me the quick version. What's going on?"

Riley pulled a box of hockey pucks off a shelf with a grunt. "There is no quick version."

"Come on."

"We were friends, and now we're not."

"I *know* that."

"There's nothing else to know." Riley handed her the box.

"Jesus, this is heavy." She put the box on the table behind her. "And fine. Don't tell me. But I think it would do you some good to talk about it. All I've pieced together is that things got bad for you after you stopped talking to him. I'd like to know if I should go out there and punch him or what."

Riley snorted. "You don't need to punch him."

"I will, though. If that hockey superstar is bothering you..."

Riley smiled at that. "Thank you." He remembered that Lindsay had been the one to listen to him when he'd hit rock bottom, and she'd been the one to convince him to come home. He owed her a lot. He glanced quickly at the door, lowered his voice, and said, "The thing with Adam is that I was in love with him for years."

Lindsay placed a hand on his shoulder. "Unrequited, I take it."

"Yes."

"I'm sorry. Does he know?"

"Yes."

"Oh." She was silent a moment, then said, "But he's here."

"So?"

"I mean, he must not be horrified by your feelings for him, if he's here."

Riley stared at her. "He's a bit late."

"Is he?"

"For fuck's sake, Linds, *yes*. I was twenty-four years old when I told him. I've moved on. We both have."

"If you say so."

With a huff, Riley turned back to the shelf to grab another box of pucks.

"I'm just saying," Lindsay said, "what I see is a handsome man who obviously cares about you a lot. There are worse places to start."

"Start *what*?"

"Start letting someone in, Riley."

Riley dropped the box of pucks next to the first one on the table with a thud. "No thanks."

"I know the timing isn't great, but I wish—"

"Nope. But if you love Adam Sheppard so much, you should head to the Dropped Anchor tonight. Apparently he's going to be the guest of honor."

Lindsay wrinkled her nose. "Yeah, I'm not going there."

"I forgot you're big city now. Too fancy for us townies."

"I'm too fancy for *that* place. But so is, like, a bag of trash. Are you going?"

"Fuck no."

"You should go! Go relive your glory days with the boys." She playfully punched his arm a couple of times. "Go talk about all the goals you scored and all the undiagnosed concussions you had."

"Sounds horrible."

Her expression turned sad again. "I hate that you're not proud of your NHL career."

"I *am* proud of it," Riley argued. "I just don't want to talk about it." *Or think about it*, he added silently. "I also don't want to talk about Adam. Or anything right now. Like, what the hell, Linds? You really think I'm looking for a date?" He flapped a hand in front of his face. "Fucking look at me. I can't sleep, I can't eat, I can't go more than a few hours without crying. A matchmaking sister is the last thing I need."

He went to open the door, but Lindsay stopped him with a hand on his arm. "I get it, and I'm sorry. Maybe I'm a little desperate for something good to come out of this nightmare. I want you to be happy."

Riley rolled his eyes. "Adam Sheppard will never make me

happy." Then he ended the conversation by opening the door and grabbing both boxes off the table.

By the time the shop closed, Riley was exhausted. He'd spent most of the day fighting back tears, and the rest of it being intermittently charmed by, and angry about being charmed by, Adam.

As he drove home, he wondered how exactly Adam had managed to invade his life so thoroughly in only a few short days. Riley had been sure he'd kept his guard up and hadn't even been nice to him. And yet, here Adam was, helping at the shop, living in his house, and, apparently, volunteering his time for the local minor hockey banquet.

When Riley and Lucky entered the house, Lucky immediately started barking, alerting him that there was an intruder.

"I know, Lucky," Riley grumbled. "We have a guest, remember?"

But Lucky tore off up the stairs, on a mission.

Riley turned on the oven, figuring they may as well have lasagna again. Assuming Adam didn't have dinner plans.

He heard Lucky barking upstairs, and Adam saying, "Oh, hey, boy. You're home."

Lucky kept barking, so Riley sighed and went upstairs. He stopped short when he saw that Adam wasn't in his own room, but was, in fact, exiting the bathroom wearing only a towel around his waist.

"Lucky," Riley said, then lost his train of thought. Adam was still carrying a lot of muscle, especially in his chest. His belly was softer than Riley remembered, and he had a surgical scar on his left shoulder. There were a few gray strands mixed into his dark chest hair.

He blinked, and said, "Come on, Lucky. Leave him alone."

Lucky seemed satisfied that his detective work had paid off, and slipped between Riley's legs to go downstairs. Adam, in what looked like a self-conscious gesture, tugged the towel up a little higher, covering most of his belly. Was he ashamed of it? Ridiculous. He looked incredible.

"That's a nice shower," Adam said.

"Thanks."

"Good water pressure," Adam continued. "I hope I didn't use too much hot water."

Riley watched a drop of water slide down Adam's neck, landing in the hollow of his throat. Adam's skin was flushed and glistening. "It'll replenish," Riley said. He couldn't rid his imagination of a clear image of Adam in his shower, the water hot enough to fill the room with steam and turn Adam's skin pink. He heard himself say, "Take all the showers you want."

For the first time in over a week, Riley's cock was getting hard, and he didn't miss the way Adam's gaze dropped to the growing bulge in his jeans.

Adam clutched the towel tighter, the muscles in his fore-arm bulging.

"Lasagna," Riley blurted out. "I'm heating up the rest of that lasagna. If you're hungry."

Adam's eyes flew back to Riley's face. "Sounds good. Or I could just eat at the Dropped Anchor. You don't have to keep feeding me."

"Don't eat at the Anchor. The kids will be disappointed if you die before the banquet. I'm sure Cathy has told the whole town by now."

Adam smiled. "All right. I'll get dressed and be right down."

Riley's gaze took another quick tour of Adam's body, then he turned his back to him and headed down the stairs.

Chapter Sixteen

A few hours later, against all reason, Riley was standing outside the Dropped Anchor.

Adam had left shortly after eating. Dinner hadn't been unpleasant, though he had tried to convince Riley to come to the bar. He'd clearly been disappointed when Riley said no, but hadn't pushed it. After Adam left, Riley had felt an odd pang of regret, not because he wanted to go out, but because he'd wanted Adam to stay in.

He was still wrestling with those confusing feelings when, about forty minutes later, Adam sent him a text: I got our table, followed by a dark blurry photo of their two jerseys, hanging beside each other above where Adam was probably sitting. Riley decided that going out might be a better plan than lying in bed, staving off the urge to jerk off to thoughts of Adam, and then inevitably jerking off to thoughts of Adam.

The Dropped Anchor was an ugly freestanding brick rectangle with an ancient light box sign on the front that had the name of the bar in a basic black font next to a beer logo that had been covered with electrical tape after a sponsorship had ended. Riley avoided the place as much as possible, especially since he'd stopped drinking. It was, however, comfortingly familiar, the way it hadn't changed since Riley had tried to order beer here in high school—as if everyone in town hadn't known exactly who he was and how old he was. Despite its lack of charm, the Anchor was one of the cornerstones of life in Avery River. It was where people celebrated and made friends and fought friends and drank to forget, and it was a rite of passage to have your first legal beer bought for you here.

But, still. It was a gross dump.

The Anchor was crowded when Riley walked in, and he had no doubt as to why. A cluster of men were standing near the bar, Adam at the center. Everyone laughed loudly as Riley approached, Adam having no doubt just shared a self-deprecating hockey story. He'd always been good at holding court. He was the type of man that other men wanted to be: handsome, confident, and impressive.

"Riles," Adam called out cheerfully when he spotted him. "You made it."

"Yeah. Decided I may as well." Someone had made a sign on neon yellow poster board that had *Welcome Adam Sheppard* written in black marker. It hung on the wall under the TV. It was possibly the most decorative thing Riley had ever seen in the Anchor.

"I was just telling them about the fight you had to bail me out of," Adam said.

"Against Fournier?"

"Right! Yeah. I was ready to kill him."

"He would have taken your head off." Adam had always been shit at fighting.

"Probably." Adam smiled at him, eyes twinkling. Riley wondered how many beers the boys had bought him already.

"How's the game going?" Riley asked.

"They're already down two-nothing," said Benny, who'd been tending bar here for as long as Riley could remember.

"Shit," Riley said.

"They need you back there, Captain," said Arnold from his stool at the end of the bar.

Everyone murmured their agreement.

"I think they're just fine without a busted-up old man on the blue line," Adam said, still smiling.

"What can I get you, Riley?" Benny asked.

"I'll take a Pepsi," Riley said, because it was safe. It came in cans, meaning it wouldn't be dispensed through the Anchor's filthy taps.

Benny handed him a can from the fridge and a thin plastic straw. "No charge. How are you holding up, son?"

Riley's chest clenched. "You know."

Benny nodded. "We all miss him."

"I know."

"That was a hell of a speech you made at the funeral," said Charlie, a man who Riley knew had gone to high school with Dad. "Harv would have been proud."

Riley could only nod as his throat tightened. He barely remembered the speech. Adam caught his eye and said, "Let's sit and watch the end of the period, okay, Riles?"

Riley nodded again.

"If you need anything," said Benny, "you let me know, all right?"

"I will." Riley held up the Pepsi can. "Thanks for this."

He felt the eyes of everyone on him as he followed Adam away from the bar. As soon as they were seated, Adam said, "I didn't think you were going to come."

"Yeah. Well."

"I'm glad you did." Adam smiled at him. He didn't seem like he'd had much to drink at all, actually. The pint glass he was holding was almost full.

"Have the boys been taking care of you?" Riley asked.

"Yeah, but—" Adam held a hand next to his mouth, shielding it from the view of the bar "—the beer here is terrible."

Riley managed part of a smile. "I know. I think it's half water."

Adam lifted the glass and squinted at it. "I *hope* it's water."

Riley cracked open his Pepsi. "They've got bottled beer. I recommend that."

"Good tip." Adam pointed at the wall above their heads. "Look."

Riley glanced at the jerseys. "Yep."

"Sheppard and Tuck," Adam said wistfully.

"Beauty and the Beast," Riley said. It had been a popular joke about them.

Adam waved a hand. "Never agreed with that. As if you're ugly."

"I think it had more to do with our style of play," Riley said, because Adam had been known for his incredible skating and his play making, where Riley had provided the brute strength, hitting hard, blocking shots, and keeping the crease clear. Though the nickname had probably also been inspired by Adam's pretty eyes.

"You *were* a beast on the ice," Adam agreed. "Fucking unreal. Never had a partner like you again. No one even close."

Riley shifted in his worn wooden chair. "What about Thompson?" Adam had been paired with Kit Thompson for most of six seasons after Riley left Toronto.

"Nah. Tommy was solid, but we never had that thing, y'know? That magic." Adam set his beer glass against the wall and put his elbows on the table. "When we played together— you and me—it was like I could read your mind on the ice. And you could read mine. Right?"

"I guess," Riley said mildly, even though yes, it had always been exactly like that.

"Magic," Adam repeated. "Fucking magic. I missed it every game after you left."

Riley hadn't managed to get his straw into the Pepsi can and was now bending it out of shape. "I think it was gone before I left."

Adam's brow furrowed. "What? No. We won the Cup together that last season."

Riley held his gaze. "I remember."

Now it was Adam's turn to shift in his chair. Good. Riley wasn't going to sit here and chat about the good times as if he hadn't been falling apart for years leading up to that Cup win. Adam, of course, had been happily distracted by his new family, and probably never noticed that Riley had lost his love of hockey and had leaned into the violence of the game. Neither the team nor the fans had minded that, loving how hard he'd hit, and how brutally he'd fought. None of them knew that after games, and on nights off, he'd drink. Sometimes he'd feel daring enough to find a man to fuck, though he hadn't really thrown himself into that until he'd been in Dallas, away from the microscope of the Toronto hockey world. More often than not, he'd just drink alone in his apartment, feeling very sorry for himself. It hadn't felt magical at all, by the end.

"I loved winning that Cup with you," Adam said quietly.

Riley wanted to choke him. "It was a really memorable fucking night."

He enjoyed the way Adam's cheeks darkened with shame. Then he remembered where they were, and that he really didn't want to talk about any of this. He leaned back in his chair and said, "Whatever. It was years ago."

"Riley—"

"It was *years ago*." Riley said firmly. "Watch the game."

Adam took a sip of beer, winced, then looked at the TV in

the corner over Riley's shoulder. Riley turned to look too. It was still 2–0.

"I invited you here to cheer you up," Adam said. "I'm not doing a great job, am I?"

"Nope. And I don't think the Northmen are going to, either, by the looks of things." Riley needed to keep the conversation focused on hockey.

"Could be nerves," Adam said.

"Mm."

"I was never nervous."

Riley actually laughed. "The fuck you weren't."

Adam smiled. "I can say that, now that I'm retired. I was never nervous, I made no mistakes, and I absolutely blocked that Bernier shot on purpose and not just because my foot happened to be in the right place at the right time."

"You didn't even know Bernier had taken a shot."

"Shh. I think I won the best defenseman trophy for that play alone that season."

"It could have been for that time you took the puck behind the net for a line change, then fell down."

"Fuck you for remembering that, and there was something on the ice!"

Riley took a sip of Pepsi.

"There was!" Adam insisted.

"Yeah. You."

Adam laughed, his eyes crinkling, and Riley was struck for the one billionth time in his life by how handsome he was. He was wearing a dark gray shirt that was unbuttoned at the collar, the sleeves rolled up to expose his forearms. The color made his eyes look even bluer. Riley absolutely didn't need any of this right now.

During a break in play the broadcast showed one of the luxury boxes in the arena. It was full of elite Northmen alumni.

A few were guys Riley had played with, but most were much older.

"You weren't invited?" Riley asked.

"I was."

Heat creeped up Riley's neck. Of course Adam had been invited. He'd chosen to be here instead. "Oh."

"You must have been too, weren't you?"

What planet was Adam living on? "No."

Adam's brow furrowed.

"What?" Riley said.

"I don't understand. It's not like you did anything."

"Sure I did. I asked for a trade, had a breakdown, then quit hockey. I don't think I can ever set foot in Dallas again. They gave up a lot of draft picks for me."

"Toronto fans still love you," Adam argued.

"They should. They got all those draft picks. They got Bergman with one of those."

Adam shook his head. "Would you *stop*? You were a fan favorite in Toronto, and I wouldn't be half the player I was if I hadn't been paired with you."

"If you say so."

Adam leaned in. "Of course I say so. Jesus, Riles, anyone who knows hockey would say so. And stop talking like you did something terrible just because you...uh..."

"Went nuts?" Riley suggested.

Adam pinned him with one of his fierce captain stares. "Don't say that."

Riley shrugged but didn't look away. "It's true, though. Ask anyone."

"I never have, and I won't. I want you to tell me about it. If you don't want to, then fine, but I'm not interested in gossip."

Riley swallowed, unexpectedly touched by Adam's respect for his privacy.

"I've been worried about you for twelve years," Adam said. "I know you probably don't want to hear that, but I have been."

Riley absolutely didn't want to hear it, but his stupid heart swelled anyway. "Why?"

"Riley."

Tears pricked at Riley's eyes. He blinked and looked away. *Not now*, he thought. At that moment, the bar erupted in cheers. Toronto had scored.

"Riley," Adam said again.

"You shouldn't have worried. Let's watch the game." He managed a small smile. "You're right. You suck at cheering me up."

Adam didn't smile back. He looked confused and sad.

"Come on," Riley said, tilting his head toward the TV. "Toronto's about to tie it up."

Adam let it go, though Riley could tell he wasn't happy about it. During the first intermission he went to the bar to mingle some more, and Riley thought about leaving.

Just before the second period was about to start, Adam returned to the table, and Riley could tell just by looking at him that he had something to say. Riley turned his attention to the TV, and his back to Adam.

After a couple of minutes, Adam said, "Things were different, by the time I retired."

Riley rolled his eyes and turned back to face him. "What things?"

"Hockey, the league, the way people, I dunno, talk about things. It's still not perfect, obviously, but some things were better."

"Like Pride nights?" Riley asked flatly. "Did those fix everything?"

Adam flinched slightly. "No. I know they didn't, but that's not even what I'm talking about. Like, some of the kids on the team during my last few seasons blew my fucking mind. Talking about anxiety and panic attacks and shit no hockey players ever would have admitted to when we both started out."

"No," Riley agreed quietly, "definitely not."

Adam looked at him seriously. "That's what I mean. I wish it could have been more like that when you played."

Riley shrugged as if it didn't matter. "Well. It wasn't."

When it was clear Riley still wasn't going to talk about it, Adam smiled weakly and said, "Those kids made me feel like a dinosaur. They were so into their health—physical and mental. There were three vegans on the team during my final season. Can you believe that? Three!"

Riley huffed. Chicken was practically a vegetable when he'd started in the league.

Adam got quiet again. "I thought about you a lot, during those last few seasons. About how things could have been better for you."

Riley was two seconds away from flipping the table. He pressed his palms into his thighs, digging his fingers in until it hurt. "How things could have been better for me," he repeated.

"I know I fucked up the night we won the Cup, but you could have stayed. We could have gotten past it. It kills me to think you threw everything away because of a stupid decision I made when I was drunk." He laughed humorlessly and gestured to the jerseys above them. "I mean, it was the dream, right? We got there. We were the best D-pairing in the league."

Riley leaned in, his pulse pounding in his temples. "I'm not talking about this."

"Why?"

"Because it doesn't. Fucking. Matter." Riley stood. "Enjoy your party, Shep. I'll leave a light on for you at home." He stormed out of the bar before Adam could reply.

Chapter Seventeen

Riley hadn't even made it out of the parking lot before he saw Adam leave the bar and get in his rental car.

"Asshole," Riley muttered as he turned onto the road. He was seething with anger the whole way home, mostly at Adam, but also at himself. Why was Adam asking these questions? And why was Riley still so mad at him? Like he'd said in the bar, it had been years ago. They'd been in their twenties, and Adam could hardly be blamed for being scared about any feelings he may have had for Riley. *If* he'd had feelings for Riley. Maybe Adam just needed closure. Maybe he just needed to hear that he had nothing to do with Riley quitting hockey.

Too fucking bad.

He could see Adam's car close behind him, but he ignored it. The road, dark in front of him, started to blur, and Riley hastily wiped at his eyes.

"Stop it," he growled at himself. "Stop fucking crying."

Ten minutes later, he was in his driveway. He exited the truck, slamming the door behind him, and stalked toward the house.

"Riley," Adam called behind him. "Wait."

Riley kept walking.

"Riley," Adam said again, and then Riley could hear him running.

Riley wheeled on him. *"What?"*

Adam spread his arms wide. "Why don't you just get it over with?"

"Get *what* over with?"

"Tell me off. Hit me. I don't know. Whatever you need to do. I fucking can't stand this anymore."

"Then go back to Toronto."

Adam stepped closer. "Why are you being such an asshole to me? I'm trying, Riley! I'm trying so fucking hard."

"What do you *want*, Shep? What the fuck is it that you want from me?" Riley was yelling now. "Do you want me to tell you it wasn't your fault? Fine. It's not. It's not your fault that I'm mentally ill, and it's not your fault you weren't in love with me. It's all on me."

Adam looked like Riley *had* hit him. His mouth hung open, and his eyes were wide and confused. And that was the last thing Riley saw before the headlights on Adam's car turned off, plunging them into darkness.

"I could have helped you," Adam said. His voice was shaking. "You were my best friend. Do you have any idea how much it fucking hurt when you left? You didn't give me a heads-up, or a goodbye. You just left after nine years of you being, like, my whole fucking world."

Riley snorted. "I think we both know I was *not* your whole fucking world." He began walking toward the house. He wasn't going to yell at Adam in the dark all night.

Adam followed. "I made a choice, all right? I made a choice that seemed right at the time. It wasn't because I didn't care about you."

Riley rounded on him. The lights from the front porch partially illuminated Adam's angry face, and seeing it only made Riley more furious. "Yeah, and then you made another choice. You chose to fuck me when we won the Cup. After years of not touching me, you chose to do *that*." He rolled his hands into fists, then released them, then repeated it until finally a surge of anger swelled and they just remained fists. "Can you imagine how any of that felt? Wanting you, knowing I couldn't have you anymore, and then suddenly you decide to fuck me because you're feeling things you don't want to? And then *humiliating* me as soon as you shot your load?" He was being unnecessarily vulgar, but it felt good. "You didn't care about me, Adam. You didn't."

There were tears in Adam's eyes now. Good.

"I don't know what I can say about that night," Adam said, "except sorry. I'm so fucking sorry. I know I fucked up."

"Yeah. You fucked up." In his heart, Riley knew that he'd fucked up too. He'd gone to bed with Adam, knowing he was married, knowing they were both drunk, and knowing that Adam wasn't going to leave his wife for him. But in the moment, it had been so easy to ignore all of it.

"I'm sorry," Adam said again. He reached a hand out in an awkward, pleading gesture. Riley stared at it.

"Well," Riley said sardonically, "I guess it all worked out for the best." He turned and walked to the front door.

On the porch, Adam grabbed his wrist. "I'm sorry I hurt you, but you hurt me too."

Riley clenched his jaw and opened the door.

"I kept hearing these rumors about you," Adam continued, as they entered the house. "I knew you weren't playing well, and everyone was saying you were drinking, missing practices, and getting in fights with your teammates. I was in agony, knowing that no one there understood your moods or how to take care of you."

"Take care of me like you did?" Riley snapped. "Fucking

me, telling me you wanted me, then telling me it never happened? Laughing at me when I finally worked up the courage to tell you I loved you? That was taking care of me and my *moods*?"

Adam shook his head and released Riley's wrist. His shoulders slumped in defeat. "No." Then he met Riley's gaze, his face determined again. "But we were so much more than that."

Riley wanted to argue, but he couldn't. Their friendship had been so easy, and maybe the rest could have been easy too, if they'd existed in a time and in a career that would have allowed it to be easy. "We were," he agreed. "And I tried. For years after you were married, I tried. I get that part is my fault, but Jesus Christ, Shep. The way you just ignored my feelings was fucking *mean*."

They heard Lucky stir from his bed in the living room, so Adam dropped his voice to a hissing whisper. "I was scared. Not just for me, but for *you*. The way we were going, we would have been caught. And then what?"

Riley shrugged.

"Maggie was *safe*," Adam said, sounding desperate. "I didn't understand what exactly you wanted from me."

"Because we never *fucking talked about it*," Riley snarled back. "And then you took the easy way out."

"*Easy?* There was nothing fucking easy about it. I needed to stop you from throwing everything away for me. I wasn't worth it. We couldn't have been together like you wanted. Not back then, and you know it. So yeah, I made a choice. I married Maggie and started a family, but I still needed you in my life."

"Right. So you get to have it all, and I get to have scraps whenever you're drunk enough to touch me. Sounds perfect."

"I wanted you to have what I had! I know now how stupid that was. I do. You were never going to marry a woman, even for appearances, because you always understood who you were and what you wanted. But I imagined living next door to you, our kids playing together, and I thought it wouldn't be a bad life."

Riley huffed in disgust. Had Adam really been that delusional? Riley had imagined them living *together*, raising *their own kids*. Maybe not until they were both retired, but it had still been something they could have done, if Adam had wanted it at all.

"I was stupid, okay?" Adam said. "I was awful and selfish, but you have to know I was in love with you too. Of course I was."

Adam may as well have stabbed Riley in the heart. Everything was blinding pain. "Shut up" was all he could say.

"I loved you. I—"

"Shut *up*." Riley was panicking now. He jabbed a finger into Adam's chest. "You can't just say that now. You can't make up how things were. It's not fair."

Adam gently wrapped his hand around Riley's angry finger. "I loved you. And it terrified me. I was a fucking coward, and I hurt you. I hurt Maggie. I know I can't apologize enough for the choices I made, but I was in love with you, Riley."

"Stop," Riley said desperately.

"I was in love with you," Adam repeated, "and then you were *gone*."

Riley turned and walked toward the stairs in a daze. He vaguely registered Lucky standing in the living room, looking concerned. He ignored him and went upstairs.

From his bedroom, he heard Adam talking softly to Lucky. Then he heard footsteps on the stairs, then in the hall, and then a quiet knock on his door, even though it wasn't closed.

"Riley?" Adam's eyes were red, and his shoulders were drawn. He took a cautious step into the room.

Riley turned on his bedside lamp, then walked to the window. Adam closed the door, probably for Lucky's benefit. When Adam was right behind him, Riley spun around and said, "You fucked me up, and it took years to get over it. So don't tell me you were in love with me! Not now."

Adam spread his arms. "Do you want me to lie?"

"It's what you're good at."

"I never lied to you."

Riley let out a strangled, humorless laugh.

"I didn't," Adam insisted. "I lied to myself, maybe. And I lied to Maggie. But I told you the truth, always. Or at least what I believed to be the truth at the time. It just...took me a while to figure out some things."

"So I should have waited, is that it? Given you another ten or twelve years to figure your shit out?"

Adam let out a frustrated groan. "I know! We've been over this! I was stupid and selfish and scared. I was also twenty-four when I married Maggie. That's fucking young, Riles."

"Maybe you're the one who should have waited."

"What else could I have done? She was pregnant! She loved me. I thought I loved her."

"You could have used a condom."

The way Adam glared at him was effective; Riley quickly filled with shame. "Fuck," he said, as he ran a hand through his hair. He walked past Adam to the middle of the room.

"I will never regret my kids, Riley." Adam's voice was tight and angry. "Don't try to make them sound like a failure of any kind."

"I'm sorry. I'm—" Riley took a deep breath, then exhaled in a whoosh. "I'm upset."

"I know."

"I can't fucking think when you're around."

"I'm sorry."

"My dad died, Adam. He died *last week*. And then you show

up at the funeral four days later and then you're fucking helping me at the shop and telling me you missed me. It's fucking too much."

Adam stepped toward him. "I didn't mean to overwhelm you."

"That's all you've ever done, Shep. You overwhelm me. It's terrifying."

"I know. I feel the same way. Always have."

In the lamplight, Adam looked soft and tired and achingly beautiful. Riley closed his eyes. He felt like he was about to shatter into a million pieces.

Riley's hands were curled into fists again at his sides, and Adam wrapped a hand around one of them. "I always hated watching you fight."

"It was part of the job."

"I mean against yourself. I just wanted to jump inside your head and tell whatever demons were in there to fuck off."

Riley huffed, then opened his eyes. "Sometimes it felt like you did."

Adam's smile was so tender, it made Riley forget why they were arguing. All that existed in the world, suddenly, were Adam's lips, his sad but hopeful eyes, his hand on Riley's.

"Riley—" Adam whispered, but Riley cut him off by kissing him.

Chapter Eighteen

For a few dizzy seconds, Adam couldn't think. His brain was completely consumed by Riley's lips on his, and the staggering blend of relief and excitement that came with it. Riley was kissing him, and Adam, after a brief moment of surprise, was kissing him back. Riley's hands were on Adam's face, and Adam was being walked backward until he bumped against a wall. Then Riley was *everywhere*, his tongue in Adam's mouth, his moans in Adam's ears, and his thigh between Adam's legs. Adam was hard almost instantly, and he grabbed at Riley's shirt, trying to pull him impossibly closer.

You overwhelm me.

Adam could feel the desperation in Riley's kiss, and in the way he was now rocking against him. The familiarity of it was both thrilling and terrifying. As Adam's senses returned, he knew he had a choice to make: he could think with his dick and let this happen, or he could finally make the right decision when it came to Riley Tuck.

He broke the kiss and gently shoved on Riley's chest, creating space. "Riley," he said, somewhat breathlessly, "I don't—"

That was all he was able to say before Riley let out an anguished sound that was close to a howl, then staggered away from him. Riley gripped his own hair with both hands, as if he was trying to tear his skull open. Then he crumpled to the floor.

Adam went to him immediately, crouching beside him and placing his hands on Riley's shoulders. He'd helped Riley through emotional overloads like this before, but he'd never witnessed one he'd been the cause of. God, how many had he been the cause of? "Hey, hey, no. Riley, look at me."

"Why am I so fucking *stupid*?" Riley said in a horrible, broken voice.

"You're not stupid. You're not. You're amazing."

"Shut *up!*" Riley practically screamed the words. "Why do you keep doing this to me?"

"Riley," Adam said, barely above a whisper, trying to sound calm even though his heart was racing. "Riley. Listen to me. Please. I'm not rejecting you."

Riley tucked his head down farther, burying his face in his forearms while he continued to pull at his own hair.

"I'm not rejecting you," Adam repeated, some of the panic he felt leaking into his voice now. "Riley, I want to kiss you. I want to do so many things with you, but not like this."

"Fuck you."

"It's not what you need right now."

Riley raised his head enough that Adam could see his eyes. They were wet and red and furious. "I need to feel something *good*. Why can't you let me have that?"

"I want to. I want to so much, but not like this. Riles— Riley, I don't want to make the same mistakes as before."

Riley's fingers dug harder into his scalp, and he moaned like someone who was bleeding out from an abdominal wound. And then Adam realized what Riley was thinking.

Adam wrapped his arms around him and pulled Riley's head against his chest. "Riley, no. I don't mean kissing you is a mistake. I'm so sorry about the things I said in the past, but that's not what I mean now. I want to do this *right*. I want to earn it, and I won't take advantage of you." Impulsively, he kissed the top of Riley's head, and then the white knuckles of the fingers that were still digging into his scalp. Riley was shaking against him, possibly sobbing, and Adam realized his own cheeks were wet with tears. "Do you hear me, Riley? It's not because I don't want you."

Adam kissed his hair again and rubbed his back until finally Riley's fingers relaxed. Slowly, Riley lowered his hands and wrapped them around Adam's back.

"I've got you," Adam whispered, and kissed Riley's temple. "It's okay." He rested his cheek on the top of Riley's head and exhaled. For a long while, they held each other, Riley's face buried in Adam's shirt. Eventually, the burn in Adam's thighs from crouching became too much.

"Hey," Adam said softly. "Come on up here." He placed a hand on Riley's elbow, helping him up. When they were both standing, Adam got a good look at Riley's face. He looked hollow with exhaustion, and messy from crying. Adam imagined he didn't look much better himself.

Riley sat heavily on the end of the bed and stared at the floor.

"I'm going to get you a facecloth, okay?" Adam said.

Riley didn't reply, so Adam left. He quickly went to the bathroom and took a facecloth from a small, tidy stack. He splashed warm water on his own face, then wet the cloth. As he was wringing it out, he realized he was trembling. He hated himself for causing Riley so much anguish, for pushing him over the edge like that. He only ever wanted to be the person who guided Riley away from the edge.

When he returned to the bedroom, Riley was lying on his

side, his head on a pillow. His eyes were open, but he didn't seem to notice when Adam was standing in front of him.

"Here," Adam said, and held out the cloth.

Riley blinked, then took the cloth. "Thanks." He held it in his clenched hand but didn't bring it to his face. Adam watched as a wet spot blossomed on the duvet.

"I'll get you some water?" he suggested. Again, Riley said nothing.

Lucky was pacing the living room when Adam went downstairs. "It's okay," he said. "You can go back to sleep. I'll take care of him."

When Adam returned to the bedroom with two glasses of water, Riley was in the same position as before. The wet spot was huge now. Adam gently took the cloth away and brought it back to the bathroom. He frowned at his reflection in the mirror above the sink.

"Great job, idiot," he scolded himself.

He went back to the bedroom and saw that Riley hadn't moved. Unsure of what to say or do, Adam took a sip of his own water and walked to the window. There was a perfect sliver of moon, high in the sky.

"Are you going to leave?" Riley asked in a hoarse voice.

Adam whipped around. "What?"

"Tomorrow."

Adam crossed the room and knelt beside the bed so he was eye level with Riley. "Of course not. Unless...do you want me to?"

Riley's voice was steady, and almost emotionless, when he said, "I don't know."

Without thinking about it, Adam began combing Riley's hair with his fingers. "I want to stay."

Riley closed his eyes. "I'm so tired."

"Should I let you sleep?" Adam's hand had made its way

down to Riley's cheek, and he stroked his soft beard. "Or can I stay with you?"

"Stay," Riley said on an exhale.

Adam's heart swelled. "Okay," he said, as if it wasn't a big deal.

He didn't waste time. He crawled on the bed to lie behind Riley. They were both fully clothed and on top of the blankets, but none of that seemed important. Adam carefully wrapped an arm around Riley, spooning up to him, and rubbed his nose against the back of Riley's neck.

This was—well, no. Adam wasn't going to pretend it was better than sex, but it was more important than sex. It was what Riley needed. And feeling Riley relax in his embrace, listening to his breathing slow until it turned into soft snoring, was what Adam needed.

Chapter Nineteen

Riley woke early the next morning, as always, and enjoyed a triumphant moment of realizing that he'd gotten a good night's sleep before he remembered everything else about last night.

He rolled over and found Adam crashed out on top of the duvet next to him. Like Riley, he was still wearing his clothes from last night. He was on his back, one hand resting on his stomach and the other on the pillow. Riley remembered that he'd fallen asleep with one of Adam's arms wrapped around him, unsure of what it had meant but too exhausted to care anymore.

I was in love with you too. Of course I was.

Last night, Riley hadn't been capable of processing those words. Now, in the quiet of early morning, watching the even rise and fall of Adam's chest, he could hold on to the words and examine each one.

The word "was" couldn't be ignored. It provided important distinction and made the entire earth-shattering statement less exciting and more frustrating.

Also frustrating were the words "of course," which implied there'd been something obvious that Riley had missed. Or maybe Adam had only just realized and was saying it to himself.

Riley could analyze the words all day, and it wouldn't change the fact that hearing them had caused him to basically explode emotions all over the place. And then he'd kissed Adam and, well. It all could have gone a lot better, probably.

But Adam was still here. He'd held him through his meltdown, and he'd held him after. Riley had offered frantic, urgent sex, and Adam had said no.

I'm not rejecting you.

He hadn't, right? Riley still wasn't sure. It had certainly felt like a rejection at the time. But Adam had kissed him back, he was sure of it, and he'd been hard. It had felt like old times, kissing Adam messily against a wall after a night out, thrilling at the speedy arrival of Adam's erection and the enthusiastic, drunken way Adam kissed him back. Except Adam hadn't been drunk this time—not even close—and Riley wasn't sure if that made him feel better or worse.

Riley, it seemed, didn't need to be drunk to make terrible decisions about Adam Sheppard.

He could hear Lucky pacing around downstairs, which meant Riley needed to leave the bed. He moved carefully, not wanting to wake Adam. He crept out of the room and into the bathroom, where he proceeded to make himself look and feel as human as possible.

Lucky greeted him happily as always when Riley descended the stairs.

"Good morning," Riley whispered. "Let's go outside, huh?"

The morning air was cool and the grass was covered in dew, but the sky was clear and blue. Riley stood on the deck and gazed out at the ocean while he waited for Lucky to do his thing. He could see two fishing boats out in the bay and the lighthouse at the end of the point.

Going to the Dropped Anchor had been a mistake. He should have let Adam enjoy his evening of being adored, then made sure to be in bed by the time Adam had come home. Then there wouldn't have been any fighting or crying or unwanted kissing. Then Riley wouldn't have anything to feel mortified about.

Well, at least now Adam had seen the truth of it: Riley was still a mess, and sometimes that mess turned into a scary, unhinged, sobbing monster. Sometimes that monster would tell you to fuck off when really he just needed you to stay and hold him.

Adam had stayed, and he'd held him.

He heard the door open behind him, and then footsteps.

"Hey," Adam said quietly.

"Hi."

Adam stood beside him and rested his forearms on the railing. "Sleep okay?"

"Yeah. Thanks."

"Good." A long silence passed, and then Adam said, "Hey! Boats."

"Yep."

"Are they fishing boats?"

"Yes."

"You know exactly who's on those boats, don't you?"

Riley smiled slightly. "Yes."

"I think that's cool. It's probably nice to be a part of a tight community."

"I think you basically *are* part of it now."

Adam huffed. "Nah. But—" Instead of finishing his sentence he said, "You going to work today?"

"Yep."

"Oh." The single syllable was loaded with concern.

Riley exhaled. "I'm sorry about last night."

"Don't be. But are you sure you're good to go to the shop? No one would blame you for taking more time."

"I'll be okay. And I don't work tomorrow, so."

"All right."

He could tell Adam had questions that he wasn't letting himself ask. Riley took a guess at some of them.

"I've been getting professional help for my, um, stuff. I have a therapist I've been talking to for years, and I take medication. I was diagnosed with clinical depression and an emotional dysregulation disorder. Probably not a big surprise, but yeah. That's me."

"Emotional dysregulation," Adam repeated quietly.

"Right. I've been mostly managing okay since moving back here and getting diagnosed and all that, but then, well. Things got bad last week."

"God, Riley. I'm so sorry. I made it so much worse, didn't I?"

"No," Riley said quickly, then amended, "Okay, yeah. You did. But...I'm not sorry you're here."

"You're not?" He could feel Adam's surprised gaze on him, so he turned his head to meet it.

"Not anymore."

Adam's lips curved into an achingly sweet smile.

Riley found it hard to tear his attention away from those lips. He had a muddy memory of Adam saying something last night about wanting to earn Riley's kisses. About wanting to do things right. Had he meant it? Riley was too scared to ask.

And if he did mean it, what exactly was Adam hoping for? A fling while he was in town, or more? What would "more" even look like? A long-distance relationship with Adam visiting as often as possible? Would Riley go to Toronto? And if Riley *did* go to Toronto, what would that be like? Would they hide in Adam's house the whole time? Would they go on dates? Would Adam be open about their relationship?

Relationship. Jesus. Was that possible?

Riley couldn't quite imagine a world where Adam Sheppard, one of the most celebrated Toronto Northmen players ever, would publicly be in a relationship with Riley Tuck. He was sure no one else could either.

But could Adam picture that? *Did* he picture that?

"Um," Riley said, still staring at Adam's lips, "you got plans today?"

"I'm meeting Cathy later to talk about the banquet."

"Right." Because that was something else Adam was doing for him. Another sweet, stubborn gesture that showed Riley he cared about him. Despite everything Riley had said to him this week, Adam was still here, and he was trying so hard. Riley didn't need to ask him if he'd meant what he'd said about wanting to get things right between them. He was showing it constantly.

Suddenly, Riley really wanted Adam to meet his friends. "Do you want to go to the farmers market before I go to work?"

Adam lit up. "There's a farmers market? Hell yes I want to go."

"It's not peak season for the market," Riley said as they crossed the parking lot.

"I'll manage my expectations," Adam said, leaning into him slightly, hoping it seemed playful and not touch starved.

The market was housed in a large blue building that sort of resembled a barn but looked fairly new. The parking lot was nearly full, though it was only nine in the morning.

Once inside, Adam was instantly delighted. When was the last time he'd been to a farmers market? He'd been to a couple with Maggie, or maybe those were craft markets. This one had a table featuring local honey and another with smoked salmon and another piled high with fresh bread.

Farmers markets were fucking awesome.

He went to the honey table and picked up the largest jar they had. "You make all this yourself?" he asked the woman behind the table.

She laughed and said, "The bees do most of the work." She was Black, probably a few years older than Adam, and was wearing actual overalls, like a *farmer*.

"Right," Adam said, feeling stupid. "But you take care of the bees?"

"My wife and I do." She pointed to a white woman with curly pink hair who was talking to a man at the table across the aisle from them. "You visiting?"

"Yeah. From Toronto." He put the honey down. A giant jar of honey would never be permitted in his carry-on suitcase. "I'm visiting my friend..." It was then that he noticed Riley wasn't with him. He glanced around and spotted him talking to three people near the entrance.

"Uh-oh. One second, ma'am." Adam strode over to Riley with his listening ears on, making sure he wasn't about to rescue his friend unnecessarily. After a few seconds of hearing an older woman, who probably meant well, tell Riley how awful his father's death was for the town, Adam said, "There you are, Riley!"

"Uh, hi. Sorry, I was just..."

Adam turned to the woman who'd just been speaking, "I need his opinion on some honey."

Riley's brow furrowed, then he got it. "Right. Thanks. I mean, sure." To the woman he'd been talking to, and her companions, he said, "Have a good morning. Say hi to Terry for me."

As he walked Riley away, Adam said, "Sorry. I got distracted by honey. I should have done a better job running interference."

"It's okay." As they approached the honey table, Riley said, "Hey, Bea."

The woman—*Bee?*—smiled at Riley, then came around the table for a hug. "Aw, Riley," she said. "It's so good to see you."

"You too. Where's Nell?"

"Getting me a coffee, or at least she's supposed to be." Bea said the second part loudly enough that her wife—Nell, Adam assumed—turned around and made a face at her.

"I'm going!" Nell said. "I just needed to ask Trent something."

Bea shook her head, then turned back to Riley. "So who's your handsome Toronto friend?"

Adam smiled, both at being called handsome and at not being recognized. "I'm Adam." He extended his hand, and she shook it. "Is your name really Bea?"

"Yes. And the jokes have all been made, believe me." She glanced at Riley, then back at Adam. "So, have you guys known each other…long?" She looked confused, which is how Adam puzzled together the fact that she and Riley must be close, and that Riley had never mentioned him.

"We used to be teammates," Riley said.

Though his description was accurate, it was also kind of brutal. "Right," Adam managed.

"Cool," Bea said. "Welcome to Avery River, Adam."

"I've been here before," Adam wanted to say. *"I used to look forward to summer so I could be here with Riley. I had sex with him here."*

Adam spotted the ornate candles at one end of the table. Now *those* could probably travel in a carry-on bag. He picked up a tall, golden-yellow pillar candle with flowers carved into it and held it to his nose. It smelled like honey. Beeswax, right. That was a thing.

"Can I buy this?" he asked.

Bea's eyes went wide. "Not that one. That is the cursed candle!"

Adam began to put it back on the table. "What?"

"Nah. I'm joking. It's normal and it's thirty dollars."

Adam laughed nervously and got his wallet out. Bea was the clever kind of funny that he could never keep up with.

"I think Maggie will like it," he said to Riley as Bea wrapped the candle in tissue paper.

Riley looked surprised, like he didn't expect Adam to still buy Maggie gifts. And maybe Adam shouldn't, maybe that was Ethan's job now, but Maggie still meant a lot to Adam.

"So you guys really are good, then?" Riley said.

"Who? Me and Maggie? Totally."

"I'm glad." It sounded like Riley really meant it, no hint of jealousy or bitterness in his voice. Adam had always suspected, despite everything, that Riley had truly liked Maggie. He wondered if that had made things easier or harder for him.

Riley chatted with Bea for another minute, then he and Adam got out of the way when a new customer approached. They roamed from stall to stall, Adam wanting to see everything. They got in line for coffee, which Riley promised was excellent, and by that time Adam had bought the candle, a half dozen shortbread cookies, a half dozen thumbprint cookies, a packet of smoked salmon, a dozen chocolate macaroons, and a large Avery River Farmers Market tote bag to put it all in. Riley had wordlessly taken the bag from him, relieving the strain on Adam's shoulder.

"I love the idea of making something like honey as your job. Living on a bee farm, selling your products at the market. It's so…nice."

"Nice?" Riley asked.

"Yeah! Just…making stuff. And selling it. It's a nice life, I'll bet."

Riley's lips tilted up on one side. "Probably. I know a lot of people here who have that sort of life."

"I don't know anyone who does that. Literally no one."

They got their coffees, and as Riley was adding milk to his, he said, "There are some other friends of mine here I'd like you to meet." He gave Adam his subtle, amused smile. "They make stuff. And sell it."

"I'd love to meet any of your friends. All of them. Bea seemed cool. I didn't really get to talk to her wife."

"Nell's awesome. We love her."

Adam was confused by "we" but he nodded.

"Here," Riley said, and began walking toward a table just past the coffee stand.

The sign above the table read North Shore Maple Syrup, and Adam was immediately on board.

"Riley," called a loud and very excited voice. "Oh my god, darling. I didn't expect to see you here!"

The man dashed out from behind the table, like Bea had, and engulfed Riley in a hug. He was tall—about Adam's height—but very slim and blond. He was probably around Adam's age, but could pass for younger. He was attractive and, unless Adam really was clueless about this sort of thing, gay.

"Are you okay?" the man asked. "Oh, no. Never mind. Forget I asked that. How awful of me. But are you okay?"

Riley smiled. "I'm okay. I want you to meet someone."

The man then noticed Adam and gave him a very obvious once-over. And then a twice over. He looked back at Riley with wide eyes and hissed, "Is this *him*?"

Riley blushed, which made Adam think that he was, indeed, *him*. He wondered if *him* meant "the hot guy who's visiting me" or "the absolute piece of shit who broke my heart." Probably the second one.

"Darren," Riley said, "this is Adam."

There was a definite note of "you know, *Adam*. The guy I *told you about*" in Riley's tone. At least he'd mentioned Adam to at least one of his friends.

"Nice to meet you, Darren," Adam said, and extended his hand.

Darren's eyes kept darting between Riley and Adam as he shook his hand. "Adam," he said. "You two used to be teammates, right?"

"Yes," Riley said, and now the note in his tone was one of warning.

"And you lived together, am I right?"

"That's right," Adam said, pleased that Riley had given his friend at least two pieces of information about him.

"And now you're here! That's wonderful." He made a face at Riley that Adam couldn't interpret. Riley shook his head. "Are you staying with Riley?"

"I am."

"Oh!" He stretched the syllable out with a hefty amount of interest. "Riley has a beautiful home."

"He does," Adam agreed. He knew Riley was uncomfortable, so he distracted Darren by asking, "So you make maple syrup? That's awesome. How do you even do that?"

"A tremendous amount of drilling and tapping," Darren said with a wink.

"God," Riley grumbled.

Then Darren snapped his fingers, "You could come to the farm. Riley, what are you doing tomorrow night? We're having people for dinner. We only didn't invite you already because we assumed you weren't ready for company, but you're here, and you could bring Adam. We'd love to have you."

"Oh, um," Riley said. "Tomorrow?" He glanced at Adam, who wasn't sure if he wanted approval, or if he wanted out of this invitation.

"Yes, but early. For dinner. Not a late night at all," Darren insisted. "Bea and Nell will be there. And Jackson and Marcel are visiting from Halifax, that's why we're having the dinner. Please come. Eight people is so much better than six, and we miss you."

"I don't want to complicate things for Tom."

Darren waved a hand. "You know Tom is going to cook for twenty people anyway."

Again, Riley looked at Adam. Again, Adam had no idea what Riley wanted him to say. Slowly, carefully, Adam said, "If you feel up for it, Riles, I'd love to get to know your friends."

Something flashed in Riley's eyes that made Adam think he'd said the right thing. "Okay, yeah. We can go, then. It would be nice, I think, to be with friends. Good energy."

"The best energy," Darren agreed. "And don't bring a thing. Just your...Adam."

Now it was Adam's turn to blush. "It was nice meeting you. See you tomorrow."

They left the market shortly after. "So, I assume Tom is Darren's...?"

"Husband," Riley confirmed. "He's great."

"How did you meet them? I mean, obviously it's a small town, but..."

"Darren and I went to school together. I wouldn't say we were good friends back then, but I've known him since we were both five years old."

"Oh," Adam said. "Wow."

They got into Riley's truck, and Riley placed Adam's bag of treasures in the back of the cab. Then he said, "I know you're wondering, so I'll just tell you: yes, Darren and I used to hook up."

Adam had definitely been wondering that. "You did? Yeah? Like...when?"

"In high school a bit. And after, when I'd come home in the summers. But then he moved to Halifax and met Tom."

"Oh. Was that...hard? For you?"

"What? No. We weren't like that. We were just the only gay kids in town, at least that's what we thought at the time, so we got a little practice in, y'know? And we became friends. Just friends," he emphasized, for some reason. "It wasn't like—" Riley stopped talking.

Adam finished the sentence in his head. "It wasn't like us." His heart swooped. "I couldn't tell if you actually wanted to go to their house. If you'd rather not, that's fine with me."

"No, I would, I think. Those are all good people, and it might do me some good to be around friends."

That stung a bit, but Adam ignored it. "It'll be fun," he said, and hoped he was right. He was very curious about Riley's friends, and about his rural gay life in general. He was also legitimately curious about the process of making maple syrup. He imagined the dinner being nothing but stacks of pancakes. He wouldn't hate that.

"I'm starving," he announced.

"If only you had fifty or sixty cookies."

"Those are for later."

"If those aren't gone by noon, I'll be surprised."

Adam smiled. "I'll pace myself. I'm not exercising like I used to. I've gotta watch it." He patted his stomach.

Riley glanced at him quickly, before he began backing out of the parking spot. "You look all right to me."

Adam rode that high for most of the drive back to Riley's house. They'd left things in a weird place last night. He'd told Riley he'd been in love with him, Riley had kissed him, Adam had told Riley he wanted to do things right this time, yet somehow all of that added up to a lot of uncertainty about what they were doing now.

At the house, Riley dropped Adam off, and Lucky took his place in the passenger seat. Adam stood beside the truck and talked to Riley through the open driver side window.

"Text me if you have any questions," Riley said, "or if…"

"If I get lonely?" Adam tried.

Riley's cheeks darkened as he smiled. "Sure."

"I will. Have a good day."

"Thanks. Don't let Cathy bully you."

"I won't."

"And, um…" Riley's hand kneaded the steering wheel anxiously. "We can maybe talk. Later."

"I'd like that."

Riley nodded. "Okay. See you later, then."

Adam wanted to kiss him goodbye, but he settled for quickly squeezing Riley's shoulder. "See you."

Adam resolved, as he watched Riley back out of the driveway, to try to woo the man a little. He wanted to give him all the open affection and adoration that he deserved, and that Adam had been too scared to offer before, all those years ago. To let him know, without pushing, that he was serious about wanting to earn whatever Riley was willing to offer.

Chapter Twenty

The first thing Riley noticed as he walked into his house after work was that it smelled like fish.

"Shep?" he called out. Lucky barked, once again alerting Riley that they had an intruder. "I *know*, Lucky."

He heard Adam swear, and then say, "In the kitchen!"

Riley mentally prepared for the possible total destruction of his kitchen as he approached the room, but was shocked to see the opposite. Adam was standing by the stove, wearing an apron and stirring something in Riley's largest pot. Fresh parsley was chopped on a small wooden cutting board, and, most startlingly, there was a large bouquet of flowers on the kitchen table, arranged in one of Riley's vintage green glass vases.

"Hi," Adam said, smiling shyly.

It was probably a symptom of Riley's age, or maybe the fact that he was, at his core, a deeply boring man, but he realized in that moment that he was looking at his ultimate fantasy.

"Hi," Riley said. "Um."

Lucky barked once, letting Riley know he'd discovered the intruder, then left the kitchen to inspect the rest of the house.

"I made dinner," Adam said. "I'll warn you now, I'm not

much of a cook, but I found this cookbook and thought, hey, I can probably manage a fish chowder."

It was then that Riley noticed the cookbook Adam was working from: *Out of Old Nova Scotia Kitchens*. "I mostly just have that for decoration. It's super old."

"That's a relief. There's some very gross-sounding stuff in there. I was going to make lobster stew, but I had no idea what a rolled cream soda is."

"Me neither." Riley crossed the kitchen to peek in the pot. "Wow, that looks really good, actually."

Adam's smile grew. "Right? I think I nailed it. I used bacon instead of whatever salt pork is."

"That's fine."

"Do you have paprika? I'm supposed to sprinkle paprika on it before serving."

"I do."

"A woman named Janet who works at the grocery store was very helpful. She told me the right kind of potatoes to use."

"Janet's nice, yeah."

"I did create a bit of a scene there, though. Everyone in the store wanted to give me their opinions on how to make fish chowder properly. Things got a bit heated between them."

Riley laughed. "It's a controversial subject." He glanced at the recipe. "You used crackers to thicken it? Nice. That's what Mom does."

Adam was standing so close to him, and he was unfairly handsome, even with his hair a mess and what appeared to be cracker crumbs around his lips.

"I picked up some rolls from Paula's too. And a pie. You like strawberry rhubarb?"

Unfair. This was all horribly unfair. How was Riley supposed to deal with any of this? A man he absolutely did not want to be in love with making him dinner and buying him flowers and *pie*? His *favorite* pie?

"Yeah," he said, "I like it." Then, as if his hand was controlled by someone else, he reached out a thumb and brushed the cracker crumbs from the corner of Adam's mouth.

Adam's lips parted slightly, his eyes widening in surprise. Riley snapped out of it and pulled his thumb away. "Sorry. You had...crumbs." He turned away, his face burning with embarrassment. "I don't know why I did that."

"It's okay." Adam wrapped a hand around Riley's wrist and tugged gently, urging him to turn back around. "It was sweet."

Riley did turn around and wished he hadn't. Adam's eyes were dark and intense, as if the simple brush of Riley's thumb had ignited him.

Oh god. Riley was in trouble. He closed his eyes in an attempt to put up some sort of defense. Adam was using his own thumb now, rubbing gentle circles on the inside of Riley's wrist and turning his legs to jelly.

Riley stepped away. The steam from the soup was too hot. Everything was too hot. He left the kitchen, unbuttoning the top of his shirt as he walked.

He wouldn't ruin this. He would eat the lovely dinner Adam had made and he wouldn't be weird. He sat on the couch and took a few slow breaths, grateful that Adam hadn't followed him to the living room.

Lucky found him and pressed his body against his legs. Riley rubbed his soft fur while he waited for his own heart rate to slow.

A few minutes later, Adam joined him on the couch. He'd taken the apron off, and Riley did his best to ignore the way his gray T-shirt clung to him perfectly. It had probably cost a fortune.

"You wanted to talk," Adam said as he stroked Lucky's back.

Riley had said that, but now he had no idea what to say.

"Maybe I should start," Adam suggested.

Riley nodded. Adam had always been the talker.

Adam turned slightly toward Riley, bumping their knees together. "I'm hoping for a chance to do things better."

Riley's heart trembled. "I don't know what that means."

"It means…" Adam's brow furrowed as if he wasn't sure either. "Well. I guess I'm hoping we can figure that out together. But to start, it means I made dinner."

And bought me flowers, Riley wanted to add. *And helped at the shop. And stayed when I told you to leave. And held me last night until I slept well for the first time in over a week.*

"It was a long time ago," Riley said weakly. "Whatever we had."

"Too long ago?"

The obvious answer was yes, of course. But sitting here now with Adam, even with their gray hairs and the gulf of years they'd both lived without each other, it didn't seem like long at all. "I don't know," he said, because it was all he could offer.

Adam's lips formed half a smile. "I'll take it for now. Come eat."

He stood, and Riley followed him to the kitchen. They ate at the table, the flowers pushed slightly aside so they could see each other. The chowder was delicious, despite the recipe being pretty basic. It was buttery and warm; perfect comfort food.

"I'm really impressed with myself," Adam said. "Like, I should open a restaurant."

Riley smiled. "There's a retirement plan: Shep's Soup Shack."

"Yes! Perfect." He reached for another roll. "How was work?"

"Fine. I think a lot of people were disappointed that you weren't there."

"Aw, now I feel bad."

"Don't. You've done plenty." And then Riley realized how rude he'd been. "Is your shoulder any better? You shouldn't have been cooking—"

"It's a little better today. And the cooking was fine. I'm lucky it's not my dominant arm."

"You're sure?"

"I'm sure."

"Good, but you should be resting it. You said you're getting more surgery soon?"

"Very soon, I think. I meet with my doctor on Wednesday, and I'll probably get a date then. I'm getting the joint replaced."

Riley winced. "That'll be rough to recover from."

"No doubt, but much better in the long run, I hope."

He ran his finger along the gilded edge of his dessert plate. "I saw that game. When you got hurt."

Adam huffed. "Which time?"

"The first one. That weird hit where your arm got twisted behind you."

"Yeah. That was the bad one."

"I should have called you, while you were recovering. Or at least sent a text to let you know I was, I don't know. Concerned."

Adam smiled. "Concerned?"

Riley leaned back in his chair. "I felt sick about it. I was mad at you, but I also wanted—" He stopped himself. What he'd wanted to do was fly to Toronto and take care of him.

"I would have liked that," Adam said quietly. "For what it's worth."

Riley swallowed.

"I thought about you a lot," Adam continued. "All the time, during those years."

Riley felt like Adam was holding his heart in his hand, alternating between caressing it and squeezing until Riley wanted to scream in agony. "I tried not to think about you at all," he said.

The hurt was obvious in Adam's eyes, but he nodded. "I guess I deserve that."

He did deserve it, but right now Riley couldn't remember why.

"Fuck," he said, and scrubbed a hand over his face. "I'm sorry. You made dinner and…" He gestured to the flowers. "And you're here, and you're *gay.* Like, I haven't even talked to you about that, really, because it fucking terrifies me for some reason."

Adam's eyebrows shot up. "Terrifies you?"

"It's just, are you—I mean—" Riley gave himself a moment to gather words together. "You said you've been with other men, but you don't have any gay friends."

"That's right."

"I hate that."

Adam's lips quirked up. "Which part?"

"Not having friends!" Of course it was also the other part, but Riley wouldn't admit that. "That sounds terrible. How are you even, like, dealing with it all?"

Adam shrugged his good shoulder. "How did you deal with it?"

"Horribly."

Adam let out a tired, rueful laugh. "Yeah. Well, same."

"Do your parents know?"

Adam grimaced. "They know. I think they're mostly choosing to ignore it."

Riley wasn't surprised. "I'm sorry."

"Anyway," Adam said. "It doesn't really matter. I'm forty-one, they're in their seventies and spend most of the year in Arizona. I mean, who cares what they think, right?"

Adam cared. That's who. And Riley wanted to drive to Arizona to yell at the Sheppards.

"What about your brother?"

"Cal's been okay about it. He didn't really understand why I'd want to tell anyone."

Riley rolled his eyes. He'd only met Adam's younger brother a few times, but he wasn't a big fan. Cal lived in Vancouver and had a job that had something to do with finance. "Let me guess: be gay if you want but don't rub other people's faces in it?"

"I wouldn't say it was that bad, but something in that neighborhood, yeah. I think he's mostly just worried about me. Or about my legacy, anyway. Like I'll be a joke instead of a future Hall of Famer as soon as I come out publicly."

"Do you plan to come out publicly?"

"I guess. I don't know what the alternative would be. I don't want to hide forever."

Riley absorbed this information. It was surreal, talking about this with Adam. He'd never in a million years imagined Adam Sheppard being out and proud. "You don't have to make a big announcement, if you don't want."

"I know, but wouldn't it be helpful if I did? Like, it could change the way some people think, maybe. Or inspire some kids to stick with hockey."

"It could be helpful," Riley agreed. "But do it because you want to, not because you think you need to."

Adam tilted his head. "I guess you're out but not, y'know, *out*."

"I live a small life here. No one in the hockey world pays any attention to me anymore. I'm as out as I need to be."

"I'd like to live a small life, I think," Adam said wistfully. "My life is way too complicated."

"Sorry you're so rich and famous."

Adam laughed. "Fuck you. My point is that I'm trying to decide whether or not to come out in a big public way. I made a pros and cons list. Look." He reached to grab his phone off the kitchen counter, then tapped at it before handing it to Riley.

Riley held the phone away from his face, squinted, and read:

Pros
1. *Good role model*
2. *Make people think/big fuck you to bigots*
3. *No hiding at all*
4. *Easier to be in a relationship/date*
5. *Would probably feel amazing*

Cons
1. *Lots of attention*
2. *Lots of pressure?*
3. *Could be hard on Lucy and Cole?*
4. *I'd have to figure out how to do it/what to say*
5. *Hall of Fame?*

Riley handed the phone back. "The Hall of Fame thing really matters to you, eh?"

"Well, yeah. I earned it."

"You're right. And I don't think they'd take your induction away if you came out. I'd cross that one off."

Adam frowned at his phone, then began tapping. "All right. Deleted. That's one down."

"You've never been afraid of lots of attention, or lots of pressure," Riley reasoned. "You were the captain of the fucking Toronto Northmen. That's plenty of pressure."

"Different kind of pressure, though."

"Where would the pressure come from? The queer community? The hockey world? You don't need to be the World's Best Gay Man, Shep. There's no Hall of Fame for it." Riley hesitated. "Or maybe there is. I don't know. I'm not online much."

"Well, I certainly don't know. At the moment I'm not even going to make the gay playoffs."

Riley's lips twitched. "Well, you're a new expansion to the league."

Adam's laugh was full of surprised delight. His nose and eyes crinkled adorably, and Riley let himself look. He let himself enjoy the simple pleasure of making Adam Sheppard laugh.

"I really don't know what I'm doing," Adam said. "You should have seen me on my first...date? I don't know if that's the right word."

"Depends," Riley said with forced mildness.

"I mean, we weren't really trying to get to know each other. It was pretty...goal oriented."

This time Riley laughed. "Goal oriented."

"Yeah. You know."

"Sure. Just stay focused, play your game, get pucks to the net..."

"Wow, that's exactly what I said to the guy. Did I do it wrong? Is that not sexy?"

Riley shook his head. "I still can't believe this."

"I didn't actually say that."

"No. I can't believe we're even talking about this. I never thought it would happen."

Adam's expression turned serious. "You're not surprised that I'm gay, though, are you?"

Riley shrugged. "I didn't think you were straight. But you were so sure about it, so..."

"So."

They were quiet a moment. Adam's leg was jiggling under the table, and Riley could tell he was working up to saying something important.

"It must help, right? Having people you can talk to about... stuff?" Adam asked.

In that moment, Riley saw a completely new side of Adam Sheppard. Not the hockey legend, not the beloved Canadian celebrity, not the proud father of two, and not even the man who broke his heart. What Riley saw now was a man who was lost; a man who lived alone in what was probably an oversize house, mustering the courage to message a guy on a hookup app. A man who had no idea what he was doing and had no one to talk to about it.

"You can talk to me about it," Riley said. "Even after you go back to Toronto, if you want."

Adam held his gaze, then blinked a few times, as if he might cry. "I'd really like that," he finally said.

"Okay." Riley could do that. He could be Adam's gay friend. Maybe it would be good for Riley, to hear about Adam's adventures with men seventeen hundred kilometers away. It made more sense for Riley to play that sort of role in Adam's life than to attempt any kind of romantic relationship with him.

"I started taking, um, PrEP." Adam blushed as he said it. "I'd never heard of it until I was asked if I was on it."

"That's good," Riley said, as evenly as possible. "I take it too."

"Cool. Yeah. Good." Adam tore off a tiny piece of bread and began rolling it into a ball between his finger and thumb. "There haven't been that many men, honestly."

"Did any of them recognize you?"

"I don't think so." Adam laughed nervously. "Except the first guy I sent a photo of my face to thought I was lying. He said, 'Fuck you, that's Adam Sheppard'."

Riley laughed. "Really?"

"I'm serious. Then he blocked me."

"His loss."

"I guess."

Riley imagined that, even without knowing who Adam was, his hookups must have been pretty thrilled when they'd first laid eyes on him. Riley had certainly never had anyone hotter. "So what's your profile picture? Naked torso?"

Adam flicked the tiny bread ball into his empty soup bowl. "There's a bit of chin in there. You know. Flattering angle."

"Like you have a bad angle."

"These days? More curves than angles."

"As if."

"I'm serious. I need to get this shoulder sorted, then get back to a serious fitness routine. Right now all I'm lifting is burgers." He seemed to study Riley for a moment. "You're doing something right, that's for sure."

"I run," Riley said. "Usually, I mean. Not lately, but maybe tomorrow if I get another decent night's sleep. I've got a little weight room in the basement and a treadmill for the winter. I do a lot of yard work, and work on the house. Keeps me active enough."

Adam seemed to be staring at Riley's arms. "You look good. Like, really good. The beard, the hair, the body. You're a fucking dreamboat, Riley."

Riley knew he was blushing, but he also felt a more pleasant heat gathering low in his belly. He'd felt far from sexy all week, but the way Adam was gazing at him now was exciting.

Still, Riley ducked his head and muttered, "A dreamboat who can barely stay afloat, maybe."

They'd decided, later, to watch the Washington versus New Jersey game. At first they'd sat on opposite ends of Riley's couch, keeping the conversation in the safe zone of hockey. During the first intermission, Riley had filled a bowl with chips for them to munch on, which had brought them closer together. Now, during the third period, Adam was barely registering what was happening on the television, because Riley was asleep against his good shoulder.

Adam doubted, even if it had been his bad shoulder—even if he'd been in immense pain—that he would have woken Riley up. It was all so wonderfully familiar: the weight of Riley's head, the tickle of his soft hair where it just barely touched the side of Adam's neck, the sweet, peaceful sighs.

As happy as he was to have Riley pressed against him, he was just as happy that his friend was getting more sleep. He was happy that Riley felt comfortable enough with him to fall asleep like this.

Adam had lowered the volume on the TV almost all the way and had turned off the lamp beside him. In the corner, on his dog bed, Lucky was snoring much more loudly than his owner. Adam felt a swell of affection for him. Riley had found a good companion in Lucky.

Riley's hand was resting lightly on Adam's knee, his fingers curled and occasionally twitching. Adam, helpless, brushed them with his own.

It was absolutely baffling that Riley was single. That no one had snatched him up over all these years. Besides being a former NHL star (yes, star, no matter what Riley said), he ran a business, had a gorgeous home, and he was extremely handsome. More handsome with age, Adam thought. He was fully out of the closet, he didn't drink, he didn't seem to have any vices at all. His only active addiction, as far as Adam could tell, was to antiques. Had no one noticed how perfect he was?

Their loss was Adam's gain. Not that Adam was clear on what exactly Riley wanted from him. And Adam wasn't sure what he could realistically offer Riley at this point. Probably not enough. He was tied to Toronto, at least for now, and he hardly expected Riley to want to spend time there. Adam would be willing to do something long-distance if that's what it took. He'd come to Avery River as often as he could. Whatever Riley wanted.

Adam was getting way ahead of himself. His method of problem solving had always been heavy-handed. Riley had once jokingly described him as someone who would smash a window before looking for a door. And that's exactly what Adam had done to their friendship; he'd had scary feelings for Riley, and instead of facing them, he'd latched onto Maggie.

Smash.

He was now fully holding Riley's hand, stroking his thumb over his knuckles. He realized that the game had ended and another was about to start. He had no idea who won.

Riley jerked suddenly, then said, "Was I asleep?"

Adam released his hand, hoping Riley hadn't noticed him holding it. "A bit, yeah."

Riley sat up, rubbed his face, then stared at Adam's shoulder. "Sorry."

"No problem."

"I should go to bed."

"Okay." Adam turned off the TV, then followed Riley up the stairs. He felt woozy, his head filled with a weird mixture of guilt and infatuation, like he'd just awoken from a sexy dream about Riley. While Riley had dozed on the couch, Adam had been holding his hand and falling more deeply in love.

They paused awkwardly outside the guest room, Adam hoping that Riley would invite him to share his bed again. But why would he? Last night had been...well, weird and intense. Today had been good, but it hadn't made anything clearer about what they were doing. He didn't think Riley hated him anymore, so that was progress, but as for trying anything resembling a relationship...

Also, Adam had taken casual sex off the table last night, so it would probably be strange for Riley to invite him to literally sleep together. Still, he couldn't stop himself from saying, "You slept well last night."

"I did, yeah."

"And you fell asleep pretty easily on the couch there."

Riley's lips twitched. "True."

"I was just wondering...do you think it has anything to do with me?"

"It's possible."

Adam's heart soared. "Maybe we should stay close then, y'know?"

"If you want." Riley rubbed the back of his neck. "I probably will fall asleep right away. So if you're thinking—"

"I'm not. Really. I just want you to sleep. And if you want to know what I'm getting out of it, well. I like being close to you."

"God," Riley mumbled. Then he took a step forward and kissed Adam on the cheek. "You don't make it easy."

"Don't make what easy?" Adam asked around a giddy smile.

"Being normal about you. I can't do it."

Adam reached out a hand, and Riley took it. "I've never been normal about you. Don't want to be."

Riley smiled at him, unguarded and boyish. It made Adam's legs weak. "Let's fall asleep together then, weirdo."

A few minutes later, Adam entered Riley's bedroom wearing pajama pants, a T-shirt, and his glasses, and carrying one of the paperback spy novels from the bookshelf in his own room. Riley was wearing shorts and a T-shirt, and was already sitting on the bed, looking at his phone.

"I missed a text from Lindsay," Riley said. "She's leaving tomorrow."

"Oh. That's too bad."

"I'm going to go to Mom's tomorrow before she leaves. You don't have to come, but...you can. If you want."

Adam smiled and sat beside him. "I'd like that."

Riley stared glumly at the floor. "I hate thinking about Mom being alone."

"I know."

"She's strong, but still. I wish I could be stronger for her."

Adam took his hand. "You're strong as hell, Riley. You've fought through so much. And based on what I've seen this past week, I don't think the town is going to let your mom be alone if she doesn't want to be."

Riley smiled a bit at that. "True."

"And Lindsay will be back, right?"

"Yeah. As soon as she can, I'm sure. With the kids, probably. Mom can't get enough of those girls."

"And...maybe...I could come back? Sometime soon?" Adam shifted on the bed. "I mean, if that would be helpful. For you."

Their eyes met, briefly, before Riley looked away again. "I wouldn't hate that."

Adam considered this a massive win. "Cool," he said, as if fireworks weren't going off in his chest.

"Well," Riley said. His hand slipped out of Adam's as he stood. "I need to sleep."

He pulled back the duvet to reveal crisp bedsheets with a delicate floral print. Adam was absurdly charmed by this. "Are we trying this under the covers tonight, then?"

"It's usually how I do it, yeah."

As he got into bed, Adam took a moment to admire Riley's bedroom. It had a high, sloped ceiling with exposed dark wood beams, a bay window facing the ocean, and another smaller window facing the front of the house. A large chandelier that

looked like branches holding candles was suspended over the
bed. There was a vintage armchair and ottoman in one corner,
upholstered in dark blue velvet. A large mirror hung over the
dresser, and another wall showcased a moody seascape painting.
Like the rest of Riley's house, it was immaculate and beautiful. It warmed Adam's heart, thinking about Riley choosing
to surround himself with beauty. To create a home where everything looked and felt pleasing. Adam sighed as he slipped
between the cool, sleek bedsheets and wondered if Riley had
ironed them. Probably. And Adam loved that.

He rested his head on a perfect pillow and waited for Riley
to turn out the bedside lamp. He was surprised when Riley
said, to the ceiling, "I do have good memories about hockey,
just so you know."

Adam rolled to his side to face him. "Yeah?"

"Some of the best memories. It took me a while to remember the good times, after I left, but there were a lot of good
times. Some fucking great times."

"Hell yes there were. I know I played for another decade,
but all my best memories were with you, Riley." Then, because he had to, he said, "I'll never forgive myself for ruining
the Cup win for you. I'm so sorry for that."

Riley turned his head and met his gaze. "I made a bad call
that night. I should have rejected you. I shouldn't have let you
come back to my place. I knew what was going to happen."

"No, Riles. It was my fault. All of it. Everything I said
after—"

"We were drunk," Riley interrupted. "We were high on
adrenaline, and we were drunk. It leads to bad decisions."

"I wanted it to happen," Adam said quietly. "I'd wanted it
for years."

Riley closed his eyes. "It was exactly how I wanted to celebrate that Cup win."

"Until I freaked out."

"Yeah, well. I should have expected it." Riley sighed heavily, opened his eyes, then said, "Anyway. We can leave it in the past."

"Are you sure?"

"Maybe we can talk about it someday, but I'm barely hanging on right now."

"Right. Sorry."

Riley's hand found Adam's, under the blankets. He hooked their index fingers together, then said, "I just wanted you to know: I remember the good times too."

Adam brushed his thumb against Riley's. "Me too."

"Good night, Shep."

"Will you show me the beach tomorrow?"

Riley smiled, then closed his eyes and said, "Yeah. You'll love it."

Chapter Twenty-One

November 2003

"They're angry," Adam said cheerfully.

"I would be too," Riley said over the noise of twenty thousand unhappy New York hockey fans, "if my team blew a four-nothing lead."

The score was 5–4 for Toronto with just under two minutes to go in the game. New York would pull their goalie for the extra attacker as soon as they got the chance. Adam and Riley were on the ice to make sure nothing would come of that chance, if they got it.

With fifty seconds left, New York was set up in the Toronto zone, six skaters on the ice and their net empty at the other end. New York passed the puck back and forth while Riley and his teammates did a good job of blocking their lanes. Finally, New York got a shot through, but Toronto's goalie, Jonah Page, got a pad on it. The puck ricocheted back to New York's top sniper, Kolar, who was looking at a wide-open net on Page's glove side. Riley threw himself in front of the net and took the shot hard in his right shin. It fucking hurt, but the puck stayed out. It bounced to Adam, who fired it down the ice and into the empty net for the game-clinching goal.

Riley was still on his knees when Adam skated over to celebrate.

"Are you okay?" Adam shouted. "Fucking incredible block, Riles. Are you good?"

"I'm good," Riley said, then took a few slow breaths through his nose.

"Come on," Adam said. He waited for Riley to stand, then stayed close to him as they went to the bench.

Riley grunted as he sat, his leg throbbing. Adam threw an arm around him and knocked their helmets together. "Now they're really mad," Adam said.

Riley pressed back against his friend and grinned up at the ceiling of the historic arena. He was twenty years old and, yeah. This was fucking cool.

Later, in the rowdy locker room, Riley's good mood began to deteriorate. "Sounds like you guys are going out," he said to Adam, trying not to let his bitterness show. "Have fun."

Adam frowned. "You're coming too, though, right? It's New York, Riles. You gotta come out."

Riley shrugged. "I'm not twenty-one yet."

Adam's eyes narrowed like he was doing math. When he solved the equation, he said, "Fuck."

"America, man. What are you gonna do?"

"You'll be twenty-one in three weeks, though."

Riley nudged him. "I don't think that matters."

"Yeah, but…" Adam glanced around the locker room, as if someone magically had three weeks of life experience they could give Riley. "There's gotta be a way."

"Sure," Riley said. "Maybe we can convince everyone to get ice cream or something instead." He went back to removing his gear, hoping he was doing a decent job hiding his jealousy.

About a minute later, Adam said, "I'll bet New York has great ice cream."

Riley huffed. "Yeah. It's the first thing people think of."

"They probably have flavors we've never even—"

"Shep. Stop. You don't have to cheer me up like I'm a fucking five-year-old. I'm fine. I'll probably fall asleep as soon as I'm back in the room anyway."

Adam ducked his head, but Riley could see the flush on the back of his neck. "It just sucks. That's all."

Riley didn't argue, because it did suck. It fucking sucked that he couldn't celebrate this win with his teammates in the coolest city in the world. It sucked that he couldn't celebrate with *Adam*. And it sucked that Adam looked so hot after games, all sweaty and vibrating with adrenaline.

An hour after they got back to their hotel room, Adam still hadn't left to go out. He hadn't even changed out of his postgame suit, or done anything except lie next to Riley and talk his ear off. Riley wasn't complaining.

"How's your leg?" Adam asked for the third time.

"Fine." It still hurt, but whatever. It was just a bruise.

"You feel like taking a walk, maybe?"

Riley couldn't stand it anymore. "Aren't you going out?"

Adam rolled to his side to face him. "Thought I might stay in."

Riley held his gaze, fighting an eye roll and a grin at the same time. "Stay in and take a walk, you mean?"

Adam's lips curved into a shy smile that made Riley want to do very stupid things. "Yeah. Maybe. You wanna?"

Riley would do anything Adam wanted to do. It was his embarrassing secret, and it wasn't even a secret because he was so fucking obvious about it. Adam could suggest they swim to Staten Island and Riley would be putting on trunks. "Where are we walking?"

"I don't know. Anywhere! It's New York."

Riley chewed the inside of his cheek. "You don't have to do this. You should go out with the guys."

"They won't miss me." Adam poked Riley's bicep. "Let's have an adventure together."

"It's eleven o'clock," Riley argued, even as his blood fizzed with excitement.

Adam waved a dismissive hand. "I've heard this city never sleeps. Come on."

Ten minutes later they'd both changed their clothes—Adam into the black jeans that Riley secretly loved, a Nike sweatshirt, and Adidas sneakers. Riley used the bathroom, and when he walked out, Adam was talking to someone on the phone that sat on the table between their beds.

"Just gonna hang with Riles," Adam was saying. "You guys have fun." He laughed at something, then said, "I don't see that happening."

Riley pretended to be ignoring the conversation by unnecessarily adjusting his pink-and-yellow-striped polo in the mirror. It didn't matter how he looked, he told himself. It was just Adam, and Adam wasn't looking at him like that. Not ever.

Adam hung up and then moved to stand behind Riley. He fussed with his own hair in the mirror a bit, then leaned into Riley's neck and said, "You smell good. Is that new cologne?"

"Yeah. Lacoste."

"I like it."

Riley couldn't look away from how close Adam's lips were to his neck. He could feel Adam's breath, and he helplessly tilted his head, just slightly. "You can use some," he said in a near whisper, "if you want."

Adam stepped back, smiling. "It's okay. I can just smell it on you."

Sometimes Riley wanted to shake Adam, because fine. He

got it. Adam wasn't gay and was oblivious to how flirtatious he often sounded. He somehow didn't notice the constant battle Riley fought to keep himself from kissing him: at home, at work, in these hotel rooms. Whenever Adam chose to lounge on Riley's bed when they watched TV instead of staying on his own bed (often). Whenever he pressed their foreheads together to murmur words of encouragement or praise before, during, or after games (more often). Whenever he laughed at something Riley said (fucking constantly, Riley was in serious trouble).

Riley was going to buy a crate of Lacoste Pour Homme.

"If I win the million dollars, I'll split it with you," Adam said.

"It's more likely that you'll win another Coke," Riley said, as he handed Adam one of the two bottles of Cherry Coke he'd bought.

"Then I'll share that with you."

"Deal."

They stepped out of the bodega onto…somethingth street. Or avenue. Riley wasn't sure. He'd lost track of where they were several blocks ago.

"It's fine," Adam had said when Riley had pointed out they were lost. "We can use the Empire State Building to find our way back. Or get a cab."

Riley wasn't overly concerned with being lost. He was tired, his leg hurt, and the night was cold—he should have worn a hat—but he was in no hurry to get back to the hotel.

"I'm pretty sure Times Square is this way," Adam said, and began walking.

"Is that where we're going?"

Adam smiled and shrugged. "Why not, right?"

Riley was sure Adam had no idea where Times Square was, but he didn't care. If they ended up in Philadelphia, so be it.

"Did you win?" Adam asked.

Riley read the inside of his bottle cap. "Nope."

"Me neither."

"Sorry."

A moment later, Adam said, "I was thinking we should get a plasma screen TV."

"I don't even really know what that is."

"They're sick. It's, like, supergood picture. Like crystal clear. Jakey got one. He said it's like being *at* a football game."

Riley didn't think there was anything wrong with the TV they had, but he indulged him. "Do you even follow football?"

"Sometimes. But you can watch anything!"

Riley's lips twitched. "That *is* a good feature."

Adam elbowed him. "I'm just saying they're dope and we should get one."

"How much are they?"

"I dunno. Like ten grand, I think?"

Riley struggled not to spit out his Cherry Coke. "Seriously?"

Adam spread his arms. "We're young and rich, Riles! Who else are they making these things for?"

"Maybe don't tell all of New York that we're rich," Riley said, glancing around the dark sidewalks. "Where even are we?"

"We're almost there."

"Where?"

"Times Square!"

"Then why are the streets getting darker? Times Square is bright, Shep."

Adam waved a hand. "We're fine. So yeah, when we get back home, I say we hit up a Future Shop and upgrade our TV. We could watch the Super Bowl on it!"

"We're in Anaheim that day."

"Oh yeah." Adam's disappointment didn't last. "That's okay. We can just have really sweet movie nights together."

Riley's heart did a weird little flip, and he decided ten thousand dollars might be a reasonable price for a television after all.

A few minutes later, they found themselves looking at water. Adam had led them to a park along what Riley assumed was the Hudson because it didn't have any of the iconic bridges that spanned the East River.

"So this is it, huh," Riley said flatly. "Times Square."

But Adam wasn't bothered. "This place is so cool!" He grabbed Riley's wrist and tugged him toward the river. "Come check it out."

They leaned together on the railing that lined the promenade, gazing across the dark water at, if Riley's geography was correct, New Jersey. The park's lights glowed all around them, making the place feel safe. It also felt, he couldn't help but notice, romantic. Riley's right hand was so close to Adam's left on the top rail that it would have been nothing to hook their fingers together.

He watched Adam, enjoying his profile against the lights. When they'd first met, Adam's hair had been spiky, with the remnants of bleach blond at the tips left over from Adam's junior team's Memorial Cup run. Now his hair was shorter, more tapered, and fully dark. His jaw was sharper, and he'd added muscle over the summer. Riley wondered if he was doomed to watch his roommate grow more handsome every year.

Adam noticed him watching and smiled. "What?"

"Nothing." Riley looked away. Not far from them, a man and a woman were against the same railing, kissing. He felt like the background extra in a movie.

"So where's the Brooklyn Bridge?" Adam asked.

"Other side."

"Other side of what?"

"Manhattan. It's over the other river."

"There's another river?"

"Jesus Christ, Shep. You know Manhattan is an island, right?"

There was a long silence, and then Adam said, "I knew that."

Riley huffed. "Sure."

"So where's the Statue of Liberty then?"

"I can't fucking believe I let *you* be the guide tonight."

Adam bumped his hip against Riley's. "How are you a New York expert? You're from the smallest town in the world."

"It's *New York*. Haven't you ever seen a movie?"

Adam laughed. "So where's the statue?"

Riley gestured to their left. "That way. In the harbor."

"Oh. Right." Adam squinted in that direction as if he might catch a glimpse of it. Riley's heart flipped again. He was so easily charmed by this idiot.

He turned his attention to his bottle cap, reading the writing on the inside as if it might have changed and now told him he was a big winner.

"How's your leg?" Adam asked.

The question reminded Riley of how this night had started. That Adam had turned down the chance to party in New York with his NHL teammates in favor of hanging out with Riley; a man that he lived with both in Toronto and on the road. A man he saw every single day, and most of the hours of those days were spent together. There was no one on earth that Adam should want to hang out with less tonight, but he was here. And Riley was being a dick to him.

"It's fine," Riley said honestly. "And, um, thanks. I liked this."

Adam smiled. "Well, it's not over yet. Let's go to that twenty-four-hour diner we passed."

In that moment, Adam looked so beautiful that Riley couldn't breathe. "Yeah," Riley said faintly. "Cool."

They never found the diner again, of course. After several blocks of Adam insisting they were retracing their steps, Riley finally persuaded him to stop. "Let's just, like, get our bearings."

They definitely hadn't been here before, and Riley knew that because he certainly would have noticed the bar with the rainbow flag waving outside. He knew the moment Adam spotted it too because he let out a quiet, "Oh."

And then Riley spotted the two men kissing across the street, and knew Adam saw them too because Adam said, "Um, yeah. Okay. We should go."

It took Riley a moment to get moving. He was rooted by a mixture of shock and fascination and embarrassment. He and Adam were intruding, witnessing something they weren't meant to. Later, he would let himself be angry that he'd felt none of these things when he saw the man kissing the woman by the river. When he saw some version of that so many times every day. Watching these men kiss shouldn't feel different, but it did. It was terrifying and exciting.

Riley was so wrapped up in his own crisis that he momentarily forgot about Adam. When he finally glanced at his friend, he saw that Adam hadn't moved either and was staring at the two men.

What are you thinking? Riley desperately wanted to ask. Was he disgusted? Horrified?

Finally, Adam started walking, quickly, back in the direction they'd come from. Opting, probably, to retreat rather than risk finding gayer terrain ahead.

They walked in silence for a few blocks, then Adam said, "We should get a cab back to the hotel."

"Okay." So that was it, then. Their New York adventure was over.

Adam was able to flag a taxi a few minutes later. They didn't speak during the ride back to the hotel.

"*I've done that,*" Riley wanted to say. "*I've kissed boys. That's me.*"

He'd often wondered how Adam would react if Riley came out to him. He knew he wouldn't get the reaction he wanted most—a delighted smile, a kiss, a love confession—but maybe he'd win the consolation prize of having his best friend truly know who he is, and accept him. That would be enough, he tried to convince himself.

By the time they were back in their hotel room, Riley had grown annoyed by Adam's continued silence. Was it really such a big deal, seeing two men kiss? Adam was acting like he'd witnessed a murder.

Riley took a risk, a very small one, and said, "It's cool that those guys felt safe doing that." He held his breath, waiting to find out if he'd be able to stay friends with Adam Sheppard.

He nearly collapsed with relief when Adam said, simply, "Yeah."

That single word assured Riley that there would be no homophobic tirades from Adam, and that at least was something. Some of their teammates would have reacted very differently to Riley saying that.

Later, when Riley was in bed and Adam still had his lamp on, Adam said, "Do you think they *were* safe?"

Riley raised his head, then turned to face his friend. Was Adam worried about those two strangers?

"Safer, maybe," Riley said. "Safer than most places, anyway. Toronto has a big gay village where you see that sort of thing." Heat crept up his neck. "I mean, I've heard that there is. In Toronto."

Adam seemed to contemplate this as he stared at the ceiling, hands clasped together on his stomach. He was still fully dressed. "It must be scary, being gay."

Riley's heart stopped. He just stopped himself from blurting out, *"It is."* Instead, he said, "Probably."

Adam turned his head and looked at him. "Sorry we never made it to Times Square. Or the diner."

"It's okay. I'm tired anyway."

"I wanted to show you a good time."

"You did." Riley raised himself up on an elbow. "I still don't know why you chose to hang out with me when you could have gone clubbing with the guys."

Adam's smile was soft and sleepy. "Wouldn't have been fun without you, Riles."

And that was when Riley fell the rest of the way in love with him.

Chapter Twenty-Two

April 2024

"You usually go a lot faster than this, don't you?" Adam puffed.

Riley smiled mysteriously while looking straight ahead, his cheeks barely flushed as he jogged beside Adam on the sand. Adam couldn't remember the last time he'd done a beach run, and he was struggling on the uneven surface.

Also, Riley was in really, *really* good shape. Possibly better shape than when he'd been a professional athlete, and certainly better than Adam's current condition. And if Adam fell a few strides behind just so he could admire Riley's ass in his tight jogging pants, well. Everyone had their own fitness journey.

Lucky was joining them too, though he occasionally became distracted by various objects and then would have to sprint to catch up. They'd gone the length of the beach and were now about halfway back to where they'd left their water bottles and sweatshirts. Adam was looking forward to that water bottle.

The tide was out, and the beach was veiled in fog, making the place seem magical and very remote. Adam loved it. And despite the fact that he was struggling a bit, he was loving the exercise too. It felt good to really work his body after several days off. He knew, despite his bad shoulder, that he was lucky to be able to do this. Lucky to have both of his knees and his hips and his ankles. He knew other former NHL players who had less to work with.

When they were a few strides away from their belongings, Adam dug deep and cranked up the speed, pushing himself ahead of Riley.

"Are you fucking serious?" Riley said.

Adam laughed as he raised a fist in the air in victory, then fell to his knees on the sand. "I win," he panted. Then, "Fucking hell."

Riley stood over him, hands on his hips, and shook his head. "Unbelievable."

Adam fell to his back, his arms and legs spread out like a starfish. "Just gonna let the sea take me."

Riley grabbed his water bottle and took a long drink. Adam enjoyed the view from below.

Then Lucky arrived and started licking Adam's face.

"Ugh, stop. I'm alive, I'm alive," Adam sputtered.

"Lucky," Riley said sternly. "Here." He poured some water into a small metal bowl he'd brought, and Lucky began to drink happily.

"I should probably do that too."

"You'll have to wait until Lucky's done first."

"Ha." Adam held his right hand out, and Riley took it and pulled him up. Adam scooped up his own bottle and soon decided slightly cold tap water in an aluminum bottle was the best tasting thing in the world.

"You all right?"

"Yes," Adam said testily. "I *can* run, you know."

"I mean your shoulder."

"I wasn't running on my hands." Adam grimaced. "Sorry.

My shoulder's fine. I'm just grumpy because I'm not good at running on sand."

"It took me a while to get good at it."

"Well," Adam said, then decided not to finish the sentence. He didn't have a while to spend here, running beside Riley on the sand. He would be leaving the day after tomorrow.

"It's beautiful here, with the fog and stuff," he said instead. "I should take a picture."

He fished his phone out of the pocket of the hoodie he'd left on a rock, then walked toward the glistening mud-like sand that stretched way out to where the tide had pulled back. He snapped a few photos that didn't do the place justice at all— he was a terrible photographer—but he decided to send one to Lucy and Cole anyway.

They had a group chat together, years of photos and earnest declarations of encouragement and love from Adam, which were sometimes followed by replies of a single word from one of the kids. More often it was a single letter: *k*, or *y*. More often than that, even, there would be no reply at all. Adam tried not to take it personally, even when he watched his kids type endless messages to their friends. There were days when they stayed with him that they barely looked away from their phones. It wasn't like they weren't *seeing* his texts.

Maggie had told him teenagers were just like that these days, but when he'd asked her if they ignored her texts too, she'd changed the subject.

Now he typed out: *Wish you were here*, then immediately deleted it because it was cheesy as hell, and also because it wasn't exactly true. He loved his kids, and he'd be happy to explore a beach with them another day, but today was for him and Riley.

And also Lucky, who was going absolutely bananas barking at something.

"Hermit crab," Riley called out to Adam, as an explanation.

"Ah," Adam said, then, "Wait, really?" He'd never seen one before.

He crossed the short distance to Riley, then looked where he was pointing. There, just in front of Riley's damp sneaker, was a little curly shell scooting along the sand.

"Oh wow." Adam crouched down to get a better look. "Look at that."

"The beach is full of them."

Lucky barked again, and Adam held his arm out to protect the crab. "It's okay," he told the dog, "we like him."

Lucky huffed, which sounded to Adam like exasperation. Adam held his phone over the crab and took a short video.

"You a filmmaker now?" Riley said.

"I thought the kids might like it. They're hard to impress."

"I heard teens are pretty wild about hermit crabs, yeah."

Adam elbowed him in the shin. "They're always watching animal videos on the internet. So I'm making one."

Above him, Riley chuckled. "Do you even know how to send a video?"

Adam ignored him. Sure, he'd always been shit when it came to technology, but he wasn't a hundred years old.

"Can I send them a photo of Lucky?" Adam asked. "Do you mind?"

"Go ahead. Lucky loves a camera."

Adam took some slightly blurry photos of Lucky, then sent the best one to the kids. He wrote, *This is my friend Lucky.*

"I regret that I didn't get to see Lucy and Cole grow up," Riley said.

Adam's head whipped around to stare at him. "You do?"

"They were great kids. I loved playing with them. I kind of always assumed I'd never have kids, so it was nice, being Uncle Riley."

"Why did you assume that?"

Riley shrugged. "Seemed at the time that I would be living life in the shadows, y'know? If I wanted to keep playing hockey. And by the time I quit I was such a mess I couldn't even imagine being in a relationship with someone, let alone raising kids."

"And now?"

Riley looked out to sea. "I've made my peace with it. I don't think it was ever my destiny. I'm okay with that, and I have my nieces now."

"I wish you'd seen Lucy and Cole grow up too. I wish my kids knew you." Silently, he told himself that they still could get to know Riley. There was time.

"Seems like they turned out okay without my help."

"Thanks to Maggie, yeah."

"You're a great dad," Riley argued. "I mean, probably."

"I do my best, but you know what the life is like. Barely home, weird hours, laid up with injuries for at least part of every season, and sometimes recovering from surgery in the summers. I'd get moody and stressed when the team was shit." He scoffed. "Seems like a stupid thing to get so worked up about, really. Hockey."

"Yeah, well. If you've got a cure for that you could make a fortune in this country."

Their gazes met, and Adam smiled at Riley's slight smile. "Anyway. They're not hurting for money, so I was good for something at least."

"There you go."

"And I'd like to say they'd give up the money in exchange for more time with their dad, but hell no. You should see Cole's gaming computer."

Riley laughed.

"I *am* trying, though," Adam said. "These past couple of years, since I retired, I've been showing up for everything.

Maybe too much. Lucy actually told me once that it seemed forced." He sighed. "That fucking hurt."

"Sorry."

"Teenagers, right? Everyone tells me it's normal, but it still stings." He hesitated a moment, then said, "Harv was my role model for fatherhood, you know."

Riley's eyes turned soft. "He was a good one."

"The best. I'm not saying I'm even half the dad he was, but he was who I wanted to be. Basically the opposite of my dad."

Riley grunted in agreement as he kicked at a pebble.

"And Maggie's a great mom. We both aimed to support our kids in whatever they wanted to do but not push them too hard. Dad thinks being a hard-ass is the only way for your kid to succeed, but you're proof that it isn't true. There's a ton of proof that it isn't true."

"I doubt your father considers me a success."

"Well, I do. I hope you do too. And I'm a thousand percent sure your parents do."

"I guess," Riley said, then looked at the sky. "Yeah. They do. Dad was always proud of me. Maybe he still is, somewhere."

"He's probably bragging about you to everyone in Heaven right now."

Riley huffed, then looked at Adam again. His eyes were misty, but he was smiling. "Definitely. And seeing if anyone needs a ride anywhere."

"Do they have Ford F-150s in Heaven?"

"Of course they do. Otherwise it would be Hell."

They both laughed, then Adam took another pull of his water bottle. He noticed, as he was wiping his mouth, that Riley was still looking at him, and his gaze seemed…interested.

When he noticed Adam noticing, he looked away.

"We still on for breakfast at your mom's?" Adam asked.

"Yeah. We should head back and get ready."

As they were walking to the stairs that led to the road, Adam found something interesting.

"Look at this fancy thing." He picked up the white, spiraled shell and rested it in his palm.

"That's a moon snail shell. Is it empty?"

"Yeah."

"You should keep it. Maybe Lucy would like it. We can wash it at the house."

Adam wasn't sure if a snail shell would win his daughter's heart, but he kept it anyway. If nothing else, it would be a nice souvenir of this roller coaster of a week.

Chapter Twenty-Three

"I hear the hockey banquet has a celebrity host," Mom said as she greeted Riley and Adam with hugs.

"Well," Adam said, "they have me. I hope I don't embarrass myself too much."

Riley scoffed. He knew Adam could quack like a duck for the entire banquet and everyone who went would still say it was the most exciting night of their life. He still couldn't believe Adam was actually going through with it.

"I'm not sure what you're thinking," Riley said, "but it's not a glamorous event."

"I'll cancel my tux fitting then," Adam said with a wink.

Damn Adam and his winks. He could wield those things like a sexy weapon. They always sliced right through Riley.

"Are you going to be there?" Adam asked Mom.

"Yes, of course. I always went with Harv, and I'm sure he'll be in the room tomorrow night too."

Riley smiled at that. Dad *would* tell God he couldn't miss the banquet. Then he imagined Dad's ghost benevolently haunting the rink and wondered if Dad wouldn't prefer that to Heaven.

"I'm sure he will be," Adam agreed, then he laughed. "Now the pressure is really on, if he's going to be watching."

Mom patted his arm. "He would be so happy you're here." She looked at Riley. "Have you boys been having a nice few days?"

"Uh, yeah," Riley said awkwardly. "Pretty good." He thought of one detail that would interest her. "Shep made fish chowder yesterday."

Mom looked delighted. "Go on! You did not."

"I did," Adam said proudly. "It was edible and everything."

"How'd you thicken it?"

"Crackers," Riley and Adam said at the same time.

"Good boy. I like a man who can cook. Don't you, Riley?"

Riley blushed as he remembered how smitten he'd been by the sight of an apron-clad Adam stirring soup in his kitchen. "Sure."

"Where's Lindsay?" Adam asked.

"Watching the eggs," Lindsay called from the kitchen. "Get in here and help, Riley."

As they went to the kitchen, Adam put his lips close to Riley's ear and said, "Before we leave, can you show me around the house again? I always loved this place."

Riley's heart skipped. "Okay."

"My god, is that the actual host of the Avery River Minor Hockey End of Season Banquet?" Lindsay teased as they entered the kitchen.

"The one and only," Adam said.

Lucky, of course, was already in the kitchen because he loved both Lindsay and food. He was sitting at Lindsay's feet, gazing mournfully at her as she stirred the eggs.

"I'm sorry I'll be missing it," Lindsay said, "but I have clients and, you know. Kids."

"I understand. I'm leaving on Tuesday because I have appointments and kids."

"Aw, are you?" Lindsay shot Riley a sympathetic look. "That's too bad."

Riley narrowed his eyes at her and said, "He can hardly stay here forever."

Adam, to his surprise, looked a little wounded by this.

"All right," Lindsay said, "these eggs are done. Let's eat."

Within minutes the table was loaded with scrambled eggs, bacon, ham, toast, baked beans ("Patty dropped those off"), coffee, and orange juice. Adam looked deliriously happy.

"Riley took me to the farmers market yesterday," he said. "It might be my new favorite place."

"He bought all the cookies," Riley said.

"Not *all* of them. And I met some of Riley's friends. Do you know Bea? She makes honey!"

"Bea is lovely," Mom said. "Nell too."

"I don't think I know them," Lindsay said.

"They're a little older than me," Riley said. "But they're great."

"Do you know Darren?" Adam asked Lindsay. "I met him too."

"Oh, I know Darren," Lindsay said with a smile. "Did he flirt with you?"

"I don't think so," Adam said with a nervous laugh. "Isn't he married? We're going to their house tonight."

"Are you?" Lindsay asked with interest. She locked eyes with Riley. "Just the two of you going?"

"There are a few people. It's a dinner party, or whatever," Riley said.

"Couples, mostly?"

"I guess."

Lindsay smiled, then took a triumphant bite of toast.

Since everyone at the table, excluding Riley, was naturally chatty, the rest of the meal passed with a lot of upbeat conversation and gentle teasing. Riley quietly enjoyed it, loving how normal it felt. Not that having Adam at his parents' kitchen table was normal, but it still felt like a Tuck family meal.

He also quietly enjoyed how handsome Adam looked, especially when he smiled. Riley was obsessed with the creases that appeared beside his sparkling eyes now when he laughed. He'd been admiring them on the beach too, when Adam had been flushed and sweaty from the run. Well, he'd been admiring most of Adam on the beach.

He was undeniably attracted to Adam, but he still wasn't sure if anything beyond simple friendship was a good idea for them. But he also wasn't sure if it mattered what he thought about that, because his idiot heart didn't seem to care if falling for Adam all over again was a bad idea.

"There's more bacon, Adam," Mom said as she held out a small blob of scrambled egg to Lucky.

"Oh, I couldn't," Adam said, then eyed the platter that still had at least ten strips of bacon left on it. "Well. Maybe."

Riley bit the inside of his cheek as he watched Adam happily transfer three strips to his empty plate. He wondered if there was any chance that, this time, falling for Adam might not be a terrible idea.

"Well," Lindsay said as she pushed her chair back. "I should hit the road."

Riley couldn't blame his sister for being eager to leave, but he'd miss having her around. "You planning on coming back anytime soon?"

"I'm sure I will, but you could always visit me in Halifax, you know."

"I will," Riley said, feeling guilty. The last time he'd gone to Halifax he hadn't told her he was in town because he'd been there for purely selfish, single-minded reasons related to having as much sex as possible in a three-day window.

"I'll clean up," Adam offered, already gathering plates from the table. "You three can say goodbye. It was nice seeing you again, Lindsay."

"What a gentleman," Mom gushed. She looked at Riley when she said, "An absolute sweetheart."

He tried to look annoyed, but he knew the color of his cheeks was telling.

Later, the three surviving Tucks gathered next to Dad's truck. Riley couldn't believe it would be the last time he'd see it.

"Is there enough gas in it?" he asked stupidly, stalling for time.

"If there isn't, I know where I can get more," Lindsay said.

He nodded. "You gonna be okay? Driving."

"I will. Are *you* going to be okay?"

Riley could only shrug, his throat already growing tight.

Lindsay threw her arms around him. "I love you. Mom loves you. And I think Adam might have some warm feelings about you."

"Stop."

"Or maybe he looks at all his former teammates that way."

"You're imagining things."

"Oh, she is not," Mom said. "Denial isn't just a river in Egypt."

"Okay, Dad."

They all laughed at that, though it was followed by a heavy silence. Mom and Lindsay had always used humor to defuse big emotions. Dad had always expressed them openly and easily, without shame. Riley simply couldn't deal with them at all.

Lindsay hugged Mom. "You know I'll be back here in a minute if you need me, okay?"

"Two hours, more like," Mom teased. "But I know. Thank you, sweetie."

"You too, big brother. Call me anytime."

Riley wrapped his arms around her. "I will. Love you, Linds."

"Love you too. Don't make me cry. I have to drive."

As they watched her drive away, Riley said, "You want us to stay awhile?"

"No, no. Adam's only in town for a couple more days. Enjoy him."

Riley's heart raced at the first way he interpreted her words. "You could stay at my place tonight, or I could stay here." It would be her first night alone.

She squeezed his arm. "Don't worry about me. Ruth is coming by with dinner, and tomorrow some of the girls are coming to the house. I don't think I'll be lonely much."

"But if you ever are, call me, okay? Or come to my house, or the shop. Don't be alone."

"I could give you the same advice."

"I'm not alone. I have a guest." Riley gestured to the house, where Adam was washing dishes. "And when he's gone, I've got Lucky. Maybe you should get a dog. That would be nice, right?"

"We'll see. That could be a good idea."

They went back inside, and Riley helped Adam finish the dishes.

"You okay?" Adam asked.

"I'm okay," Riley assured him, because in that moment, he was. Maybe later he'd feel like crying again, but for now he was good.

He put away the last of the dishes, then he and Adam went to the living room, where Mom was tidying while Lucky supervised.

"Do you mind if I show Adam around the house a bit?" Riley asked.

"Of course I don't mind. He's always been welcome here." She straightened a throw pillow on the sofa, and Riley was hit by the memory of making out with Adam on that same sofa, nearly eighteen years ago.

He glanced at Adam to see if he might be having similar thoughts, but Adam was inspecting a cluster of framed photos on the wall over the fireplace. One was of Adam handing Riley the Stanley Cup, both men looking young and jubilant and sweaty. They were both in profile, smiling at each other like nothing bad had ever happened to them, or ever would.

"I don't think I've seen this photo before," Adam said.

"Harv ordered prints of a whole pile of photos from that night. I can't remember which photographer it was who took that one."

"It's a good one," Adam said quietly.

Riley had always hated having to look at that photo when he visited his parents, but Dad had loved it, so he'd never said anything. He wasn't sorry it was here now, though.

"We were so proud that night," Mom said. "I mean, it was enough of a thrill for Harv that Toronto had finally won the Cup, but for his own son to be on the team. Well, it was really special."

"It was," Adam agreed. "I'm glad we were able to win it for him."

A few minutes later, Riley led Adam up the creaky stairs to the second floor, and then into his childhood bedroom. It was still full of Riley's old hockey trophies and medals, and a poster of the Stanley Cup was still tacked to the wall. His old twin bed with the blue-and-green quilt his grandmother had made was against the same wall it had always been against.

Adam had sucked Riley off for the first time on that bed. They'd had the house to themselves for a short window and had been making out when Adam had shocked him by taking two of Riley's fingers into his mouth and sucking them. Riley hadn't dared to hope for more, but then Adam had released his fingers and said, "I want to blow you. I want to try."

And he had. On his knees in Riley's childhood bedroom while Riley sat on the bed. Objectively, it had probably been a terrible blow job, but Riley had only lasted about a minute anyway.

Adam sat on the edge of that bed now, legs spread, and Riley had to look away.

"Looks the same," Adam said.

"I don't spend much time here."

"I have good memories of this room."

Riley wondered if he was talking about the blow job—or the other furtive sexual experiences they'd enjoyed in here—or if he meant the more innocent nights when they'd talked and laughed in the dark, Riley on his bed and Adam on an air mattress on the floor. Riley had always offered to take the floor, but Adam always refused. What Riley had really wanted to offer was to share the bed, even though it would have been uncomfortably small.

"Me too," Riley said, which made Adam smile. Which made the eye creases appear. Which made Riley's heart bounce. He sat beside Adam, and the ancient bed creaked ominously. "I loved those summers."

"They were the best. Does your family still have the boat?"

"I bought Dad a newer one a few years ago. I guess maybe it's mine now."

"Maybe next time I'm here you can take me for a spin," Adam said as he bumped his shoulder against Riley's.

Riley smiled, picturing it. "Maybe I will."

That afternoon, Riley showed Adam his greenhouse.

"This is amazing! You grew all this? From seeds?"

"Mostly, yeah."

"What's this one?" Adam leaned down and sniffed one of the larger herb plants that Riley had managed to keep alive through the winter.

"Sage," Riley said. "And those ones are basil."

"And you'll plant these outside?"

"I keep those ones potted so I can move them easily, but most of the stuff in here will get planted."

"What are those?" Adam asked. "Another herb?"

"Bell peppers."

"Shit, really? Green, or red?"

"Well," Riley said, "green peppers are usually just under-ripe red peppers."

Adam's eyes went wide like Riley had just proved god was real. "Are you serious? Is that why green peppers taste like garbage?"

"They have their uses."

"If you say so. Hey, tell me what everything is. I want the full tour."

So Riley gave him the tour, happily explaining which plants would yield fruit this year, and which would take at least another year or two. He explained which ones needed lots of sun, which needed shade, which ones might keep deer away, and which ones he was trying to grow for the first time.

"You have deer?" Adam asked, immediately turning his gaze to the yard outside, searching.

"Unfortunately," Riley grumbled, then amended, "They're nice, they just eat everything."

"Still," Adam said with a note of wonder, like deer were unicorns.

They left the greenhouse, joining Lucky in the yard. Riley showed Adam the rhubarb growing in one corner of the yard, and the small lavender patch, still dormant from the winter.

"You know how amazing this is, right?" Adam asked.

"It's just a garden."

"Yeah, but you made it. You did all this work, and it'll turn into something beautiful and useful. That's inspiring, Riley."

Riley really, really wanted to kiss him. Instead he said, "It's just a hobby."

"Well, it's a good one." Adam gazed at the ocean. "Man, this place is beautiful."

"I like it."

Over by the trees that lined one side of the yard, Lucky started barking.

"What's his problem?" Adam asked.

"Probably saw a rabbit."

"You have *rabbits*?"

"Calm down. Those fuckers eat everything too."

Adam laughed. "I love how you traded Kevin Kroeker for rabbits. Your new nemesis."

"Oh *fuck* Kevin Kroeker," Riley said, with feeling. "Is he still alive? No one killed him?"

"He's alive."

"Only because I retired early."

Adam was beautiful when he laughed, especially now, in the sunshine, in Riley's garden. "Well," Adam said, "wherever that asshole is, I doubt he's got a view like this."

Riley's gaze stayed on Adam's face. "Probably not."

Chapter Twenty-Four

"We're going to miss the Toronto game tonight. Are you okay with that?" Riley asked as he stepped out of his bedroom.

Adam poked his head out of the bathroom. "I don't think they need my help anymore. I'll just check the score lat—wow. You look...wow."

Riley was wearing his best outfit, and it was because he wanted Adam to look at him exactly as he was now. Riley had splurged at an upscale menswear store in Halifax on the impeccably tailored aubergine trousers, the shiny black leather belt, and the flattering black jacket made from a sleek cotton sateen. Under it, he wore a simple black T-shirt that he knew showed off his broad chest.

"Thanks," Riley said. He was excited about tonight, and it felt good to be excited about something. He wanted Adam to meet his friends. He wanted his friends to like Adam. And after...well, Riley couldn't be sure, but the air between them seemed to buzz with the promise of something thrilling and sexy, the same way it had when they'd been younger. Riley wanted so badly to let it happen, even if it was a bad idea. Even if the timing was all wrong. He wanted to lose himself in Adam and deal with the consequences later. It felt inevitable, that they would end this day by giving in to what they both wanted.

"I'll just be a minute," Adam said.

"Okay. I'll be downstairs."

For a moment, they both smiled at each other. *He must feel it too*, Riley thought. *He has to.*

"Do they live nearby?" Adam asked as they pulled out of Riley's driveway.

"No. They live in West Avery. It's about twenty minutes away."

"*West* Avery? Where's that?"

Riley didn't look away from the road, but Adam could tell that teasing smile was there. "West of here."

"This Avery guy really got his name around."

"Yep. Avery River, Avery Harbour, Avery Mountain, West Avery, Avery Point, Avery Point South…"

"Jesus."

"May as well have been, yeah."

"Give me the rundown. Who all is going to be there?"

"Bea and Nell, who you met. They also live in West Avery, and they've been married for longer than I've known them. Bea's from New Glasgow, and I think Nell's from around Truro. I forget. They met in Truro for sure, at the agricultural college."

"And Darren's husband is…Tom?"

"Right. Really sweet guy. An enormous teddy bear, really. Darren met him when he was living in Halifax. Tom was a big shot at one of the major hotel chains, originally from Ontario somewhere. Darren worked at the bar across the street from one of the hotels Tom was in charge of. Tom started crossing the street as much as possible, always sitting at the bar so he could flirt with the cute bartender. Then Darren asked him out, and the rest is history."

"And now they make maple syrup?"

Riley laughed a bit. "And now they make maple syrup. I guess they both dreamed of a more rural life, and the farm was for sale, so here they are."

"That's a big change."

"It is," Riley agreed. "But they've made it work."

Adam could imagine a future, maybe when the kids were grown, when he might live here with Riley. Helping at the shop and in the garden. He was, again, getting way ahead of himself, but the vision was nice. "Who else is going to be there?" he asked, trying to stay in the present.

"Jackson—he's an artist, and a professor at the art university in Halifax. And his husband is Marcel, who does something related to IT. I never really understood it."

"I'm sure I won't either." Lucky poked his head over Adam's shoulder from the back seat. "Shit, I forgot you were there, Lucky."

"He's being quiet, but he'll get excited when he sees his girlfriends." Riley had already told Adam about their hosts' fancy French dogs.

Adam was both nervous and excited, and not only for the party. He'd already decided he wouldn't drink at all tonight, because he was almost sure that something was going to happen between Riley and him later, and he wanted to be sober when it did. He wanted Riley to know that he didn't need alcohol for courage anymore.

Riley looked fucking hot tonight. Adam kept stealing glances at his thighs in those excellent pants. Adam had done his best with the limited selection of clothing he'd packed, settling on his navy sweater and dark brown slacks, but Riley

was definitely outshining him tonight. Which was just fine
with Adam.

When, nearly twenty minutes later, they pulled up in front
of Darren and Tom's large cabin-style house, Adam was instantly charmed. "Are these maple trees?" he asked as they exited the truck.

"Yeah. They tend to make the best maple syrup."

Adam lightly elbowed him in front of the truck. "Oh, is
that their secret ingredient?"

"They tried palm trees, but..."

"I can't stand you," Adam lied.

Lucky ran ahead of them, barking excitedly. Adam knew
how he felt. The door opened and two large, beautiful dogs
ran out to greet Lucky. Then Darren appeared in the door-
way, waving and smiling. "Our favorite hockey players are
here," he called out.

"He doesn't watch hockey at all, does he?" Adam said quietly.

"Not a minute of it, as far as I know. I don't think anyone
here has. Maybe Tom."

Adam wasn't used to being in rooms where no one knew
who he was, but he was pretty sure he'd like it.

They were the last to arrive, so Adam was introduced
quickly to everyone once they'd reached the living room. He
was surprised to find that Marcel was significantly younger
than his husband, Jackson. He was a light-skinned Black man,
originally from Montreal, who was very slim and stylish, with
thick-framed glasses. Jackson, by contrast, was a large white
man with shoulder-length curly gray hair, and he was wearing
a white T-shirt that just said Yes I Am in a plain black font.
Was the shirt art? Adam was already in way over his head.

Adam liked Tom right away, though. He was chatty, which

Adam always appreciated, and, he quickly learned, had grown up not far from Adam's own hometown in Ontario.

Bea remembered Adam from the market, of course, and introduced him properly to her wife, Nell. Even though no one in the room recognized Adam as a hockey player, they all seemed very interested in him. Adam wondered what Darren had told everyone about him.

They all lounged on the living room furniture, grazing from an exciting spread of snacks on the coffee table. Riley was drinking soda water with lime, so Adam was doing the same. Everyone else was drinking wine. Adam was used to people wanting him to tell them hockey stories, but tonight he stayed mostly silent. Riley seemed the most relaxed Adam had seen him since…well. Probably ever. He smiled a lot, laughed easily, and even got animated a few times when recalling a funny story from his recent past. The more these friends talked, the clearer the picture became to Adam: Riley had lived a whole life without him. He'd lived a life full of hookups with men, some disastrous and some hot; a life full of parties and celebrations with queer friends; a life full of community and family that had nothing to do with hockey.

These were the people who had been there for Riley when he'd been at his lowest. When he'd gotten sober and gotten professional help with his mental health. And they'd been there when he'd bought his house and adopted Lucky and started working at the store again.

Adam was only visiting.

He tried not to let the melancholy that had settled in him show on the outside as they gathered in the dining room for dinner. He realized that no one here even knew that Adam was gay. Did they assume? Maybe Riley had told Darren, but Adam doubted it. Riley would ask first, he was sure.

Why did they think he was here, with Riley? What did

Adam want them to think, and, more importantly, what did *Riley* want them to think?

Adam started to wish he was also drinking wine, but dismissed the idea immediately. He realized he'd zoned out of the conversation that was happening, and when he snapped back to attention, he heard Jackson and Marcel trashing Halifax's newest gay bar.

"It's not accessible at all," Marcel complained. "Like, really? In 2024?"

"It's hard to get to?" Adam asked in a weak attempt to enter the conversation.

Marcel frowned at him, confused. "It doesn't have a ramp, and there's no elevator. The dance floor is up a flight of stairs. It's terrible."

Adam hoped he wasn't blushing. "Oh, right. I get it."

Jackson smiled warmly at him. "But like all things in downtown Halifax, it's also not easy to get to."

That launched most of the table into a rant about Halifax's abysmal mass transit system and the endless construction that blocked sidewalks.

Finally, Riley changed the subject by saying, "Adam helped me a lot this week in the shop, getting it ready to reopen."

"Oh, that's so sweet of you, Adam," said Nell. "I'm glad you weren't alone doing that, Riley."

"Me too," Riley said quietly. Adam's heart glowed.

"So," Jackson said, "I have to ask—you two have been friends for a while?"

"Yeah," Riley said. "A long time."

"I think what you're really asking," Adam said with a slight smile, "is where the hell have I been before now?"

Everyone laughed. "Right," Jackson said. "Thank you for seeing through my bullshit."

Adam wasn't sure how to answer. What did Riley want him

to say? "We didn't talk much, for a while there. But it's been really great, seeing Riley again."

That seemed vague enough to be safe, while also being true.

"They were roommates," Darren said. And there was definitely *something* in his tone. Mischief, maybe.

"We were," Adam confirmed, cautiously.

"Riley was so cute back then," Darren said. "You're a total fox now obviously, Riley, but you had such a baby face and all those muscles. Absolutely deadly combination."

Adam felt a ridiculous pang of jealousy, remembering that Darren had gotten to touch Riley before he had. "He was cute," Adam said, as mildly as he could manage. "But now he's gorgeous." He punctuated his declaration by taking a sip of water. Let them draw whatever conclusions they wanted from that. Adam was done with hiding.

He could practically feel the heat of Riley's blush beside him, but he didn't look at him.

Jackson broke the tension by clapping his hands together with delight, then saying, "Well, thank god that mystery has been solved."

"What mystery?" Riley grumbled.

"You can't show up here with the World's Most Beautiful Man and not expect us to have questions."

Adam sputtered a bit at that. "Um, thank you?"

"We're friends," Riley said firmly. Which, yes, was true, but also: ouch.

"But, if what you're really asking is if I'm gay," Adam said, then pointed to Jackson's T-shirt. "Yes. I am."

Everyone loved that, laughing and cheering. Adam laughed too, feeling relieved. He still wasn't used to saying those words.

"I'm new at it, though," he added. "So go easy on me."

Bea pressed her fingers to her cheeks. "A baby!"

"Welcome aboard, Adam," Tom said.

Adam did turn to Riley then, and found his friend smiling at him in that unfamiliar relaxed way. A smile that wasn't tinged with sadness or regret or longing. Just happiness, and maybe pride.

Under the table, Riley put a hand on Adam's knee and squeezed, once, before taking it away. Adam wanted to grab it back.

The conversation moved on, and Riley said, low enough so only Adam could hear, "Gorgeous?"

"Well," Adam said, feeling a little lightheaded even without wine, "it's not like you're the World's Most Beautiful Man or anything."

Riley had been worried during the dinner that Adam wasn't comfortable. He'd been uncharacteristically quiet all night, and Riley had been cursing himself for dropping Adam into an awkward situation. But then Adam had surprised him, and then surprised him again. He'd told everyone he was gay, and he'd said that Riley was *gorgeous*. Riley's heart was still fluttering.

After dinner, the group had begun to separate into pairs and trios. Darren had Riley alone in the kitchen and was, of course, losing his mind.

"He's so hot for you. You know that, right?"

Riley folded his arms across his chest and leaned back against the counter. "I don't know where you're getting that from."

"Oh, I don't know," Darren glanced up from where he was loading the dishwasher. "Maybe the way he's always caressing you with his eyeballs."

Riley scoffed. "Caressing."

"Oof, those eyes, though, right? Breathtaking. I can see why you were head over heels."

"It wasn't because of his eyes." Riley sighed, and amended, "It wasn't *only* because of his eyes."

Darren closed the dishwasher, grabbed his glass of wine, then perched on one of the stools at the island. "Go on."

"He was…" Riley couldn't think of how to summarize everything he'd loved about Adam. "We were…" he tried again, then shook his head.

"I get it," Darren assured him. "Like with Tom, I can't even remember the why of it. I met him, and I fell in love."

"Yeah," Riley said, loving how simple the explanation was. "The why doesn't matter."

"So *why* don't you take that hunk home and love him all night long?"

Riley glanced at the entrance to the kitchen to make sure Adam wasn't within earshot. He spotted him in the far corner of the living room, talking to Bea. "I want to, believe me, but it might not be the best idea."

"Oh, come on."

"Hey, the other day when I told you about him you called him a monster."

"But that was before I *saw* him," Darren argued.

Riley huffed. "You're a terrible friend."

"No! Let me rephrase that: It was before I saw how he looks at *you*."

"Caressing me with his eyeballs."

"Right! Anyway, he's in love with you. Deal with it, *gorgeous*."

Now Riley was really blushing, but he was smiling too. "He lives in Toronto," he pointed out, needing to keep things grounded.

"So what? So did Tom. There's a cure for Toronto."

"He has kids there."

Darren frowned at this. "Oh. Well, that's a bit tricky. How old?"

"Fifteen and sixteen."

"Pfft. I thought you said *kids*. They probably haven't noticed he's gone."

Riley shot him a withering look.

"Seriously," Darren insisted. "You know what I was doing at that age? Smoking weed and making out with you. I didn't care what my parents were doing. And you moved away to play hockey when you were how old?"

"Sixteen," Riley mumbled.

"See? All grown-up."

"Hardly. And anyway, he's not abandoning his kids, and I'd never want him to."

Darren sighed. "Fine. And I never said *abandon*. He could fly to Toronto once a month, or, you know…FaceTime."

Riley pushed away from the counter. "You made the right decision, not having kids."

"God, I know."

"I'm tired, so I'm going to see if Shep's ready to go."

Darren's brow furrowed. "Who's Shep?" Then he smiled. "Is that your little nickname for Adam? That's sexy."

Riley rolled his eyes. "It's what everyone calls him."

"What does he call you? Tucky?"

"Good night, Darren. Thank you for a lovely evening."

"Wait. Does he call you Ri-Ri?"

Riley flipped him off, then left the kitchen. He found Adam still talking to Bea. Lucky was resting at Adam's feet.

"Riles," Adam said, all smiles. "I'm learning about honey!"

Riley's heart fluttered again at the nickname. He'd told Adam not to call him that, but it wasn't because he hated it. It was because he fucking loved hearing it again. He crouched to scratch Lucky's head while Adam asked a few more questions about bees.

Finally, Adam said, "You tired?"

"Yeah."

"Okay, let's go."

They said goodbye to everyone, Adam even getting a few hugs. Riley was standing beside him when Tom hugged Adam and said, "Remember what I told you."

"I will," Adam said. "Thank you."

That certainly captured Riley's attention.

When they were back on the road, Lucky's head peeking over Adam's shoulder again, Riley asked, "You had an okay time?"

"I had a great time. Your friends are awesome."

"They are. You had some good conversations then?"

"I did."

Riley waited for Adam to elaborate. Finally, Adam said, "I always knew honey came from bees, but I'd never really thought about how it was actually made, y'know?"

Riley sighed.

"Did you know they use smoke to put the bees to sleep?"

"Yes, Shep. Everyone knows that. What did Tom tell you?"

"Tom? Oh! That."

Another silence passed where Riley tried not to scream.

"Tom wanted me to know that he was in his thirties when he came out, and that he'd actually been engaged once. To a woman."

Riley nodded. He'd known all this, though Tom rarely talked about it. It had all been before he'd met Darren.

"He said that he felt guilty sometimes, about how happy he was after coming out. To do it, he had to hurt the woman who'd been planning to marry him. And he told me that if he'd waited longer, if he'd married her and had kids, and then came out, he probably would have felt even worse about it."

"Oh," Riley said, understanding now.

"Then he said that letting myself be happy now, being who I really am, doesn't have to mean I regret Maggie, or the amazing kids we raised. People might think it does, or that I'm freeing myself from my family, but it doesn't matter what they think. Because I'm not. I would never do that. I wouldn't want to."

"I know," Riley said quietly.

"But," Adam continued, "I think I've been caring too much about it seeming that way. Maggie has been seeing someone for a while now, but I've been...stuck. I live in the same neighborhood—which I don't mind, I do like being close to Maggie and the kids, but it's probably not necessary. Honestly, we barely see the kids these days, either of us. But it felt like, if I really do this, if I fully come out and, I don't know, move downtown to a swanky condo, and live my new gay life, I'll look like an asshole."

"To who?"

Adam sighed. "I don't even know. I just don't want that gossip, y'know? Did you hear Adam Sheppard left his family and now he's having gay orgies every night in his penthouse?"

Riley's eyebrows shot up. "Every night?"

Adam laughed. "I'd take Mondays off, probably."

Riley snorted. "Maybe there's something between living next door to your ex-wife and nightly penthouse orgies." He glanced at Adam and saw him smiling as he stared straight ahead.

"Maybe," Adam said.

Chapter Twenty-Five

"Did Toronto win?" Riley asked as he returned from upstairs.

"They did," Adam said, and set his phone on the coffee table. "I told you it was just nerves. They've got this." He stood from where he'd been sitting on the couch. The living room was dimly lit by a single table lamp, and Lucky was asleep on his bed in the corner. The room felt very peaceful and cozy.

Riley still looked incredible. He'd removed his jacket, and now wore only a snug black T-shirt, tucked into those sexy pants. His hair glowed like embers in the golden lamplight.

"So," Adam said. He bounced on his toes, once, then commanded his body to be cool.

Riley crossed the room to the record player and crouched to flip through his LP collection. He selected something, then put it on the turntable. Adam waited, wondering if he should sit again. Wondering what would happen next.

A few seconds later, soft, twangy guitar began playing, followed by a female voice that Adam recognized but couldn't place. Not Dolly.

Riley set the album sleeve on the coffee table. Emmylou Harris. Right. He'd gone with Riley to see her perform once, in Toronto. Riley had been mesmerized by her, and Adam had been mesmerized by him.

"I remember that show," Adam said. "When we went."

Riley smiled. "I loved that night."

"Me too." Then, feeling brave, Adam extended his hand. "Dance with me?"

"Dancing is not one of my gay superpowers," Riley warned, even as he tugged Adam closer.

"Riles, I don't care. I'm just trying to get your hands on me."

Riley laughed, and now they were so close that Adam could feel his breath on his temple. "How's this?" He placed one of his giant hands on Adam's hip, and tangled the fingers of his other hand together with Adam's.

Adam closed his eyes. "Perfect."

They didn't do much more than slowly rotate together in the space between the coffee table and the record player, but Riley was nuzzling Adam's hair, making Adam's heart race and his legs melt. He wanted to respond somehow, without it being too much, so he let his hand slide up Riley's back, on top of his T-shirt, following his spine until he could press his palm against the back of Riley's neck. He was being so careful, knowing that Riley needed to be the one to ask for more, but trying to make it clear that the answer would be yes.

Then Riley dipped his fingertips under the hems of Adam's sweater and undershirt. Adam shivered as Riley teased the skin he found there with exhilarating featherlight touches. *"Keep going,"* Adam wanted to say. *"You can touch me anywhere."*

"Shep," Riley whispered. He kissed Adam's forehead, then the knuckles of the hand he held.

"Yes," Adam replied, as if there'd been a question. He kissed Riley's temple and waited.

Riley exhaled, then kissed behind Adam's ear, and then

again. The second time, his tongue flicked against the sensitive skin there, making Adam shiver again.

Riley pulled back, but only enough so their gazes could meet. His gray eyes didn't hold the exhaustion or sadness Adam had seen in them all week. Instead they were intense, and questioning.

"Tell me what you're thinking," Riley said, his gaze already dropping to Adam's lips.

"That I want to get this right," Adam whispered back.

Riley let go of his hand, but only so he could press his palm to Adam's face. "This feels right to me."

The first brush of Riley's lips made Adam gasp, and then, to cover it, he let out a nervous puff of laughter. Riley laughed too, then tried again. This time, they connected, soft and careful, like they were doing something dangerous. Then Riley's fingers dug into Adam's hip as he angled his head and kissed Adam like he meant it. He tasted like toothpaste, and Adam wished he'd also brushed his own teeth when they'd gotten back but he also didn't care because he was *kissing Riley*. And it did feel right. It felt so fucking right and wonderfully simple but also like the most amazing thing to ever happen.

He tightened his hold on Riley's neck, maneuvering him where he wanted him. Riley growled into his mouth and pressed his fingertip into the hinge of Adam's jaw, opening him wider as the kiss grew hungrier. No one had ever kissed Adam the way Riley always had, with this fierce desire mixed with wonder.

He cataloged everything that was new: Riley's beard, soft against Adam's skin, the scent of the fancy grooming products Riley used now, the confidence in the way Riley handled him. Adam loved all of it, like he loved this beautiful room that Riley had created and had invited Adam into and now was kissing him in.

Riley tugged at his hair, pulling Adam's head back as he took his mouth again. Adam had always loved that Riley was taller than him, not by enough to make kissing awkward, but enough to make Adam feel surrounded by him.

Distantly, Emmylou Harris kept singing. Riley kissed along his jaw, making Adam lose what was left of his mind. "God," he rasped as he fought to keep himself still. He was so hard already and was desperate to grind himself shamelessly against Riley. He needed Riley to be the one to escalate things, if he wanted.

Riley slid his hand off Adam's hip and onto his ass, urging Adam's hips to come forward.

"Fuck, Shep," Riley said in a low voice when their erections bumped together.

Adam rolled his hips without meaning to and groaned with how good it felt. It had been a long time since he'd had sex with anyone, and it had been an eternity since it had been with Riley.

To his relief, Riley began moving too. He took his mouth again, kissing Adam deeply and swallowing his moans as they ground together. They were both fully clothed and standing and barely doing anything, but Adam had never felt so turned on in his life. He was shaking with need.

A thumb stroked over Adam's cheek, soothing him. "What do you want?"

God, what a question. He tried to think, but couldn't. He felt like he might start crying. He didn't think he'd have this again. He wanted to believe he'd earned it, but had he?

Lucky woofed quietly in his sleep, which made both of them laugh.

"Maybe we should go upstairs," Riley said, then kissed the corner of Adam's mouth.

"Yeah."

They didn't move right away, choosing instead to kiss some more, but without the grinding. Adam ran his fingers over Riley's beard, getting to know it. He wondered if Riley's body hair looked the same as it had before. He wanted to find out.

With effort, he pulled away. "Upstairs," he said.

They climbed the stairs, not bothering to turn off the lamp or the record player. They kissed in the hall at the top of the stairs, Adam against the wall. He pressed his thigh against Riley's cock, and Riley groaned, rocking against it as their kisses turned messy. He wanted to let Riley keep going like that, and loved knowing that he was just as excited as Adam was.

"Fuck," Riley said as he gently pushed Adam away. "Bed. Now."

Finally, they were in Riley's bedroom, and for an awkward moment after Riley turned on a lamp, neither of them seemed to know what to do.

"Should I...?" Adam asked as he tugged at the hem of his own sweater.

Riley nodded, his eyes dark and his lips slack and swollen.

Adam pulled his sweater off, then, after only a moment of hesitation, he removed the T-shirt he'd been wearing underneath. Riley watched him with keen interest.

Adam brushed a nervous hand over his soft belly. "Not the same as you remember, probably."

"It's better," Riley said.

"Come on."

Riley stepped toward him. "It's better," he repeated.

Adam reached for him. "That's nice of you to say."

Riley ran a hand down Adam's right side. "You're so sexy, Shep. It's fucking ridiculous."

Adam tipped his head back as Riley kissed along his jaw. "You know," he said breathlessly, "I like it when you call me Adam."

Riley paused. "Yeah?"

"Everyone calls me Shep. Everyone from hockey, anyway. Adam sounds...special. At least when you say it."

"Adam," Riley said, then began kissing Adam's throat. "Call me Riles."

"But you said—"

"Forget what I said. I like it. I hadn't heard it in a long time, before you got here."

That made Adam smile. "Riles," he said, "take your shirt off."

Riley did, and Adam's mouth went dry. His chest was still broad and strong, and the hair there was as perfect as it had always been: dark and coppery, and heavier between his pecs. His waist was trim, possibly even more so than when he'd played hockey, and his arms were ridiculous.

He also had a tattoo of a ship on his right bicep. Like a sailor.

"You have a tattoo," Adam said.

Riley touched it as if this was news to him. "Oh, that. Yeah, I was not sober when I got that."

Adam leaned in to inspect it. It looked very old-school, a tall ship with sails—a frigate?—breaking through some waves. No color, just slightly faded black line art.

"Did you get this...at sea?" Adam teased.

"No. Shut up. I got it in Dallas. I missed Nova Scotia or something. Who knows."

"Nova Scotia...two hundred years ago?"

"Would you shut the fuck up about it, please?" Riley's voice was gruff, but he was smiling, and the combination made Adam very aroused.

"Aye, aye," Adam said, then winked.

Riley stepped into him. "You're such a dick," he said, then kissed him like he was starving for it. They kissed like that for a long time, taking breaks only long enough to take a breath before catching each other's eye and diving in again. It was like, now that they'd started, they'd never be able to stop kissing each other.

Eventually, Adam dipped his head to kiss and lick at Riley's neck and to nuzzle his beard. Riley stroked his back, his touch light and curious, as if he was relearning Adam's body. It felt electric.

Riley sat on the edge of the bed and pulled Adam into his lap. Adam straddled him as they kissed some more, and explored his chest with his hands, which Riley seemed to love. When Adam lightly pinched Riley's left nipple, Riley sucked in a breath, and then laughed.

"Good?" Adam asked.

"Yeah. Fuck. Keep doing that."

Adam did, kissing him and pinching his nipples until Riley was grinding up against him. Then Riley fell back on the mattress, and Adam followed him down. He started kissing Riley's chest, capturing one stiff nipple between his teeth.

"Yes," Riley said on an exhale. He rolled his hips again.

"Fuck, that feels good," Adam rasped.

Riley let out a shaky laugh. "It feels too good."

"I'm, uh. I'm pretty keyed up here," Adam confessed. "It's been a while."

He only had a split second to see Riley's smile before they crashed together again. They moaned into each other's mouths as their hips found a rhythm.

"We should—*fuck*—I need to take my pants off, Adam."

Adam rolled off of him, and they both scrambled out of their pants and socks. Riley left his underwear on—boxer briefs in a vibrant floral print—so Adam did too.

"I like these," Adam said as he gently tugged Riley's waistband. They were both on their knees on the bed, facing each other.

"I like this," Riley replied, running a thumb over the bulge in Adam's black briefs.

Adam sucked in a breath. "Fuck."

Riley did it again and then leaned in to kiss Adam again. He cupped Adam in his enormous hand and began massaging him through his underwear as they kissed. Adam rocked helplessly against his palm as he lost the ability to kiss with any kind of finesse.

"Can I," Adam panted, "touch you?"

In response, Riley took hold of Adam's wrist and guided his hand to his cock. They both groaned when Adam made contact. Adam could think of so many things he wanted to do to Riley's cock, but he was in real danger of coming before he could do any of them.

"So good," Riley said.

"Yeah," Adam agreed, because it was good. It was fucking perfect.

Still kissing, Riley guided him down until Adam was on his back. Adam wrapped his legs around Riley's hips, pulling him closer as he ground against him.

"What do you want?" Riley murmured against his lips.

"Just keep kissing me. Don't stop."

Riley moaned. "I might come," he warned.

That sent a jolt through Adam's whole body. "Y-you wouldn't be alone if you did."

"Fuck, Adam." Riley moved faster against him.

"Can I—?"

Riley didn't need further explanation. He reached between them and tugged Adam's waistband down, and then his own, just enough to free their erections. They both moaned in relief, and then with pleasure as their bare cocks slid together.

They gave up on kissing in favor of panting against each other. "Don't stop," Adam pleaded mindlessly.

"I won't," Riley promised. "But you've gotta—*ah*—you've gotta hurry."

"I'm right there. Holy." Adam fumbled for Riley's hand, needing an anchor. Riley grabbed it and held him tight as Adam began to shatter apart. "Yes. Fuck. Gonna come."

He dug the fingers of his free hand into Riley's back as he came, shooting hard against Riley's stomach. Distantly, he heard Riley grunt, and then he felt the hot bursts of his release against his skin.

"Fucking hell," Adam said hoarsely.

Riley laughed, then kissed his chin. "Yeah." He rolled off of him and lay on his side next to Adam.

"I'm a mess," Adam said.

"Mm." Riley dragged a finger lazily through the come on Adam's chest. "You sound the same as you used to. When you come."

Adam covered his face with his forearm. "Oh god."

"No. I like it. It's…nice."

Adam removed his arm. "The way I sound when I come is *nice*?"

Riley ducked his head shyly. "The way it made me feel is nice. I missed it."

Adam's heart somersaulted. "Oh." He wished he'd been paying closer attention to Riley's orgasm. Next time, he promised himself. Because surely there would be one, right?

Riley kissed his forehead. "I'll be right back."

He left the bed and headed for the door, removing his underwear on the way. Adam got his first look at Riley's ass in years, and he was not disappointed.

He gazed up at the wood ceiling beams and smiled. He felt dangerously, deliriously happy, and he hoped Riley felt the same way.

Riley returned in a minute with a damp cloth, and wearing, to Adam's delight, a silk floral-print robe that hit Riley about midthigh.

"What?" Riley asked when he noticed Adam staring.

"I was hoping you'd still be naked but, uh. I like this better."

Riley ran a hand over the robe. "Yeah?"

"It's fucking sexy, Riles. Come here."

Riley smiled as he approached the bed. He cleaned Adam quickly, then let Adam pull him down for a kiss.

"You love beautiful things," Adam murmured as he slid a hand up Riley's thigh.

"I do," Riley agreed as he gazed into Adam's eyes.

"I want you to have every beautiful thing."

"I don't need everything."

Adam swore the unsaid words were there, lingering in the inches between them: *I just need you.* He almost said them himself because he felt them with his whole body.

"I can stay, right?" Adam asked. "I can sleep with you?"

Riley brushed his fingers through Adam's hair. "You always could have."

"I wish I had." Christ, they'd lived alone. What had Adam been so scared of?

Riley kissed him. The silk felt like cool water against Adam's heated skin. "Stay," Riley said.

Chapter Twenty-Six

Riley woke the next morning with Adam Sheppard in his arms.

He'd thought, as he'd drifted off to sleep last night, that he may feel overwhelmed in this moment. Maybe he'd even start panicking or spiraling or be taken on some other involuntary emotional adventure. He'd never been good at navigating highs or lows.

Instead, with his body curled around Adam's, his arm draped across Adam's chest, both men completely naked, Riley only felt wonderfully, uncomplicatedly calm.

Adam was lying on his good shoulder, his back to Riley. The bad shoulder was close to Riley's lips, so he kissed it, very gently. Last night had been perfect in so many ways. He'd loved introducing Adam to his friends, and he'd loved Adam being brave enough to come out to a room full of near strangers simply because they were people who were important to Riley.

And later, at home, dancing with Adam in his living room, holding him, kissing him. Then taking him to bed for sex that was, yes, not unlike the frantic rutting against each other that they used to rely on, but had also been so different from anything they'd done before. For the first time, there had been no signs of panic from Adam. They'd been able to take their time, to check in, and to enjoy the afterglow.

And now Adam was still here. Riley wanted to stay in bed all morning, but Lucky was pacing around downstairs and needed to be let outside. With a sigh and a final kiss to Adam's shoulder, Riley dragged himself out of bed.

Outside, he whistled the Emmylou Harris song he had danced to with Adam. He smiled at the hyacinths beside his deck that were just about to bloom. He smiled at the sunny sky. He smiled at Lucky inspecting the yard. He smiled while he cleaned up after Lucky. A few days ago he'd thought he would never smile again, and now he couldn't stop. He knew it was temporary, but it felt so fucking good to be happy. Just like it had felt so fucking good to have Adam's hands on him, to kiss him, to lose himself in the rush of sex. He wanted to do it again.

Back inside, he gave Lucky his food, then hurried back upstairs. Adam was sitting up in bed, hair disheveled.

"Hi," Adam said. He blinked, and for a moment he looked confused. "I thought you'd left."

"I was just letting Lucky out. I'm back now." Riley climbed back on the bed and leaned into Adam. The bedsheet slipped, revealing Adam's erection. "That for me?" Riley asked, then kissed Adam as best he could. He really couldn't stop smiling.

"Riles, wait."

Riley's stomach dropped. This was it. This was when Adam would get weird about what they'd done. The thought hit him so forcefully, Riley almost scrambled off the bed and out of the room. Everything he'd been so happy about a moment ago crumbled apart.

Then Adam smiled. "Sorry. I just really need to pee."

"Oh," Riley said. Then, *"Oh."* He rolled off Adam, but still felt gripped by anxiety. Even as Adam kissed his cheek before leaving the bed, naked. Even as Adam gave his ass a playful wiggle before he left the room.

Riley exhaled into the empty room. Things were going to be okay. Adam was still here, and he still wanted Riley.

He'd settled himself by the time Adam returned. Now Riley could fully appreciate how stunning Adam looked, naked in the morning sunshine.

"I feel like either I should put clothes on, cr you should take clothes off," Adam said. He stood beside the bed, hands on his hips, and his cock mostly soft now.

Riley removed the sweats he'd pulled on to go outside. "Better?"

"Unless you want to put that hot little silk robe on again."

"You liked that, did you?" Riley had never known Adam to wear anything but drab, conservative colors. He wondered if his clothing choices had been motivated by fear too. Maybe Adam secretly wanted to drape himself in splashy flowers and jewel tones.

"Mm." Adam planted one knee on the bed, then leaned in to kiss him. "I like you in anything."

Riley was so relieved by the kiss that he let out a deranged-sounding giggle. Adam pulled back. "You all right?"

"Yeah, I'm good. I'm good. I'm just… I don't know. Never mind." He tried to kiss Adam again, but Adam pulled back farther.

Riley closed his eyes, but opened them again when Adam placed a hand on the side of his face. "Hey," Adam said gently.

Riley blinked and swallowed. He was pretty sure he was trembling. Fuck, he wished he could process a single emotion without feeling like he was going to explode.

"I wish I didn't have to go to work today." It was the easiest thought he could share. Easier than *"I don't want you to leave,"* or, *"Does this end after you leave?"*

"I wish you didn't either," Adam said with a sympathetic smile. "It's okay, though. We have tonight. And…"

"And…" Riley smiled as Adam leaned in.

"We have right now," Adam said, then captured Riley's lips.

Riley fell back on the bed and pulled Adam on top of him. Adam laughed against his mouth, then kept kissing him. His lips were soft and he tasted like mouthwash. Riley's brain, never one to just enjoy a moment, tried to compare the way Adam kissed now to how he'd kissed *then*. In their twenties, Adam's kisses had always felt tinged with something: fear, or anger, or shame. But there'd also always been a hunger to them, something wild and desperate that Riley had fucking loved.

The way Adam was kissing him now—when both of their smiles were contained enough to actually kiss—was different. There was no fear, or anger, or shame. There was hunger, but it didn't feel like desperation. It felt like reverence.

Adam let out a grunt that didn't sound like pleasure. Carefully, Riley rolled them so Adam was on his back. Then he wedged a pillow under Adam's left shoulder.

"Good?" Riley asked.

"Yeah. Thanks. Come here."

Riley kissed him, taking control. They were both hard, but Riley was in no hurry as he explored Adam's mouth. Their hands were clasped together, next to Adam's head, and Riley used his other arm to prop himself up. Adam's left hand caressed Riley's lower back, making Riley's blood sing. He moaned as Adam kissed his neck, loving that Adam remembered how much Riley loved that.

Adam moaned too, and Riley realized Adam was thrusting against him. Riley raised his hips, just out of reach. "Be patient," he scolded.

"Why?"

"Because I want you to be patient."

Adam's eyes widened, and for a moment he stared at Riley, lips parted. Then he said, "Fuck, that's really hot."

Slowly, Riley lowered his hips until their cocks were touching again. "Are you going to behave?"

Adam smiled. "Is this what you're like in bed now? Bossy? I'm really into it."

Riley brushed his lips against Adam's ear. "You have no idea how much I wanted to boss you around in bed before."

Adam gasped, then said, "I'm an idiot."

Riley kissed behind his ear, then down the side of his neck, loving how Adam squirmed underneath him. He'd always been different with Adam than he'd been with other lovers. Timid, or maybe too overcome with gratitude whenever they'd had sex to push things. He did like being bossy in bed, though, and it was good to know that Adam might be into it.

He raised his head so he could admire Adam's face for a bit. "God, you're pretty," he murmured as he stroked Adam's lips with his thumb.

On the third pass, Adam captured his thumb in his mouth, and sucked.

"Mm," Riley rumbled. "Yeah. All right."

He dragged his wet thumb over Adam's chin, then began to kiss a trail down to his stomach.

Adam let out a shaky "Oh," when Riley kissed below his belly button.

"Yeah?" Riley asked.

"Yes," Adam said on exhale.

Riley gave the head of his cock a tender little kiss, greeting it like an old friend. "I always wanted to have you in the morning like this, Adam."

"You have me." Adam writhed as Riley licked at his leaking slit. "You have me, Riles."

They both groaned when Riley took him into his mouth.

Riley went slow, at first, simply because he could. He let all of his senses fill with Adam.

It didn't take long, once Riley really got going, to get Adam close to the edge. When Adam was reduced to whimpers and free-form profanity, Riley pulled off.

Adam groaned in frustration, which made Riley laugh. "You want me to finish you off, then?"

"Yes. No. Fuck, I don't know. Yes."

Riley kissed his stomach. "Pick one."

"I can't."

Riley raised his head and held Adam's gaze. Adam looked dazed, his eyes soft and so fucking pretty. Riley kissed him, slow and commanding, because, yeah, he was fucking bossy in bed. He kissed him and kissed him, and only when Adam starting whimpering did Riley begin a slow grind of his hips. He kept a steady, controlled pace, knowing it was making Adam lose his mind.

"Riles," Adam panted. "Please. Fuck. I need it."

"Oh, did you make a decision?"

"I—ah fuck—yes—"

"You want my mouth?" Riley's voice was shaky. He hadn't even realized he'd lost control of his slow, even thrusts. He was jerking his hips quickly, gliding his cock against Adam's and against Adam's stomach.

"Yeah…no. Fuck. No, it's too late. Keep going. I'm so close."

Riley went faster, shocked by how close his own release suddenly was. "Yeah. Fuck, Adam."

Adam shuddered beneath him, then came against Riley's stomach. Adam grabbed his face, surged up, and kissed him hard, and Riley moaned into his mouth.

"Fuck," Adam panted. "Let me." He pushed him to his back, then went to his knees between Riley's spread thighs.

Riley took a couple of deep breaths, trying to pull himself

back from the brink so he could enjoy this. Adam gazed up at the ceiling, then said, bizarrely, "This is a really nice room. I like the ceiling beams. And did you build the headboard?"

Riley huffed out a surprised laugh. "Are you serious right now?"

Adam smiled, then dipped his head low to kiss along Riley's shaft. Riley was already trembling by the time he began sucking him. Adam still wasn't the most skilled cocksucker in the world, but he didn't need to be. Not for Riley.

Fuck, did Adam really need to leave tomorrow? Could they spend every minute until then in this bed?

Adam found a rhythm that was absolutely working for Riley, and after a few short minutes he had to issue a warning. "Adam," he gritted out, his cock already swelling. "Now. Fuck."

His orgasm ripped through him, and Adam surprised him by staying on him, swallowing, and then sputtering, and then taking the last of it across his chin. It made Riley laugh, even as his body was still rocking with pleasure.

When it was over, Adam flopped on his back and wiped a hand over his mouth. "You sound the same," he said hoarsely.

Riley was still trying to catch his breath. "Yeah?"

"I'm still bad at swallowing, by the way."

That made Riley crack up, which made Adam crack up. When they finally calmed down, Riley said, "So you were asking about the headboard."

That set them off again. By the time they'd stopped laughing, they were both on their backs, boneless and breathing heavily.

"That was nice," Adam said.

Riley smiled at the ceiling. "It was."

Adam searched blindly for Riley's hand, found it, and held

it. "I wanted that too, by the way. All of it. The morning sex, sleeping together, taking our time. I wanted it so much."

Riley turned his head and looked at him, surprised. A jumble of emotions surged inside him, but the one that was in the lead was sympathy. He felt sorry for the scared young man Adam had been.

He squeezed Adam's hand. "Good to know."

Adam smiled, a bit sadly. "You would have been such a good boyfriend."

"I don't know. I was kind of a mess back then." He rolled his eyes. "Not like now."

Adam brought their joined hands to his lips and kissed Riley's knuckles. "We're all messes, Riles."

They showered together and kissed nearly the entire time. Then Riley made breakfast, and they kissed during most of that too. They kissed again for a long time when Riley was leaving the house, Lucky pacing impatiently outside.

"What do you have planned for today?" Riley asked, then kissed Adam's jaw.

"I'm helping Cathy set up for the banquet, but first I have some farewells to make."

Riley huffed. "Paula's?"

"Obviously."

Riley kissed him, then said, "If you need any sporting goods…"

Adam laughed. "You just want a cinnamon bun."

"I want to kiss you when you taste like cinnamon."

Lucky barked as if he was reminding Riley that they had somewhere to be.

"In a minute," Riley barked back. Then, to Adam, he said, "I'm going to leave now."

"Okay."

"Yeah."

And then he was kissing Adam against the doorframe, pressing their bodies together, wanting to dive inside of him and never think about anything else.

With an enormous amount of effort, Riley broke the kiss and staggered back a couple of steps. "Jesus," he said as he ran a hand though his own hair. "Okay. I'm going. I have to."

Adam nodded, his lips dark and wet, his hair a mess. He looked dazed and debauched and, god. How was Riley supposed to walk away from this?

He did, adjusting himself in his pants as he exited the house. "I'll see you later," Adam called after him.

Riley waved as he got into his truck. Adam smiled at him from the front porch the entire time Riley backed out of the driveway. When he was on the road, and couldn't see Adam anymore, Riley exhaled and told Lucky, "It's going to hurt like hell when he leaves."

Chapter Twenty-Seven

Harvey Tuck's grave was easy to find; it was absolutely covered in flowers. The one next to Harv's belonged to a married couple, who Adam guessed were his parents. The thought crossed Adam's mind that Riley would be buried here someday. He pushed it away.

"Hi, Harv," Adam said. "I was at the funeral but I never got a chance to…" He scrunched his nose and tried to think of the least weird way to say what he meant. "As you can probably guess, your funeral was packed. I arrived right before it started and barely got a seat. And then, well, I kind of ran off. We don't need to get into it, but Riley wasn't thrilled to see me. Anyway. We've worked it out now."

Adam glanced around to confirm he was alone. He knew people talked to graves like this, but it still felt weird. And personal. He'd been lucky enough to have never lost anyone close to him before.

He blew out a breath and said, "Okay. A few things. First, I wanted to tell you that I always thought you were the best dad I've ever met. I was so jealous of Riley, having a dad like you. And I tried to—" Adam had to swallow hard. "Shit, okay. I tried to be the kind of dad you were. As soon as Maggie told me she was pregnant, I thought, 'I'm going to be like Harvey Tuck. My kids are going to get that kind of dad.'" Adam laughed. "Okay, my real first thoughts were 'Holy shit, pregnant? What are we going to do?' but once the shock wore off, I thought about what kind of dad I wanted to be."

Adam picked up a carnation that had fallen and tucked it randomly into one of the arrangements. "I'm not saying I succeeded. I try to be a good dad, but obviously I wasn't around all that much. And when I was around, I felt like an intruder, kind of. Maybe that was all in my head, though. Anyway, Maggie did a great job with them, and I didn't get in her way. So that's something."

"I also wanted to thank you for inviting me to stay with your family here during those summers, way back. Summers at home were never great for me, and I think you guessed that. Well, you met my parents. And, yeah, I could have fucked off to Italy or somewhere with some of the guys, but Riley never wanted to do that, so I didn't want to either." He huffed out a sardonic laugh. "Probably should have figured that meant something but, you know. Hockey IQ doesn't translate to the real world, unfortunately."

"Which, um, yeah. I also want you to know that I love your son." He glanced up at the sky, then back at the tiny temporary grave marker poking through the flowers. "I don't know how you feel about that. Maybe you don't think I deserve him, after everything, and I get that. I made a lot of mistakes with him, but I've been trying to fix them. I want to deserve him."

Riley had probably never told his parents much about Adam, but Harv had been a perceptive man. "I'm going to do my best to deserve him, from now on. I don't know what our future looks like, but if there's a chance we can be together, I'm going to fight for that."

Adam had to blink a few times to stop his vision from blurring. "I promise I won't hurt him again, and I'm sorry I did before. He deserves to be so happy, and I hope I can give him that."

He let out a shaky laugh, then said, "So all of that is just to say, yeah. Good job on raising Riley. And Lindsay, because she's awesome. They were lucky to have you, and I know you're proud of them both."

"Oh, and I'm hosting the hockey banquet tonight. Maybe you heard, I don't know. I've got big shoes to fill, though." He laughed again. "I'm actually nervous about it. Although the kids probably just see me as the opening act for pizza. I'm sure it'll be fine."

Adam felt good about hosting the banquet. He liked having a chance to honor Harv in some small way and to help out the town Harv had loved so much. The town that Adam loved too.

"I didn't bring flowers, but I thought you might like this." He pulled the moon snail shell he'd found on the beach out of his coat pocket, then placed it at the edge of all the flowers. "It's pretty, right?" He hoped it wasn't a weird thing to leave.

"Okay, well. Susan said you'll probably be in the room at the banquet, so see you tonight, I guess. But if you decide to skip it in favor of, I don't know, playing a game of pickup with a bunch of NHL legends in Heaven, I don't think anyone would blame you."

Adam gave an awkward wave. "Bye, Harv."

Riley still could barely believe what he was witnessing.

Adam Sheppard was standing at a podium in front of a yellow-and-black balloon arch, next to a screen that displayed a slideshow of photos from the most recent Avery River Minor Hockey season. He was wearing his glasses and reading the achievements of various teams and players with the same amount of grandeur someone might use in a speech for a Hockey Hall of Fame induction.

"Brady Mosher not only led his team in goals this season, he not only led the *league* in goals this past season, he set a new *record* for goals scored by a U13 player in the entire North Shore hockey system!" Massive cheers and applause broke out, and Adam applauded along with them. "That's right. We are in the presence of greatness tonight. And Brady, that's why you've been named the U13 MVP for this season. Come on up here, hotshot."

Adam maintained this level of enthusiasm and awe for even the youngest house league players who could barely skate. It was sweet, and the kids were clearly loving it. Even from his seat at the back of the room, next to Mom, Riley could see that. This would be a memory these kids would have for the rest of their lives. And Riley didn't think he'd be forgetting it anytime soon himself.

Because Adam was doing this. For Dad, for him, for kids he didn't even know, for Riley's hometown. Tomorrow he'd be back in Toronto, but tonight he was here. And later tonight, if Riley had anything to say about it, he'd be in Riley's bed.

"He's wonderful," Mom whispered.

"Yeah," Riley agreed. "He is."

Cathy had said a few words about Dad at the start of the banquet, and that had been emotional. But Adam had done an excellent job bringing the mood back up and making the night about the kids. Dad would have approved.

After the awards were all given out, Adam announced that pizza was available in the adjoining room. This led to a stampede of kids charging out of the banquet room, except for the ones who charged up to Adam for a photo and an autograph. Riley stood, but stayed at the back of the room.

"I'm going to see if they need help managing those kids," Mom said.

"Okay. I'll be over there in a minute." He didn't take his eyes off Adam.

It was probably twenty minutes before Adam was finally alone and noticed Riley at the back of the room. He smiled and walked toward him. When he reached him, he pretended to wipe his brow. "Phew, I got through it okay, I think."

"You were awesome," Riley assured him. He took Adam's hand, and leaned in slightly before he realized where they were. He released his hand and stared awkwardly over Adam's shoulder. "Um. Yeah. Good job."

"Thanks." Adam took a step closer. "Actually, would you mind giving me a hand with something?"

"Sure. Of course."

He followed Adam out of the room and down the hall. The top floor of the rink housed the banquet room, a smaller meeting room, a few offices, and a storage room. Adam led him to the storage room.

"I was getting stuff from here earlier with Cathy," Adam explained.

"And what do you need now?" Riley asked as the door closed behind them.

"This." Adam lunged at him, kissing him hungrily against the door.

Riley huffed out a laugh, even as he kissed him back. It was pitch-black in the room, but he didn't need to see. He grabbed at Adam's shirt, his face, his neck, his ass, wanting to hold all of him. He loved that Adam had been wanting him as much as he'd wanted Adam during that long banquet. Riley kissed his throat, making Adam moan more loudly than was safe. They probably shouldn't be doing this at all. Not here.

"God, Riles," Adam groaned, just in case anyone who might be listening needed to know exactly who was making out in here.

"Shh," Riley said, but even that sounded comically loud. They both started laughing.

"We're going to get in trouble," Adam whispered against his ear.

Any blood that wasn't already in Riley's cock rushed there at those words. "God," he rasped. "Shut up."

Adam was rock-hard too, and Riley really wanted to do something about it, but that was a line he wasn't willing to cross at a youth hockey banquet in his hometown arena.

"We gotta stop," Riley panted against Adam's mouth after another bone-melting kiss.

"Mm," Adam agreed, then kissed him again. He rocked his hips against Riley and pressed a thigh between Riley's legs.

"Oh, fuck," Riley gasped. It was so easy to rut against Adam's muscular thigh as he lost himself in the heat of Adam's mouth. The darkness elevated every sensation, and he knew he could easily come from this. Might possibly come from this in just a few seconds.

He forced himself to stop. "We can't. Later, okay? Fuck. *Fuck.*"

Adam stopped and took a step back. "Yeah. Okay." For a long moment, they both breathed heavily in the dark. Riley tried to think of *anything* that might make his dick soft. He could *not* go back out there like this.

"My *mom* is here," Riley said.

Adam laughed. "Okay, yeah. That's helping. Keep talking."

"Um… Bridgeman! Remember that guy?"

"Tyson Bridgeman? Ugh."

Tyson had easily been one of the worst teammates they'd had. Loud and hateful, he'd also had some of the worst hygiene habits Riley had ever witnessed. "He accused me of being gay because I flossed my teeth."

Adam scoffed. "Is washing your hands gay too? Because he never did that either."

"Probably. And I'm guessing being good at hockey was also gay."

Adam laughed, and it sounded like he'd taken another step or two away from Riley. "He was garbage." He exhaled loudly, then said, "Okay. I think I'm presentable."

Riley quickly adjusted his own wilting erection. "Same. I hope so, at least."

They both laughed because it was ridiculous, being in their forties and making out in a storage closet. But Adam was leaving tomorrow, and Riley was feeling a little reckless.

He opened the door and made sure the coast was clear before they stepped into the hallway.

"Oh, man," Adam said. "You look like you were getting groped in a closet."

Riley glanced down at his clothes, then at Adam. "So do you." Adam's hair was a mess and his shirt was close to being untucked. His lips were swollen and his cheeks were pink, and Riley hoped he didn't look quite as ravished.

"Here," Adam said, and began smoothing out Riley's hair with his hands.

"We're too old for this," Riley said as he attempted to make his shirt look less rumpled.

"I don't ever want to be too old for this." Adam's eyes were glinting with joy and mischief, and Riley wanted to haul him right back into the storage room.

"Oh, there you are," said Cathy's voice from behind them.

Riley closed his eyes, as if that might make him disappear.

"Hey, Cathy," Adam said smoothly. "Need help with something?"

"No, no. It's just that Warren was hoping to talk to you for a minute. He writes local news stories for CBC. Is that okay?"

"No problem. I hope he's in the pizza room because I'm starving."

Cathy smiled. "I'll tell him to meet you there. And Adam, you did such a great job tonight. We really can't thank you enough. Wasn't he great, Riley?"

"He was."

"Can we book you for next year?" Cathy laughed and briefly placed a hand on Adam's arm. "I'm just kidding."

Adam looked at Riley. "I might be available."

Riley bit the inside of his cheek to keep himself from grinning like a lovestruck fool.

Chapter Twenty-Eight

"Am I a bear?" Adam asked out of nowhere as they drove home after the banquet.

Riley glanced over from the driver's seat, then back at the road. "No."

"Oh. Are *you* a bear?"

"I wouldn't say so, no."

"You have a beard."

"I think it takes more than that."

Adam was silent a moment, then said, "Tom is a bear, right? Darren's husband?"

"Yes."

"Okay, yeah. That makes sense."

"Why are you interested in bears all of a sudden?"

"I'm not. I just find so many things confusing. What would you say I am then?"

"An idiot," Riley said fondly.

"Come on."

"Do you want to know which theme nights to go to when you're back in Toronto or something?"

"Sure, okay. Which ones should I go to?"

"Whichever ones you want. Depends on what you're into, and how you self-identify."

Adam was quiet another moment, then said, "Which ones do you go to?"

"I rarely get the chance. I went to a cowboy-themed night once in Montreal, and I've been to a few jock nights."

"Is that jock as in…"

"Both. Sporty dudes and dudes wearing jocks. Mostly sporty dudes wearing jocks."

"Did you wear a jock?"

Riley smiled at the windshield. "Maybe."

"Fuck," Adam muttered. "Wish I'd seen that."

"I was wearing pants over it. I'm not that bold."

"Still…"

Riley slowed the truck and pulled into his driveway.

"Do you still own a jock?" Adam asked as he exited the truck.

"Maybe," Riley said again, then closed the driver side door behind him. The noise echoed in the quiet night.

"I haven't actually been to a gay bar yet," Adam said.

"No?"

"I almost went once. A few months ago—holy shit. Look at the stars."

The night was chilly but clear, and the moon was still a sliver; ideal conditions for stargazing. Riley walked up behind Adam and wrapped his arms around him. "You'd do well in a gay bar. You'd turn every head."

Adam tilted his head back. "You think?"

"I know." He kissed Adam's hair. "You'd have your pick."

Adam tilted his head, and Riley accepted the invitation to kiss his neck. Adam squirmed happily in his arms, then said, "I'd like to go to one with you."

Riley didn't think he'd like watching Adam pick up other

men, and he was scared to hope that wasn't what Adam meant. He kissed behind Adam's ear and waited for more information.

"They could all watch me leave with you," Adam said.

Riley's heart sped up. "Yeah?"

Adam turned in Riley's arms. "No one else would even come close." They kissed, slowly this time, not like the fevered kisses in the storage room. This was careful and quiet, as if they might disturb the silent beauty around them if they rushed. It was, Riley thought, possibly the most romantic moment of his life.

But the night *was* very cold, so after a few more minutes, they went inside. Lucky greeted them enthusiastically as they removed their shoes and coats.

"Hey, buddy," Adam said as he scratched Lucky's ears. "I know you were worried, but I think the banquet went okay."

"I think the town might elect Shep mayor," Riley added.

"Does this town have a mayor?"

"Nah. There's a county mayor. But you could probably have that job too if you asked for it."

"Sounds like a lot of paperwork."

"Mm."

"But I could see some perks too." Adam attacked him with one of his winks.

"Yeah?" Riley put a hand on Adam's hip and guided him closer.

"I'd probably have to test the quality of the fried seafood pretty regularly," Adam mused. "Y'know. As mayor."

"Very important."

"And I could create a new holiday where you just make out with a handsome shop owner all day."

"Got your eye on Allan at the hardware store, do you?"

Adam laughed. "I could make you my deputy."

"No thanks."

"Special advisor?"

"Nope." Riley kissed just under Adam's jaw, which made Adam gasp.

"Come on," Adam said shakily. "I need someone to tell me important stuff. Like what the name of the county is."

Riley chuckled against Adam's throat, then kissed a trail down to his shoulder.

Lucky wedged his way between their legs, tail knocking against Riley's shin. "Go to bed, Lucky," Riley said between kisses.

Lucky sighed heavily but obeyed.

"Maybe we should go to bed too," Adam suggested. His pulse was racing against Riley's lips, and his cock was straining against the front of his pants. Riley wanted to sink to his knees right here, but Lucky was making things weird.

"Yeah. Okay."

Adam practically ran up the stairs, which made Riley laugh.

Riley took his time downstairs, watering a couple of plants and turning off lights. All he could think about all night was taking Adam to bed, but now that the moment was here, he was anxious. He didn't even know why; they'd had sex twice in the past twenty-four hours, and both times had been incredible. Everything he'd ever wanted, really. And maybe that was the problem: when things were good, Riley's guard went up.

He filled two water glasses and brought them upstairs with him. Adam was sitting on the edge of the bed, wearing only a pair of black boxer briefs and palming the bulge of his erection.

"Oh," Riley said.

Adam's lips tilted into the sexiest smile Riley had ever seen. "Thought I was gonna have to do this myself."

Riley set the water glasses on the dresser. "Nope." He took his shirt off, then popped the button open on his jeans.

"Come here," Adam said. He spread his legs wide, inviting Riley to step into them.

And yeah. Okay. Maybe this could be easy. Maybe Riley could let himself have this without overthinking it.

Adam greeted Riley by kissing his stomach, then again and again. Gentle kisses with electric little flicks of tongue that were making Riley crazy.

"God, you're fucking sexy, Riles," Adam said as he slowly pulled Riley's zipper down. He kissed his cock through his underwear as he pushed Riley's jeans down to his thighs. "You smell so good." He began to mouth at Riley's erection, his breath hot against the damp cotton. Riley tilted his head back and groaned.

Adam kept going until the front of Riley's briefs were soaked and his cock was dying to be released. "Come on," Riley complained.

"Tell me what to do," Adam said. "Get bossy with me."

Riley sucked in a breath. "Take my dick out and suck it then, superstar."

Adam gaped for a moment, then whispered, "Shit. Okay."

Riley grunted in relief as his cock was freed from the wet fabric, then grunted again as he sank into the wet heat of Adam's mouth. Within seconds, every bad feeling that lived inside Riley drifted away as he lost himself in pleasure. He kept himself still, letting Adam set the pace.

"That's good. That's perfect," Riley said.

Adam hummed around him in reply.

Riley stroked his cheek. "You think maybe you wanna fuck me tonight?"

A moan this time, and then Adam pulled off. He gazed up

at Riley with those gorgeous eyes and said, "Or you could fuck me."

Riley's heart stopped. "You serious?" They'd never even come close to that before. Adam's ass had always been, as far as Riley had been able to tell, off-limits.

"I'm really fucking serious. I want you to fuck me, Riles."

"Have you…?"

Adam shook his head. "But I've been…practicing. With toys. I like it."

Well, there was an image. Riley needed a second to remember how to speak, then he said, "Yeah?"

Adam smiled at him. "Yeah."

In the next second, Adam was flat on his back, Riley on top of him, kissing him and kissing him. They stayed like that for a while, making out and grinding against each other, until finally Riley said, "Lie on your stomach. Gonna get you ready."

"Okay, but hurry," Adam said as he rolled over.

Adam's ass was still incredible, thick with muscle and lightly dusted with dark hair. "Don't worry," Riley said as he palmed one of Adam's ass cheeks and squeezed, "you're going to like this part."

He draped himself over Adam, kissing his shoulder, then the back of his neck, then kissed a trail down his spine. He kissed one ass cheek, then the other, then spread those cheeks wide.

"Oh god," Adam whimpered. "Yes. Please." He bent his knees slightly, raising himself up in offering to Riley.

It was so hard to believe this was real. It was much easier to believe it was a fantasy, or a wonderful dream that Riley would wake up frustrated from. It certainly wouldn't be the first time.

Adam jolted when Riley flicked his tongue against his hole, but then he moaned when Riley did it again. "Holy. Fuck. Riles, that's—yes. Keep doing that."

Had no one ever done this to Adam before? If not, then what a waste. Riley would happily do this for hours, listening to Adam's blissed-out noises while feeling his hole relax against his tongue.

"That's it," Riley murmured after a few minutes. "Let me in."

"Want you in me. Want it," Adam panted. His hips were grinding against the mattress and back against Riley's mouth.

Riley lightly swatted his ass. "Stop that. Be patient."

"Patience is overrated."

Riley laughed, then wriggled his tongue inside.

"Oh my fucking—what the fuck? That's so good."

Encouraged, Riley kept at it. He slipped a hand between Adam's legs and wrapped it around his hard cock, giving him a couple of strokes as a reward for staying still.

Adam hissed, then said, "Riles. Careful."

Riley let him go and pulled away from his hole with a parting kiss. "Already, huh?"

"Fuck you. You know how good that fucking feels."

"First time?"

"Yes. Obviously." Adam took a slow, deep breath, then exhaled. "I want to last for you."

Riley stroked Adam's back soothingly as he admired his ass. "What makes you think *I'll* last?"

Adam laughed. "Maybe it's not important."

Riley kissed between his shoulder blades. "Just a sec." He left the bed to retrieve the lube from his nightstand. His hand hovered over a second item. "I have condoms if you want. But you said you were on PrEP?"

"Yeah. And I got tested since my last time. It's up to you, but I'm good without a condom."

Riley shut the drawer. "Me too."

Adam rolled to his back. "Can we do it like this?"

"Better for your shoulder?"

"Yeah. And...I want to see you."

Riley melted a bit at that. "Okay."

He got to work, opening Adam up with his fingers.

"Oh fuck, that's nice," Adam said as he squirmed against the sheets. "Your fingers are so thick."

"You like being filled, huh?" Riley added a second finger. Then, needing to know, he asked, "Did you want this before? When we used to fuck? Did you wish you were under me?"

"I don't know," Adam rasped. "Probably. Yes. I was so fucking stupid."

"Not stupid," Riley corrected him. "Just scared. Are you scared now?"

"No," Adam said quickly. He met Riley's gaze, his eyes dark and fierce. "I'm not scared at all."

Riley swallowed and wished he could say the same. He was scared of what would happen tomorrow, when Adam left. He was scared it might break him.

"Stroke yourself," he instructed, forcing the dark thoughts away. "Get yourself close, then stop."

Riley sat back on his heels, between Adam's spread legs, and watched him. Adam was stunning like this, flushed and glistening with lube and sweat and saliva. His cock looked painfully hard, his balls heavy and tight, as he carefully jerked himself off.

"Just like that," Riley praised. "Beautiful."

"You're playing," Adam gritted out, "a dangerous game here."

Riley smiled, then added a third finger inside.

"Oh shit," Adam gasped. "Shit. Shit."

Riley cupped Adam's balls with his other hand and gave them a gentle squeeze. "Keep going."

Adam threw his head back on the pillow, his neck straining as he continued stroking his cock. "Please."

Riley pulled his fingers out. "You want it?"

"I want—yes. Oh! Oh fuck." Adam took his hand off his cock and groaned in frustration.

"You good?" Riley asked as he slicked his own cock with lube.

Adam flopped an arm over his eyes. "Give me a minute. That was way too close."

Riley stroked himself, watching the heavy rise and fall of Adam's chest, and admiring how tortured Adam's cock looked. Riley would bet he could blow on it right now and Adam would shoot off.

"Tell me when you're ready." Riley hoped he didn't sound as impatient as he suddenly felt. He'd been waiting so long for this moment.

Adam pulled his arm away so he could see again, and his gaze fell right to Riley's cock. "Oh wow."

"I'll go slow," Riley promised. "And we can stop anytime."

Adam nodded. "Okay."

Riley grabbed a pillow. "Lift up." He wedged it under Adam's hips. "That's better." He lined himself up. "Tell me to stop if you need to," he reminded him.

"I will."

Riley pushed against his entrance. "Try to relax for me."

Adam exhaled, and Riley pushed inside.

If Riley had thought Adam had overwhelmed him before, it was nothing compared to this moment. He watched in amazement as his cock slowly sank into Adam's—*Adam's!*—body.

Adam's eyes were squeezed shut, and he was biting his bottom lip hard. Riley stopped. "You okay?"

"I think. Yeah." He laughed nervously. "You're huge."

"I'm a pretty standard size."

"You *feel* huge. Keep going."

"You sure?"

"Keep. Going."

Riley pushed in farther. He wasn't sure how much longer he was going to be able to be the one in charge here. He could feel his brain breaking apart as he sank deeper. "God, Adam. So fucking good."

"Yeah," Adam panted. "Yeah."

Riley pulled out a bit, then pushed back in. Adam's eyes went wide with surprise, then he moaned out a string of profanity and slurred compliments. Riley smiled and did it again. He was going to make this so good for Adam. He knew he was good at topping—Adam had been one of the only men he'd ever bottomed for. Riley wasn't particular, but most of his partners wanted him to top. He'd never expected Adam to be one of them.

"You're so," Riley said as he gave Adam another slow thrust, "fucking beautiful."

"God, that's good. You're so good. So hot. Riles, please."

Riley went a little faster, a little harder. He planted a hand on the mattress, bracing himself so he could find a rhythm. He fucked Adam the way he'd always dreamed while Adam gazed at him with dazed wonder.

Riley pressed his lips tight together, scared of the truths that might rattle out of him.

I don't want you to leave.

I want to go with you.

I can't be without you again.

I love you so much. I never stopped. I couldn't stop.

He felt those words with every thrust.

Adam was stroking himself again, still gazing at Riley's face. "Riles," he said. Then repeated his name twice more. Riley loved hearing it. He never wanted to stop listening to a blissed-out Adam Sheppard chanting his name like a prayer.

"You gonna come?" Riley asked with effort. "Shit, Adam. I'm so close."

Adam answered his question by going rigid and coming all over his own chest. "Oh fuck. *Fuck.* Riles."

Riley lost all sense of rhythm after that, fucking Adam wildly as he drowned in pleasure. Then, like the sea being dragged back from the shore to form a monster wave, he shivered and braced for impact before being smashed apart. He exploded inside Adam with a choked howl of relief and ecstasy. It seemed to go on and on, delicious ripples rocking through him as he continued to lazily thrust. Now that he was finally inside Adam, he didn't want to leave.

He lowered himself carefully and kissed Adam until his dick softened and slipped out on its own. Then he sat back on his heels so he could admire the mess that was now Adam Sheppard.

Adam spread his arms wide on the mattress and smiled sleepily. "Gotta say, that was fucking great."

Riley smiled back at him. "The best."

"I probably need a shower."

"You look all right to me."

Adam laughed, then said, "Shower with me?"

"You just want someone else to do all the work scrubbing you down."

Adam closed his eyes, still smiling. "You made the mess."

Riley huffed. "Guess I've gotta clean it up then. Come on."

The shower was ninety-eight percent lazy kissing and two percent scrubbing, but they got the job done. Later, when they were back in bed, Adam tucked snugly under Riley's arm, Adam said, "Thank you. For doing that for me."

It took Riley a moment to understand what he was talking about. "It wasn't exactly a hardship, fucking you."

"I mean… I'm glad it was you. I needed to really trust the person who did that to me for the first time, so thank you."

Riley's brain told him two things at once: that it was really nice hearing Adam say that, and also that it might mean Adam was now ready to bottom his way through gay Toronto.

He pushed the second thought away and kissed Adam's temple. "I'm glad it was me too."

He wanted it to keep being him. He wished they had more time. He wished this could have happened during a better week, one where Riley wasn't choking on grief. A week when Adam could have seen him at his best, instead of his absolute worst.

But Adam *had* seen him at his worst, and he was in Riley's bed anyway.

Riley kissed his temple again. He hoped, if nothing else, he'd given Adam some good memories over the past couple of days. If this was where things had to end, then at least they could both move forward without the ghosts of the past haunting them.

As Adam fell asleep in Riley's arms, Riley let himself imagine a different future, where things didn't have to end. He thought about what that might look like, what he'd be willing to give up. He could be patient, he thought, if a life with Adam was the prize.

Chapter Twenty-Nine

"How long is the drive again?" Adam asked between kisses.

Riley smiled. "It's still about ninety minutes. Same as when you asked last time."

Adam sighed and slipped his hands under the hem of Riley's T-shirt. He was obsessed with Riley's stomach: the solid muscle, the soft skin, the sexy dip of his belly button. "What time is it now?"

"Almost ten. Your flight is at one. You need to leave."

They were in the kitchen, attempting to say goodbye for the second time today. The first time had been an hour ago, but then Adam had spotted a deer in the backyard, and Riley had found his excitement adorable. So they'd ended up blowing each other on the sofa. This time Adam had his coat on, and his suitcase beside him. This time it was real.

"Maybe there's a later flight," Adam murmured against Riley's neck. "Like, maybe one in October."

Riley laughed. "You have to see your doctor tomorrow."

"I guess."

"Your kids would miss you."

"I doubt it."

"You'd miss them."

Adam rested his forehead on Riley's shoulder. "I would. But I'll miss you too."

You could have had this, you idiot, he scolded himself. *This could have been your life.*

"Come on," Riley said gently. "Let's get you in the car."

He carried Adam's suitcase for him. Lucky was already outside and bounded over when he spotted them.

"Thanks for letting me stay with you, Lucky," Adam said as he rubbed Lucky's face with both hands. "You take care of Riles, okay?"

"He will," Riley assured him. "He's good at that."

Adam took a moment to admire the view of the ocean one more time. It was a beautiful sunny day, and the blue water sparkled like a tourism ad for Nova Scotia. A small boat sat right in the middle of the bay, and in the far distance, at the end of one arm of land, Adam could see the white lighthouse glinting in the sun.

"I won't be seeing much of this in Toronto," Adam said.

"You'll be able to get, like, Thai food, though," Riley pointed out.

Adam laughed, even though his eyes were starting to burn with tears. "Are you going to be okay, Riles?"

Riley shrugged. "I'll keep busy."

It wasn't an answer, but at least Riley wasn't lying to him. Adam took a steadying breath and asked the most important question. "So what now? For us, I mean."

"You go back to Toronto, and I stay here," Riley said. It was a brutal answer, but it was honest and, Adam suspected, careful.

Adam took his hand and turned slightly so he was facing him directly. He said, "I don't want to push you, but—" at the same time Riley said, "I can't—"

They both laughed nervously, then Adam said, gently, "You can't?"

Riley sighed. "Sorry. I just… I need time. I need to *think*."

"I get that," Adam said, even as his heart crumbled.

Riley stared at their joined hands. "The past few days have been so good. Like, so fucking good, Adam. But I'm still such a mess. I can't make big decisions right now."

"Sure," Adam managed. "Makes sense."

Riley raised his gaze to meet Adam's. "Tell me what you were going to say."

"Oh." Adam wasn't sure how to say it now. Would it be too much? He tried a watered-down version. "You're right. It's not a good time to jump into anything, but if you ever think maybe you'd like to…with me. Well, I can wait a really long time if that's something that might be on the table someday."

Riley's eyes softened. "I think it will be."

Adam blinked a few times, trying to unblur his vision. "But yeah. Until then, whatever you need."

"It's not just what I need. You need to think about what you want too. Look at that list of yours again, about coming out. Figure out a plan."

"I'll come out," Adam said quickly. Too quickly. "I'll tell the whole world if that's what you—"

Riley held up a hand. "I just think it's…safer if we don't make promises right now." A small, sad smile twisted his lips. "But thank you."

"I won't hurt you," Adam blurted out.

"Yeah. That's the kind of promise we shouldn't make. Not now." Riley's lips tilted into a shy smile. "But, um. Stay on me, okay?"

Adam exhaled in a relieved whoosh. "I'll text you when I get home. I'll call you. What's the number for your landline? I want to call you and know you're in your kitchen, talking to me on that adorable pink phone."

Riley's smile grew. "I'll text it to you." He tugged on Adam's hand and started walking toward the car. "Come on."

At the car, they kissed one more time. Adam rested a palm on Riley's cheek, against his soft beard. "This town loves you," he reminded him. "If you need help, ask for it, okay?"

"I will."

"I'll text you when I get to the airport. And when I get home."

"Thanks."

Adam opened the car door. He knew he shouldn't tell Riley he loved him, but he needed to say *something*. "Riles, I—I'm just really glad I came here. I'm glad we..." He stopped himself because the words were horribly inadequate. He tried again. "It was awful when you weren't in my life. I don't want to lose you again."

Riley's eyes glistened, then he looked away. "Fuck, Adam."

"I wanted you to know that. In case I haven't been clear."

Riley blew out a breath. "I'm glad you didn't listen when I told you to leave."

Adam smiled sadly and wished for the millionth time that he hadn't listened when Riley had pushed him away the first time, when he'd gone to Dallas. "This isn't the end," he promised. "I'll see you soon."

"Yeah. Okay. Go home and get that shoulder fixed."

Adam got into the driver's seat. "Goodbye, Riles."

"Bye, Shep. Drive safe. And, um, thank you. For everything this week."

Riley took a step back, and Adam closed the door. He waved one more time before he backed out of the driveway, and left Riley Tuck behind.

Chapter Thirty

"I got all your favorites," Adam said cheerfully. "Basil chicken, pad Thai with shrimp, mango salad, massaman curry." He snapped his fingers, "Oh, and the spicy fish one we liked last time. Remember?"

"Cool," Cole said disinterestedly as he opened the fridge. "Do you have Sprite?"

"Oh shoot," Adam said. "I forgot to get Sprite. Sorry, buddy."

Cole closed the fridge door with a heavy sigh. "Well, what *do* you have?"

"Um… I haven't really had a chance to go grocery shopping yet." Adam had only returned home from Nova Scotia last night.

"You can get groceries delivered, you know," said Lucy from one of the stools at Adam's kitchen island. "Like, everyone does that."

"I *know*," Adam said. "And you're right. I'll place a grocery order later. Sorry."

"It's fine," Lucy said, her gaze fixed on her phone. "I'm not hungry anyway."

"But I have all this Thai food…" Adam gestured to the two

large paper bags that had been delivered minutes before his kids had arrived.

"I don't really feel like Thai food," Lucy said.

"Me neither," said Cole. "Can we get a pizza?"

Adam knew his kids didn't behave like this with Maggie, and he knew they hadn't behaved like this before the divorce. This was punishment. "Come on," he said with a forced smile, "I'm not ordering a pizza. I got Thai food because I know you guys like it."

"You could have asked us what we wanted before you decided for us," Lucy said.

Adam's heart sank. "I wanted to surprise you."

Lucy didn't reply. Cole grumbled, "I wish you'd surprised us with pizza."

Adam couldn't fake the smile anymore. "I'm sorry about the food, but can't we have a nice meal together anyway? I haven't seen you guys for a while."

Neither kid replied.

"Are you seriously mad at me because I went away for, like, a week? I was at a funeral."

"You were away for a week?" Cole asked.

Lucy laughed, though it may have been at something on her phone.

"Yes," Adam said. "Didn't you get all my texts from Nova Scotia?"

"Oh yeah," said Cole.

"Who died?" Lucy asked, and because it was an actual question that showed some interest in Adam's life, he answered enthusiastically.

"A man named Harvey Tuck. He was my friend's dad, and he was a really great person. You probably don't remember Riley Tuck, my old teammate? He used to play with you when you were little."

"No," said Cole.

"Weird," said Lucy.

"Anyway, Harv was a pretty important guy in Avery River. Everyone loved him there."

"Wherever that is," Cole said.

"Nova Scotia! I told you."

Cole opened the fridge again. "Do you have iced tea?"

"No, I don't."

Cole closed the fridge. "God, this place sucks."

All right. That was enough. "What is your problem? Both of you."

Lucy put her phone down. "I don't know. Just…why do we still have to come here?"

Adam gaped for a moment, then said, "Because I'm *still* your dad?"

"Yeah, but coming here is weird and sad."

Adam looked to Cole for support, but Cole only nodded in agreement with his sister.

"You don't want to see me?" Adam asked as evenly as possible.

"We can *see* you, but why do we need to sleep over here? All our stuff is at our house. Our friends come over to our house."

"Your friends could come over here," Adam argued.

"Uh, no," Cole said.

"What would they even *do* here?" Lucy asked.

"They could eat Thai food," Adam said, almost through gritted teeth. "Watch TV?"

"Oh my god, Dad," Cole moaned.

"I have a pool! You could swim here with your friends in the summer."

"We have a pool at home too."

"And Sprite," Cole added.

"Would you stop saying 'home' as if this house isn't your home too? I'm your *dad*."

"This house doesn't even have, like, decorations," Lucy said. "It's depressing."

"It has some," Adam argued weakly.

"Dad," Lucy said, her tone softening as if she was talking to a small child, "we love you and everything, but we don't need to have sleepovers with you anymore. We're just, like, too old for that."

Adam wanted to snap back that these weren't "sleepovers," this was a shared custody arrangement, and they were supposed to live with him for something close to half the time. But the kids had been less and less interested in spending time with Adam as they'd gotten older, and he hadn't fought them or Maggie on it. But he wanted to have them here *sometimes*.

"I miss you guys, though," Adam tried.

"But couldn't we just come over for dinner or whatever and then go home? Like, we can walk there from here."

"You're not walking anywhere at night."

Lucy rolled her eyes. "Dad, we do it all the time."

Adam didn't like hearing *that*. "What? Where? Alone?"

"With friends, or whatever. Anyway, can we just eat the food?"

"You're not leaving after you eat."

"But—"

"No. I'm sorry, but you're stuck with me tonight. I planned this with your mom, and—"

"Great," Cole grumbled.

"So Mom doesn't want us to come home?" Lucy asked angrily.

Oh god. Adam had no idea what to say here. "Of course she wants you at home. She might have plans tonight, though."

"So?" Cole said. "We stay home alone all the time."

"Maybe she wants the house to herself," Adam blurted out without thinking.

"Oh," Lucy said. "Gross."

"What?" Cole asked.

"Nothing," said Adam.

"She's having a romantic evening with *Ethan*," Lucy said.

Cole wrinkled his nose.

"I thought you guys liked Ethan," Adam said. "I like Ethan."

"Sorry. Mom saw him first," Lucy said dryly.

Adam let out a surprised laugh. "Was that a joke?"

Lucy shrugged.

"For the record, I'm not into Ethan."

"If you say so." She smiled, and it was the first warm expression Adam had seen on her face since she'd arrived.

He smiled back and said, "Shut up."

They both laughed, and it felt like dark clouds disappearing. Adam began to open the bags of Thai food and set the containers out on the island. Cole got plates from the cupboard without being asked, and then forks.

"Are you into *anyone*?" Lucy asked casually a few minutes later.

Adam swallowed his mouthful of pad Thai and said, "What do you mean?"

"Like, are you dating or anything?"

He knew he was blushing and hoped it wasn't obvious. "I don't know. Maybe."

Lucy's eyes lit up. "Are you?"

"Ugh. Yuck," Cole groaned, then quickly said, "That's not because you're gay. It's because you're my dad."

"Noted," Adam said. "And, yeah, we don't have to talk about this."

"But I want to," Lucy insisted. "Do you have a boyfriend? You can tell us you know."

"Thank you," Adam said sincerely, "but I'm not really—I mean, I don't know if 'boyfriend' is the right word…" He realized too late that this sounded like he was telling his teenage kids that he had a fuck buddy. "We're taking it slow," he amended. "It's a long-distance kind of thing. Someone I reunited with recently."

"I wonder where he lives," Cole said sarcastically.

Adam pointed his fork at him. "Listen." And when he couldn't think of any way to finish that sentence, he said, "All right. Yes. He's in Nova Scotia."

"Dad," Lucy said. "It's obviously that Ryan guy."

"Riley," Adam corrected her, then cringed at himself. "Not that—okay. Yes."

"Aw, you're dating your old teammate," Lucy cooed. "That's cute. Love that for you."

"Again, I don't know that we're 'dating' exactly. But I really like him."

"Are you going to move to Nova Scotia?" Cole asked.

"The other guy could move here," Lucy pointed out. "He'd probably move here, right?"

"Why would he move here?"

"Uh, because it's Toronto and you're rich? Is there even anything to do in…whatever his town is called?"

"Avery River. And yes, there's lots to do. There are beaches, and there's a farmers market. Riley does a lot of gardening. Um…"

Both kids stared blankly at him.

"It's really beautiful there!" Adam insisted. "I'll take you there sometime. You'll see."

"No offense, Dad, but I can think of like a million places I'd rather go," said Cole.

"I want to go to Costa Rica," said Lucy.

"Ethan said he'd take me to New York," said Cole.

"*I've* taken you to New York!"

"Yeah, but we didn't go to the Nintendo store," said Cole. "Ethan's a gamer too."

Adam sighed. Was there even anything at the Nintendo store that Cole didn't own already? "We can go on a trip somewhere if you want. I'd love to do that. Really."

"When?" Lucy asked. "We're going to France with Mom and Ethan this summer."

"I *know*. And I probably can't travel this summer anyway. I'll need a few weeks to heal after my surgery."

"When's that?" Lucy asked.

"July seventh. Got the date today, actually."

"That's when we're in France."

"Well. That's okay."

"But won't you need help?" Lucy said.

"I'm sure I'll manage. I've got friends who will help out."

"What about Riley? Can he help?"

"Oh, well. Probably not. He runs a store, so he's pretty busy. And I don't think he's a fan of Toronto, really. And summers are so gross here."

Lucy scoffed.

"What?" Adam asked.

"He sounds like a shit boyfriend. He won't look after you after surgery?"

"He's *not* my boyfriend. And I haven't *asked* him to look after me. And I don't *need* someone to look after me."

"You do, though," Lucy said. "You've been, like, really depressing since the divorce."

"I have not."

Lucy's tone turned more serious. "Yeah, you have. You were always busy when you played hockey, but now you're just, like, this bored, lonely guy."

"I'm—maybe a little."

"You need a boyfriend," she concluded. "And a hobby."

Adam considered this and realized he didn't have a single hobby. "Well. Maybe I'll take up...model trains?"

Cole laughed. "I can't believe anyone thinks you're cool."

"I'm very cool. And, fine. You suggest a hobby then."

"MMOs," Cole said without hesitating.

"M M whats?"

"It's a video game thing," Lucy sighed.

"Oh. No thanks."

"You might like it," Cole argued. "It's like being captain of a hockey team except it's, like, a whole army. Well, depending on the game."

"You could *garden*," Lucy said in a singsong voice. "Like your *boyfriend*."

Adam blushed again. "I regret telling you anything."

"I'm glad you told us," Lucy said. "We're all worried about you."

"Worried about me? And who's 'we're all'?"

"Us. Mom. Ethan."

"I'm sure Ethan isn't losing any sleep over my love life." God, were they really all talking about him over at Maggie's house?

"Ethan said that change can be hard," Cole said.

"Very insightful of him," Adam muttered. He liked Ethan, really, but he didn't like Ethan weaving theories about Adam's happiness. Or lack thereof.

"Why do you even live here? Isn't it super boring?" Lucy asked.

"I want to be close to you. And your school."

"But you don't *need* to be."

"It would be cooler to visit you if you lived downtown," Cole said.

"Yeah!" Lucy said excitedly. "Oh my god, if you had a penthouse downtown, that would rule."

"I'm not buying a penthouse in Toronto! I'm a hockey player, not a baseball player."

"Well, it could just be a regular apartment. But a cool one."

"You guys would be okay with living with me sometimes if I had a cool apartment then?" Adam asked flatly.

"Yup," Cole said at the same time Lucy said, "Totally." Then they both laughed, so Adam laughed too.

Later, they watched a movie together and Adam thought seriously about selling the house. Maybe the kids were right: maybe they'd all be happier if he lived somewhere more exciting. In this neighborhood he was basically providing a weird satellite version of Maggie's house, and of course the kids didn't like living here. *Adam* didn't like living here.

But the only place Adam wanted to live right now was a cranberry-colored house by the sea, and that wasn't going to happen. Not soon, anyway.

He texted Riley: Lucy and Cole think I'm uncool and depressing.

A minute later, Riley wrote: You're not depressing with a winky face emoji.

Adam laughed.

"What's so funny?" Cole asked. Adam glanced at the screen and saw that a child actor was crying. So he couldn't use the movie as an excuse.

"He's texting his boyfriend," Lucy said with a smile.

"Ugh," said Cole.

Adam wrote: The kids are roasting me because they think I'm texting my boyfriend. Then he erased it, because he didn't want Riley to know he'd told his kids about him. And also because he was scared that Riley would deny it in some way. Laugh it off as ridiculous.

But as far as Adam was concerned, he *was* texting his boyfriend.

Chapter Thirty-One

Riley had braced himself for total emotional and mental collapse after Adam left, but he found, as each day passed, that he was doing...okay.

It had now been five days, and Riley had stayed busy for all of them. He'd gone to work, he'd visited Mom, he'd taken Lucky for runs on the beach, and he'd worked on his garden. Yesterday he'd talked to his therapist, and although he'd spent a good chunk of the hour crying about his dad, it had been helpful. He'd booked another appointment at the end of the session.

He'd also been sleeping reasonably well and eating when he was supposed to. He'd been texting his friends and Lindsay, and was trying to run more errands around town, just to talk to people.

And he talked to Adam. They texted, mostly, though there had been a couple of short phone calls. Just casual stuff: about hockey, about Adam's kids, about Lucky, about the shop. Sometimes Adam would send him a blurry photo of something. Adam was doing exactly what Riley needed: he was giving him space, while also staying in touch, and Riley appreciated that more than he could say. He missed Adam like crazy, but being able to talk to him again, knowing they were friends, felt wonderful. Being apart hurt, but not as much as the agony he'd carried before, when he'd cut Adam out of his life. He wouldn't do that again.

Now Riley was on his couch, watching the Northmen game. They'd managed to win another game, and now the series was tied at two wins each. Game five was back in Toronto.

As he watched the opening minutes of the game, he found himself transported back in time, remembering the rush of the playoffs. When every second of every game mattered so fucking much. Riley had loved the playoffs; he'd been able to let his emotions off the leash because *everyone's* emotions were cranked up to a million. Losses were devastating, clean body checks invoked blood vengeance, bad calls by the refs made everyone see red, and wins made grown men scream with triumph and sob with relief. Playoffs were the only times he'd felt normal.

Suddenly, the broadcast was showing the team's private box, and there was Adam, flanked by two other former Northmen. Riley's heart stopped as he watched Adam wave and smile at the crowd. He must be on the big screen at the arena.

"And you can hear the love from the fans for Adam Sheppard, who's in the building tonight after being absent for games one and two," said Charlie Pullman, a longtime Northmen play-by-play announcer, on the broadcast.

"I was talking to Shep before the game," said the commentator, Grant Rollins, "and he told me he was in Nova Scotia for the funeral of Riley Tuck's father."

"Riley Tuck," said Pullman with a laugh. "I haven't heard that name in a while."

"Jesus Christ, Charlie," Riley said, which made Lucky briefly raise his head at the other end of the couch.

"Nope. Not someone I'd thought about either," said Rollins.

"But condolences to him and his family, and I hope he's doing well. Nice to hear that Shep still keeps in touch with him."

"Well, that's just the kind of guy Shep is, right, Grant? He was known for helping his teammates, and even when—well, we know Tuck had his difficulties, but Shep would be there for guys like that. He was a hell of a captain, and that's why he's getting this ovation right now. I don't think there's ever been a hockey player more beloved in this town than Adam Sheppard."

"No sir. And that is saying something."

Pullman laughed. "It sure is."

Great. So now the nation had been reminded of Riley's existence, and his "difficulties," via an on-air appeal for the sainthood of Adam Sheppard.

It seemed suddenly impossible that Adam had been here, in Riley's house, only a few days ago. Riley couldn't connect the smiling god being worshipped by thousands on his TV screen with the man who'd been giddy about spotting a deer in Riley's yard. The man who'd released some of that deer-fueled adrenaline by blowing Riley on this very couch.

The man who Riley was definitely in love with, possibly in a vague relationship with, and who absolutely wasn't here right now. In that moment, Adam felt very far from Riley, in every sense of the word. Because *this* was Adam's life: luxury boxes and standing ovations and hockey broadcasters gushing about his greatness. He likely lived in a house that people around here would call a mansion. He was a *dad*. He was *important*. Riley's life had once been glamorous, but now it was just a life. Did he really expect Adam to live here, even part of the time? Adam was meant for better things than a sporting goods store, minor hockey banquets, and dinners with Darren and Tom. He was meant for better things than Riley.

His phone lit up with an incoming text.

Adam: Did you eat dinner?

Riley stared at the message. Had Adam really sent that *now*? While he'd been receiving that standing ovation, had he actually been worried about Riley not eating?

Riley wrote back: yes.

Adam: I miss you.

Riley smiled, and wrote: Are you not being adored enough at the Northmen game?

Adam: I'd rather be watching the game on your couch.

It couldn't be good for Riley's heart, the way Adam kept making it bounce wildly against his ribs. Riley wrote back: I'd probably fall asleep on you.

Adam replied: I know, punctuated with a smiley face emoji.

The broadcast briefly cut back to a shot of Adam, and Riley could *see him* smiling softly at his phone.

God, Riley's heart was going to burst out of his chest.

He wrote: You look good.

Adam: Send me a pic.

Riley snapped a photo of Lucky and sent it.

Adam: You look good.

Riley laughed, then turned his camera on himself. He happened to be wearing his silk robe with only a pair of boxer briefs covered in little pineapples. They clashed terribly, but

Adam didn't need to see his underwear right now. Riley re-
clined a bit and snapped a photo. It was, he had to admit, very
sexy. Maybe too sexy, considering his request to keep things
platonic for now.

He sent it.

A moment later, Adam replied: You bastard.

Riley smiled. Was Adam all hot and bothered in that luxury
box? He wished the broadcast would show him again. Maybe
this was exactly what they weren't supposed to be doing, but
it felt good, flirting with Adam.

Adam: You can't just send that and not expect me to look up
flights to Nova Scotia.

Riley laughed again, but he wrote: Not yet.

Adam: I know. Fuck, though.

Riley agreed, but he was determined to resist temptation.
Because he was still too messed up to know for sure that these
good feelings were the safe kind, or if they were the dangerous kind, like the ones alcohol used to give him.

He needed to be sure, before he offered his heart to Adam
Sheppard again.

Three nights later, Toronto had been eliminated from the
playoffs. The next morning, Riley went to console his dad
about it.

He approached the grave warily, with a handful of hyacinths
from his garden. His breath caught when he read Dad's name,
etched into the small, metal grave marker. He almost turned
away, but forced himself to speak.

"Hey, Dad," he mumbled. "Sorry about the Northmen. It wasn't their year."

"They need stronger defense," he explained, as if Dad didn't know. As if Dad hadn't complained about that all the time, though never in a way that had made Riley feel guilty about asking for the trade. "They've got some decent young guys. I dunno. We'll see how they develop."

He laid the flowers next to the marker and noticed the moon snail shell that someone had placed there. Riley picked it up, turned it over, recognized the chip that was missing from the bottom.

Adam had been here.

Riley closed his fingers on the shell, holding it tight. He wasn't sure about many things, but he was pretty sure someone who was bad for him wouldn't have taken the time to visit Dad's grave. To leave him something beautiful.

"I still love him," he told his dad. "And I think we have a chance to be happy together. Like, really fucking happy."

There was no sign; the clouds didn't part, a butterfly didn't land on the grave, no gentle breeze swept over Riley. But he knew, in his heart, that Dad agreed.

"A *book*?" Riley exclaimed. "You're going to write a *book*?"

"Well, no," Adam said from his sofa in Toronto. He'd called Riley specifically to talk about this, but it had taken him nearly thirty minutes to finally bring it up. "I'm not actually going to write it. There's a ghost writer. It would just be…about me."

Riley paused from where he'd been yanking weeds out of the ground over twelve hundred kilometers away from Adam and smiled at the camera. "Sounds like a real page-turner."

Adam laughed. "Hey, it wasn't my idea. Obviously someone out there wants to read it because they're offering me—I mean, this publisher thinks it would be a good seller. In Canada, at least."

Riley went back to weeding. He had earbuds in so he could work and talk at the same time, while also leaving his actual phone in a spot that allowed Adam to watch him work. It was raining in Toronto, but in Avery River it was a beautiful June day, and Riley was wearing a tank top. Adam had always loved him in a tank top.

"You gonna do it?" Riley asked.

Adam hesitated. He'd only told Riley about the book because he'd wanted to tell him this next part. But the next part was a lot, and he wasn't sure how Riley would react. "No," he said. "At least not yet."

"Why not?" Riley was kneeling in the dirt, wearing kneepads and very short shorts. He had a smear of soil on his right forearm.

"Because..." Adam said carefully, "I want to be sure the story has the ending I'm hoping for first."

Adam could see the exact moment Riley realized what he'd said. He stopped working, sat back on his heels, and looked directly at the camera. "Adam—"

"It just made me think," Adam interrupted. "If there's going to be a book about me, it should be about all of me, right? Or at least the important parts." He laughed. "They don't need to know that bananas give me heartburn."

"I thought you liked bananas."

"I *do*, Riles. My life is hell."

Riley smiled at that.

Adam kept going. "I don't want to write a book that doesn't mention that I'm gay. That's all. But I also don't want the book to be how everyone finds out either. That feels sleazy to me. I dunno."

"Sure. Okay." Riley wiped his brow with his arm, leaving a smudge of soil on his forehead.

Adam took a breath, and said, "My life has been amazing, really. I know that. And I could tell a hundred hockey stories to a ghost writer, and we'd probably get a decent book at the end. Honestly, until recently, I really did think my best years were behind me. That my story was done, maybe, y'know?"

Riley's lips parted, but he didn't say anything.

"I know we're not deciding things right now," Adam said, "so feel free to ignore this, but since I was in Avery River, I've been thinking retirement isn't going to be so bad. That maybe I've got some really good years ahead of me. Some great years."

"Oh," Riley finally said.

"Sorry."

"No," Riley said quickly. "No, that's—really?"

Adam smiled. "Really."

Riley looked away—toward the sea, Adam was pretty sure.

"You don't have to—" Adam started.

"Your surgery is July seventh?"

Adam was confused by the topic change. "Yeah."

Riley nodded, then turned his gaze back to the camera. "Okay. I'll be there."

"What?"

"I'll be there. Whatever it takes. Lucky can stay with Mom. We've got a full staff at work. I'll be there."

"You don't have to—"

"Adam," Riley said sternly, "I fucking miss you and I want to see you and take care of you while you're recovering. I'll be there."

God. Adam probably looked like the biggest sap, the way he was smiling at the camera with a lump in his throat. "I fucking miss you too."

Riley smiled back. "Then I'll see you in July."

"What about your garden?"

"It'll be here."

"But—"

"Shep, it's a garden. It's a hobby. You just told me you want me to be the happy ending to your life story, so yeah. I'm choosing you over beans." He paused, eyes going wide. "That *is* what you were saying, right?"

Adam laughed soggily. "Yeah, Riles. That's what I was saying."

Chapter Thirty-Two

Riley arrived in Toronto the day before Adam's operation. He spotted Adam right away in the domestic arrivals section of the airport because there were at least six people gathered around him, getting autographs and selfies.

Adam's face lit up when he spotted Riley.

"My friend is here," Adam said, politely but firmly. "Excuse me." He stepped out of the circle of fans and into Riley's arms.

"You need a fake mustache," Riley said as he wrapped Adam in the kind of friendly, manly hug that wouldn't raise eyebrows.

Adam patted him twice on the back. "I was thinking about growing a beard. I might get recognized less."

"Still hoping to be a bear, are you?"

Adam laughed, then his lips brushed Riley's ear as he said, "God, you look good."

"Same."

They broke apart and began walking toward the parking garage, Riley wheeling his small suitcase behind him. "How was your flight?"

"Fine. Short. No legroom."

"I really appreciate you being here. I know you're busy, and

I know you'd probably rather be anywhere on earth than Toronto in July, but I'm glad you're here. Thanks."

Riley nudged him with his elbow. "I can think of worse places to be."

Adam smiled, but it didn't last. "I feel bad, making you give up the best part of the year in Avery River to be my nurse for two weeks."

"You're not making me do anything. I have my whole life to enjoy summers back home. Being here with you is important." Riley nudged him again. "And it's not two weeks. It's three."

"What?"

"Surprise."

"Riles, no. You can't—"

"I did a bit of research, and it sounds like you'll need help for at least three weeks, and I know that's when the kids get back from France, so I figure you might have some extra hands then. But until then, I'm staying. So deal with it."

Adam's pinkie brushed against Riley's hand. "Well, I guess that's okay."

"You did say you live alone, right?" Riley asked as he stared up at Adam's giant house.

"Yes."

He glanced at Adam and then back at the house. "Just checking."

"I know it's big for one person, but the kids stay with me sometimes."

"Remind me how many kids you have again? Twenty-six?"

"Okay, fuck off."

Riley laughed. The house was exactly what he'd been expecting: a recently constructed brick luxury home that looked a lot like the one Adam had shared with Maggie. It also looked like every other house in the neighborhood, with the same tidy patch of lawn, wide cement driveway, and three-car garage. Riley had never been a fan of the style, but houses like this one had been popular with his teammates.

Adam had parked his dark blue Porsche Cayenne in the driveway, maybe so he could introduce Riley to his home through the front door, rather than through the garage. It was a hot afternoon, the sticky kind of humidity that Riley wasn't used to anymore. Even the walk from the car to the front door made his T-shirt cling to his back.

The inside of Adam's house was blissfully air-conditioned. Riley sighed in relief as he walked through the door.

"I have a pool too," Adam said. "If you're looking to beat the heat. I won't be able to use it for a while after tomorrow, but I won't mind watching you."

Riley smiled. "Is that what I'm here for? Eye candy?"

Adam closed the door and stepped toward him. He was wearing blue shorts and a white linen shirt and had a bit of a tan. "My doctor said it was important."

"He did, did he?" Riley placed a hand on Adam's hip. Goose bumps erupted all over his forearms, from the aggressive air-conditioning and from anticipation.

"*She*, and I'm pretty sure she said something about how having a hunk around the house would speed recovery."

"Can't hurt," Riley said, then kissed him. Adam surged against him, quickly transforming the kiss from hopeful to spine melting.

"Thank god," Adam said when they broke apart. "I was worried we might not be doing that right away."

Riley smiled. "I was going to try to hold out longer."

"Fuck that," Adam said, and then they were kissing again.

They kissed until they were both breathless, then Adam rested his forehead against Riley's and said, "We have to have so much sex tonight."

"Yeah?" Riley was on board with that. He, of course, hadn't been with anyone since Adam had left, and the grief that Riley had slowly been working through had been spiked by horniness. It had been a confusing and intense cocktail of emotions.

"I'll be out of commission after tonight," Adam explained. "I've got to stockpile orgasms."

"Is this your doctor's advice again?"

"She's a really good doctor."

Riley laughed. "I forgot. I brought you a cinnamon bun."

Adam gasped. "From Paula's?"

"No, from the airport. Of course from Paula's."

"And you're just telling me *now*? Jesus, Riles. Sex can wait."

Mid-cinnamon bun, Adam proposed pizza from his favorite place as his "last meal," which sounded perfect to Riley.

"I'm pretty sure you can eat a few hours after your operation," Riley said. "It's not *that* long without food."

"Yeah, but it'll be hospital food tomorrow. That doesn't count."

It was expected that Adam would only need to stay one night in the hospital, and then Riley could take him home. That was if everything went well. Riley wasn't letting himself think about any other possibilities.

"Are you nervous?" Riley asked later, as they were eating pizza at Adam's kitchen island.

"Nah," Adam said. "I'm a pro at operations at this point."

Riley wasn't sure he believed him, but Adam wouldn't be the first hockey player to pretend he wasn't scared, so he let it go. "You have your bag packed?"

"Yep. And you can just drop me off at the hospital. You don't have to come in and wait around."

Riley narrowed his eyes. "The fuck I don't."

"It'll be boring. Come on. Who wants to hang out in a hospital? Do something downtown at least. See the aquarium!"

"I'm not going to a fucking aquarium while you're in surgery, Adam."

"But you'll—"

"Adam," Riley said sternly. "I'm not leaving you."

Adam's lips twitched, then curved into a wobbly smile. "Okay."

Riley nodded, satisfied that he'd won.

"You can hang your stuff up in my closet, if you like," Adam offered. Given the usual crisp state of Riley's clothes, he assumed he wasn't keen to live out of a suitcase.

"Thanks."

Riley had his suitcase open on Adam's bed, rummaging for the gift he'd apparently brought. Adam had his fingers crossed for five more cinnamon buns.

"Here," Riley said finally, then turned around. "Thought you might like one of your own."

He held out a silk robe, similar to the one he'd tantalized Adam with back in Avery River. This one was black with large white flowers. "Oh wow," Adam said as he reached for it. "For me?"

"You don't seem to do color," Riley explained. "I also think it'll make your eyes look sexy." He paused, then corrected himself. "Sexier."

"I love it." Adam rubbed the liquid fabric against his cheek. "And what do you mean I don't do color?"

Riley counted on his fingers. "Black, gray, brown, navy, white."

"Those are all colors."

Riley sighed. "Technically."

At the moment, Riley was wearing a pale purple T-shirt and teal shorts that couldn't have had more than a five-inch inseam. He'd changed into them before the pizza had arrived and Adam had been losing his mind about them ever since.

"It's just what I'm used to," Adam argued. "And those colors all go together."

"Hm."

"You want me to try this on?" Adam asked. "You packed yours, right?"

"I did. But I have to warn you," Riley said gravely, "once you put that on, you are officially super gay."

Adam laughed, then unfastened his belt.

"Need help?" Riley asked, then started unbuttoning Adam's shirt.

"I might need lots of help, after today," Adam said. "Dressing, undressing, *bathing.*"

"That doesn't sound as hot as you think it does." But the way Riley kissed him then suggested otherwise.

Eventually, they broke apart and Riley carried a small stack of shirts toward the closet. The double doors were already open.

"*This* is your closet?" Riley asked. "Jesus, no wonder you didn't want to leave it."

Adam laughed so hard he had to sit on the bed. He was still laughing when Riley returned from the closet.

"I'd worry about never finding my clothes again in there," he said, "but they kind of stick out."

"I get it. It's big."

"Big? It's fucking huge. There's a *couch* in there. You take rests on that thing while walking across the closet, or what?"

"I like clothes, okay?"

"Yeah, me too, but that's like Céline Dion level."

Adam snorted and started laughing again.

"I've never seen so much navy and brown," Riley continued. "It was like being in a lake."

"Then take me shopping, asshole. Since you're the expert."

Riley lit up. "Could we? Before I leave? If you feel up to it?"

Adam smiled at him. "Sure. We can go shopping."

"The fashion options aren't great back home. Halifax is okay, but it's not Toronto."

Adam stood. "Okay. I'm putting the robe on." He'd been wearing only underwear since they'd kissed. He slipped the robe on and let out a weird little sigh. "Oh, that's nice."

"Shit," Riley murmured. "Yeah."

Adam examined himself in a mirror. He'd never worn anything like this. Had he ever worn a floral print? Probably not; he barely wore prints at all. He'd always focused on looking classy and stylish and, well, straight.

"Oh, hello," he said to his reflection. "I like this."

Riley came up behind him and their gazes met in the mirror. "You look really fucking hot."

Adam tilted his head back against Riley's shoulder. "Yeah?"

"Mm." Riley slid a hand down Adam's bare chest and kissed his neck.

"Riles," Adam breathed. He dropped a hand down to the hem of Riley's little shorts and dipped his fingertips under. He teased at the soft hairs on Riley's thigh while Riley sucked on his neck and circled a finger over Adam's left nipple. Adam never took his eyes off the mirror. They looked so good together.

He watched the way Riley's lips pressed against his skin, the way his huge hands slid along Adam's skin, and the way his own cock grew hard in his black briefs. The robe slid off Adam's right shoulder, and Riley kissed the exposed skin there.

He turned his head and captured Riley's lips in a messy, frantic kiss. Riley's erection bumped against his ass and, yeah. Adam wanted it.

"Oh fuck," he moaned when Riley reached down and

cupped the bulge in Adam's briefs. He watched their reflection, watched Riley's eyes grow dark as he massaged Adam's cock.

"Look at how fucking sexy you are," Riley rumbled in his ear.

Adam mostly wanted to look at how sexy Riley was. "Want you," he managed.

Riley slipped his hand inside Adam's underwear and pulled his cock out. Adam gasped from the relief of being free, and from how fucking debauched he looked in the mirror.

"You wanna get fucked, Shep?" Riley asked as he stroked him.

"Yes." God, it was pretty much all he'd been able to think about since Riley had fucked him the first time. "I loved it."

Riley growled. "You wanna see how close I can get you first? You wanna watch that happen in the mirror?"

Oh, Christ. "Yeah. Fuck."

Riley kept the pace slow and easy, reminding Adam of how much time they had. Three weeks. Of course, Adam wouldn't be in peak sexual condition during that time, but still: three weeks!

But it was the idea of everything after those three weeks that was really making Adam's heart race. This could be his life from now on. Riley and hot sex and silk robes and a home that Riley filled with beautiful things.

Riley snapped Adam's waistband. "Take these off." Then he pulled his own shirt off. In a few seconds, Riley was naked. Adam left the robe on.

"Don't get it dirty," Adam warned.

Riley chuckled. "Then don't come." He went back to stroking him, and Adam melted against him. They both watched their reflections, Adam's gaze darting between where Riley's hand was working him, and Riley's face. Riley's eyes were hazy with arousal, his jaw set as if he was struggling to hold back. He was rocking his erection against Adam's ass, against the silk, and, god, that probably felt incredible. Adam would have to try it.

"So good. I missed you so much, Riles."

"Missed you too. Fucking dreamed about this."

"Yeah? Me too. Couldn't stop thinking about you."

Riley grunted and stroked him faster.

"Fuck," Adam panted after not nearly long enough. "I'm getting close."

For a moment, he thought Riley, seemingly lost in his own bliss, hadn't heard him. Adam was quickly reaching the moment when warnings wouldn't matter anymore, when, with a frustrated huff, Riley released him and took a step back.

Adam squeezed his eyes shut, trying to come back from the brink. "Holy shit," he gasped.

"Yeah. Fuck. Me too."

Adam opened his eyes and saw Riley squeezing the base of his own erection. Adam turned to face him properly and put a hand on Riley's hip.

"Don't," Riley gritted out. "Wait."

"Really?"

Riley laughed shakily. "You look too fucking good like that."

Adam let the robe drop to the floor. "How about now?"

"Fucking hell."

This time they tried it with Adam bent over the bed, his forearms resting on a big pillow, and Riley standing behind him. It was, Adam was happy to learn, extremely successful, with Riley holding him with firm hands and driving into him with exactly the right balance of strength and caution. Yes, Adam's shoulder complained a bit, but he would be throwing it in the garbage tomorrow, so who cared?

After, they cuddled in bed, both naked and sleepy. Despite

Adam's earlier desire to have "so much sex tonight," he wasn't in his twenties, and neither was Riley. Instead, he rested his head on Riley's chest and mourned all the lost years he could have had this every night.

"I'm sorry I was such an asshole to you," Adam said.

"What? When? I've got no complaints about what we just did."

"Back when we played together."

There was a tense silence, then Riley said, "We were young. We were both assholes."

Adam raised his head. "I was definitely worse."

Riley held his gaze. "It doesn't matter. I'm not angry anymore. I forgive you, and I forgive myself. And, Shep? That's a fucking amazing feeling."

Adam swallowed hard. "I'm really glad to hear that." He wasn't quite ready to forgive himself, but knowing Riley had let go of his anger would help. He wanted to give him something in return; something honest and sweet.

"The first time I ever kissed you was terrifying. It felt so huge and *good* and, I don't know. It was scary, but it was also, like, the best thing I'd ever felt."

Riley's fingers paused where they'd been stroking Adam's stomach. "Same. All of that."

"You'd kissed guys before, though."

Riley was silent a moment. "You were different," he said finally.

Adam snorted. "I was probably a much worse kisser."

"No," Riley said seriously. "It was perfect."

"It was," Adam agreed. He hadn't meant to darken the afterglow by dragging their past into it, but it felt important. "I just wanted you to know. Despite how I acted after, that first time together meant everything to me."

Another long silence and then Riley said, "Thank you."

He went back to gently stroking Adam's skin. He didn't need to tell Adam what that first time had meant to him. Adam knew.

And he also knew that, now, nearly twenty years later, he was in the arms of the man he loved, and if Riley would let him, he would devote the rest of his life to letting him know that he still meant everything to Adam.

Chapter Thirty-Three

Riley probably should have guessed that the wait while Adam was in surgery would be agony. Somehow, despite knowing that he was terrible at managing feelings, and knowing that he was still reeling from the sudden loss of his dad, Riley hadn't considered that he'd spend the entire two hours—now two hours and eighteen fucking minutes—terrified that he was about to lose Adam too.

It's just an operation, he reminded himself. *He's had tons of them, you've had a few yourself. The surgeon has probably performed a million of them. He's fine. He's fine.*

He hadn't brought a book or anything. He'd spent most of the past few hours texting Lindsay, because she was the closest person to a doctor that he knew.

Lindsay had, lovingly, told him to chill the fuck out after the first hour. As if Riley knew how to do that.

Finally, *finally*, after nearly three fucking hours had passed, a man wearing scrubs entered the waiting room and beamed when he spotted Riley. "It really is you," the man exclaimed. "Riley Tuck. It's a pleasure to meet you. I'm Dr. Pandev, I performed Shep's surgery." He extended a hand to Riley. A hand that had just replaced Adam's shoulder joint and had possibly taken his pain away for good.

Riley shook it. "He's okay? He's...okay?"

"Absolutely fine. I think his life is going to be much easier now. After he recovers, of course."

Riley nearly collapsed with relief. "Thank you."

"Well, I could hardly let anything bad happen to him," the doctor joked. "The city of Toronto would have my head."

Riley couldn't quite manage to smile at that. Dr. Pandev looked to be about Riley's age, maybe a bit younger.

The doctor gave his bicep a chummy pat and said, "I was a huge fan of yours. I was sorry when you left. You're doing well?"

"Thanks, uh, yeah. Doing well."

"That's great. Good to hear." He laughed. "I couldn't believe it when Shep told me you were in the waiting room. It's cool that you're still close."

"Yup," Riley said uneasily.

Dr. Pandev beamed at him for another few seconds, then said, "So I'll be checking in with Shep later today when he's in his room, but a nurse will come let you know when you can see him."

"Okay. Thanks."

The doctor left, and Riley returned to his plastic chair. Adam was fine. It was over, and he was fine.

The nurse—a young man with kind eyes named Hassan—arrived about twenty minutes later.

"Can I see him?" Riley blurted out immediately.

Hassan smiled in a way that seemed...knowing. "Yes, you can come with me. He's settled in his room, and he was asking about you."

Riley's heart swelled. "Yeah?"

"He is very tired still, and he needs to rest," the nurse warned him.

"Of course. Yeah. But he's good?"

"He's very good. And it seems that he will be well taken care of at home."

Riley blushed. "He will be."

He followed Hassan onto an elevator, then down a hall, and then, finally, into the room where Adam was resting in bed, his chest and shoulders slightly elevated, his arm in a sling. He was pale and looked exhausted, but he managed a weak smile when he saw Riley.

"Hey," Adam rasped. "How was your morning?"

A relieved laugh tumbled out of Riley as he approached the bed. He gently combed Adam's hair with his fingers and said, "You look amazing."

Adam laughed.

Hassan was still in the room, checking the monitors Adam was attached to, but Riley didn't care about having an audience. He wished Adam had a free hand he could hold, but the one that wasn't in a sling had an IV needle in the back of it and a heart rate monitor clamped to his index finger.

"How are you feeling?" Riley asked as he continued to stroke Adam's hair.

"Brutal. But the drugs are nice." Adam closed his eyes and tilted his head into Riley's touch. "That feels nice."

"We'll be getting you out of bed and walking around a bit later today," Hassan said. "But for now you rest, and I'll make sure you're comfortable. If the pain feels like too much, let me know and I can make adjustments." He gestured to the call button.

"Thanks," Adam mumbled.

"And I mean it," Hassan said. "Tell me if you are in pain. This isn't a hockey game."

Riley smiled. "I'll make sure he tells you."

"He will," Adam assured Hassan sleepily. "He's bossy."

Riley bit the inside of his cheek.

After Hassan left, Riley pulled a chair beside the bed and continued stroking Adam's hair. He thought Adam had fallen asleep, but Adam surprised him by murmuring, "Hockey makes us into liars."

Riley's fingers stopped. "Hm?"

"Liars," Adam repeated without opening his eyes. "About how much pain we're in. Mental health, addiction, all of it." He opened his eyes, gaze locked on Riley's. "I lied about who I was. About my feelings for you."

Riley swallowed and waited.

"Look where it got me," Adam continued. "Divorced, fucked-up shoulder, lost you for years."

Though none of what he was saying was news to Riley, it was shocking to hear Adam say it. Riley had never heard him say a bad word about hockey before. He didn't know how to react to it now, so he just said, "I'm here now."

Adam closed his eyes again. "I should have said it back to you. Should have been honest."

It took Riley a moment to figure out what he was referring to. When he realized, he said, "Adam. Don't. It doesn't matter now."

"I think we would have been happy," Adam said, barely above a whisper. "I think we would have been fucking unstoppable together."

"You need to rest," Riley said desperately. This was all too much, for this moment. And, besides, Adam was probably high as a kite. "We can talk later."

"Yeah," Adam sighed, then smiled, just slightly. "We've got time."

Chapter Thirty-Four

"Can I get you anything?" Riley asked for probably the fiftieth time that day, and probably the one billionth time that week.

"Not a thing," Adam said sleepily. He was sitting in the shade under an awning, watching Riley swim laps in the pool. He already had a glass of ice water on the table next to him, along with his glasses, his book, and a plate of sliced fruit.

"Are you sure?"

Adam flicked the hand that wasn't in a sling. "Swim. I'm fine." Frankly, watching Riley slice through the water like a dolphin was the highlight of Adam's day. Especially given how short Riley's bathing suit was.

It had been an exhausting week. Adam had just done a round of the physio exercises he'd been given to do at home, and it had used up all the energy he'd had, which hadn't been much to start with. Sleeping on his back while wearing a sling was challenging, which only added to the wooziness he already felt from the shock of surgery and from the painkillers.

He couldn't be much fun to be around, but Riley had barely left his side. Riley had made the week much less horrible.

After a few minutes, Riley hoisted himself out of the pool.

Adam enjoyed the rivulets of water that followed the lines of his pecs and stomach. He really was ridiculously handsome.

"You want to take a nap, maybe?" Riley sounded concerned, which told Adam that he must look as rough as he felt.

"Nah." Adam attempted a flirtatious smile. "I'd miss you."

Riley rolled his eyes but couldn't hide his grin. "I'll still be here when you wake up."

"I know."

Riley plucked a strawberry off the fruit plate and popped it in his mouth. Adam blatantly ogled him, particularly in the area where his wet bathing suit clung to his skin. They hadn't done anything sexual since the night before the operation, and Adam definitely didn't feel up to it yet, but it was nice to look. It was nice to be *allowed* to look.

Besides the sling, Adam was wearing a tank top and loose shorts that Riley had helped him put on. That combo had become his uniform this week. Except for the times he wore his silk robe. Riley also assisted him in the shower, took care of every meal one way or another, and helped him text Maggie and the kids in France.

And, most importantly, sometimes he kissed him.

With some effort, Adam got himself out of the chair. He rested his free hand on Riley's chest. "I want to take you on a date."

Riley's eyebrows shot up. "Tonight?"

"I wish. No. But before you leave."

Riley's grin returned. "Dinner? Dancing?"

Adam winced. "Probably not dancing."

"I was kidding."

"Someday, though. I'd like to."

"Yeah?" Riley seemed to blush, as if he still couldn't understand that Adam wanted to do literally everything with him.

Forever. And, to be fair, they hadn't really talked about this, since Riley had arrived.

Adam decided to lay his cards on the table.

"Riles," he said. "I want to do this for real."

"Dancing?"

"Us. Everything. I want to be together, even if we need to deal with a bit of distance at first."

To his surprise, Riley's smile faded.

"Riles?"

"Maybe we should talk about this when you're not…" He gestured at Adam, as if presenting evidence.

"You think I'm not of sound mind right now or something? I'm a little tired, not delirious. I want you to be my boyfriend. Or partner. Or… I don't know. I want to be with you all the fucking time for as long as you're willing to put up with me."

Riley looked at the ground, hiding his expression. When he finally tilted his face back up, his eyes were damp. "I need you to be sure."

"I'm sure."

"No, I mean, about all of it. Are you ready to let everyone know that you're dating a man? That you're dating…me?"

"I—"

"You need to really think about that. Because, Adam, I can't—" He exhaled heavily. "I'm already in way too deep here, I know, but I'm trying to be careful. I want everything you want, but I need you to be sure."

Adam moved his hand to Riley's cheek. "You seem to think I'm making a snap decision here or something. I've been thinking about this pretty much constantly for weeks—*months*. I'm sure, Riley. I'm fucking nervous about coming out, but I'll get through it."

"I've been thinking about it all the time too."

"And?"

"And I decided I shouldn't get my hopes up."

"What? Why? Get them up!"

Riley's lips twitched. "I mean, they are. That's the problem."

"It's not a problem. I want to be with you. I want everyone to know I'm with you. I want to spend the rest of my life with you." He hesitated. "Was that too much? Fuck it, I don't care. I love you, Riley. I've always loved you so much, but I'm finally able to love you the way you deserve. I'm sorry it took so long."

For an intense moment, they stared at each other. Then Riley said, "You could have waited a little longer. At least until I'm not wearing a wet bathing suit."

Adam laughed. "Have you *seen* you in a wet bathing suit?"

Then they were kissing. Riley was careful with him, bracing him with a firm hand on his back as they kissed through their smiles. Then Riley pulled back and, with a steady hand on Adam's cheek, said, "I love you, Adam."

"I love you," Adam said back, finally, *finally* getting that right.

Their kisses got deeper, more passionate, and Adam groaned when he started to get hard. "God, I wish we could fuck."

Riley, to his disappointment, stepped back. "Motivation to rest and do your physio and get better."

"But—"

"Right now, I am taking you to your bed, and you are going to try to nap. And after that, we can watch *Gladiator*."

Adam smiled. "Until you fall asleep on me."

"That would be terrible for your shoulder."

"Something to look forward to," Adam said. "A lifetime of you falling asleep on me while watching stuff."

Riley laughed, but Adam had meant it with his whole heart.

Epilogue

Five Years Later

One part of the job that never got old for Riley was watching a kid get their very first set of hockey gear.

Today it was Emily, a four-year-old girl who was grinning from ear to ear after trying on hockey pants. Riley remembered that feeling, the simple joy he used to get from hockey. He loved being able to relive it.

"Those aren't too big?" Emily's mother, Kim, asked Riley.

"I know they look huge, but no. Those are perfect."

Emily purposely fell back on her butt. "It doesn't hurt!"

"Nope," Riley agreed with a smile. "Your butt will be invincible."

"I want to wear these to school!"

Riley was able to find most of Emily's gear in the shop's secondhand section, which smart parents knew to raid early. It was now the first week of August, and by September there wouldn't be much left. He sharpened Emily's new skates and trimmed her stick to the right height for her tiny body.

"And when she outgrows her gear, you can bring it all right back to us for credit toward her new stuff," Riley reminded

Kim later as he handed her the debit machine. "Even her stick if it's in okay shape." He made eye contact with Emily. "Though I'll bet you've got a really hard slap shot, don't you? Your stick will probably be in five pieces by the end of the season."

Emily giggled.

They were less than an hour away from closing time on a Tuesday. It had been an enjoyable day at work, but Riley was keen to get home. For one thing, Adam had just returned home last night after being away for a week doing speaking engagements. For another, today was their first wedding anniversary, and Riley had plans.

They'd been married in their backyard, surrounded by flowers and the sea and a small group of close friends and family. Riley had never given much thought to what his dream wedding might be like, but he couldn't imagine a better one. He was often struck by sudden moments of disbelief that Adam Sheppard was truly in his life again. That they were together. That Adam was his. But he'd never felt it so strongly as he had when they'd stood fearlessly in the sunshine and vowed to love each other always and forever; when Adam had kissed him for the first time as his *husband*, in front of his kids and Maggie and even a couple of his closest hockey friends.

Adam's parents and brother hadn't been there. Adam had felt obligated to invite them, but he hadn't seemed disappointed when they'd declined. His parents hadn't spoken to him much since his book came out.

Adam and Riley had kept things quiet for the first year of their relationship. Adam had traveled frequently to Nova Scotia, and Riley had gone to Toronto a couple of times to visit Adam in his new downtown apartment. Near the end of that first year, Adam came out to a small group of close hockey friends. He'd told Riley after that it had gone okay. When

Riley had pressed for more details, Adam had smiled sadly and said, "They just need some time, y'know? It's a shock."

Some of them had needed time, and some of them, it had turned out, were assholes.

A few months later, Adam came out publicly and, with Riley's blessing, announced their relationship. Riley never paid much attention to hockey media, and he paid even less attention to social media, but according to Adam, the hockey world "lost their fucking minds" about the news. There had been a lot of support, but there had been—and still were—plenty of loud bigots making gross jokes.

Adam was interviewed by just about every news outlet in Canada and asked to speak at events all over the place. Riley had been asked to join Adam for some of those interviews, but he'd declined. He'd never been very comfortable with the celebrity side of being a hockey pro, and he preferred not to be back in the spotlight, though he appreciated the support. Adam understood, but he still—to Riley's embarrassment and delight—talked up Riley in every interview. When he was inducted into the Hockey Hall of Fame the following November, he gave a speech where he'd described Riley as the love of his life. Riley still teared up whenever he thought of it.

The year after that, Adam's autobiography was released, and it was an instant national bestseller. The book was remarkably raw and honest. Adam openly talked about his mistakes and regrets, but was also critical of hockey culture and the way it encouraged men to hide important things about themselves. And he'd also called out his parents a bit for being overbearing perfectionists, but he'd stopped short of using the word *abusive*. Riley felt he'd gone easy on them. The Sheppards had felt otherwise, but they'd already shut Adam out almost entirely anyway since he'd told them he was dating Riley. It was no great loss, but he knew it was still painful for Adam.

Feeling braver by then, Riley had joined Adam for part of the book tour. Now that his sexuality, his mental health struggles, and his long, complicated history with Adam was (mostly) public knowledge, he'd received a lot of support and sympathy from hockey journalists and fans. One journalist even devoted an entire column to apologizing for accusing Riley of being lazy and undisciplined during his final season. Adam had been thrilled because, more than anything, he wanted the world to be in love with Riley.

Riley had never cared much about the world. His town loved him, his family loved him, and Adam loved him. That was all he needed.

And Lucky, of course.

Once both Lucy and Cole had gone off to university, Adam moved in with Riley. That had been two years ago, and Riley's life had been more or less perfect ever since. Of course he still missed Dad every day, but the pain had softened over the years. People around town had really stepped up to take on the tasks that Dad had, somehow, always managed to do himself every year. Riley had thrown himself into managing the shop, introducing new product categories like kayaks, and adding a bike shop expansion. Not being much of a bike expert himself, Riley had hired a young woman named Grace who regularly did triathlons to run that side of things. She'd done a great job. At first he'd felt guilty, making changes to the shop, but both Mom and Steve had assured him that Dad would have been proud of him.

Finally, it was closing time. Steve teased Riley for rushing through the closing duties, then got stern with him. "Go home to your husband, boss. I'll finish up here."

Riley didn't argue.

He'd hoped to sweep his husband into a bone-melting kiss

as soon as he got home, but those plans got put on hold when he saw Mom in the kitchen with Adam.

"I'm leaving!" Mom said immediately. "I know it's your anniversary. I just dropped by to exchange jam with Adam. I'd meant to be gone before you got home."

"It's my fault," Adam said. "I'm chatty."

"You both are." Riley gave Mom a hug, and then Adam a quick kiss on the cheek. "You don't have to run off, Mom."

"Nope. I'm going. I've got what I came for." She held up a jar of red jam.

"What'd you make?" Riley asked Adam.

"Raspberry jam with thyme."

"Fancy." Jam and pickles had become Adam's passion. Once he'd learned how to make them, he couldn't be stopped. Not that Riley wanted to stop him; his spicy dill pickles were incredible. "It's a hot day for making jam, isn't it?"

"Yeah, well." Adam gestured to his sweat-damp shirt. It was the aqua linen one that Riley had picked out for him when they'd been in Montreal in May for Lucy's university graduation. It was a great color on him. Adam's hair and stubble were more salt than pepper, now, and his belly was a little larger than it used to be, but to Riley he'd never been more handsome.

"Susan brought us blueberry jam," Adam said. "Fair trade, I think."

"Agreed," said Riley.

Lucky wandered into the kitchen and greeted Riley with a mild woof. He wasn't as energetic as he used to be, but he still took his job as inspector seriously.

"Hey, buddy," Riley said, and bent to scratch Lucky's ears. He still came with Riley to the shop sometimes—as did Adam—but Riley didn't blame Lucky for wanting to loaf around the house most of the time in his old age.

"I took him to the beach this morning," Adam said. "He gave us a crab shell for our anniversary."

"Aw. Thanks, Lucky."

"Okay, I really am leaving now," Mom said. Then, without budging, she said, "My god, I drove by the Anchor on the way here—or whatever they're calling it now—and the people! Jam-packed on the patio, and there wasn't a parking spot. Cars were parked along the street! Imagine."

"It's popular," Riley agreed. The Dropped Anchor had been sold a couple of years ago to a couple who'd turned it into the Avery River Brewing Company. The locals had been wary of the change—especially since the new owners were from *Halifax*—but were quickly won over by exciting new features like clean floors, good beer, edible food, and windows.

The one thing that hadn't changed was that Riley and Adam's jerseys still hung beside each other on one wall. Riley had insisted it wasn't necessary to display them if they didn't match the new vibe, but the town—and the new owners—had very strong opinions about keeping them. Avery River was proud of Riley, and of the town's adopted son, Adam.

"What are you up to tonight, Mom?"

"Oh. I don't know." She blushed slightly, which probably meant she'd be spending time with Lyle from pickleball. "We'll see."

After she left, Adam said, "Lyle is *so* her boyfriend."

"I know. It's cute." Lyle was a nice man and a widower, so he had that in common with Mom. Riley liked him because he made Mom very happy, even if she seemed to be embarrassed about it.

"I was thinking we could go to the brewery for dinner," Adam said. "But it sounds like there'd be a wait."

Riley took him in his arms. "What if…" He kissed his neck. "Your husband took you to the finest restaurant in town?"

"Paula's?"

"Of course."

Adam laughed, then kissed him. "Am I dressed up enough for Paula's?"

"I don't know. They've got a pretty strict dress code. Do you have anything in Mossy Oak?"

"I have a T-shirt with paint stains on it."

"Perfect." Riley kissed him again. "Are you hungry?"

"Always. But, um, kiss me like that some more and I may forget about food for a while."

Riley kissed his nose. "Later. Let's eat."

After they'd both finished off Paula's deluxe fried seafood platters—hey, they were celebrating—Riley said, "I have a surprise."

Adam's face lit up. "Yeah?"

Riley glanced out the window beside their table. The sun was setting, but he'd like it to be darker. "Let's go for a walk first."

They walked down Main Street, greeting anyone they passed. The shops were all closed for the night, but plenty of people were out for a stroll. They did end up at the brewery, but the only available table happened to be, to Riley's mortification, the one directly under their jerseys.

"Did you plan this?" Adam teased.

"Definitely not."

"Hey! It's the real guys!" Dustin, one of the owners, said cheerfully as he approached the table.

"Business is good, I see," Adam said.

"It's nuts," Dustin agreed with a huge smile. "We've got a new nonalcoholic Belgian wheat beer on tap."

"Sounds good," Riley said.

"Make it two," Adam added. He didn't abstain from alcohol completely, but he rarely drank these days.

Later, when they were halfway through their pints, Adam said, "I can't believe this is the same place."

"I know."

"Like, who knew it was so big?"

"Just needed some light."

"So what's the surprise?" Adam asked.

"Not telling."

Adam kicked him gently under the table. "Come on."

"Nope."

Adam sighed, then leaned in. "Okay, then I'll tell you mine."

Riley raised his eyebrows. "You have a surprise?"

"It's more of an idea than a surprise. Here it is: let's go to Iceland."

"Today?"

"This winter. I still want to sit in a thermal pool and watch the northern lights with you."

"Still?"

"Yes, Riles. We talked about this, remember?"

"No. When?"

Adam's cheeks turned pink. "I guess it may have been a while ago."

"Like when we were twenty-two?"

Adam mumbled something.

"Pardon?" Riley said.

"Twenty-*three*," Adam said. "And, okay, yes. It's weird that I still think about it."

Riley put his hand on Adam's wrist. "It's not weird. It's sweet. And I'd love to go to Iceland with you."

"Yeah?" Adam's eyes crinkled. "Cool. We haven't gotten to travel together much."

"I know. We've been busy. But we should."

Adam glanced up at their jerseys. "I wish I could go back

in time and tell the guy who signed that jersey that, one day, he'd be married to you."

"Seems mean."

Adam kicked him again. "Stop it."

They stayed for another drink, and by that time Riley felt it was dark enough to finally reveal his surprise, though he worried about Adam's raised expectations.

Adam guessed his plans when Riley turned onto an unpaved road.

"Hey, wait. Are we going to that little beach?"

"Thought we could have a bonfire," Riley said mildly, though his stomach was full of butterflies.

"Riles!" Adam exclaimed. "That's so fucking romantic."

Riley smiled. He liked being romantic. He'd been trying to be romantic the first time he'd brought Adam to this beach, nearly a quarter century ago.

"I was really charmed that first time," Adam said, as if reading Riley's mind. "Obviously I didn't deal with my feelings very well at the time, but, yeah. I was swooning."

"It was one of my favorite nights ever," Riley admitted.

"Mine too. But tonight will be better."

"Will it?"

"Yeah, because tonight I can swoon openly. I'm gonna swoon all over you."

"I think you swooned all over my hand last time."

Adam laughed. "God, and then you made me go in the dark, scary ocean."

"It's a shallow cove, Shep. And I didn't *make* you."

"You lured me with your naked body."

"Well. I can't promise I won't do it again tonight."

"Does that mean you plan on shoving your hand down my shorts?"

Riley laughed. "Honestly, I mostly wanted to do this because there might be shooting stars tonight."

"Oh, *this* star will certainly be—wait, really? Shooting stars?"

Riley nodded. "Meteor shower."

"You're a master of seduction, Tuck."

They reached the beach and struggled to carry the supplies Riley had hidden in the back of the truck over the rocks to the sand. Had the climb down always been this steep, or was he just getting old?

"Here," Adam said, reaching out to him. "Give me the cooler. You're carrying too much. Let me use my bionic shoulder powers."

Riley scoffed, but he handed Adam the cooler. Adam's shoulder had been pain free since his replacement surgery, and he loved opportunities to use it. Adam still had issues with his back, and his right ankle complained sometimes, but overall he was in decent condition now for someone who'd played pro hockey for twenty years.

When they reached the sand, Riley began digging a firepit while Adam laid out the blanket. Once the fire was blazing, Riley joined him on the blanket and accepted the cold Avery River Brewing Company nonalcoholic beer Adam handed him. They clinked their cans together and Adam said, "Happy anniversary, gorgeous."

"To my husband—the World's Most Beautiful Man."

They both laughed and then drank.

"This is nice," Adam said, after they'd both watched the fire for a few minutes. "Thank you."

Riley gazed at his profile in the firelight. Jokes aside, he truly was the most beautiful man in the world to Riley. And now he could admire his husband as much as he wanted, not having to quickly look away whenever Adam noticed.

"I love you," he said, because that was something else he could do now.

"I love you too, Riles." Adam smiled mischievously. "Wanna make out?"

He ended up underneath Riley as they kissed each other breathless.

"Are we too old for this?" Adam asked giddily as he pressed his erection against Riley's.

"I don't ever want to be too old for this." He unbuttoned Adam's shorts and slid his hand inside.

"Oh, fuck," Adam gasped. "Yes."

For the next several minutes, the hermit crabs and any other beach creatures around were treated to the sounds of two middle-aged men panting and moaning and laughing as they jerked each other off. It was probably the most Riley had ever giggled during sex.

"Riles, shit. I'm—fuck, I've gotta—" Adam frantically yanked his shirt up under his chin, then came all over his exposed stomach and chest.

Riley groaned, then aimed and added to the mess there with his own release. After, he flopped to his back and grinned at the stars.

"That took me back," Adam said sleepily.

"Mm."

"Except this time I don't know how I'm going to get up."

Riley chuckled. "I'll help you."

"I'm so glad I married a younger man."

Riley kissed his cheek, then, in a demonstration of his enduring youth, sprang to his feet.

"Show-off," Adam complained.

Riley pulled his own shirt off, then his shorts and underwear.

"Oh," Adam said, and sat up.

Riley extended his hand. "Let's get you cleaned up."

For a moment, Adam only stared at him. Then he said, "Goddamn, I'm lucky." He took Riley's hand, and, when he was standing, let him remove his clothes. They ran to the water and waded in until they were chest deep.

"This is nice, actually," Adam said. "Not as freezing as I expected."

"Shallow cove," Riley reminded him.

They kissed, under the stars and a sliver of moon, as the water lapped gently against their bare skin.

"Tell you a secret?" Adam murmured. "I loved that summer here so much—the one with the bonfire. I sometimes wished, after, that I could stay in that summer forever."

Riley smiled. He'd felt the same way. "Yeah?"

"I feel like I did it. Being with you feels like that summer every day." He touched their foreheads together and pressed a wet palm to Riley's cheek. "You make me so happy, Riles."

Riley squeezed his eyes shut because he didn't want to cry. Of course Adam made him happy too, but the most important thing he did was make Riley feel *steady*. "You walked into that church on the worst day of my life," he said, "and made me stronger. Happier. Better."

"Eventually," Adam reminded him.

Riley huffed out a laugh. "Eventually." He kissed him. "Thank you for being brave enough to come find me."

"Thank you for being brave enough to love me, way back when it terrified me. I know it didn't seem like it at the time, but it helped. I don't think I could have gotten to where I am now if I hadn't heard those words then."

Riley's throat tightened. "Fuck," he said. "You're making me cry."

Adam took his hand under the water and squeezed it. "You can, if you need to."

The truth of that made Riley's chest relax. He could always be himself with Adam.

Eventually, they left the water and lay together naked on the blanket, with another blanket over them. Riley's head was tilted against Adam's shoulder as they both watched for shooting stars. He held Adam's hand and occasionally nuzzled his hair and let himself be overwhelmed by how much he loved him.

"Hey, there's one," Adam said excitedly. "Make a wish."

But Riley couldn't think of a single thing he needed.

★ ★ ★ ★ ★

Acknowledgments

Romance about male hockey players falling in love with other men is my brand, but I seem to have accidentally veered into the very specific (and super fun) sub-brand of Grieving Nova Scotians. It seems to be all I want to write about these days, and I should probably unpack this with my therapist soon.

I have lived in Nova Scotia my whole life (except for my adventurous university years when I lived about ten minutes over the Nova Scotia/New Brunswick border). I am, however, a city girl who grew up, and still lives, in the Halifax area. I invented the small town of Avery River as a tribute to the many Nova Scotia towns and villages I love and often dream of moving to. I placed Avery River on Nova Scotia's beautiful (and, in my opinion, underrated) North Shore in the vicinity of Tatamagouche, but I sort of mashed a few real towns together to create my fictional one. I really enjoyed writing a book set in Nova Scotia and I'm not sure why it took me this long to do it.

There are some specific Nova Scotians I would like to thank. My husband, Matt, who not only gave me all the time, space and encouragement that I needed, he also read the first draft and loved it, which was truly the only feedback I wanted. My kids, Mitchell and Trevor, for their patience and their ideas (sorry I wasn't able to work a pet frog into this book). My parents for their enormous support, even if hockey romance isn't necessarily their preferred genre. Matt's parents for showing my kids a fun time on weekends when I had to write. Melissa for listening to me complain, and letting me bounce ideas off her.

There are some non–Nova Scotians I would also like to thank. My editor, Mackenzie Walton, who is just the best and I love working with her. Eight books strong! The team at Carina Press and Harlequin, especially Stephanie Doig, for being great to work with. My agent, Deidre Knight, for making big things happen. Everyone on my Discord server, especially the hardworking mods, for being awesome. To my author pals, especially Jenn Burke and Allie Therin, for their support, feedback, good chats, and vent sessions. And, of course, thank you to my readers. I would never have gotten this far without your overwhelming enthusiasm for my sad hockey players.